"My secret in exchange for yours."

Tantalizing. He was drawing her into his snare, but she couldn't resist asking, "How do you know I've a secret?"

"To begin with, you're hiding in a tree. What from, a wild beast?"

"Near enough. You."

He smiled. "Was I to think you a large red bird, or overlook you entirely?"

Drawing her remaining shreds of dignity around her like a mantle, she said, "This isn't one of my best hiding places."

"Indeed? Where are the others?"

"That would be telling."

The strengthening breeze tossed the branches around them as he considered. "You never could keep secrets from me, Cricket. I'll discover them and you."

An assertion she found both disturbing and oddly heartening.

His lips curved as if the deed were already done. "Why were you hiding? Am I so very frightening?"

"Oh—I feared you were some sort of warrior."

The humor faded from his eyes. "I am."

Praise for Beth Trissel

ENEMY OF THE KING: "Beth Trissel is a skilled storyteller and scene-builder. She immediately plunges the reader into action and excitement with a vivid sense of time and place."

~*Historical Romance Author Kris Kennedy*
~*~

"I love historical romances. They are one of my favorites and anymore when I think of a historical I think of Beth Trissel."

~*Bella Wolfe, You Gotta Read*
~*~

2008 Golden Heart® Finalist
2008 Winner Preditor's & Editor's Readers Poll
Publisher's Weekly BHB Reader's Choice Best Books of 2009
2010 Best Romance Novel List at Buzzle
Five Time Book of the Week Winner At LASR
2012 Double Epic Award Finalist

Kira,
Daughter
of
the Moon

by

Beth Trissel

Kira, Daughter of the Moon

Cover Art by *Rae Monet, Inc. Design*

The Wild Rose Press, Inc.
PO Box 708
Adams Basin, NY 14410-0708
Visit us at www.thewildrosepress.com

Publishing History
First American Rose Edition, 2012
Print ISBN 978-1-61217-419-8
Digital ISBN 978-1-61217-420-4

Published in the United States of America

Dedication

To my mom,
whose wholehearted support encouraged me to
go the distance and finish this novel.

Chapter One

May 1765
The Allegheny Mountains of Western Virginia

Green-gold light streamed through the rippling
leaves while high overhead a yellow warbler trilled
sweet, sweet, sweet and the warmth of hay-scented
fern wafted on the mild breeze. A rush of
exhilaration swept through Kira McClure and a
fluttering of hope stirred inside her as it hadn't in
years. She wasn't certain why. Granted, it was a
glorious day, the sort when she could almost hear
the trees speak and if she listened closely enough,
sing the song of the woodlands in springtime.
Instead of tree song, warning rumbled from the
small brown and white beagle at her ankles.

She glanced down at the high-strung little
hound. Was he just being overly nervous—again—or
had he cause for alarm?

Plainly Bawtie thought he did.

How swiftly her Garden of Eden could transform
into a sinister place. Danger might lurk in the
deceptive beauty, like a coiled rattlesnake. She
swept her gaze over drifts of fern and trees cloaked
in delicate shades of green. Nothing seemed amiss,
but she might have overlooked something.

"Calm down, Bawtie. We'll leave in a bit."
Keeping an eye on the underbrush, Kira took the
young crow from her shoulder and thrust him up
toward the patch of blue peeking from between the
wind-tossed branches. "Your wing's mended,
Ebenezer. Go, boy!"

Rays of late afternoon sun touched the bird's iridescent wings as he fluttered briefly then settled back onto his usual perch. "Go boy," he mimicked in his throaty voice.

Groaning in frustration, she wriggled to dislodge him. Aunt Alice had banished the crow from the Houston homestead saying, "All those creatures of yours, filling your pockets with chipmunks and squirrels. And that bird is downright sassy."

The bristling dog growled with more insistence.

She strained to see through the leaves. "What is it, Bawtie?"

As if in reply, he broke into full cry and bounded up the stream bank. Startled ducks flapped from the water in a frenzy of wings while the scolding crow flew high overhead.

Good heavens. Snatching up her crimson petticoats, she picked her way across lichen-encrusted stones and scaled the gentle incline to pause beside the quivering hound, baying so loudly he hurt her ears. Was all this commotion over some dire threat or a harmless shadow?

There. Through the lavender blush of redbud and white-flowering dogwood, she spied the source of his alarm—a man advancing through the trees. Not anyone she knew, but likely a passing frontiersman who'd be on his way.

Then again, maybe not.

Hand to her throat, she peered at the stranger. His hunting shirt, the hue of deer's fur, blew in the breeze to reveal an elkskin breechclout and blue cloth leggings more in keeping with warrior's garb. True, some frontiersmen had adopted Indian dress after the recent wars, but the stealth in his manner reminded her of a brave.

Yet he wasn't one. Dappled light played over the loose reddish-brown hair falling to his well-muscled shoulders.

2

Chills prickled down her spine. Was he a renegade come to spy out their settlement? Lawless men sometimes ran with bands of warriors. Too many settlers in these mountains had been killed and captured for her to believe the uneasy truce made with the tribes last autumn would last. If the newcomer were in league with hostile Indians, she didn't want to be detected alone with only an incensed beagle for protection.

She clenched fingers gone cold. Perhaps her fears were foolish and he was a harmless stranger.

And perhaps not.

His long strides brought him nearer to her with each step. Her usual hiding places were out of reach and her skirts as red as a cardinal's wings—easily spotted.

Everything in her urged concealment. *Now*!

Heart thudding, she sprang behind a broad maple tree and flattened herself against the furrowed trunk.

Had he seen her? He'd have to be stone-deaf not to notice the commotion emanating from her side.

She bent down, pushing at the little dog and hissed, "Shh, Bawtie. Go home."

Clearly, the steadfast beagle considered this poor judgment on her part and refused to budge. If he wouldn't distance himself from her, she must remove herself from him. With the instincts of a bear cub, she leapt up and clamped her fingers around the tree's lower limb. Kicking her legs, she heaved herself up onto this first level and scrambled onto the next. The bark scraped her knuckles and she stepped on her hem, throwing herself off balance.

Clumsy. All she needed was a tumble from the tree and a broken ankle. But she had to get higher.

Chest heaving inside her skirted bodice, she hoisted herself onto a third limb then a fourth. She flung her leg over the next branch and clambered up—

Her skirts snagged.

"Ooohhh," she grunted, clinging to the branch above her with a length of petticoat suspended overhead. Both legs were exposed above the knee. Tugging only wound the fabric more tightly.

Damn it all, she was snared like a bird in a trap with that man rapidly closing the distance between them. He'd be here in a—

Too late. He'd come. Kira could only pray he'd think her frantic dog alone. And that he wouldn't look up.

The intruder stopped a few yards beyond the tree and bent down. Hand extended to the blaring hound, he crooned, "Steady on, fellow. What's all the fuss about?"

He sounded amiable enough, but that might be a ruse. From her awkward perch, she watched him dip into the fringed pouch hanging from his woven belt.

"How about this?" He tossed the tidbit to her sentry.

Bawtie gulped his offering in mid-yelp.

"Liked that, did you?" The man offered another treat.

The little beggar ceased hostilities and wagged his rear-end. The next thing Kira knew, the stranger was kneeling beneath her lofty hideout while the tail-thumping traitor had his ears stroked.

"Now then, where's your mistress gotten to?" Humor tinged the newcomer's low voice.

She stifled a groan, her fear fast changing into red-faced embarrassment as heat flooded her cheeks. He must've spotted her before and Bawtie was only too glad to assist him now with a soulful upward gaze.

"Thought as much." He lifted his head, eying her in amusement.

God help her, she could die of mortification. And

oh, was he handsome. What she could see of him anyway. She felt miles above the forest floor. Even that wasn't distant enough, though, as he smiled up at her and the spectacle she'd made of herself. Why had she worn crimson today? She should've donned her mud-colored petticoats and blended in better, or run in the first place—

"Hullo there!" His call disrupted her internal tirade.

Ebenezer chose that particular moment to land on what he could reach of her shoulder and answered, "Hullo!"

The man chuckled. "Another defender?"

Kira nodded, all she could manage in her awkward state.

"Have you others?"

She lifted her chin—sort of—and blew a dark strand of hair from her eyes. "Not at hand."

He cocked his head to one side. "Pardon my intrusion, Miss, but you seem in want of aid."

Refusing any acknowledgement of her situation, she said, "No. Just resting," as if clinging to the tree in this absurd manner were a common occurrence.

"Indeed? I could swear you were stuck up there."

"I'm quite comfortable."

"Ah. Would you like me to go, then?"

Heartily. She felt an utter fool.

"Very well. I shall bid you good day." With a cheery wave, the frontiersman turned and started down the ferny path.

Returning the gesture was impossible; she didn't dare move. It occurred to her, rather strongly, that perhaps on this particular occasion it might be best to pocket her pride. Not readily done, but Kira called after him "Wait!"

He stopped on the trail and pivoted. "Yes?"

"Please—would you be so good as to free my skirts?"

"You don't intend them arranged in that fashion?"

Cheeky fellow. "I fear they'll have to be cut loose!"

"Fear not." He propped his long musket against the trunk. Taking his tomahawk from where he'd slung it at his belt, he laid it on the ground then swung himself up into the tree. With catlike grace, he climbed to her perch and scaled the branch above that she'd failed to master. She saw the top of one moccasin reaching mid-calf on his muscular leg.

"Only cut a bit off," she pleaded. Cloth was dear, and Aunt Alice would have fits if she returned with her petticoats in shreds.

"I think we can forego the blade." He left the knife in its sheath and freed the stubborn cloth with his fingers.

Crimson homespun and white linen spilled down over her face. The indignant crow flew while she floundered beneath the folds. Her champion restored order with unseen hands and she found herself gazing up into the most amazing pair of gold-flecked brown eyes. A strange sensation rifled through her. "I thank you, sir."

Abundant humor warmed his appraisal. "My pleasure, Miss. 'Tis a service I can honestly say I've never rendered."

No doubt. She cringed at what he must've seen during her immodest display and could kick herself for the impetuous climb. But how could she possibly expect to encounter such a man out in the woods today—or ever, for that matter. His vibrant presence charged the very air with masculinity.

He swung himself down beside her and balanced on the stout branch with ease, his ruggedly attractive face framed against the rustling leaves. Only the nick of a scar on his forehead and chin detracted from an otherwise unmarred

countenance—plainly he'd been in a fight or two—
but pox had left him untouched and his looks were
wholly pleasing. A smile enhanced his powerful
appeal and he was smiling at her now. She had to
remember to close her mouth and not gape back
while fingering the drawstring at her neck. Her shift
should've been more snugly drawn, and she'd
neglected to don a jacket over her bodice. Most
unseemly. Despite her self-consciousness, she
couldn't look away from him. Not only because he
was mightily attractive, but hauntingly familiar, his
face, his voice...

He returned her scrutiny with open, even bold,
appreciation. "Do you often climb about in trees?"

She replied absently. "Now and then."

"Rather unusual for a young woman."

"Is it?" she asked, intrigued by the bits of gold in
his eyes, like hidden treasure. How many men could
possibly have this unique feature? She knew of one.
But he couldn't be whom she suspected, not after all
these years.

Fingering a chin dusted with brown whiskers,
he asked, "Why did you fancy a climb today? Not
that I mind."

She lifted her shoulders and let them drop. "'Tis
Tuesday. I often go climbing on Tuesdays."

Not an arch of his brow or the slightest
indication of the surprise she was accustomed to.
"Any particular reason?"

She pursed her lips in the thoughtful manner
she'd found effective. "Seeking for the little folk."

"Found any, yet?"

His unruffled question took her aback. "Oh—I'm
not to tell. Fairies wouldn't like me sharing their
secrets."

He threw back his head and laughed.

Disconcerting. Most people simply stared at her
or shook their heads when she acted peculiar, not

this undisguised mirth. "I can't imagine why you're taking on like this."

"No?" He succumbed to another paroxysm of laughter. "I must admit you're good."

A lift of her chin. "At what, pray tell?"

"Play acting."

Stiffening her reply, she said, "I haven't the faintest notion what you mean."

He wiped his eyes on the wide sleeve of his loosely belted shirt. "Haven't you, now?"

Her eyes strayed to his browned chest where the earth-colored cloth gapped open at his neck. "Not at all."

"If you truly wish me to think you *tetched*, dim the brightness in your gaze. Try for a more vacant expression."

"I can manage quite well without direction from you." She hesitated. "I mean—"

"I know what you mean. I see you're quite the actress."

Shifting her gaze from the intensity in his expression to the swaying branches, she asked, "How so?"

"I could always see right through you."

An odd flop in her stomach and she slid her gaze back to his penetrating eyes. "Always?"

"Don't you know me, Cricket?"

"Good heavens," she breathed out, and leaned weakly against the tree. She could have toppled to the forest floor. Only two people had ever called her by that name and this definitely wasn't her brother. The teasing youth she'd adored had returned a man in warrior's clothing, hardened now, tested by wind and fire. "Logan?"

He smiled, no longer in teasing, but a deep down grin that ripped right through her. "I was beginning to fear you'd forgotten me entirely."

"Never."

Eyes flashing with that irresistible twinkle, he reached out to steady her. "Took you long enough to say."

She answered shakily. "I can't believe it's you. You're so changed."

"And you. How you've grown."

The warmth of his hand flowed through her shift and sent tingles down her arm. "Did you think to find the waif your relations took in?"

"I didn't know what I'd find. You're a far cry from that mite. You filled out nicely."

"So have you." She faltered at her unintended candor. "I—you—were gone so long, Logan."

"Did you miss me?"

Every interminable day. "You know how I felt about you."

A hint of regret crossed his expression. "Poor lass. I teased you shamefully."

"And treated me like a little sister."

"Was I to regard you as the love of my life when you were barely thirteen and I a strapping lad of seventeen?"

"I suppose not." But how she'd wished.

Head tilted to one side, he appraised her with a keen eye, approval in his gaze. "The years between us don't seem to make such a difference now, do they?"

A shiver darted through her. "Not like they once did."

He ran his fingers lightly over her cheek. "I'll have to make amends for my past neglect."

Her chest thudded wildly. "Will you?"

"Oh, yes."

As though she'd issued an invitation, Logan slid closer to her so they were pressed thigh to thigh, nearer than she'd sat to any man. He turned, circling an arm around her waist, and drew her into his hard chest. His low voice a shivery whisper in her ear, he said, "This'll do for a start."

Too stunned to speak, she wondered if her galloping heart might give out altogether. This must be a dream. He couldn't be real. Yet he felt wonderfully solid and smelled of the sun-warmed earth mingled with his own appealing essence, heightening her acute awareness of him. But he was overtaking her with the sudden fury of a gale.

She found her tongue. "I hardly know what to think."

He didn't loosen his grip. "Don't think just yet."

"But you've told me nothing—"

"Shh...just feel."

Too dazed to do anything else, she pressed her cheek against the inviting hollow of his shoulder. Was she truly conscious? How was it possible that Logan was here holding her? She lifted her head, searching his face. He did the same in wind-swept silence and she could scarcely breathe.

Loosening her braid, he slipped his fingers through the unbound lengths. "Ah, Kira. What a beauty you are, hair as black as night and past your waist now. Your eyes haven't changed, still colored like violets and filled with questions. Tell me, in all the years I've been gone, how many lads have kissed you?"

"Tried or succeeded?" She gulped out.

A smile turned up the corners of his mouth. "Succeeded."

"None has claimed more than I've been willing to give."

A devilish twinkle. "And what was that?"

"The back of my hand. My cheek if I were generous."

His smile broadened and his eyes sparkled at her. "High time you were properly kissed."

"That's what I've been trying to avoid—"

"Quite right. But I'm back now."

"And you're the proper one to do the kissing, are you?"

"The very one for whom you professed undying love."

Shame still seared her. "I hoped you'd forgotten that."

"Such a heartfelt declaration?"

"Whispered in the dead of night when I thought you fast asleep. You laughed."

"To my deep regret. Just allow me one small kiss upon those sweet lips that uttered the vow."

Part of Kira yearned for his kiss. She'd dreamed of him often enough, Lord knows, but the part of her drilled in caution wanted to flee far away. Flight not possible in her present state, she shrank back against his shoulder.

He cupped his hand under her chin and tilted her face toward him. "You can't hide from me that easily."

But hiding was what Kira did best.

A towering figure flashed through her mind, offering her another way out. "Josiah Campbell will thrash you if he discovers you've kissed me."

Logan drew chestnut eyebrows together in a hard line. "Laying claim to you, is he? We'll just see about that."

"Josiah's as big as a barn," she warned.

"Then Mister Campbell had better find himself a cow and leave you to me."

A cloud of butterflies took flight in her stomach. "I don't know if I want to be left to you."

The flint in Logan's expression softened. His gaze caressed her as he stroked one finger over her cheek. "Close those wide eyes, Cricket. Trust me, for old times' sake."

"I never really trusted you then."

"But you cared for me."

To the depths of her soul. Not that she was about

11

to make that admission. Still…she warily shut out the blowing leaves and his mesmerizing eyes. Shivers coursed through her. Would he act at once or wait?

He didn't leave her long in suspense. Warmth enveloped her as his lips stole over hers in tender invitation, stirring to the core. *Dear Lord.* A hundred drums beat in her chest—shocking sensation. Surely, she'd jar them from the tree.

Logan held her to him and the tantalizing pressure on her mouth increased, conveying a sense of urgency as contagious as a fever. Heady desire swelled up in her like water from a spring…wondrous, all-consuming.

Overwhelming.

Awash in this new sensation, she clung to the little reason she had left before swirling away, enveloped by Logan. Nor was it lost on her that although this was *her* first real kiss it couldn't possibly be *his.* From his initial caress he'd rapidly taken possession of her. With whom had he gained such proficiency while she'd dodged suitors and prayed for his return?

Accusation boiled up inside her, indignation lending her the much needed impetus to tear free from his seductive mouth. "You have some cheek, Logan. You can't just reappear after all these years and play the lover. I never thought to see you again this side of heaven. Other captives returned last fall." How devastated she'd been at his absence.

Regret etched his face, reflected in those extraordinary eyes. "I'm sorry, Kira. More than I can say."

His entreaty was nigh irresistible. But she didn't relent. "Why didn't you come home sooner?"

"I have my reasons."

Much was implied in his quiet tone, along with the hint that he'd had some control over his destiny.

"What do you mean? The return of all captives was a condition Colonel Bouquet demanded in his treaty with the chiefs."

Logan's jaw tightened. "Some captives evaded this *condition* and rightly so."

Hurt needled her. "I don't understand."

Grim lines crimped the edges of his mouth. "I don't expect you to."

"You've not given me a chance yet."

Silence. And his eyes were veiled.

His reluctance rose between them like a wall. "Don't cut me off without an explanation. Please Logan. You owe me this much."

He parted tight lips. "Many captives were spared torture and adopted into the tribe. To return home after living all these years with the Shawnee can be terribly painful."

A red haze roiled through her. "How can anyone form attachments to such a fierce enemy?"

"They're not always fierce. I was shown much kindness."

"They killed my father! And yours. Likely my brother as well. A wounded grizzly has more compassion."

"I thought that once. But they treated me as an equal."

"You were an equal here. More highly regarded than many. You sound like the Williams boy, home six months and still raving about his Indian family."

Logan hardly seemed to hear. His eyes grew distant as if he were looking beyond her. "I've much affection for my adopted father and others. Did you think I could live seven years with them and form no bonds?"

She recoiled. "By heavens, I could. Is your heart so full for these savages you found it painful to return?"

He tensed beside her. "I'm here now, aren't I?"

13

"And would have been far sooner had you escaped—seems that wasn't uppermost in your mind."

"At first I badly wanted to run, but was too well guarded. Then…I no longer wanted to go."

She could have shoved him out of the tree. "How dare you make such an outrageous declaration?"

"You demanded an explanation."

"I never thought to hear this!" At least before his reappearance, she'd held his memory dear with the assurance that he'd surely return if he could. Now, her world crashed around her. She wanted to pound his chest with her fists and rail at him, but tears threatened to choke her.

Blinking furiously, she pressed her forehead against the rough bark. "Go away."

"Wait, Kira. Hear me out. I never meant to wound you."

The hell he didn't.

He clasped her shoulder with one hand. "Look at me."

"No."

"I don't blame you for being upset."

Swiping at her cheeks, she rounded on him. "*Upset* was when your aunt banished my creatures from the house. I'm well beyond that!"

"Distraught then."

"There's no word strong enough for this. Am I forever to be abandoned?"

"I didn't intend to abandon—"

"All those years, Logan. Did you spare me a thought? You care nothing for me."

"Not true." He gathered her, struggling, in his arms.

"Leave me be." She would have given her life for him. Now, she scrabbled at the tree with her foot in her effort to free herself. Her shoe slid off, dropped through the branches, and *thunked* onto the ground as she was about to.

She clutched at him. "Logan—"

He kept her in place with unflappable balance. "Be still. I've got you."

A sob shook her. "Don't want you to."

"I won't have you weeping without comfort."

"What in blazes do you think I've been doing all this time?" she demanded, sounding very like her gruff guardian, Logan's Uncle Peter.

"I'm sorry for all the pain I caused you, Cricket. I had no idea you'd wait so long for me. I'm flattered—amazed—"

"Oh, hush. I wish you had never come."

"You don't mean that. What about our kiss?"

"You started it," she forced past the lump in her throat.

"And you kissed me back, the sweetest I've ever had."

"Ever?" The word arrested her.

He traced her downturned lips with his finger. "Ever."

A spark shimmered through her; she tightened her defenses. "I'll not kiss you again. I'd sooner slap you."

"Maybe so, but you will. Before the night's out."

She squeezed her eyes against the gleam in his. "Won't."

"Want to wager on that?"

"You've nothing to wager with."

"I wouldn't be so certain."

She cracked her eyes and peered at him. "What?"

"My secret in exchange for yours."

Tantalizing. He was drawing her into his snare, but she couldn't resist asking, "How do you know I've a secret?"

"To begin with, you're hiding in a tree. What from, a wild beast?"

15

"Near enough. You."

He smiled. "Was I to think you a large red bird, or overlook you entirely?"

Drawing her remaining shreds of dignity around her like a mantle, she said, "This isn't one of my best hiding places."

"Indeed? Where are the others?"

"That would be telling."

The strengthening breeze tossed the branches around them as he considered. "You never could keep secrets from me, Cricket. I'll discover them and you."

An assertion she found both disturbing and oddly heartening.

His lips curved as if the deed were already done. "Why were you hiding? Am I so very frightening?"

"Oh—I feared you were some sort of warrior."

The humor faded from his eyes. "I am."

Chapter Two

Kira's dark brows arched and her blue eyes widened. Logan wasn't certain why he'd made that shocking disclosure. She'd already gotten more from him than he meant to reveal initially—possibly ever. He supposed somewhere inside him he wanted her to understand how he felt about his Shawnee ties. He also knew that she wouldn't.

Even now, she was shrinking back against the trunk like a ravishingly pretty kitten. Frightening Kira wasn't at all what he'd intended, but then he never expected to be so taken with her in the first place. She was the one person, though, whom he owed at least some portion of the truth.

The strengthening wind rocked the tree and whipped glossy black hair across her stunned face. Then she seemed to come to her senses and a torrent of protest rushed from her bonnie mouth. "You can't be a warrior! You're white."

"I'm adopted into the tribe. A white warrior."

A vehement shake of her head. "No! How can you deny your family? The blood of the clans flows in your veins." She regarded him with the censure of generations of Scots. "Have you forgotten everything you ever were? You're a McCutcheon, for God's sake. Logan McCutcheon."

His name uttered in her accent struck a twinge in him. "I haven't been called that in ages."

"Good Heavens. Have you a Shawnee name?"

"Alaquoi."

"I can't believe I'm sitting up here with a warrior." Faint hope lit her gaze. "Did they force you

17

to become one?"

"*Nay*. I asked to be taught. My adopted father and his brother took pains to instruct me. I wasn't treated any differently than one born into the tribe. I have many friends in the village. I fought by their side."

Knuckles white, she gripped the branch beneath them. "Against who?"

"Mohawk."

She exhaled in evident relief.

"Until we got caught up in a battle with redcoats."

Her fair skin blanched even whiter. "You fought against *British* troops?"

"I couldn't leave my friends to fight alone. Not that I was much help on that occasion. My Shawnee father had to battle twice as hard just to keep me alive. I owe him, all of them, a great debt."

"Dear God, Logan. The chatter of squirrels makes more sense. You're far crazier than anything I ever pretended."

He pounced on her words. "So you admit to pretending?"

"Fine. I admit it. 'Tis a puny effort in comparison to your doings."

He let her scathing comparison pass. She'd always been unusual, but seemed bent on being odd. "Why do you playact?"

A haunted look crossed Kira's eyes. She waved him aside. "We're not discussing me. Your madness was the subject. And don't think I'm going to start calling you Alaquoi."

"Logan suits me fine. I've rather missed hearing my English name, now that I think of it."

"At least that's a step in the right direction. Your behavior is disgraceful. Despicable. I'm shocked. I'm—" she halted, apparently at a momentary loss.

He smiled. What a hissing, spitting little fury. Not at all the timid girl he recalled and marvelous to watch.

She glared at him. "Are you listening to a word I've said?"

"Every single one."

"Then stop grinning at me like a lunatic. Your uncle would thrash you within an inch of your life if he knew, and believe me, he could. He's still as strong as an ox."

"Undoubtedly," Logan answered, observing the play of emotions across her expressive features.

A quizzical arch of her brow. "Have you forgotten his temper?"

"It's not likely I'd forget that hothead."

"Then why are you so unconcerned? Uncle Peter and Will are away from home, but we expect them back any hour."

Logan shrugged at the mention of his cantankerous uncle and mettlesome cousin. "I don't intend telling them a thing."

Challenge flashed in her eyes. "What if I tell?"

"You won't. You don't want to see us come to blows."

"Maybe Uncle Peter could knock some sense into you."

"Wouldn't be the first time he tried."

"I begged you not to get on his bad side," she reminded him. "You have his temper. It just doesn't show as often."

"You have ample temper of your own, Miss."

"I'm not the one turned traitor."

Anger flared in him. "Those words would never pass your lips unpunished were you a man."

She thrust her chin inches from his. "Don't let that stop you. Pitch me out of the tree. Go ahead. I dare you."

The volatile emotion firing in him dwindled at

her outburst. He chuckled. "You're wonderful, Kira. You really should be a redhead, but I prefer you as you are."

Her irate gaze softened. "Don't scold me, then."

"Don't call me a traitor. I was only aiding my friends."

The corners of her eyes creased in exasperation and she threw her hand up. "You're not supposed to have those sorts of friends."

He caught her fingers. "You may be glad enough I do."

Conflicting emotions crossed her face. "You mean if we're attacked? Are they plotting something?"

"Not that I'm aware of."

"Then why—"

"I can't say."

"But you'd sound warning, if you knew, wouldn't you?"

"Kira, I'd never let harm come to you or my relations."

Eyes on his all the while, she considered for a long moment, shivering in the rising breeze.

"You're cold." To shield her, and as an excuse to keep her near, he tucked her between himself and the trunk. "This is rather like the tree house we played in as children, don't you think?"

"A bit. But you're nothing like you were back then."

"Nor you." How soft and feminine she was, far more alluring than any woman he'd ever known.

He thought she might insist he let her go, but she remained quietly against him, possibly too overcome to act. Whatever the reason, he reveled in the sheer feel of the girl, not too thin, with delectable curves. The smell of soap clung to her, the kind his aunt made scented with spiceberries. He knew Kira had no idea the havoc she played with his emotions, but that only made her all the more enticing.

What on earth was he to do? His plans were laid out and she didn't figure into them. Not far into the future, anyway. He slid silky strands of her hair between his fingers. "Holding you like this, I don't ever want to let you go."

"Are you luring me into some sort of seduction?"

Smiling at her innocent suspicion, he pressed his lips to her smooth cheek. "Not up here in this tree." A sigh escaped him. "Ah, Cricket, I loathe the thought of parting from you."

She stiffened. "You'll be staying with us, won't you?"

"Not for long."

"Oh." Such a small sound. Lifting her head to look at him, she asked, "Will you reclaim the McCutcheon homestead?"

He flinched at the mention of his family place and the secret task awaiting him there.

"There was a fire and the cabin burned," she continued.

"I heard."

"How could you possibly have?"

Another slip on his part. "I don't recall."

She had to know that wasn't true.

Regarding him closely, she said, "The site is overgrown, but the land's good and the men would help you rebuild."

He hated to think of all he'd known burnt to cinders. "I'm not a farmer anymore. I scarcely remember that life."

Pleading glistened in her eyes. "You could learn again."

He could hardly look her in the face and speak two words together. "I don't belong here."

"What are you saying?"

"I can't be what I'm not."

Her lips trembled. "You haven't even tried."

"There's no use. I must return to my friends."

Breath escaped her in short pants. "You still have friends here. You're not forgotten. Please, Logan. You've only just come."

"I'll stay. For a time."

Reproach narrowed her gaze. "Long enough to take all I have to give, then leave me?"

"I didn't mean—I'm not heartless."

"You give every appearance." Up went her chin with the innate pride he sensed in her and she bit out, "Go then. Back to your Shawnee friends. I can't prevent you."

"You can make it very difficult."

She fairly bristled at him. "I'm certain you shall manage quite well without me. You've done so for years."

"It's different now."

"Everything's different now, you wretched man! Get me down from here this instant."

"Calm yourself. I'm willing." *And the sooner, the better, before he disclosed any more.* He swung down to the branch below. Steadying himself with one hand, he reached up to her with the other. "Easy. It's quite a drop."

Blinking at tears, she reached for his outstretched fingers then hesitated, staring at the forest floor with a strange expression on her face. "Perhaps I'll fly down."

Fear seized him with an ice cold hand. There was no telling what this unpredictable girl might do in her distress. Before she twitched, he plucked Kira from her perch with the suddenness of a hawk snatching a dove and held her against him, his heart pounding. "Don't ever let me catch you contemplating anything so daft again."

She gasped in his near fierce hold. "You're leaving me, remember?"

"I'm not gone yet." He pushed her down onto the

22

limb. "Wait here."

Lips clamped together, he climbed down to the next branch and beckoned. Just let her dare try to refuse.

Annoyance in every taut line of her face, she bent toward him. He dragged his eyes from the rounded breasts peeking above her fitted bodice, minus its jacket, and closed his hands under her shoulders to lift her down beside him.

She glowered at him from beneath dark, beaded lashes. "What gives you the right to order me about?"

He closed his arm around her waist. "You belong to me."

"Impudent fellow. How on earth did you arrive at that?"

"I've possessed your heart since you were a wee lass."

"Quite the contrary, sir. I detest you."

Logan held her to him a moment longer than necessary. Even in her wrath, she was pliant in his grasp. "Loathing is not what I feel in you, Miss." He descended to the branch below them and stood her on the lowest limb, then sprang to the moss. "Come on."

"I can't break my neck from this height." Sitting on the branch, she leaned back against the trunk. "Go away."

"Not without you."

"Ah well, might be a while. I may set up camp in this tree." She pointed at the pinkish-brown toadstools circling the base. "A fairy ring. I'll be in good company."

"You're talking nonsense."

"You're a fine one to judge."

Bawtie leapt up, tail wagging, and scratched at the bark. "Your friend's waiting for you," Logan coaxed.

"Useless little beggar. It's all your fault, Bawtie, bringing this renegade to me in the first place."

The dog flopped down, peering from between his paws with sorrowful brown eyes. Logan bent to pat his floppy ears. "Don't scold him. I'd have found you anyway. Aunt Alice told me where to look."

She sat bolt upright. "You already visited the house?"

Her unease was apparent, and he pressed his advantage. "Oh yes. My dear aunt was delighted to see me. Poor woman is fretting over you, gal, says you've been acting strange. Fancy that?"

Kira shrugged in a feeble attempt at casualness.

"She wants me to look out for you as a sort of guardian."

Lurching forward, Kira dug her fingers into the bark. "You can't—you're not even going to be here."

"I am, for a time."

"How long? Hours, days, weeks?"

Logan straightened. "Can't say. I've divulged enough and you've not yet won our wager."

"There's more to your secret?"

"Like the layers of an onion, you must peel me away to get to the core."

She wrinkled her nose. "Uncle Peter is guardian enough."

"Aunt Alice intends persuading him to entrust you to me."

"He won't," Kira scoffed. "There's too much bad feeling between you."

"Uncle Peter is a bad-tempered old coot, but he dotes on his bonnie wife." Aware of Kira waiting in palpable tension, Logan plucked her shoe from the toadstools and handed it to her. "Besides, she fears he'll marry you off to the first man who asks."

"Your uncle might as well toss me to the wolves as to entrust me to you."

"Come now, I'm not so bad. Aunt Alice says I'll

do you a power of good and she doesn't trust that Campbell fellow," he said, mimicking his aunt's brogue.

No smile from Kira. "Uncle Peter likes Josie well enough."

The familiarity of the name cut through Logan. "You're to call him *Mister Campbell*."

That mulish glint shone in her eyes. "I can call my beau what I like."

Logan clenched his fists. "Now he's your beau, is he? You dislike Josiah Campbell and you know it, Kira."

"Is that so?" Revealing a well turned ankle, she slipped stocking-clad toes into the shoe. "He's a perfect gentleman in comparison to you."

"He throws his weight around like some clan laird and pummels anyone who gets in the way. You would fare better with wolves than with him."

Kira crossed both arms over her distracting bust. "I need a man devoted to me, not one allied with savages."

Molten anger flowed through every sinew of Logan's being, but she paid no mind. With a toss of her head, she added, "*Josie's* calling this evening. Maybe I'll let him take my hand, even kiss—"

"And maybe I'll take you captive!" Panther like, he sprang and jerked her down from the tree. "Just like that."

She shrieked and twisted in his arms. "You can't be serious!"

Bawtie whined and pawed his legs. "Your little dog thinks I am."

She beat at his chest. "You wouldn't dare carry me off."

"Then why are you so frightened? You're not a large lass, Kira. I could haul you part way."

Eyes wild, she argued, "Someone would see."

He grabbed up his musket and slipped the strap

over his shoulder. "Who?"

She swiveled her pale face at the trees. "Uncle Peter would come after me. Will and Josiah too."

The familiar tomahawk slung at his side, he strode through rippling fern. "The Shawnee taught me to lose myself in these ridges and not leave a trail. And I know my way."

"You're out of your mind entirely."

"So you've said." The nervous beagle at his heels, he bore her down the stream bank. "My moccasins leave no mark, nor will the water when I ford it."

Her eyes fixed on him with the intensity of a trapped badger. "Where are you taking me?"

Orange lichens covered the log he stepped over. "Haven't I said?"

She clutched at him like a drowning woman. "You can't mean it. I don't believe—Oh, Logan— please don't."

Damn, she was adorable. He almost relented. But she needed a lesson. "You'll come to like living with Indians, sweetheart."

"The hell I will."

Disbelief slowed him. "Since when do you swear, Miss?"

"Since now."

"Well you can stop that kind of talk right now. Aunt Alice would be shocked."

"Who's going to tell her?"

"I will if you keep it up."

Kira regarded him shakily. "You aren't hauling me off?"

He stopped beside a clump of sassafras trees, their mitten shaped leaves blowing in the wind. "I promised her I'd fetch you back, didn't I?"

Breath escaped Kira in a great sigh of relief. "You never had any intention of taking me away?"

"I didn't say *never*."

"Logan! You can't just carry me off."

"Didn't I just prove I could?" He lowered her to her feet.

She glared up at him, standing more than a head taller than she. Her wrath filled the gap between them. "You beat all! I'd be hard pressed to find any man with more cheek. I've a half mind to tell Aunt Alice about you."

"She won't believe you." He knelt by moss-covered stones and cupped his hands into the clear cold water to drink. "You've made such a pretense of being peculiar, I doubt anyone will."

Kira squatted beside him and scooped the water to her lips with near ferocity. "I am not a liar."

"No, *given to strange fancies* were Aunt Alice's words. It amounts to the same thing in the end."

A strangled cry broke from Kira and she leapt up. "You will drive me to distraction." She swept moist fingers at him dismissively. "I've finished with you entirely."

Wiping his mouth on the back of his hand, he rose. "Most inopportune as I've only just begun with you."

Crimson petticoats awhirl, she spun away and fled through a patch of heart-shaped violets. He followed at her heels. "After so many years apart don't you want to become better acquainted?"

She darted to the side of the path behind a chestnut.

Logan waited, one hand propped on the wide trunk. As expected, greenbriers forced her back onto the path. "I find you fascinating. Have you no wish to know more of me?"

"I know enough. Let me pass, sir. I'll not be carried off to any damn Indians."

He stepped aside. "Your language is rapidly worsening."

She hurried past him through gold daisies no

27

bigger than his thumbnail. "I'm not speaking to you, remember."

"Pity. I adore listening."

Pink and white trillium flanked the trail she sped over. She stumbled on her hem and he lunged forward to grasp her shoulder and prevent her from falling on the stones scattered at her feet. "Are we racing?"

"Not with me in these stupid skirts."

"Tell you what, hitch up your petticoats and we'll race like we used to. I'll even give you a head start."

As if weighing the odds, she slanted her eyes down the length of his legs. "Even so, I'm not likely to outrun you."

"You came close, as I recall. Unless, you're slower now," he baited.

"No." Still, she hesitated. "Did I really catch you, or did you just let me?"

He smiled. "I'll let you now."

Eyes wide, she blurted, "I don't want to catch you!"

"Am I so very alarming? Apart from my threat to carry you off, I mean?"

The rapid pulse in her throat beat out a reply.

"I could be extremely soothing if you'd allow me."

At that, she snatched up her skirts, whirled around, and pelted away through the trees. Allowing her the head start he'd promised, Logan sidled from foot to foot.

Confound it. How was he to know the most desirable woman of his acquaintance would turn out to be wee little Kira McClure? No longer so wee and quite a handful to boot.

Chapter Three

Just wait. Kira would prove to Logan how fast she was then he'd see she couldn't be hauled off like some captive. *The traitor.* That wretched word pounded in her head and churned in her gut. Stretching out her legs for all she was worth, she tore through the woods and left Logan behind— physically. He was still very much in her mind.

His eyes had an almost hypnotic, decidedly unnerving, effect on her; she vowed never to look into their gold-flecked depths again. She'd hide until he went away, as he inevitably would. If only that thought didn't hurt all the way down to the pit of her aching belly.

Forget him! Just run!

Meadowlarks trilled from the tall grass as she burst out of the trees and sprinted toward the split rail fence encircling the meadow. Her petticoats disappeared halfway to her knees in the lush blades. No time to stop and unlatch the gate. Without pausing to catch her breath, she scrambled over the zigzagged rails and took off again.

The grass was shorter here from the flock of black-faced sheep that grazed in the enclosure, which made running easier. But a wide swathe of green lay between her and the stone house up on the hill. Despite the sharp stitch growing in her side, she raced on, panting, skirts swishing, the soggy earth squelching beneath her shoes. She'd run till she dropped if need be.

Startled ewes scuttled aside at her coming while frisky lambs joined in her supposed game. One

29

playful baby kicked up his heels and sprang directly across her path. Veering to avoid the infant, she smacked headlong into its sturdy mother. The impact flung her flat on her back, knocking the wind from her. She lay gasping like a stranded fish while curious matrons gathered around her and Bawtie nosed her face.

"Cricket!" Logan's head appeared above the wooly assembly.

She moaned in pain and mortification. Why was it that she seemed destined to appear a fool in front of him?

He made his way through the sheep to where she was sprawled. "Are you all right?"

A coherent reply beyond her, she moaned.

His anxious gaze scanned her for injury as he laid his musket down and knelt beside her. "Does this hurt?" he asked, and ran gentle hands over her arms and shoulders.

She fought to recover her breath and shook her head.

"Good. What of this?" He shoved up her skirts and pressed his fingers over her lower legs.

"No—don't." She struggled to push his hands away.

"I'll not see anything I haven't already been privy to. Are you certain you haven't turned an ankle or something?"

"I'm not made of glass," she gasped, neglecting to mention the growing ache in her knee.

The tension in his eyes eased. "Glad to hear it. You took quite a spill."

"Was I much ahead before?" she managed between pants.

He considered her in bemusement. "Does it truly matter?"

She gave a nod.

"You're the fastest woman I know, Kira

McClure."

"But you're faster still?"

"I've outrun warriors who race horses for sport."

She swallowed hard.

A knowing grin spread over his face. "You wanted to see if you could escape me, didn't you?"

Gathering as much dignity as she could under the circumstances, she countered, "There are other ways."

"Ah, yes. Your hiding places."

"And my defenders."

His widening smile showed white teeth. "The ones who won't believe you?"

She eyed him frostily. "Not all are human."

He gestured at the worried dog and inquisitive sheep. "What? This lot?"

"That's not all."

"Right. I'm forgetting your crow."

She itched to smack the smirk from his face. "You don't know everything about me."

"Yet." Logan rose, picked up his musket, then bent and held out his hand. "Let's see if you can stand."

"I can manage without your help. Go on."

"I'll wait."

She stifled groans as she got to her feet under his quizzical gaze. Walking was more of a challenge; she was forced to adopt a peculiar hop.

He frowned at her. "Out with it, Kira. What have you done to yourself?"

"Nothing." She stopped, balancing on her sound leg, her sore limb bent to try and keep the weight off. "Much."

"You're standing like a bloody heron. You'll not reach the house before nightfall at this pace."

"No doubt Josiah will gladly assist me when he arrives."

The hair whipping across her eyes obscured the

annoyance in Logan's, but it resounded in his voice. "Of all the pigheaded nonsense. Are you gonna wait out here for him?"

Kira lifted her chin to match the jut in his. "Maybe I prefer Josiah's guardianship to yours."

"Aunt Alice prefers me."

"Only out of sheer ignorance."

Logan considered her, the pull at his mouth lessening as the irritation in his face diminished. "Another has made this request. One who knows me well."

He seemed in earnest. She pushed aside lengths of her hair to study his apparent sincerity. "But you've not seen Uncle Peter or Will yet."

"It's not one of them." No trace of teasing sounded in his quiet reply.

"Who, then?"

That veil again shadowed his gaze. "I shouldn't have said."

Anger sparked in her. "Why do you torment me with these bits and pieces?"

"I'm sorry. You're not ready to hear this yet."

"I've not been ready for a great deal you've thrown at me! What do you know that I don't?"

His lips twitched. "Quite a bit. You'll have to wait to learn."

Kira shifted her injured leg in mounting discomfort. "Never mind, then."

"Oh stop being stubborn. Tell me what you've hurt."

"I'm not speaking to you, remember?"

Those eyes she'd swore to avoid glinted with promise. "Fine. Then you'll not utter a sound while I strip off your stockings and have a look."

"Logan—don't—" She turned away, staggering at the pain.

A squeal escaped her as he swept her up off the ground and into his arms. "Tell me, Kira, or I swear

I will."

"My knee could do with a poultice," she admitted.

"There. Was that so difficult?"

Telling him anything riled her when he was being so maddeningly furtive.

"I'd better carry you back to the house before you make yourself any worse."

"But Aunt Alice will fear I've been stricken if I return like this."

"You don't look the least bit stricken. Your eyes are bright, cheeks pink, and hair all tumbled about as though..." his voice trailed off, a smile at his mouth.

Immediately on her guard, Kira asked, "What?"

"Nothing. You never looked lovelier."

"Aunt Alice won't be alarmed?"

"Trust me. Alarm won't even cross her mind."

He seemed genuine enough, but Kira suspected he'd left something unsaid.

Chapter Four

Logan followed Kira's uncertain gaze across the rolling pasture to the stone house on the hill above them. The trees rising on either side of the weathered home helped buffet the nearly ever-present wind. Tangy wood smoke drifting from the massive chimney evoked pleasant thoughts of supper and a warm hearth in him, as doubtless it did in her. The gray clouds banking across the sky and apple blossoms scattering in the orchard like snow flurries signaled a change in the weather; not one for the better.

Trembling in the chill, she closed hesitant arms around his neck. "Perhaps you'd best take me in after all."

"I fully intend to," and he'd be damned if he'd leave her out here for that rogue Campbell to find. Still, her concession pleased him and her tentative hold was very nearly an embrace, although she didn't realize. He smiled. "I'm glad I have your approval, darling."

She squirmed delightfully in his grasp. "Must you call me that?"

"Sweetheart, then," he teased.

"You make us sound as though we're—" she halted, clearly reluctant to speak the word.

"Lovers?" he suggested, without a trace of hesitation.

"Logan!"

"Haven't we always behaved as brother and sister?"

"That was before."

He chuckled and bore her across grass bending in the wind. Satisfied his mistress was safely in tow, the little dog followed at his heels and inquisitive sheep tagged along. Ever hopeful of a handout, two cows and a calf bawled from the other side of the pasture. He unlatched the gate, swung it open and walked through, then penned the sheep in behind them.

Stiff breezes tossed Kira's hair as he walked with her past the barn, smokehouse, and other outbuildings. The homestead had fairly sprawled since he'd last seen it. A fat sow and half a dozen pink porkers grunted from their aromatic sty. Black, red-combed chickens, their tiny peeps, and a strutting bronze rooster scratched in the yard. The sight, sound, and earthy scents of livestock, the hickory smoke from the hearth, the log and stone structures built with hard sweat and toil...were achingly familiar in a place he'd buried deep inside him, like awakening the dead.

"Kira! Cousin Logan!" Childish voices carried above the wind and animals.

Kira made an impatient noise. "Here come D and D," she said, referring to his eight-year-old twin cousins by their initials. "They're as curious as raccoons with twice the cunning."

The pair had been off doing only Lord knows what when Logan first stopped by the house so he hadn't yet met the identical little boys swarming at them like bees from a hive. Coppery curls fell around cherubic, freckled faces as they peered up at him, their hazel eyes intent. Even without Kira's caution, he doubted they were as angelic as they appeared. Small boys rarely were.

One child spoke first. "Why are you hauling Kira about?"

"She battled a sheep and lost. Hurt her knee."

Laughter pealed from his keen observers.

"She's always doing silly things," the second lad offered with a giggle.

His brother doubled over with mirth. "One time she got stuck in a hole and we had to pull her out. She's got these hiding places. You should see."

The pair amused him. "Show me?"

Two burnished heads nodded eagerly.

Kira scolded, "D and D! It's a secret."

"Aw, Logan won't tell. He's our cousin. Mama said."

"And that makes him bloody perfect, I suppose, Donald?"

The second imp, whom Logan assumed must be David, clapped grubby fingers to his mouth. "Kira swore."

"Did not."

"Bloody's swearing," the more outspoken Donald confirmed.

"I don't need sermonizing from you two heathens. And you broke our pact. Go away."

They regarded her impassively. She was no immediate threat with a bad knee, held by Logan. He almost laughed at the imps, but pointed to the chestnut tree jutting up behind the house.

"Run and gather leaves for a poultice."

The twins scrutinized him as if determining whether or not this new relation required their cooperation.

Keeping a straight face, he said, "I lived seven years with Indians. Care to discover what happens to lads who dawdle?"

Their short legs came to life and they hurtled through the grass in the direction of his insistent finger.

"Probably afraid you'll scalp them," Kira said.

Logan smiled. "Not before supper. Puts me off my food."

He walked on, slowing at the garden, so like the

one his mother had lovingly tended years ago. Silvery sage, English thyme, and wooly white horehound flourished among other fragrant culinary and medicinal herbs. Spring onions, beet tops, lettuce, and new peas thrust up from the freshly-hoed earth. Just as she'd left it before she'd died. Melancholy washed over him and he lingered beside the large clump of reddish-green leaves.

"I've missed rhubarb," he found himself saying. "Mama used to stew the stalks with honey."

"Mine too. Anything else you've missed?"

"Violet-colored eyes."

He turned away, carried her to the house, and bounded up the steps to the back stoop. Stopping before the door, he sniffed the meaty aroma. "That stew sure smells good. It's been ages since I haven't had to shoot my dinner."

"Aren't you glad to be home?"

Her transparent hopefulness only added to the nostalgic assault he'd come under. "This isn't my home."

"It could be if you weren't so all fired stubborn—like you always were!"

"I'm not the one who got hung up in a tree."

"I wouldn't have if you—"

"Look who I found, Aunt!" he broke in, opening the door.

"I heard. And spitting at each other like cats."

Her back to them, the petite woman in striped petticoats bent before the stone hearth adding chopped onion tops to the steaming black kettle. The savory stew mixed with the pungent scent of dried herbs hanging in bunches from the blackened beams overhead and filling baskets here and there...the welcome appeal of the cozy room very like the distant home he'd known.

Another stab of sentiment ran through Logan. If he didn't take care, he'd be as awash with emotion

37

as his aunt. God forbid he got weepy. He'd known it wouldn't be easy coming back, but never expected to be shot through the heart.

Steeling himself against debilitating sentiment as he might a physical blow, he slipped the woven strap off his shoulder and propped his musket against the log wall. "Kira needs a poultice."

Aunt Alice wiped her hands on the white apron she wore over her skirts and turned toward them. Fine eyes colored the same gray-green as the twins widened in her flushed face. "Kira, what on earth?"

Explanation tumbled from her lips. "I fell—twisted my knee."

"From the tree Logan spoke of?"

"No, Ma'am. Racing."

"At your age?" Clucking disapproval, Aunt Alice tucked fiery tendrils into the braided coil atop her head.

"Cricket wanted to see if she could outrun me," Logan interjected.

The mature woman leveled her knowing gaze at Kira. "'Tis said a young man chases after a girl until she catches him."

Kira jerked in his arms. "I don't want to catch him."

"Indeed? I declare my nephew looks like he's just carried his bride over the threshold."

Relieved to find his mood lightening at the exchange, Logan smiled. "I'd have no argument with that."

Kira sputtered, "I would."

Aunt Alice arched a quizzical brow at her. "Clinging to his neck with your hair falling about you both?"

The hold on him ceased. "My hair came loose."

"On its own?" the skeptical woman pressed.

"Logan—" Kira began then bit off her defense.

His aunt gaped at her. "Good heavens."

"It's not like that! I want nothing to do with him."

"I can see you don't."

"Truly—"

"Come now, lass. You were always powerfully fond of Logan. 'Tis him I thought you've been waiting on all these years."

Kira's loose hair flew with the vehement shaking of her head. "No longer. Logan has gone quite mad."

"*Him* mad, is it?"

"He intends going back to those savages and taking me with him."

A look of vexation creased his aunt's face. "Wherever do you get such strange notions?"

"'Tisn't notions this time. You must help me."

Aunt Alice lifted perplexed eyes to her nephew. "Have you any idea why she's taking on so?"

He shrugged. "Perhaps my rough attire has alarmed her?"

His aunt nodded matter-of-factly, "I expect that's it. We're all uneasy, but Kira has a dread of savages beyond all reason. Hideouts everywhere."

"Which I see I'll need to change!" She thrashed to escape him. "Put me down!"

He lowered her onto the floorboards, closing a supportive arm around her as she staggered. "Let me help you, Cricket. I'd never do you any harm."

"There, see?" Aunt Alice encouraged. "We'll get Logan some proper breeches. You'll soon find he's the same."

Kira waved the good-hearted woman off as she might a stinging fly. "He wants to carry me away, I tell you."

"Don't be ridiculous, girl."

"You must hear me. Logan may be a spy as well."

"A spy?" The door swung wide and the twins

39

tumbled into the room. Flinging fistfuls of large leaves onto the trestle table, they rounded on Logan.

David sang out,"Will he be taken away in irons and shot?"

"Naw. Beaten first and hung by the neck," Donald said then brightened. "Papa said we could go to the next hanging."

David's small features pulled together in a frown. "We can't let soldiers hang him. He's our cousin."

A grudging nod from Donald who agreed, "Family first, I reckon." Scheming in his eyes, he added, "We'll hide him in one of Kira's places."

Logan trapped his lower lip against his teeth to keep from chuckling. "I'm indebted to you both, forfeiting your first hanging for me."

Aunt Alice grabbed each scrappy boy by the shoulder. "There will be none, do you hear? My nephew is no spy."

Identical mouths opened in outcry. "But Kira said—"

"Pay her no mind. She's having one of her funny turns."

Grins split their impish faces. "You gonna dose her?"

"Indeed I am."

"Little stinkers," Kira hissed.

Logan smothered a smile. "Poor girl. We'll see to you."

Kira narrowed those wonderful telltale eyes at him.

Throwing her hands up, Aunt Alice admonished, "See how tenderly he cares for you? How can you speak ill of him?"

Kira puckered her lips. "You don't know him as I do."

It made Logan want to laugh, kiss her, and caution her all at the same time. Not so, his aunt.

She was of one mind. If Kira had declared him a changeling exchanged for an ogre at birth, she could scarcely have caused more offense.

Hands on her hips, Aunt Alice puffed out an ample bosom. "Not know my dear sister's only boy? Like a son he is to me."

He patted the affronted woman's shoulder. "Never mind, Aunt. My pride's not harmed."

She seemed slightly appeased. "'Tis most forbearing of you, I'm sure, to be so forgiving."

"No doubt my sudden coming is a great shock to the lass."

"Must be, to set her off so. We best get her settled in my bed. She won't be climbing up to the loft for a while."

"Nor racing me," Logan couldn't resist adding.

"'Tisn't ladylike to race men, Kira," his aunt chided.

"I wouldn't have, if Logan weren't so hell-bent on—"

Donald pounced. "Kira said a bad word."

"Hell's swearing for certain sure," David added, with sanctimonious censure.

Aunt Alice pressed fingertips to her forehead as though she had a headache coming on, likely a common occurrence in this household. "Honestly, lass. What would Peter say to such talk escaping your mouth?"

"It escapes his often enough," Kira answered back.

His aunt flushed rose-red. "A God-fearing man is Peter Houston and entitled to an oath or two in his own home, though I might remind you decent folk have been hauled into court for less. Do you wish to find yourself before a judge with a fine levied against you, or worse, a flogging?"

Head down, Kira allowed she didn't with a muted, "No."

"Not that Peter wouldn't tar and feather any man who laid a coarse finger on you," Aunt Alice continued. "Still, have care not to cause offense among the neighbors. Folk already think you peculiar. And you've taken a right turn this time."

"But Logan—"

Before she uttered another sound, he scooped up Kira and held her so that his mouth was next to her ear. "Settle down. You're only digging yourself a deeper hole." He carried her to the snug bed built against one wall and lowered her onto the sheet and striped blanket covering the straw-filled ticking. "Rest quietly, Kira."

With a frown at him, she pushed up on her elbows. "I've my creatures to tend."

Aunt Alice hovered over her like an agitated wren. "You are not to move. The boys can see to those animals of yours. You've got them catching mice for that owl as it is."

"But the wee fawn—"

"They can fetch milk from the three-titted ewe that lost her lamb. Will you bide here or must I stand guard over you?"

Kira lay back down on the woven coverlet.

"I'll stay with her if you'd like," Logan offered.

A sigh of relief and Aunt Alice clasped his arm as if he were the answer to her prayers. "Praise God you've come."

He pressed her dimpled hand. "Glad to be of service."

"You always were a good lad, no matter what your uncle said. I'll just go soak these leaves and fetch her medicine." She darted to the hearth.

Kira drew her pale features together in a grimace. "I despise that brew. 'Tis all your fault, Logan."

"Hardly." Pulling up one of his uncle's hand-hewn chairs, he sat beside her and said under his breath, "I warned you not to tell her of me."

"Tell Mama what?"

Damn. The twins nosed around him like fox kits. "You two have sharp ears."

Donald whispered, "Is it true, then? Are you a spy?"

"Try renegade," Kira muttered.

David leaned in. "Is that like a spy?"

"Or a pirate."

The boys lit up and chorused, "We'll be pirates too!"

"You'll find no seas to sail in these ridges," their mother said drily. "Fetch more kindling. 'Twill be chilly tonight."

Donald considered her without enthusiasm. Logan tousled his red-gold curls and swiped fondly at David. "Off with you. Keep an eye out for strangers while you're about it."

"Soldiers, spies?" Donald asked.

"Pirates, warriors?" David added, not to be outdone.

"Any and all. Report back to me."

"He's their leader," Kira added.

The two shot out the door, slamming it behind them.

"Must you fill the lads' heads with fancies, Kira? Neither is lacking in mischief," their mother chided, and scurried to the cupboard. Standing on tiptoe, she grasped the brown crock that apparently held the noxious elixir.

Kira's voice rose in a plea. "Only give me a wee bit."

"After all that hysteria? You need a proper dose." Aunt Alice poured a dark stream of muck into a wooden cup and bore down on her hapless victim. "I want this drained."

"'Tis vile." Kira rolled over and buried her face against the bolster.

43

"Proves its power. Hold her head, Logan, and help me get this in her," his aunt directed, as if they were dosing a pig.

"I'll hate you forever, Logan," Kira ground out.

Nor would he blame her.

Rather than force her compliance, he slipped his fingers over her hair. "Leave her to me, Aunt."

Her mouth crimped. "You see what a trial the girl is."

"I've dealt with more troublesome creatures. You remember Tessa's temper."

The exasperation in her face lessened and her gaze misted. "*Aye.* Your dear sister tried me sorely, right enough."

"But I knew how to get around her."

A swipe at her eyes with her apron and she nodded. "You did that. Better than any. How you must grieve her loss."

"Always. Tessa and I were like twins." Logan's conscience chided him that he couldn't confide the entire story to this devoted relation.

"If only she hadn't strayed from the fort she might be with us still. But then, that girl always did have a mind of her own. Like you. And such a temper."

"Uncle Peter has the worst bark and bite of us all."

His aunt loosed a low wail. "Mercy. We'll be having a bout with Peter if we don't get the lass calmed down afore he comes home. Maybe you would fare better with her. Lord knows I've tried." She relinquished the cup to him. "I blame Margaret McClure, God rest her, for the girl's odd ways."

The tightening in Kira's back betrayed her tension.

"Why, that?" Logan asked.

"The fault can't be laid at her father's door. A good Scot was Robert McClure and Protestant."

44

Muffled by the bolster, Kira argued, "Mama was an angel."

"Margaret McClure had the face of an angel, I'll grant you. Still, that's no assurance of the state of her soul."

Lifting her head, Kira fixed impassioned eyes on the accuser. "How dare you judge Mama's soul?"

"You needn't take on so, lass. You know I was fond of Margaret, even if she was Papist."

"Leave her to God, then."

"We all do. Gracious child, I declare you grow more hysterical by the moment."

"Me? It's you who—"

Logan clapped his hand over Kira's mouth. "Not another word."

She fumed beneath his palm.

"Take a swig of this stuff and I'll tell you something about your mother. Something good," he bargained.

"That's the way, Logan. You coax her. I'll see to this poultice." His aunt bustled back to the hearth.

Kira reproached him with liquid eyes.

"Do you agree to my terms?"

Though she appeared more inclined to object, she grunted an assent.

He freed her mouth and she turned onto her side. "A generous swig, mind, or it doesn't count."

Screwing up her face, she choked down a gulp and shuddered. He wasn't entirely sure she'd keep it down.

"You're doing right well, Logan!" his aunt called. "See every drop's gone."

"Aye. Empty as a dog's bowl."

"Don't make me," Kira mouthed at him.

An immediate decision; he glanced at the unsuspecting matron's back and saluted Kira with the cup. In a whisper, he said, "To you, sweetheart," and raised the vessel to his lips.

She stared at him as he knocked back the loathsome contents in a few gulps. He barely suppressed a grimace, and he'd tasted some nasty fare in his day. "All gone, Aunt."

Pleasure dimpled her face as she turned. "Good. That's done. I'll soak these leaves and fetch my wash. Gather some tansy whilst I'm about it to mix with the chestnut. I like a blend of herbs for a poultice." Basket in hand, she snatched the brown cloak from a peg by the door and stepped outside.

Logan muttered, "What did she *blend* in that stuff?"

"Her own special remedy. 'Tis a secret."

"As if anyone would covet the recipe."

Like the dawning of a new age, Kira smiled up at him with tremulous sweetness he'd never before witnessed in her. "Drinking that vile brew was the kindest thing you've ever done for me, Logan."

"And the bravest."

The light in her eyes washed over him, a beam of purest sunshine. "You should smile more often, Cricket."

"You've given me precious little to smile about."

"I'll bring you a drop of whiskey. That'll settle you far better than her remedy."

"I don't need settling. At least, not before you came."

"To ease your pain then. I could do with a drop after that rot. Where does my good aunt hide Uncle Peter's bottle?"

Kira pointed to the dark corner behind the cupboard. "Tucked back there. She doesn't want the boys getting into it."

Logan stood. "As if she can keep anything from them."

Firelight played over the simple furnishings in the cozy room, so like his old home. Sentiment twisted his gut as he retrieved the brown bottle from the shadows and a pewter vessel from the cupboard. It was damn unsettling not to be the self-assured man he normally was. This place really worked on him, and Kira's staggering appeal didn't help matters any. He had to get a grip on his emotions.

Uncorking the bottle, he filled the cup and drank the potent liquid. The fiery tide washed away the repugnant taste left in his mouth. He smacked his lips. "That's more like it." After replenishing his drink, he walked back to her and sat on the bedside. He extended the cup. "Have a swallow."

"Aunt Alice says straight whiskey's too strong for me."

"A little won't hurt."

Her eyes watered at the first mouthful and she coughed.

"Another," he prodded. "Takes some getting used to."

Blinking hard, she managed several swallows and cleared her throat. "Now tell me what you promised about Mama."

"No hardship there. I remember Maggie McClure well. You're very like her."

Kira melted him with another smile.

"Rare beauties, both. It's no mystery to me why your father wed her."

"You don't mind Mama being Irish and Catholic?"

"Not a whit."

"I suppose you've kept company with worse."

Letting that remark pass, he pressed Kira to another draught before returning the cup to his own lips.

She lay back on the bolster and raised wondering eyes. "You did say something good."

"Promised you I would, didn't I? Is it so surprising I'm taken with the daughter of Maggie McClure?"

"'Tis a recently discovered passion."

"Come, now. There's always been a bond between us."

"More on my part than yours."

Fast-growing on his part now. "I was always fond of you."

"Like a favorite dog."

"Not only that. I often thought of you while I was off," he insisted, and took a swallow.

Kira passed a hand over her eyes as if having difficulty focusing. "Did you think of me when you held that Shawnee woman in your arms?"

He choked on the fiery liquid and launched into a coughing fit. When he recovered enough to speak, he demanded, "How did you come by such a question?"

She pushed up on her hands, swaying slightly. "Unless you've had more than one woman, doing only God knows what."

Such accusations escaping this chaste girl's mouth flabbergasted him. Granted, her eyes were a bit glazed and her cheeks flushed. "I think maybe I've given you a drop too much." And he had no idea what effect that herbal brew might have when taken with strong spirits.

"Must be why the room's gone wobbly."

He felt a little odd himself. "Not a word to my aunt."

Kira flopped back down. "Tell me what that Indian woman was to you then."

Frowning at her, he firmly said, "I'll tell you no such thing. It's not seemly to pry into the affairs of men."

Her eyes watered from more than the whiskey alone. "I never thought to hear *you* scold me for impropriety."

"Nor I." He softened his rebuke. "But the questions you ask, that's all in the past, Kira. We have the present and the future to embrace."

"Do you still think to take me away with you?"

"Would you have me leave you behind?"

She eyed him like one in a dream. "I'd have you stay."

He strained to hear her. "In spite of all I've done?"

In an unexpected gesture, she lifted her hand to his cheek. "I don't care, just so you stay. Begin a new life here with me."

His skin tingled at her caress. Covering her hand with his, he pressed her fingers to his lips. "Is that the whiskey talking or you?"

"Me. The whiskey just makes it easier…like being in that place between sleep and waking. I'd do more than plead, if only you wouldn't go away. Stay with me, Logan."

Such a heartfelt request couldn't have come easy, even with the drink. But there could be only one answer. Regret pierced him with razor-sharp thorns. "I can't."

Disbelief washed through her eyes like a stream suddenly devoid of sunlight. "You're refusing me?"

"Not you, dearest. Just your plea."

She regarded him with the black reproach of betrayal and wrenched her hand away. "Then you leave us only the past."

He reclaimed her fingers. "I am resolved otherwise. Can you not trust me to care for you, come what may?"

Lips tight, she shook her head.

"Not even a little?"

Refusing even to look at him, she said nothing.

"Whom do you trust, Kira?"

She turned her face to the wall.

"What, not even Will or your precious Josiah Campbell?"

"I didn't say that."

"No need. I see how it is. You trust no one."

She shook her head. "Not true."

"Who, then? Name one living soul."

"Hannah McCue."

Logan jerked as if scorched by fire. "Dear God, Kira, she's a witch."

Her eyes flashed back to his. "No—don't say that. Hannah's kind to me, always."

"And mistrusted by everyone else. Does Aunt Alice know you keep company with her?"

"No one does."

"I'll bet David and Donald do."

As if suddenly apprehensive of being overheard, Kira shifted her gaze around the room.

"Take care or you'll find yourself shunned the same as Hannah. Or worse," Logan warned. Kira was more reckless than he'd realized.

She rushed to the old Scotswoman's defense. "Hannah can't help who she is. Folks don't understand her ways."

"Nor do they understand yours."

A mulish twist of her lips. "Maybe I don't want them to."

"You think that gives you some sort of advantage? Why do you pretend as you do?"

"It's not all pretending."

"Much is. Why do you want to be thought peculiar?"

Reluctance shadowed her eyes.

"You know the reason."

She heaved a sigh from the recesses of her soul. "Mama."

He spoke gently. "Tell me."

"I can still see her lying there as if it were yesterday, black hair spilled about her white face, lovely eyes seeing, yet not seeing. 'Hide well, Kira love,' Mama said, 'like a clever bird, so none will find you. None will know.'"

"What did she fear people would do?"

"Destroy me as they did her."

"No, sweetheart. She died of pneumonia."

"Mama's spirit was broken long before the sickness came. Papa should have put a stop to the taunting."

Logan bent near. "He tried. Your father loved her."

"Her face. Not her heart. She said so at the last. Her final words."

"Ramblings caused by fever. Your father was dead by then and not here to speak for himself."

"Perhaps. I was alone with Mama when she died and for three days after," Kira said in a small voice.

"Dear Lord. I didn't realize. Who found you?"

"Hannah's brother, Joseph. He took me to live with them, but Uncle Peter said Papa wanted him to raise me. I wish he'd left me with the McCues."

"My uncle did as he thought best."

"He did wrong."

Conviction surged in Logan. "Maybe so and maybe you're not giving him his fair due. Either way, he's had his turn. It's my time now."

Refusal shone back at him through her sheen of tears. "Uncle Peter won't hand me over to you, even if I beg him. And that I surely won't."

"I don't need you to beg him. I shall leave my uncle no other choice than to concede. Nor you."

Kira weighed his assertion and slowly asked, "If I were yours, as you desire, what part of me would you love?"

"All of you."

"I believe you might—" her voice caught. She breathed in shakily and firmed up her tone. "But I'll not let you. We no longer follow the same course."

Logan was undaunted. "Might we not still converge?"

Slender shoulders sagged. "I don't see how."

"Can you stop a rushing tide?"

She arched fine dark brows at him. "Must you rush just now? I'm frightfully giddy."

He smiled. "You think to better oppose me sober?"

"At least I'll see what I'm up against."

"That will aid you little." Sliding his arms beneath Kira, he lifted her from the bed and gathered her against him. An embrace she didn't immediately protest...possibly too dazed.

Even so, he faced a host of opposition, her resistance being only one obstacle. Why was he set on having the woman he never thought he'd want, and most unsuited to his plans?

Her voice barely a whisper, she said, "I've not yet peeled away all of your layers."

"Nor I yours."

Chapter Five

Before Kira extricated herself from Logan—fast gaining an alarming hold on her—the cabin door banged open and the twins burst into the room, their small arms stacked with firewood. Like pups on their first hunt, they fastened gleaming eyes on her and Logan.

"Logan's hugging Kira real close, Mama!"

"I can see that plain enough." Aunt Alice entered behind the boys with a basket of clean linen. She set it down in the corner beside the spinning wheel and cocked her head at them.

Matters were progressing at a dizzying pace; not all as Kira intended. Shutting her eyes to Aunt Alice's scrutiny, she clapped a hand to her forehead and moaned, "I feel faint. Logan kept me from falling."

"Out of bed or his arms?"

"Both." He chuckled and laid Kira down on the coverlet.

Firewood clattered to the floor. "What do you want to hold a girl for? Wouldn't you rather a wee lamb?"

That was David.

"Or a piglet?"

Donald's suggestion.

"Men prefer lasses to livestock," their mother enlightened them.

Logan laughed. "True. But Kira is giddy, Aunt. Your tonic delivers quite a punch." He neglected to mention the whiskey he'd administered.

"I've not given her too much, have I?" The

53

concern running through the good-hearted woman hummed in her tone.

"I expect Kira will soon recover," he assured her.

"She's a mite calmer, though, don't you think?"

"Limp as cloth."

"Oh, my. Is she overly warm? Maybe I ought to brew a fever drink?"

"You're taking it if she does," Kira said under her breath.

"Not on your life," he whispered then raised his voice. "No need, Aunt. She'll be fine in a shake."

"Just grand," Kira muttered. "A few hours with you and I'm lame in one leg and too giddy to stand on the other."

"How was I to know you would run headlong into a sheep and had no tolerance for whiskey?"

"Stack that kindling, Donald. Don't scatter it about." Aunt Alice's directive intruded on their low dispute. "I fetched some woundwort and tansy while I was out." Fragrance charged the air as she pounded the herbs with the wooden mallet she used to pulverize roots and stems. "Logan, if Kira's too light-headed mayhap you would help ready her for this poultice. You ought to have the girl's shoes off."

"That and everything else," he teased in a voice only Kira could hear.

"I'll not be giving you the chance. I shall be engaged this evening entertaining a visit from Josiah Campbell."

Even with her eyes closed, she sensed Logan's mood darken. He slid off her shoe and tossed it to the floor. "Pity you won't be seeing him."

She tensed with the wariness of a rabbit. "Why is that?"

Her second shoe thumped beside its mate. "Are you in the habit of receiving gentleman callers while lying flat on your back?" he asked, projecting his voice for appreciative ears.

"I'll be better by—"

The thump of the mallet and Aunt Alice burst out with, "Gracious! I'd forgotten about his coming. There's enough gossip about her among the neighbors as it is. She's in no fit state for visitors."

"Ah well, perhaps another time." Logan patted Kira's arm in mock sympathy. "I'll tell the fellow you're indisposed and see him on his way."

"What a comfort to have you here," Aunt Alice gushed.

Kira squinted narrowly at his smug expression, and hissed, "You're the one who got me in this state."

Logan spoke in her ear. "You make it sound as though I've gotten you with child."

She nearly stuttered. "I *what*?"

"Not a bad idea," he continued, as though she'd had some part in the outrageous exchange.

"Are there no bounds to your cockiness?"

Humor glinted back at her. "Few."

"Might I remind you we are not wed, sir?"

"The deed isn't always accomplished in that order, Miss."

"'Tis with decent folk!" That escaped her more loudly than she'd intended.

Aunt Alice swiveled toward her. "What is?"

Before Logan gained more ground, Kira lied, "Receiving callers who take the trouble to see me."

A sigh heaved from his aunt. "You're not bent on seeing Mister Campbell, are you, lass?"

Kira fired a mutinous look at Logan who returned fire with a slit-eyed glare. She ignored him. "More than ever."

Still wearing her cloak, Aunt Alice darted to them carrying the chipped brown bowl and a strip of linen. She set the herbal-scented concoction on the small circular stand beside the bed. Her dimpled prettiness reflected her skepticism. "You never seemed overly fond of him."

"I'm devoted."

"'Tis a well-guarded secret."

"I didn't like to say."

"I doubt you know what you're saying now. We had best tend this knee." She jerked up Kira's skirts.

"Aunt Alice! The boys." Despite their professed lack of interest in females, they were certainly staring at her now.

Their mother pointed at the door. "Go feed that wee fawn and the orphan lamb."

Neither boy sprang to action. Logan rose and gave them a suggestive push. "Scoot. Before I give you a better reason."

They flew, grabbing a corn cake from the earthenware plate on the table in passing. Renewing her assault on Kira, Aunt Alice tugged the layers of cloth nearly to her thighs.

"Hold on!" She pushed at her ascending hemline.

"Logan's family," his aunt reasoned.

"Not *mine.*"

"Near enough. Besides, you two behave as if you're betrothed."

"We're not."

"Yet." The brisk woman unrolled Kira's muddied stocking. Scooping leaves from the bowl, she pressed them to her knee. "You're just in a right state."

Heaven help her, Aunt Alice was as determined as Logan and Kira felt backed into a corner. She needed someone on her side. "I want to see Mister Campbell."

With a distressed glance at Logan, Aunt Alice explained, "She gets like this sometimes. But I declare I don't know what to do. She's fairly dug in her heels this time."

"Leave Kira to me. I'll soon sort this out." His unruffled tone was at odds with the threat in his face.

"Bless you," his aunt breathed out. "You always were good with the girl and so patient." She bound the moist compress in place with the linen and pulled the cover back over Kira. "Try your hand, then. I've Essie to milk and eggs to gather." Floor boards creaked as she dashed to the door.

"Don't leave me with him!" Kira called after her.

"You've naught to dread. The stew's 'bout ready. A hearty supper will settle you," she soothed, opening the door.

"Oh, I'll settle her, Aunt. Never fear."

"Someone had better and soon, before Peter returns." With that, the perturbed woman scooted outside.

Kira actually found herself wishing Uncle Peter would turn up; definitely Logan's Cousin Will. Despite Will's strong opinions, the young man would be a welcome ally.

Jaw set, lips tight, Logan sat on the edge of her bed. Blocked from retreat, she slid further beneath the coverlet. "I'm not speaking to you when you're like this," she began—gasping as he clamped his hands around her shoulders.

He pulled her out from beneath the blanket, leaving her no alternative other than to face his stern regard. "You've already said plenty for one not speaking. What's all this nonsense about you harboring feelings for Mister Campbell?"

"'Tisn't nonsense."

"Do you take me for a fool?"

Only a dimwitted individual would mistake him for one of limited intellect. Closing her eyes to the ire in his, she turned her face to the log wall.

He tightened his grip on her upper arms. "Look at me or I swear I'll light into your suitor the instant I see him."

She met the threat in his scowl. "Don't you dare."

He bent in more closely until their noses nearly touched. As before, in the tree, he emanated masculine vitality. His energy filled the room. Even if she hadn't known he were near, she would have sensed his presence. He was the stronger, more forceful, of the two. And she couldn't hide. He...stared...her...down.

She swallowed hard and wordlessly conceded ground, at least temporarily.

Logan released her and crossed his arms over his chest. "The truth now, Kira. Why do you insist on seeing Campbell?"

"I need him."

"In God's name, why?"

She blurted, "To keep you at bay. I can't trust you to behave properly."

"What on earth leads you to believe Campbell will?"

His blunt question startled her. "I thought—I mean—he treats me well enough."

Astute eyes weighed her assertion. "Has he ever been alone with you?"

"Aunt Alice sees to it that we're properly chaperoned. Not leaving me like she does with you." *More the fool her,* Kira was tempted to add.

A sage look in his face, Logan said, "As I expected. The fellow's just biding his time."

"Josiah wouldn't try anything unsuitable."

Logan scoffed, "You're as unknowing as a newborn babe."

The kernel of doubt he planted made her squirm, but she was loath to admit it. "And you think all men are like you!"

"No dear heart. Some are far worse. Do you truly wish to find yourself wedded and bedded by the honorable Mister Campbell?"

Kira cringed at the unsavory image.

"Taste something vile?"

"It's just—I never meant—I only wanted his protection."

A wry turn of his lips and Logan countered, "'Tis dearly bought."

"I can handle Josiah Campbell."

He huffed out his chest. "I'm vastly relieved to hear it. How, pray tell?"

His sarcasm goaded her. "I have my ways."

Logan rolled his eyes. "Your peculiarities haven't dampened his ardor any."

"Josiah doesn't know them all yet."

"Oh for the love of—" Logan threw both hands up then raked back his hair with long, tapered fingers. Despite their mutual ire, she couldn't help but admire the slight curl at the ends of his brown mane. "Do you fish out a new oddity when your supply runs low like a squirrel digging for nuts?"

"I can fend for myself. I've done so for years."

"Not against the likes of Campbell, you haven't. Most men would pale at the challenge where he's concerned."

"I can manage Josiah."

"Mister Campbell, and I'm sorely tempted to let you try."

"Fine. See my caller in when he comes and leave us be."

"Being tempted isn't the same as fool enough to do it."

The glare in Logan's eyes reminded her of a rooster's before it flew in attack. "So you're bent on coming to blows?"

"That all depends on how your suitor feels about being thrown off the place. With Uncle Peter and Will away, he thinks to find only defenseless women and children about."

"We're not all defenseless."

"No, I dare say David and Donald could manage some devious mischief. And my aunt could fell him with one of her concoctions. But you are a sitting duck."

"Logan—"

He raised his arms and his sleeves slid back revealing corded muscle. "Fortunately, I've come in the nick of time."

There was nothing the least bit defenseless about the sinewy thighs his breechclout revealed, or the knife and tomahawk at his side. The fire in the hearth blazed up, better illuminating his strong back and shoulders through the loose shirt. The sight was most unsettling both in how his enormous attraction affected her fluttering stomach and the knowledge that he fairly itched for a fight.

"Josiah is our neighbor and not coming to molest us. Couldn't you at least be civil?"

"Not remotely."

"For heaven's sake, you were boys together."

The tension returned to his jaw. "I despised him then too. Before you, Campbell had his eye on our Tessa."

"That was long ago. Your sister's been gone for years."

Every muscle in his face drew together. "Campbell's kept busy in between. Been a great Indian fighter."

She sensed a deeper cause for his animosity. "Did he kill one of your Shawnee friends?"

Logan scowled into the flames. "What do you care?"

His terseness took her aback. Josiah must have done just that. She tried to fathom his attachment to this unknown warrior. Perhaps the brave had done him good service. They sometimes did. Admittedly, Logan appeared in excellent health and couldn't have suffered too badly during his long absence. And if he had, why hide it and insist on fair treatment?

In a more subdued tone, she asked, "Was it

someone dear to you?"

"Dear to many."

"What happened?"

He shifted his narrow stare back to her. "Do you really want to know?"

Oddly enough, she did. "Yes."

He fingered his chin, darkened with the stubble from several days' beard. "I was deep in the mountains with a small hunting party when Campbell and a group of frontiersman fired on us. Campbell shot my friend, Skaki. I fired back."

Kira sat bolt upright. "That was *you* who shot Josiah?"

"I only winged him, damn it."

"He still complains about his shoulder."

Logan smiled faintly. "Good. Maybe it will slow him."

"How can you be so brash? What if he suspects you?"

"It was nearly dark. All he knows is that I'm English."

Suddenly chilled, Kira drew the blanket up around her shoulders. "He's no simpleton. He may figure out the rest."

Logan scrutinized her. "Are you fearful for me?"

She balked at full disclosure. "I don't want to see him rip you apart."

A hint of mirth crossed Logan's expression. "Not even a little to get back at me?"

"Josiah does nothing by halves and you need both of yours."

"Why are you so certain I will lose?"

"Josiah's huge. Besides, I saw him in a fight once. Awful," she shuddered. "Please don't bait him when he comes."

The glint in Logan's eyes promised otherwise. "If you are set on receiving Mister Campbell then we shall entertain him together."

If a bee had gotten under her cover, she couldn't have been more startled. "Josiah won't want you about!"

A satisfied expression accompanied Logan's reply. "No. I dare say he won't."

****

What on earth was keeping his aunt? It shouldn't take *this* long to milk and gather eggs. Likely she'd delayed on purpose and stalled the twins too, which meant she hoped for great things from her newly arrived nephew in regards to Kira. Clearly his distracted relation was at her wit's end with the stubborn girl. Logan was rather *distracted* himself. He looked up from his second bowl of stew and let his appreciative gaze roam over the trouble-maker who leaned against the bolster looking far too desirable, not to mention vulnerable, for his peace of mind with Josiah Campbell coming.

How could he persuade Kira she needed protection, all right, though not from him? Campbell was the menace. There was still so much Logan hadn't confided in her. Did he dare?

No. He couldn't take the risk. Not yet.

But he had to make her understand—

"Please help me tidy up." She broke into his thoughts.

A twinge of annoyance, like toothache, sent a spasm through him. "You're tidy enough for Campbell."

"For me, then. I can't fetch my things from the loft."

He set his bowl down on the table. "Stuck are you, sweetheart? What a shame."

"You brought my stew. Why not my brush?"

"Shall I help you into a bath as well?"

She didn't comment on his flippancy. "What about a jacket? I'm only wearing stays over my shift. 'Tis hardly proper."

A state he was acutely aware of. He considered greeting her suitor with his fist and having done with it at the start. Maybe he'd harass Campbell first and then punch him.

"I suppose we best have you decent," he grumbled, and walked across the room. He climbed the ladder. Reaching for the final rung, he asked over his shoulder, "Anything else you require while I'm about it?"

No reply.

He glanced down to see her staring up at him and realized how unaccustomed she must be to seeing a man's thighs and how much more of his she could view from below. He smiled at her.

She flushed prettily. "My balm and best stockings, if you please."

"Certainly, my lady."

"You sound a perfect gentleman. Doesn't suit a warrior."

"My father was from Scottish gentry, a younger son. His sister married high into English society, if you recall."

"Vaguely. You don't look as if you descend from gentry."

"No? How do I look to you, Kira?"

She blinked and the blush deepened. "Well—"

The word rushed from her with more feeling than he suspected she'd meant for it to. Chuckling, he climbed into the darkened loft and bent to rummage through the leather-bound trunk that held all her possessions. Not a lot. If Kira's father had lived, she would have been far more indulged. For all her resentment of the man, he'd doted on her and the wife she was persuaded he'd failed.

"The blue jacket!" she called up, as if to prevent Logan from returning with the drabbest garment she owned. Not that there was a great deal of choice among the scanty selection.

He fished out the flowered jacket, skirted at the waist. The fabric he recognized as having been presented to her by her older brother, Tom, which had to make it at least seven years old. Aunt Alice must have made the garment over to fit Kira's more womanly figure. Tucked in among her petticoats were the wooden hairbrush, comb, and small blue and white porcelain box, cherished heirlooms from her sainted mother.

Someone ought to give Kira a fine gown to suit her beauty, but the Houstons weren't wealthy. Resolving to see her properly outfitted as soon as he had the opportunity, Logan retrieved the goods and headed down the ladder. A mischievous thought occurred to him.

Instantly suspicious, Kira asked, "What?"

"Nothing. I'm come to ready you for our guest."

Eyes widening, she protested. "Oh, no."

"Surely one so grievously injured requires assistance?"

She made a grab for her things. "There's nothing amiss with my arms."

Holding the desired items out of reach, he cautioned, "Mustn't overtire yourself."

"Logan!"

"Will you chase me around this room, or accept my aid?"

"Oh, have it your way. If anyone comes I can always pretend illness."

"Or any number of maladies." He lowered himself beside her and laid the articles on the bed. It was intoxicating just being near her. He lifted the brush and ran the bristles through the black cascade flowing over her shoulders and down her back. "Such lovely hair. However did it come to be in such a state?" he asked in mock innocence.

"A bold young man unbound it in the tree."

"You ought not sit in trees with bold men, my

girl," he chided in imitation of his aunt.

A smile tugged at her enticing lips. "What should I do?"

"Hide from all but me."

"Ah, but you are the boldest."

Sobered at her words, he held out the jacket. "I wish that were so."

She pushed her arms through the sleeves and laced the ribbons up her rounded chest. He gave her a long appraisal. "That hue makes your eyes even bluer."

"My, I've never had so many compliments from you, sir."

She was so beautiful it pained him. "You would have, if I'd been here."

"But you weren't." Another pang drove through him.

Kira pulled on her stockings and shoes with a little help he was more than willing to give. Then she lifted the porcelain lid and rubbed some of the rose-scented balm onto her hands. Smelling as inviting as she looked, she reached behind her head to restore her braid.

He stilled her hands. "I like you as you are. Besides, I prefer to torment our guest."

"How so?"

Logan slipped his fingers through the ebony lengths, a stirring sensation, one only he should be allowed to savor. "The unworthy Campbell cannot touch you as I can."

"You shouldn't." Her shallow intake of air betrayed her.

He yearned to kiss her into breathless stupefaction. "We're nearly betrothed as far as my aunt is concerned."

"Not your uncle. Nor have I given my consent. For that matter, I don't recall you asking me to wed you, Logan."

"Did I neglect that? I thought one of us had proposed."

Rose again suffused her cheeks. "You refused."

"Perhaps you will be more agreeable." He closed his arms around her, nestling her against him and burying his face in her smooth neck. "Marry me, Kira. I'm asking."

A tremble rippled through her. "I don't dare. Wed another. Maybe you already have."

"No. And 'tis you I want."

"For how long?" she gasped. "You may be as capricious as the wind for all I know."

The curve of her ear beckoned and he kissed behind the tender lobe. "I'm as steady as a strong east breeze."

"You say that now," she argued with a shiver.

"I'll keep on saying it." Everything about Kira called to his innermost being, the Celtic clansman borne of heather moors and icy lochs...the Scots settler come to the New World to build a life in these rugged ridges...the primal warrior carved from dark forests and howling wolves.

He pressed his lips up her exquisite neck, spreading goosebumps as he went, and nibbled at the corner of her mouth.

"We belong together."

She ducked down against his shoulder. "We did once."

"We still do. I swear it by all I hold dear."

Lifting her face, her eyes brimming with want and overhung with fear, she implored him, "Logan, please."

"Anything, darling."

"I can't wed you."

"Except that."

Her eyes shimmered with the tears she fought to hold back. "What else matters?"

He smiled at her guileless admission. "Not a

blessed thing. Just remember, I gave you the chance to wed properly."

She shifted warily in his arms. "What do you intend?"

"Now?" Logan settled his lips over her unbearably compelling mouth, and felt Kira succumb to the tempting pressure, as though his second invitation were even more irresistible than his first. Whatever she'd meant to him before was multiplied a hundredfold now. Desire reverberated in him like the primal rhythm of drums as pounding warmth urged him ever nearer her.

Then she tore herself away, panting, "You mustn't!"

He groaned and pressed his lips to her sweet throat. "It's impossible to be with you and not want all. You feel the same. I know you do."

"But I don't intend to act on my emotions."

"I possess enough intent for us both."

Her lips quivered. "Don't press me—please."

"I'm sorry, Cricket. I can't give you that assurance and I see little purpose in waiting about here."

She jerked like one backed too near the hearth. "What are you saying?"

He held her firm. "Why should I allow you the chance to make some foolish declaration for Mister Campbell just because you're frightened of your feelings for me?"

"That's not all I fear! You said you'd stay awhile, that I had time to—"

"What? Wed that lout. Come with me, Kira."

With the panic of a snared bird, she fought to tear free from him. "Off to savages?"

"Nay. To my place."

She stopped in mid-struggle. "You haven't got one—unless—you mean the McCutcheon homestead?"

Pain pierced him at the name, and a chill hand snaked around his gut. He gave a nod.

"It lies in ruins. What can possibly await you there?"

"I've something to see to."

"And you want to start at this hour? I can barely walk."

"We'll take my horse. You can ride."

"I didn't realize you had one."

"Aye, a fine mount in the stable. He's a gift from my Shawnee father." Logan stood and scooped her up, blanket and all. "We'll stop after a while for the night."

Shock welled in her eyes. "Are you mad? What of Aunt Alice?"

"She has entrusted you to me."

"Not for this!"

"She would far rather you belonged to me than Josiah Campbell."

"But to take me off alone?"

"Trust me, Kira."

Her chest heaved like one emerging from deep water. "Trusting you is as risky as treading a foggy cliff."

"Ah, but I know where the edge lies."

"I need to know as well."

"Someday you'll understand. I promise."

"Logan! No!"

At her cry, the door flew open as if borne on a great wind. What light remained in the sky was dimmed by the bulk of the man charging inside. Josiah Campbell fixed glittering blue eyes on Logan with all the malevolence of a bull.

"Where are you going with Miss McClure, McCutcheon!"

Every muscle in Logan's body tightened, but he made no move to relinquish his hold on Kira. "Out for some air."

Josiah stopped just in front of him. "Put the lass down. You and me will take the air."

"Missed me, have you?" Logan asked coolly.

"I'll give you to the count of three to surrender her."

Eyeing the bigger man in contempt, he spat back, "I didn't know you could count that high, Campbell."

His old enemy pawed the floorboards, shifting enormous riding boots from side to side. "I'm gonna skin you alive."

"Not very welcoming, is it?"

Thick fingers ran over the red tangle Josiah had made an effort to tame by tying it back at his neck. "I'll give you a welcome that'll make you wish you'd stayed with savages."

"Appears I've found one."

"You son of a—"

"Language. Lady present." Logan lowered Kira to the bed and pressed a quick kiss to her astonished lips. "Wait for me. I've a score to settle, darling."

"You dare kiss her with me here!"

He turned to face Josiah. "I've been kissing her quite well without you."

Thick fingers reached for the knife at his waist. "I'll cut out your tongue!"

Logan whipped out his tomahawk. "Pull that blade and you won't have an able arm to do it with."

Josiah snorted, but withdrew his hand. "No man hauls my woman about."

"Then it's just as well she isn't yours. This is my uncle's home. You don't give the orders here."

"I was invited to court the lass, McCutcheon. And that's what I aim to do."

"You'll have to get past me first."

A wary eye on the tomahawk, Josiah said, "With you holding that?"

"Drop your knife. Kick it aside. I'll drop my

weapons and we'll take this outside."

Josiah's knife clattered to the floor and he booted it aside. "I've whipped more than one pitiful excuse of a man."

"Go on. Dig yourself a deeper hole." Logan kicked his weapons under the bed. "You've the arse to fill it."

Kira rose, wincing, to her feet. "For God's sake—stop!"

"Stay back," Logan cautioned.

She clutched the bed for support. "Don't fight him, Logan!"

Josiah leveled his scorn at her. "You always did have a soft spot for this fellow. When I've seen to McCutcheon, you and me are fixing a time to be wed, gal."

She thrust out her jaw. "I never agreed to marry you."

"You know what I want, Kira."

"I don't care what you want!" she shouted up at the mountain of a man.

"Where'd you come by such a mouth?" She winced as Josiah grabbed her by the arm. "High time you learned some respect."

The sight of that oaf man-handling Kira enraged Logan beyond anything he'd ever known. "By heaven, I'll teach you some, Campbell."

Like a flame shooting from the fire, he flew at Josiah and smacked his fist into his jaw with a satisfying crack. "Can't promise you'll survive the lesson."

Surprise showed in his eyes as his head snapped back. Blood trickled down his chin and he slackened his grip on Kira. She retreated to the relative safety of the bed.

With speed on his side, Logan let his fist fly again. Circling his adversary like a wolf, he darted in and punched Josiah over and over. The room resounded with his knuckles crunching against bone. His battered hand stung like the devil but he reveled in meting out long deserved punishment.

Josiah reeled back. Then he came roaring to life and swung at him. "You bastard!"

Logan dodged the blow. He spun around with the dexterity his Shawnee brothers had taught him. Kicking out hard, he caught Josiah in the gut and sent him thudding to the floor.

He crashed loudly enough to open a gap in the boards, but only shook the house. For a moment the giant lay as he was then rolled over. With the fury of a wounded bear, he grabbed Logan's ankles and jerked him down. Rock-hard knuckles caught Logan's jaw as he fell. Pain starred in front of his eyes and blood ran from the corner of his stinging mouth.

Josiah rose above him and slammed him in the face. "You'll get your own back now."

"Stop it!" Kira shrieked.

"Didn't cry out none for me, did you, gal!" he bellowed.

In a flood of rage, Logan surged up and threw him off. He sprang to his feet and drove his foot into Josiah's belly.

A grunt whooshed from him. He bent over and sank down onto one knee.

"That's for Skaki!" Logan hurled in vindication of his fallen friend.

Josiah clambered up. Again, his bulk loomed like the shadow of a menacing ridge. Logan sprang out of reach. He spun around and smashed bleeding fists under his chin. "That's for Tom McClure!"

Josiah shook his head as if to clear it. "What in blazes has Tom to do with this?"

"Asked me to look after Kira, didn't he? Reckon her big brother would tell you to stay clear!"

"Like hell! McClure's dead!"

"Looked better than you the last time I saw him."

"Liar!" Josiah cracked Logan on the side of the head.

Blasted lout. Dizzied by the blow, Logan stumbled into the table and sent the plate of corncakes toppling to the floor. The brown pottery crashed into pieces and bread flew.

Josiah slid on a shard, giving Logan a moment to collect himself. He shook off the giddiness and ducked the fist coming at him then drove bloodied knuckles into Josiah's stomach. Without pause, he landed a blow to his punished jaw. "Tom looks better all the time!"

Josiah reeled back. "Think that gives you a right to her?"

"More than you."

Still a little giddy, Logan wasn't quite fast enough to evade Josiah's next lunge. Meaty hands fastened around his throat. He stared into the slitted eyes watching his choking struggle. "How about now, McCutcheon?"

"Let him go, Josie!" Kira screamed.

"When I'm done."

Logan grappled wildly. And fought to think. What would Shoka or Meshewa do?

Never be in this tight spot to begin with. They'd have finished Josiah with that first shot and not only winged him!

Chapter Six

"Stop, Josie!" He was beyond reason.

Ignoring the stab in her knee, Kira tore across the room seeking something, anything, to use as a weapon. If she'd had a pistol, she would've shot Josiah then and there—the consequences be damned. Baskets, crockery, pots in the hearth, all swirled into view. Before she grabbed the poker, Logan rammed his knee into Josiah's groin.

Breath rushed from him in a heavy grunt and his eyes squinted in puffy folds of purpled flesh. His death hold on Logan lightened as he doubled over.

Gulping in air, Logan stumbled back. "What say you now, Campbell?"

"Bastard," Josiah croaked.

Bawtie shot through the open door. Baying at the top of his lungs, he tore into the man he'd never liked.

"Damn dog!" Josiah pitched the incensed hound at the twins running in just behind him.

"Get him!" the boys yelled, hurtling at Josiah. Puny fists, fur, and teeth flew. And not only Bawtie's.

Josiah swiped at them like an enraged bear. "Get away you little beasts!"

They hung on. Each twin had a leg while Bawtie snapped at everything in between. Winking from a swelling eye, Logan waded into the brawl. He seized a child in each hand.

Donald thrashed in his grasp. "He tossed Bawtie!"

"He didn't do me a power of good either!" Logan

bawled over the incessant barking as he wrested the boys away.

"Heaven preserve us!" Their mother rushed inside, eggs clutched in her apron, milk sloshing in the wooden bucket. She set the pail down and pointed shakily at the doorway. "Out, Bawtie! You too, Donald, David. Go!"

Bawtie scurried from the room, tail tucked between his legs. The twins bolted after him without their usual argument and disappeared into the twilight.

Aunt Alice glanced at the shattered plate and took in her bleeding, disheveled nephew. She riveted her astonished gaze on their guest. "Mister Campbell, what in God's name?"

He straightened stiffly, speaking through his teeth. "Had a bit of a disagreement, Ma'am."

With shaky fingers, she began plucking the brown eggs from her apron and putting them in the basket on the table. "Is the matter resolved?"

"No, Ma'am."

She looked questioningly at Logan.

"Not by half, Aunt," he frowned.

"I see."

Josiah swept disdainful blackened eyes over Logan. "Perhaps I ought to be on my way, Mrs. Houston."

"Perhaps you ought."

"I shall speak with your husband upon his return. No doubt he will see sense."

She stiffened. "In what way, sir?"

"I've a valuable holding. What has your nephew got to offer the girl? Nothing but trouble."

"We will leave the matter for Peter to decide."

Logan hissed, "I'm game now, Aunt."

"Enough!" Kira strangled on the sob in her throat. She crumbled onto the bed and buried her face in her arms. Now that the worst of the crisis had passed, she badly needed answers and all she got was this incessant battling.

Warmth enveloped her as Logan bent near. The hand that had pounded Josiah only minutes ago lightly patted her back.

"Don't weep, Cricket."

"Leave her be, McCutcheon!" Josiah railed at him.

"Go—just go! Both of you!" Kira cried.

Gently turning her toward him, Logan smoothed strands of hair from her damp cheeks with bloodied fingers. "Speak to me, Kira. Please don't send me away."

Her tears streamed over his battered knuckles as she choked out, "Why didn't you tell me Tom was alive?"

The regret in Logan's bruised face swam into view. "I nearly did earlier in the meadow. Forgive me. I didn't mean for you to learn about him this way."

"Tom's alive?" Aunt Alice sank onto a stool.

Boots shifting back and forth, Josiah asked, "Where's the fellow gotten to now?"

"Tom was taken captive about the same time I was. I can't say where he is at present."

Josiah stood stock-still. "Or won't?"

"Tom asked me to look after his sister. That I vow."

A small gasp escaped Aunt Alice. "We thought dearest Tom dead ages ago, killed in that terrible ambush on the militia."

Josiah glared at Logan through blackened eyes. "You have only McCutcheon's say he wasn't."

The hauteur Aunt Alice leveled at him spoke for itself. "My nephew does not lie."

"What of your husband?"

She regarded Josiah as she might a squashed toad. "Will you abuse all my relations to my face?"

"No, indeed." He swiped his sleeve at the blood on his chin. "'Tis only, Mister Houston gave me his word I'd be wedding the lass."

Aunt Alice's dumbstruck eyes mirrored the disbelief welling in Kira. "Are you quite certain Peter said that?"

"Near enough, Ma'am. We've yet to shake hands on it."

Every fiber of Kira's being silently shrieked 'no!'

In a stunned second, Aunt Alice suddenly seemed older. "This puts the matter in a different light, Mister Campbell. Still, Peter must determine what's best for our ward."

Logan opened his mouth in protest. "What of Kira?"

"Nay." His aunt shook her capped head. "'Tisn't for her to decide."

"Shawnee allow women a say in who they wed," he muttered.

Josiah growled, "The lass will do as she's told. We're not savages."

Before Logan moved to quell Josiah, Donald tore into the room, his face pale, eyes wild. "Papa's come! He's hurt!"

Aunt Alice sprang up from her seat. "How badly?"

"Stabbed! His leg's bleeding something terrible. Never saw so much blood."

Logan grasped the little boy by his shoulders. "Where is he? Where's Will?"

"Up the road. Will's hurt too. Bawtie found them. They've been robbed!"

"God help us." Aunt Alice blanched deathly white.

Logan closed a supportive arm around her. "Campbell and I will go fetch them."

"Feuding all the while?"

"A temporary truce. You better wait here, Aunt,

until we return."

"No. I'm going with you. They're my menfolk."

"Lean on me then. You look ready to swoon."

Kira struggled to her feet. "I'm coming too."

Logan glanced at her, his brow creased, eyes lined. "What on earth for? You can barely walk."

There wasn't time to explain. "I just must."

"Better see to her, Campbell," he said, with abundant reluctance in his gruff tone and drawn face.

"Come on, girl." Kira clenched her teeth as Josiah took her arm.

"Easy, man!" Logan barked, and guided his aunt out into the dusk.

Behaving more like his usual self, Josiah assisted Kira across the room. "How were you injured?"

"I fell from a tree," she lied, not about to divulge the truth.

He stopped for her cloak, hung from a peg on the wall near the door. "What were you doing up there?"

She took the wrap from him. "Hunting for the wee folk."

"There'll be none of that nonsense when we're wed."

"You wouldn't want me for a wife, Josie," she assured him, throwing the wrap around her shoulders while balancing on her good leg. "I'm stranger than any lass you know."

"And fairer. Just mind that mouth." He lifted her down the steps at the stoop then swept her up in his thick arms. And kept her there.

"Put me down!"

He only held her more closely to his wall of a chest. "Just sparing your knee."

"I can hobble—"

Rude lips silenced her as he crushed his mouth to hers. Revulsion engulfed her in utter contrast to the desire that had surged in her with Logan's kiss. Powerful warring emotions! She pushed frantically against him, like trying to shift a boulder—didn't hinder him in the least. If anything, her resistance only increased his ardor. His gamey scent made her want to retch. As much as she hated to admit it, Logan had been right. Josiah was a predator and she, his prey.

Grunting with satisfaction, he finally released her captive mouth. "I've waited some time for that. Found a far better use for those lips than hurling insults."

She wiped at her scorched mouth. "Do you think I'll keep your insult to me a secret?"

"If you want Logan to live."

Her stomach knotted. "You'll hang if you murder him."

"Maybe he'll hang. Save me the trouble."

It was as though he'd struck her full in the gut. She could've doubled over. "What do you mean?"

"McCutcheon took his time coming home."

Fighting to firm up the hitch in her voice, she argued, "He just needs a while to adjust. Some captives do."

"Not him. That fellow's different from the rest. Battles like the best warriors have trained him."

"Logan can't help what he's been taught."

"They don't teach just anyone. And then there's that friend he struck me for. I reckon he's a warrior, or was."

In mounting desperation, she reasoned, "It could be some other friend."

Josiah snorted. "Who? He's been off with Indians. They've got a hold over him. And where do you suppose your brother is? Both in league with savages, I reckon."

"They couldn't be," she argued, with the sickening realization that he probably had the truth of it.

"Think not? I ever tell you that lead ball I took come from a white man's musket?"

She had a mighty urge to fell Josiah herself. "You have no proof that man was Logan."

"Is it proof you're wanting?"

"No!" The word tore from her before she could stop it.

"I figured as much. You'll forever take McCutcheon's side, no matter how the wind blows."

"I despise savages same as you."

"But you don't despise Logan, do you?"

Denial was futile. And Uncle Peter's life might hang in the balance. "Please, we must go to my guardian!"

"Whatever my betrothed wishes."

"I'm not your betrothed. After that crude foretaste, I never shall be."

"Rather I had a word with my good friend Captain Winn? That white man who shot me was fighting with Indians, a hanging offense. Winn likes a good hanging."

The noose was tightening around her own neck. Captain Winn had commanded Fort Rudd after Fort Warden burned and Captain Bancroft was taken captive. The Virginia Regiment was disbanded now and the militia called up in an emergency, but Winn remained in the area on land awarded him by the Crown—his ties to England stronger than most.

"Reckon your renegade brother is out there somewhere. Might hang 'em both," Josiah added, further tightening it.

Damn it all, Josiah had ingratiated himself with the zealous captain who kept a sharp eye out in the event of an Indian raid and scouted the border to see that they stayed on their side of the Ohio River. All Winn needed was a hint from Josiah to summon an eager party to track Logan and Tom down. She'd been glad of Winn's watchfulness before, but now—

A spasm twisted her gut. How had she gotten caught in such a predicament, and how dare Josiah try to force her hand this way? "Blast you for a black-hearted rogue, Josiah Campbell!"

She cried out as he struck her across the cheek, and held chilled fingers to her stinging face.

"Swear at me again and I promise you'll feel worse."

"Would you take an unwilling bride?"

"I'll take you anyway I can get you. Don't fool yourself. McCutcheon would do the same."

But Logan would never strike her. Strangely, he was more of a gentleman after seven years with savages than this lout.

****

Kira spotted the figures huddled on the dark road, their dim forms illuminated in the smoky light cast by the pine knot torch Donald held over his prostrate father. Gone, the boy's usual swagger, and David was equally somber. Breaking from Josiah, she half-ran, half-hopped, to the shadowed assembly.

"Papa? Can you hear us?" Donald pleaded.

Logan knelt over his cantankerous relation, now ominously silent. "Hold on, Uncle."

"Don't leave us, Peter." Aunt Alice slumped beside her husband, weeping into the apron she clutched to her face.

Will circled his arm around his distraught mother. "He's not gone yet, Mama."

At least Will didn't seem badly injured.

How still her guardian lay, unlike the indomitable man who barked out orders like a manor laird. Kira looked from Peter Houston's ashen face to Logan's grim expression. He'd balled Aunt Alice's kerchief beneath his palms to plug the wound and pressed bloodstained hands to his uncle's leg. But his efforts seemed too little, too late. A crimson pool was spreading over the earth like an evil tide. The attacker's blade must have ruptured something vital.

Helplessness washed over Kira like the red stain. How could she halt the deadly flow?

As if spoken in her ear, Hannah's words returned. *You're a natural born healer, child. You possess the gift. Have faith.*

If ever there was a need for faith, it was now.

"Logan?" His desperation was as palpable as the smoke from the torch. Bearing the weight on her good knee, she knelt beside him.

He said under his breath, "I can't stop the bleeding."

"Let me try."

"I don't dare," he whispered. "Uncle Peter's life depends on me. Aunt Alice will never forgive you if he dies. Better it be on my head."

"He's lost too much blood already. 'Tis the healing touch he needs now."

"And you're a healer?"

"Hannah says I am."

Logan swiveled his intent gaze from his uncle to Kira. "You believe her, don't you?"

She gave a nod.

"Maybe that's what truly matters. Very well. Take my place." Lifting scarlet hands, he allowed hers to slip beneath his. "God help you."

Praying hard for Divine aid, Kira pressed the kerchief to Uncle Peter's gushing flesh. The words from the book of *Ezekiel* seemed to flow forth from her on their own. "'When I passed by thee and saw thee polluted in thine own blood, I said unto thee, live.'"

A strange tingling charged through Kira from the tips of her fingers through her innermost being down to her toes. Logan closed his hands over hers. She sensed the wonder filling his spirit, weighed only moments before by despair.

"There's power in you, Kira. I feel it." His voice held hushed excitement.

She breathed in shakily. "So can I."

He nudged her. "Look. The bleeding's stopped."

Most marvelous of all was the fragrance. Where only blood, sweat, and the scent of fear had been, the sweetness of roses now wafted around them.

"Your balm?" he asked.

"This goes well beyond that."

Logan gave a low whistle. "Good Lord."

Was it Kira's imagination or did her guardian seem less gray? Surely, the life force was flowing back into him. A moan issued from his parted lips. His eyelids fluttered.

Will bent closer to the fallen man. "Papa's coming round!"

"Peter?" Aunt Alice enfolded her reviving spouse in her arms.

Faint color tinted his cheeks and he blinked up at them owlishly. "Why in blazes is everyone perched over me like a pack of crows?"

"His temper hasn't changed any," Logan remarked.

Aunt Alice sniffed. "Ornery as ever, bless him. Oh, Logan, my dear boy, you've snatched him back from the brink."

"Not me, Aunt. Kira is the miracle worker."

"Our Kira?"

"Seems she's a healer."

Will eyed her with newfound appreciation. "Who'd have thought it?"

"Hannah," Kira answered.

Aunt Alice tore a strip from her petticoat to bind her husband's wound. "Hannah McCue said this? Whatever were you doing with her?"

"Hannah's my dear friend."

She glanced distractedly at Kira. "I thought we

told you to stay away from that old woman?"

"There's no harm in her, Ma'am."

"No harm? She's a *witch*," Josiah said roughly. "You're not to keep company with such a one."

Kira cried out as he seized her arm, jerking her up.

Bristling like an incensed wolf, Logan sprang to his feet. "Turn her loose, Campbell!"

"I'm only curbing my betrothed."

Logan thrust out his bruised jaw. "Call her that again and I swear you'll eat your words."

"I've every right."

Uncle Peter pushed up on his elbows and glared at the circle. "Has the devil himself come for me? What are you jabbering about?"

Thick fingers dug into Kira's arm as Josiah ground out. "Your ward and I came to an agreement this evening, Mister Houston."

"What have you forced from her, you lout!" Logan drew back his fist and slammed Josiah on the side of his head.

"Hold on, McCutcheon! Nothing she won't say herself. Tell him, lass."

Kira would rather sink into her grave, but she couldn't let Logan hang. "Josiah and I are engaged." Each strained word sounded like a death knell.

"Over my dead body, Cricket!"

She wanted to shout back, "that's just what I'm trying to prevent!" but was silent.

Startled quiet seized the small assembly while Josiah gloated, "Heard it from her own lips, didn't you, McCutcheon?"

"Barely," Logan bit out.

"The girl's overcome by events of the night."

"Ah, yes. *Events.* Thought it took you overlong to join us."

Josiah smirked. "Lost our way in the dark."

"And the welt on her cheek?"

"A tree branch."

"Or the back of your hand?" Logan didn't await a retort, but smacked his fist into Josiah's already bruised jaw.

"We're having this out now!" Josiah pushed Kira aside and tore into his antagonist.

"Not without me!" Undeterred by the cut over one eye or his scrapes and bruises, Will scrambled up to join sides with his long-lost cousin. His curly blond head glowed in the sputtering light as he flung himself at Josiah.

He struck out and caught the eager young man on the jaw. Will stumbled back then rallied. He barreled at Josiah and knocked him to the ground. Logan rushed to pin Josiah. The two rolled over and over into the blackness with Will diving in behind them while David and Donald cheered.

Aunt Alice sprang up, twisting her apron in her fingers. "Have you all gone mad? Peter still lies before you!"

"Give me a hand, woman. I'll not be down for long."

With Kira grasping one callused hand, Aunt Alice the other, and David tugging at his father's arm, they hauled the burly man to his feet. Donald faithfully held the torch.

Uncle Peter ran his fingers over a brown, grizzled beard. "Will someone please tell me what my nephew's doing here?"

David strained to see the forms colliding in the dark. "Fighting Mister Campbell, Papa."

"That's plain enough, lad. *When* did Logan turn up?"

"Today. He wants Kira for himself," Donald volunteered.

"Violently, by the looks of it. Why is Will fighting the fellow?"

Donald seemed puzzled. "Does Will need a

reason?"

His father puffed out his cheeks. "To brawl with that great ox, he bloody well better have a good one. Haven't we troubles aplenty without my son and nephew getting themselves pounded into the dirt?"

"Not sure they're losing," Donald pointed out.

"They're hurtin plenty, I'll wager," his father grumbled. "I figured the lass would be in the middle of all this—"

Aunt Alice broke in. "Not the girl's fault both men fancy her. Besides, Kira's healing touch saved your life."

The annoyance in his rugged face lessened. "I'm right muzzy about what happened. If it's as you say, I'm indebted to you, gal. So all our care's not been wasted on you, eh?"

"I can't say as I agree with her visiting Hannah McCue, but Kira's done you a power of good," his wife assured him.

He drew heavy brows together. "You are not to see that old woman. Still, I'm right grateful to you, Kira."

Gratitude from this man was rare. "God did the deed."

"So you'll credit the Almighty, not the witch?"

"She's not one, sir. Hannah's an angel. I swear by all that's sacred."

"Many in these ridges swear differently." He paused for a moment. "If she's innocent as you say then I'm right sorry for the poor woman. But watch yourself, my girl, or I fear you may fall under the same condemnation as her."

Strident barking intruded over the grunts, scuffles, and oaths emanating from the turbulent darkness.

"I had better put an end to this before another has need of your gift. Donald, bring that torch," his father directed.

Kira limped on one side of her guardian, Donald on his other, and David at their heels, as he hobbled nearer the combatants. He bellowed, "Campbell!"

Any response from Josiah was muffled, likely because the other two had wrestled his bulk to the ground and straddled him with a fist or two in his mouth.

"Will! Logan! Let the man go!"

Winded but triumphant, Logan clambered to his feet. He tugged Will up with him. Arms wrapped around each other like the best friends in the world, they staggered over to where Uncle Peter waited. "About done here anyway," Logan panted.

Aunt Alice joined them, shaking her head. "Look at the state of you."

Will grinned through bloodied lips. "Campbell's worse."

The feeble torch didn't reveal the extent of Josiah's injuries, but he was covered in grime and smeared with blood.

"Enjoying your visit, Campbell?" Uncle Peter asked.

Josiah heaved his bulk to an upright posture and tracked unsteadily to the group. "Houston hospitality is sorely lacking. And I can't say much for McCutcheon manners either."

Uncle Peter eyed the damage inflicted by his relations. "Scarcely home a day, Logan, and already attacking the neighbors."

He blotted a scarlet trickle on his sleeve. "I'll take on this *neighbor* again if he lays a finger on Kira."

Josiah glowered at him. "You'll not permit me to touch my betrothed?"

"No man abuses Kira while I live," Will said.

Donald thrust a finger at the big man. "He tossed Bawtie, too."

"The little beast was tearing at my breeches."

David leapt in. "You were choking Logan—"

"Enough." Their father rounded on Josiah. "Kira may be strange in her ways, but by heaven, I'll not see her suffer."

Through battered lips, Josiah argued,"Have you never disciplined her, then?"

"Nary a slap. I don't hold with using force to subdue a woman. I shan't give her to any man who does."

"We had an understanding."

"Strike her again and we surely will."

"I apologize, Mister Houston." Josiah adopted a far more condescending tone. "My temper got the best of me, but the lass is headed for trouble."

"Indeed. 'Tis a firm hand she needs, not a harsh one."

"I shall have greater care in future, sir."

"And I promised her father to look after the lass until a suitable husband be found. Seems I must look again." The patriarch shifted himself and the assembly toward home.

Josiah hastened after them, his gait a bit ragged. "I'll make amends. Anything to regain your good favor."

"I see little likelihood there." Uncle Peter stumped on.

"Wait! Please. I'm devoted to your ward and she to me."

"Kira must have come by all this devotion in the past hour!" Logan hurled over his shoulder.

"She was cool enough toward you when I left three days ago," Will added.

"Quiet down," his father rumbled. "You two are scratching for a fight like prize gamecocks." He slowed his pace and glanced down at Kira. "What say you to this, lass?"

His unexpected query trapped her like steel jaws. Some women joined convents at such dire times, but Protestants had none, an oversight that really ought to be amended. She had no choice other than to say, "Hear Mister Campbell, sir."

Her guardian grunted, "As you like," and then to Josiah, "what do you propose, man?"

He leapt at the opening. "You were robbed of much needed supplies, were you not? I shall restore your goods."

"How do you propose to do that? Have you the means to purchase a year's supply of salt, meal, powder, shot..."

Aunt Alice covered her mouth. "Oh Peter, is it all gone?"

"And both horses taken."

"Leave matters to me, Ma'am. All will be well." Josiah slid hated fingers over Kira's cheek in defiance of Logan. "For such a prize, I would do far more."

"If you do as much as this, we will speak again," Uncle Peter said grudgingly. "More than that, I cannot promise."

"Thank you, sir. Mend quickly. Be seeing you, Will, McCutcheon," Josiah added tersely, and walked stiffly on by.

Logan waved him ahead. "No hurry. Don't rush back."

"Logan," his uncle warned.

"No matter, Mister Houston. I am content to let your nephew's insults pass unchallenged."

Once again, Josiah was the controlled man Kira had known before Logan's coming. But she'd seen what he really was.

Night swallowed his vile bulk. "My dreams are all of you, lass. Never fear. We shall soon be wed!"

"Dream away! You've still me to reckon with!" Logan flung after him.

But he didn't fully realize what he was up against, that Josiah would enlist Captain Winn against him, and Tom too if her brother could be found. This Kira could not bear. Nor could she possibly wed Josiah. In that instant, she resolved to evade her eager suitor. And if this failed, her desperate thoughts turned to belladonna, and how much of the potentially fatal herb to administer to a man of Josiah's size, and the best way go about it getting him to take it...an odd undertaking for a healer, she supposed. But powerless, Kira was not.

She had been once. Never again.

****

"Fire at the north gate!"

The warning cry echoed in Kira's terrified mind as billowing smoke smudged the blue sky above Fort Warden.

Coughing in the thick air, she lifted stinging eyes to the handful of frontiersmen on the narrow walk circling the inside of the fort walls. Muskets raised, they fired over the logs at the elusive enemy dodging through the trees. Wives and daughters crouched alongside the men and hurriedly reloaded spare firearms.

Kira joined the frantic cluster of women and children tossing buckets of water onto the fire—too little to dampen the inferno. The growing blaze would soon force the men to retreat and leave their walls undefended.

"Get to the blockhouses!" Captain Bancroft shouted.

These log structures at each corner of the palisade acted as miniature forts, and Kira fled with the others inside the blockhouse furthest from the flames. A husky frontiersman bolted the heavy door behind them. Men fired through the slits in the walls while babies screamed in their mother's arms and tearful children clung to their skirts. Kira huddled beside them, her hounded senses attuned to every explosion and the all-pervasive smoke. Would the air ever smell clean again, would she ever feel safe?

Before the attack began, she'd seen some crazy woman pleading with Captain Bancroft to surrender the fort. The beautiful stranger was out in the yard with him now. She told him sixty warriors were gathered in the trees, far more men then they had at Warden. The newcomer also brought fearsome news of Logan, said he'd been taken captive. The dreaded word seared Kira's soul. How could she live without Logan?

Time apart from him threatened to be cut brutally short. Blood-chilling war whoops rose above the musket bursts and crackle of burning wood. A chorus of dismay went up from the women and children. Were warriors forcing their gates? Was the blockhouse about to erupt into flames?

Trapped! Kira was trapped. And she couldn't stand it for one more minute.

Instinct compelled her to scramble through the panicked assembly to the door. She slid the bolt and shot outside—straight into the gaping mouth of hell.

"'Tis madness! Turn back!" voices shouted at her.

Ignoring them, she sped toward the first outlet she saw. Roaring sounded. The blaze burned hotter as she tore through the west gate. The hem of her cloak flashed orange.

"I'm afire!" She shrieked, running wildly.

Unseen hands grabbed her from behind. The man—somehow Kira knew it was a man—threw her to the ground and rolled her around on the grassy earth. He extinguished the flames, but her gratitude changed to terror as she glimpsed his face.

Chapter Seven

"No! Stop! Let me go!"

Kira's panting cries reached Logan asleep in the loft. He sat bolt upright in his bedroll. The last thing he knew she'd been snugly tucked down before the hearth. Had Josiah somehow snuck into the house through bolted doors?

Uncle Peter rumbled from his and Aunt Alice's bed where Kira had been earlier this evening. "What in the world?"

"We're under attack!" The call came from David or Donald sleeping in the back room with big brother Will.

"Will—Logan! Get your muskets!" the second boy shouted. Their mother shushed them drowsily. "No. Kira's only dreaming. Go back to sleep, boys."

Uncle Peter grunted. "How in blazes can anyone sleep with the lass taking on like someone's got her by the throat?"

"'Tis Fort Warden again, Peter," his wife said.

Warden. The name was seared into Logan's mind like the fire that had claimed the wooden palisade seven years ago.

His uncle sighed heavily. "Will the girl never forget?"

"No. Never." Kira sounded badly shaken.

What was this all about?

Logan rose from the blanket wrapped around him, wearing his breechclout and the clean white shirt Aunt Alice had given him. He'd washed the worst of the blood and grime off and she'd dabbed pungent salve on his wounds before he'd fallen soundly asleep. But he was wide awake now, and climbed barefoot down the ladder. Flames from the hearth washed orange light over Kira still lying in the nest of blankets he'd made for her before the fire. She'd drawn the striped wool up over her head and quivered beneath the covers.

Kneeling beside her, he said, "You were at Fort Warden?"

She pulled the cloth beneath her chin and stared up at him, her eyes stark. "I wish to God I hadn't been."

The thought of her in that inferno made him cringe. "When did you reach there?"

"Just before the Shawnee attacked."

"You couldn't have come on your own. Who brought you?"

"I did." Will staggered groggily into the room from where he'd been sleeping in the back.

"Snuck off without asking my leave," his father grumbled.

Shadows hid Will's bruised face as he stifled a yawn. "I knew you wouldn't give your permission, Papa."

"With good reason. 'Twas pure foolishness."

"Which I have lived to regret." Will sounded both somber and annoyed. Clearly, they'd had this conversation before.

Something puzzled Logan. "I thought you all would fort up inside these stone walls. Why take Kira to Warden, Will?"

"To see you."

"Me?" Logan had no idea.

"There was no contenting her. When we reached the fort, your father said you were off hunting and hoped you would soon return. Thinking Kira safe there, I left her and hurried home to face Papa's wrath."

Logan fingered a cut on his jaw. "I never knew."

"You were a captive by then. Besides, it's behind us now. Most of us, anyway. I'm sorrier than I can say for Kira's suffering." Will smothered another yawn. "You must excuse me. I'm all in." He turned back toward his room.

"We're all worn to a thread. Be glad you live, girl," Uncle Peter admonished her. "No use stewing over the past."

Aunt Alice sat up wearily. "These dreams always leave her terribly upset. I best fetch her a drop of brandy."

"Stay, Aunt. I'll get it and sit with her."

"Mind that's all you do, nephew," Uncle Peter muttered.

Annoyance flashed in Logan. "What more do you think I'd venture with you lying there not a stone's throw away?"

"Nothing, if you have a lick of sense."

His aunt flopped back down. "Leave him be, Peter. Logan's good with the girl. Likely 'tis the only way we'll get a moment's peace this night."

"Comfort her, then," Uncle Peter grumbled, "though not as David did Bathsheba. I've not given her into your hands."

Logan straightened. "Yet."

"Can you better Campbell's offer? You've got next to nothing."

"I've more than you know." Even without seeing his uncle, he sensed him perk up.

"Did Shawnee give you silver? I hear they have mines."

He walked to the cupboard. "Aye, they do. I have an armband or two."

"Hardly enough to refurbish your homestead."

Logan rummaged among the plates and crockery. "Yet I have wealth," if he found that secret stash.

"Enough of this mystery, Nephew. Speak

plainly."

"I'll say no more for now, sir."

"And I'll believe when I see it," Uncle Peter snapped.

"Fair enough."

Aunt Alice must have fallen asleep or she'd have badgered Logan for details. He snagged the glazed jug containing a portion of her special apple brandy—the rest stored in barrels along with the whiskey in the earthen cellar—and poured some into a wooden cup. He returned to Kira. Kneeling beside her, he slid his arm beneath her trembling shoulders and held the brew to her lips. "You're shaking like a newborn foal left out in the wet."

She sipped slowly. The brandy seemed to ease her chill and the jarring tremble diminished. Doubtless her anxious mind still churned, though. He set the cup down and drew Kira to him, bringing the blankets with her. She half-lay half-sat in his embrace. How good she felt held close, the urge to protect her surged inside him like a fierce wolf guardian.

"You're safe now," he soothed.

Gradually, she grew calmer. His uncle's even snores drifted to them. It was safe to speak without fear of being overheard, and Logan had more to ask. Keeping his voice low, he asked, "Tell me how you escaped Warden."

Her voice thick with emotion, she said, "I bolted out the west gate—through the very flames."

A shudder ran through him at the horrific image and he cradled her tightly. "I'm amazed you weren't shot or burnt."

"No one fired on me, but my cloak caught fire. A warrior quickly smothered the blaze."

Logan sucked in his breath. "He saved your life, Cricket."

"But I was terrified of being taken captive and

carried away. Don't you see?"

"Yes. Why did he let you go?"

"Catawba warriors allied with the English attacked the Shawnee. The brave disappeared into the trees and I ran until I dropped. Uncle Peter and Will found me not far from here."

"Oh, Kira. If only I'd known you were at Warden. I would have asked my cousin Rebecca to bring you away with her, like she did Tessa. They fled the fort together."

Kira tilted her head at him, her eyes searching his in the firelight. "Some folk said they saw Tessa with the English lady. That was your cousin?"

"Aye, wed to Shoka, the brother of my Shawnee father."

Her eyebrows shot up. "But people said that woman was beautiful and dressed like a lady."

"She is, or was. Rebecca's father was a wealthy Englishman, but she fled his abuse and came to America."

"Still, it makes no sense for a lady to wed a warrior."

"Shoka is highly unusual and Rebecca's a bit wild."

"She truly must be. Where is this so called *lady* now?"

"In Quebec with Shoka and their two small sons. They're staying with their friend, Capitaine Renault, who wed Rebecca's younger sister."

Kira jerked. "A *French* capitaine? I hate the French!"

Logan clapped his hand over her mouth. "Your animosity is understandable after years of war, but Capitaine Renault offered Shoka and Rebecca much needed sanctuary in Canada. With an English army demanding the return of all captives, they had no choice but to flee to the French. I realize this is a great deal to take in, but keep your voice down, for heaven's sake."

He lightened his grip slightly. "Will you keep still?"

A slight, grudging nod came from Kira, likely overcome with curiosity despite her vehement objections.

He slid his hand from her mouth, prepared to return it in an instant. "Capitaine Renault inherited a vast estate from his father. The land is good and abundant with game, enough for Shoka to hunt, trap, and make a life there."

Kira scrutinized him. He squinted back at her through sore eyes, readying for her next question. It soon came, though in the muffled tone he'd insisted on.

"What happened after Tessa escaped the fort?"

"My sister is well. That's all you need know."

Eyes crinkled in determined lines, Kira argued, "Tessa was my friend. You must tell me. Is she also in Canada?"

"Nay. Closer than that," he admitted.

"Where?"

"If you speak of this to a soul, you may bring evil on her."

"I won't. I promise."

"Not good enough. I dare not risk further revelation without more assurance. This confidence requires a blood oath."

She bit her lip. "Do it, then."

He drew his knife from the buckskin sheath at his side. The blade glinted in the firelight. "Hold out your hand."

She extended her fingers, blinking as he grasped her palm. With a flick of the blade, he nicked her smooth flesh. Making a quick cut to his hand, he pressed the small slits together, mingling their blood. "Swear you'll not breathe a word of what I'm about to say."

"I swear it."

In barely perceptible tones, Logan said, "Tessa is wed to Meshewa, the younger cousin of Shoka and my adopted father."

Kira's mouth fell open.

"Hear me out. Meshewa was kind to me from the start and became like a brother. He and Tessa are in hiding from the soldiers who would haul her away if they find her."

"Are there others with them?"

He nodded. "Waiting for me."

With the stillness of a hushed doe, she asked, "Where?"

"Two days hard ride from here deeper in the Alleghenies."

"*That* near? When will you meet with them?"

"At the agreed time. When the strawberry moon is full."

"I don't understand."

"In what month do you first taste wild strawberries?"

"Late May, or June." She looked hard at him. "Soon."

"Yes. I've something to seek before I join them."

"What you spoke of wanting to find at your home place?"

He spoke softly in her ear, "A treasure's buried there."

She shivered. "Does anyone else know of this?"

"Only those who left it behind."

She searched his eyes as if the answer lay there. "What could you possibly seek in that burned-out homestead?"

"You wouldn't believe me if I told you and I'm not ready to do that yet."

A shadow crossed her intent gaze. "What of Tom, then? Why didn't he return with you?"

Here, Logan answered with extreme care. "Tom

97

couldn't."

"Doesn't he want to see me?" The hurt he'd anticipated roughened her voice.

"Very much."

"But why—" Realization puckered her forehead and her face crumpled. "Tom has a Shawnee wife, doesn't he?"

Logan made no denial. She sagged against him and he tightened his arm around her.

The barest wail sounded against his chest. "Why couldn't Tom have wed Tessa and come home?"

"That isn't where his heart led him. He loves Laneke and they have two small daughters. If he left them, there's no assurance he could return. Tom regrets being apart from you."

She wiped at the tears wetting her cheeks. "Not nearly enough."

"Tom's never forgotten you. He's deeply fond of you."

"With me thinking him dead all these years?"

"He couldn't let you know otherwise. He asked me to see how you fared and to look out for you."

"I would be foolish to think you returned for my sake alone. 'Tis this treasure that's brought you, isn't it?"

"The instant I laid eyes on you, I knew I'd found another."

Eyes brimming, she shook her head. "Not one you'll be claiming."

"Kira, listen to me."

She struggled to pull from him. "I've heard enough."

"Not quite." Restraining her with one arm, he clapped his other hand back over her lips in the event her response grew too loud. "Tom's there now, Kira. With the others."

She froze in his hold. Logan sensed her keen interest at odds with blinding hurt. "I'll take you to him. After all these years you can finally be reunited."

Longing welled in her liquid gaze. Then she stiffened and shook her head.

"I know you're afraid, but Tom and I would never allow harm to come to you. And no one wishes you ill."

Still, she regarded him as though they'd betrayed her.

In a way, he supposed they had. "Please, Kira. I'm offering you a chance to be with Tom and me." He lifted his hand a few inches from her mouth.

"By joining up with savages? Tom has made his choice. And so, it would seem, have you." Tears trailed down over his fingers, but she was insistent. "Go away, Logan, and keep on going."

Pain knifed through him. "How can you say that?"

"'Tis for your own good and mine," she sniffed. "Tom must forget me. You both must."

"And leave you to Josiah? That big oaf will pluck you like a buzzard on a chicken."

"Don't be crude."

"As if he'll be tender. I'll deal with your *betrothed*."

"I can manage. If I haven't you to worry over."

"You needn't trouble about me, Cricket."

"No? If I don't wed Josiah, he will tell his good friend Captain Winn you are a renegade spy."

So, that's what the scoundrel had over her. "I recall you making that very same accusation earlier about me."

"Not to anyone who would actually hang you for such a grievous offense. You're in grave danger. You must go."

"Not yet. And not without you."

Emotion garbled her voice. "My life is here. I know no other."

"You're young. You could learn."

"I would rather live with gypsies than among your new friends and relations."

"Listen to me, Kira. A fear faced is a fear lessened."

"And sometimes 'tis best left as it is." Her chest heaved in an anguished sigh. "Leave me to my forest creatures. At least they're true."

"So am I, if you'd give me the chance to prove myself."

She gulped back sobs and shook her head.

Damn, she was stubborn. Not that he could blame her after all she'd endured.

Nor did Logan imagine this was a good time to tell her their little band intended to join Shoka in Quebec as soon as he'd discovered the wealth at his home place, which didn't leave him a great deal of time to change her mind. But convince her, he must, or lose her forever. The thought of never seeing Kira again ratcheted through his heart like a tomahawk exactly striking its mark.

****

Breathing in the earthiness of hay and horses, Logan quietly led his stallion from the dark stable. The big chestnut was just visible in the pale pre-dawn light. Clouds further veiled the sky as he paused to look at the dim outline of the house. Smoke from the massive hearth mingled with the raw air, heavy with the promise of rain, but he was well accustomed to cold and wet.

How he wished he could've stolen a few more moments to lie beside Kira's soft warmth. What bliss, even though she was so vexed with him he hadn't been able to coax a kind word, let alone anything else, from her before she'd faded into oblivion last night. Still, he'd held her close and she'd nestled against him, now and then loosing small sighs.

To think of Kira actually telling that rogue Campbell she'd wed him rather than risk Logan's neck struck him full on. Yet, she wasn't about to entrust herself to him. Understanding the ways of women, especially this one, was exasperating to the extreme. Maybe he shouldn't bother, just put her from his mind, if that were remotely possible.

Ah, Kira. What have you done to me? He used to be so independent. Now, he just wanted her back in his arms.

Logan tore his wistful gaze from the sleeping household. No one had awakened yet to mark his absence. It was better slipping off this way. No awkward questions.

The thickening clouds parted long enough to reveal a single star hanging low on the eastern horizon. The brilliant ball shone like a promise, reminding Logan of his. He knew what he had to do. No point in further delay. Reluctantly, he swung himself up into the saddle and turned Tequi's head toward the western woods.

****

Rain drummed on the shingled roof as Kira stirred drowsily in her nest of blankets. Instinctively, she reached out for Logan, her disappointment sharp at not finding him there. A rush of memories engulfed her like a rain-swollen stream. The sense of betrayal from the night before weighed her wounded spirit. She must evade him. Evade them all.

Loathe to rise and face the day, she opened her eyes. Aunt Alice was seated by the hearth, sewing. Firelight glinted on the silver needle in her industrious hands.

She glanced at Kira. "Awake, are you? How's that knee faring?"

Kira stretched gingerly and sat up. With a yawn, she said, "Better."

"I always did swear by my blend of leaves for a poultice."

"You've got me trussed up in one," Uncle Peter muttered from his bed. "How's a fellow supposed to get about?"

"You're not." His wife was adamant.

Kira swept her eyes over the snug room, filled with vibrant life only yesterday, now sadly empty, and returned her gaze to Aunt Alice. "Where is everyone?"

"If by *everyone* you mean Logan, I suppose he's off with that stallion of his."

Feigning disinterest, Kira said, "Not only him. What of Will?"

"With Logan, I reckon. Can't keep Will down for long."

"Nor me," Uncle Peter grunted. "I'll not long endure your coddling, woman."

His wife rounded on him. "You can spend a day mending."

Though sympathetic to her guardian's unaccustomed confinement, Kira was glad he'd be out of the way while she acted on her scheme. "Where are David and Donald?"

"Out. The rain will soon drive them in," said their long-suffering mother.

No time to waste. Kira untied the cloth at her knee, discarded the dressing, snatched her shoes and stockings from the hearth and pulled them on. "I must see to my animals."

"'Tis you I worry over, lass, not those creatures of yours."

Kira got carefully to her feet. Concealing any remaining soreness, she walked to the wall. "They need tending."

"In all this wet? You've not even had your breakfast."

She took her green cloak from its peg. "I'll have

lunch and breakfast in one, later."

"Don't be overlong."

"I shan't." But Kira knew better. Guilt pricked her as she pulled up the hood and tied the cloak at her neck. Lifting the bolt, she stepped out the door.

"If it's Logan you're wanting, I'm not keen on the match!" Uncle Peter called after her.

"Did I say I wanted him?"

"No need. Remember, I have the final say in who you'll be wedding!"

He was in one of his black moods. Kira hitched up her skirts and walked stiffly down the steps, hoping her knee would limber up. Blinking in the rain, she scanned the foggy homestead. No one was in the yard or out in the meadow. Likely, they'd all gathered in the stable. She didn't wait to be discovered and limped up to the trees behind the house.

The branches overhead provided scant cover from the damp cold seeping beneath her cloak. She'd be chilled through by the time she reached Hannah's. But she had to go on. That lout Josiah, her cantankerous guardian, and Logan—him most of all—had left her no alternative other than to seek refuge elsewhere. Even her faithless brother bore some of the guilt by sending the renegade to her in the first place.

Life was abysmally cruel. She despised how easily tears came thinking about Logan and the black ache inside seemed to spiral down into an eternity of pain. Why must she long to feel his lips on hers again? Why did he possess her heart?

The wretched wind tore at her mantle as she reached the sheltered nook where she kept the injured animals. Showery droplets further anointed her head as she pushed soppy branches aside and knelt awkwardly to peer beneath. Pity touched her at the sight of two baby squirrels curled in the nest she'd made, long tails wrapped around each other. The forlorn owl with rust-colored feathers huddled beside them.

"Poor Alf." She scooped up the bedraggled bird, tucked him into the pocket she'd sewn inside her cloak, and slid the squirrels into another. Finding the tiny fawn was more of a challenge, but she spied her under the saturated leaves. Fortunately, the splint on its leg was in place. "Come on, Deirdre." She gathered the orphan in her arms.

Skirts flapping, she squelched over the winding path, awash with water and slick underfoot. Yesterday's warmth seemed an illusion, as did Logan's coming. Spring in these ridges was as variable as a woman's mind was said to be, though Kira knew her own. Surely.

Wetter and colder by the minute, she scrambled over downed branches and lichen-encrusted logs. Yellow fungus called witches' butter sprouted in the leaf mold. She startled at the wild turkey flapping from the foggy undercover, but saw no other animals. The birds were hidden away. Then why did she have the eerie sense of being watched?

She turned, squinting in the rain, and looked back through the hazy trees—nothing. If someone were behind her, he gave no more indication of his presence than a ghost. The thought of wandering spirits sent a shiver down her spine. Her mother had spoken of restless beings that haunted the hollows, especially at night. Uncle Peter declared it nonsense, but Kira knew many who held this belief.

The misty woods were ghoulishly dark. "Only nonsense," she repeated, ready to jump at the slightest provocation.

Arms aching, she hurried on. The fawn grew heavier with each sodden step. She lost her footing on a mossy stone and lurched forward. With a cry, she slid down the slope. She dug in her shoes for a toehold and clamped her hand around a sapling. Clutching the woodland baby, she jerked to a stop.

Her chest heaved as she gazed down at the shrouded hollow below. Who would find her if she tumbled down this rocky slope and broke her leg—or worse, her neck? A spirit?

As quickly as she dared, Kira climbed further down into the gloom toward Hannah's cabin. Even on sunny days, the light was hard put to filter through the heavy shadows in the McCue hollow. Mist enveloped everything now and the stream gurgled against the thrum of rain as she picked her way along its ferny bank. She could barely see to find her way.

An unsettling thought gnawed at her along with her empty stomach. She'd passed the gnarled apple tree that marked the trail some time ago and should have reached the turn to the cabin by now. If she'd veered off the path, miles of stormy woods lay between her and the Lewis homestead, the McCue's nearest neighbor. Should she retrace her steps? It was impossible to say in all this fog.

"Kira!"

Was the wind playing tricks on her, or had someone called her name?

"Kira!"

There it was again, louder and more insistent. Did the voice come from a being of this world, or the next?

"Kira Anne McClure!"

A ghost wasn't likely to shout her whole name. She turned and looked behind her—nothing. Then relief rushed up inside her as she spotted the familiar figure. His wide-brimmed brown hat and woods-colored coat blended with the trees, making him hard to distinguish at first.

"Joseph! Thank God!" She hurled herself at the older man and pressed her face to his damp chest.

His woolen coat smelled reassuringly of wood smoke and pipe tobacco.

He hugged her close. "Lost your way, have you, lass?"

"And I feared spirits were after me."

"Spirits have no liking for all this wet. They'll be tucked away in the dry, sensibly, like you should be."

She looked up at his face, weathered from years spent out in all sorts of weather. Gray streaked his beard, but his muscular figure showed no signs of age. Unlike his frail sister, Joseph McCue stood tall and straight.

"Was it you following me?" she asked.

"Since Turner's Ridge."

"I was spooked well before that."

His lined brown eyes creased in reproach. "I'll hear no more of spirits. You know better than to venture out when 'tis blowing hard. You'll worry that bonnie Alice Houston to a thread. And after all she's done for you."

Kira shifted the fawn from her aching hold into Joseph's ready arms. "Don't scold. I'm in such a lot of trouble."

"You'll be in a sight more if you catch your death. Best get you indoors, my girl." He strode ahead, humming the nameless tune he'd sung to her since her childhood.

Kira limped behind his long legs as he angled expertly through the trees.

Some folks called Joseph McCue peculiar because he kept to himself and was *the witch's* brother, but no one volunteered this opinion to his face. He was quick with his fists and had a temper, although he'd always had a soft spot for Kira and her late mother.

The haze momentarily swallowed him. He'd taken the turn Kira had missed and she scrambled to catch up, heartened beyond words as the misty clearing came into sight. There stood the log cabin and Hannah's tidy garden. Smoke drifted up from the chimney and a welcoming hearth beckoned.

The petite, shawled woman appeared in the doorway as if Kira's coming were expected. Hannah always seemed to anticipate her visits, as she did so many other things.

Hastening nearer, Kira called through chattering teeth, "Hannah! I've come!" She mounted the steps to the stoop.

Hannah's green gaze took her in and touched on the fawn. "A glad sight you are to these old eyes, indeed, but you're chilled to the bone. Get you inside, lass. Put the wee mite near the warm, Joseph."

Kira tottered gratefully into the snug room and he settled the baby on some sacking in front of the hearth.

Tucking gray tendrils beneath a white cap, Hannah said, "I'll have this cloak off you in a shake, my dear girl."

"I've brought my nursery."

"Thought as much."

A golden-brown owl followed their movements from the beam overhead; its heart-shaped face partially hidden by bunches of dried herbs. Yellow eyes widened as Hannah dipped out the squirrels and young owl Kira had brought. These joined the fawn.

"You'll get on together, Ebenezer," Hannah assured the watchful elder.

Chittering sounds came from the top of the walnut cupboard. Kira glimpsed masked eyes and whiskered faces. Two raccoon babies had retreated among the crocks and white-oak baskets. A shy young fox slinked behind a barrel of cornmeal. Kira had no idea how many animals might be sheltered beneath this roof. The count varied each time she came.

"Now then, lass." Hannah tugged at the sodden ties closing Kira's cloak. "Turn your head, Joseph. I'm having it all off."

Humor in his dark gaze, he turned away and hung his coat from a peg. "What brings you out in all this muck, girl?"

Kira drew as near to the hearth as she dared without catching on fire. She held out chilled hands to the heat. "I can't stay with the Houstons any longer."

"I thought you were content there?"

"Well enough, I suppose. Until now."

Hannah untied Kira's petticoats and spread the sopping cloth over the wooden rack near the hearth. "Would this sudden change have to do with a certain young man?"

"Josiah Campbell is bent on wedding me. I despise him."

"Can you not refuse the fellow?" Joseph asked.

"He won't take no for an answer and has fairly persuaded Uncle Peter 'tis a good match."

Joseph lifted the fox with work-worn hands and stroked its reddish fur. "Then you must persuade Peter differently. His bark is worse than his bite, with women, anyway."

"'Tisn't that simple."

"Never is," he grunted.

Her stays and shift went the way of her petticoats and left her covered only in goosebumps. Hannah wrapped a woven blanket snugly around her and picked up a linen towel. "She'll do, brother. What a state you're in, girl."

Kira sank onto a stool before the hearth while Hannah rubbed the wet lengths of her hair. "There's more than Josiah troubling you," she observed with her usual perception.

Wishing she wouldn't tear up at the mention of his name, Kira said, "Logan's come."

"Ah. At long last your prayers are answered."

"Not as I imagined. Not nearly."

"They rarely are, child," Hannah soothed. "Is he not as handsome, charming and clever as you remembered?"

"Far more so. That only makes it unbearable to be parted from him again. But he's bent on returning to the Shawnee."

Hannah didn't appear the least bit surprised. "They must seem like family by now."

"He's been with them long enough," Joseph added.

Kira couldn't believe her ears. "He has family here."

"He may come to see that in time, lass. You've still not told us all," Hannah prodded gently.

"Logan wants to take me back with him."

Joseph arched dark graying brows. "Does he, now?"

"I'm not certain where," Kira added, "but his new *friends* will be there too, I don't doubt."

"I see." With a deeply pensive look, Hannah took the wooden ladle and filled a stoneware bowl with broth from the kettle simmering over the fire. "What's to be done?"

"Nothing—except to hide." Kira took the steaming bowl from Hannah and sipped hungrily, speaking between draughts. "I shan't wed Josiah and can't go with Logan to savages. Or Quebec. He even speaks fondly of the French!"

Joseph replied, "There's worse company. Some behave more like savages than the Indians, and not all French are vile."

This was pure madness, and yet, Joseph didn't seem the least bit insane. "Have you friends among the Indian?"

"Why do you think our cabin still stands after all the years of war when so many others were burned to the ground?"

"Some people say I put a protective circle around our house," Hannah said with sad weariness, "and can change myself into an egg and float across the stream if I'm in danger."

Joseph furrowed his craggy brow in a scowl. "Rubbish."

"The tales only grow. When the Lewis's ewes took sick, the fault was laid at my door."

"By God, I'll kill the next man who accuses you of such nonsense."

"Many are women," Hannah sighed. "Mrs. Winn declares I come to her at night and transform her into a horse. She says 'tis the reason she's so weary the next day from all the riding I've put her to."

"Captain Winn's attentions in the night would never account for such fatigue. That woman has the face of a horse and temperament of a sow with bellyache," Joseph muttered.

Hannah smiled wanly. "All the same, folk hear her, especially as she's the captain's wife."

"Who will they find to blame for their misfortunes after you've gone, sister?"

"Kira, I fear." Hannah picked up the forlorn little owl and stroked his rumpled feathers. "If you remain under this roof, lass, your fate will be the same as mine."

The somber threat weighed Kira's already low spirits. "But I don't know where else to go."

"Better to go with the man you love than risk being wed to the one you loathe."

Her heart caught. "I'll stay with you and risk my fate."

Hannah looked at her with unveiled regret. "Such joy I would take in having you near. But you mustn't stay. 'Tis the life of a leper, not for a bonnie lass so filled with promise. When the storm eases, Joseph must see you back."

Dismay swelled in Kira. "What if I can't bear my lot?"

"God will preserve you. And I will be with you, even if in spirit, at your hour of greatest need."

Kira could have sworn that hour had come.

Chapter Eight

A watchful sentinel, the golden-brown owl swiveled his head as Hannah tugged the comb through Kira's tangled spill. "Such bonnie hair. I'll soon put you to rights."

"I'd rather you made me ugly. Then I'd not be plagued with suitors."

Hannah laughed softly. "That would take some doing."

"You could shear my hair or stain me with walnut juice—"

At that moment, the raccoon babies shot down from the cupboard and overturned a basket of yarn. One scuttled behind the loom while the second whirred the spinning wheel.

Joseph cupped Kira's cheek with his roughened hand. "We can't spoil your looks, lass. Like your sweet Mama you are."

"Were you very fond of her, Joseph?"

His eyes grew distant. "Beyond any other woman. I'd have wed Maggie. Your father never loved her as I did."

"Maybe if Papa had lived." Kira wasn't certain why she defended him.

"He had his chance, did Thomas. Don't go losing yours."

Kira lifted her chin. "Logan's the one forfeiting our happiness. Didn't I beg him to stay? I can't endure what he asks and there's an end to it."

A faint smile lightened Joseph's somberness. "You're a fighter, lass. So is young McCutcheon, I'll wager."

"And he doesn't fight fair."

Joseph's smile broadened. "Reckon he fights to win."

Hannah was brisk. "Enough talk of battling. Let's get you dressed. Alice Houston will be overwrought. They all will."

"But I've only just come." Kira looked longingly at the cozy room. A tiny chipmunk scurried under the bed and the baby squirrels were curled in a basket. "These creatures are given refuge. Will you make me go?"

Hannah wrapped her thin arms around Kira. How frail she was, as if she might blow away in a stiff breeze.

"I would give all to keep you, my sweet lass, but your path doesn't lie with me. Before you leave, I have a gift. One I've been saving for you." Hannah walked to the cupboard, a newfound spring in her step.

With curiosity equal to the raccoon babies, Kira watched her open the closed doors. From beneath an herbal bouquet, she withdrew a wealth of lilac-flowered cloth. "I've remade this gown for you. Feel, 'tis taffeta."

At a loss for words, Kira rose from the stool and ran her fingers over the lustrous fabric. The style was far grander than anything she'd ever seen, with a fitted bodice that laced up the front and a long full skirt. Finally, she found her tongue, "Wherever did you come by such a gown?"

"In Ulster, before we came to Virginia. 'Twas a precious gift from a dear friend."

"No use asking who. She'll not say," Joseph interjected.

Hannah behaved as though she hadn't heard him. "Let's see this on you. But first—" Laying the gown over a chair, she turned back to the cupboard with more animation than she'd displayed in ages.

Again, she opened the doors and drew out a lacy bundle. "I've tucked away my shift, boned corset, two petticoats and ivory stockings fit for a lady."

Kira smoothed the lavender bows on the corset with a sense of awe. "So beautiful. Like a dream."

"Yet some folks live in grand style. This would be only passing fair to them. Try it on. Let's see the fit."

"Turning my head." Joseph pivoted toward the wall. "How's the girl to get about in all that finery?"

Hannah pulled Kira's blanket away. "Never you mind. Just once, I'll see her dressed properly."

"Did you know some of the gentry in Ireland?" Kira asked.

"Aye," the older woman allowed. "I did once."

Before she could press Hannah for details, she found herself pushing her arms into the soft shift and standing dazedly as Hannah drew the strings at the ruffled neckline and tied them. Kira pulled on the ivory stockings and stepped into the most extravagant petticoat, adorned with ruffles. It hung to her ankles and must have swept the floor on petite Hannah. An even grander petticoat went on over the first one, beautifully embroidered with rosy knots and flowers.

Hannah tied the petticoats at Kira's waist and picked up the beribboned corset. Kira had stays, though not a corset that fitted as tightly as this one, and laced up the back.

"Takes some getting used to, lass." Hannah reverently gathered the gown. The rustling cloth whispered down over Kira. She slipped her arms into fluted sleeves that fitted at the elbow and fell in a swath of lace.

Sweetness wafted from the luxurious folds, reminiscent of a summer's day. "This smells as marvelous as it looks."

"I keep it with lavender sachets. Not an easy

herb to grow in these mountains, but I'll not be without it." Hannah laced the bodice over the corset and gave a few tugs to the creation, then trotted back to the cupboard.

She returned with a pair of lilac-colored slippers, unlike any Kira had ever worn. "These always were a mite big for me. Try them."

Kira slid her feet inside, pleased that they fit.

"Everything suits you perfectly. Now for your hair." Hannah wound Kira's black cascade into a knot on her head and held it in place with an ivory comb. Taking her by the hand, she led her to the ancient mirror on the log wall.

Firelight flickered over Kira as she admired the elegant young lady clothed in the beautiful gown. Tendrils framed her face, hauntingly like her mother's. "Mercy, Hannah. You've not made me any uglier."

"That was never my wish."

Joseph gave a low whistle. "Our little tree climber has grown into a right beauty."

"One more thing is wanting." Hannah reached behind her neck and freed something hidden beneath the kerchief tucked around her bodice. A small gold cross hung from the black ribbon she dangled in her fingers. She held it out to Kira.

"I can't accept this. The cross must be dear if you've worn it near your heart all these years."

"No one is dearer to me than you." Hannah tied the ribbon around Kira's neck.

The gown's low neckline readily revealed the precious keepsake. "Did your friend also give you this?"

"He did."

"I thought it must have been a man. Did he make you happy?"

"For a time. This gown was meant for our wedding day."

The underlying sadness that had lingered in Hannah all these years now made sense. "That day never took place."

"Nay. Promise me you will always wear the cross. And the gown on the day you're wed."

"What if I'm not?"

"Don't travel my road, lass. There are worse barriers than those you face. Logan could be dead."

Her stomach knotted. "Is that what happened to your beloved?"

"At my own father's hand."

"Their engagement was made in secret," Joseph explained.

Then Kira knew. "Your betrothed was Irish and Catholic."

A tear glistened in Hannah's farseeing gaze. "I should have gone away with Shawn when he first asked, not delayed."

Anger lit Joseph's eyes. "Our father cared not that he was well-to-do and loved our Hannah, only that he was Papist."

"Was there vengeance for his death?"

Hannah gave a sad nod. "Shawn's brothers were out for blood. Joseph took me away and Papa's heart failed soon after. Never allow hate or fear to rule you, lass." She lifted a long, gray hooded cloak from the cupboard and handed it to her. "And now, you must leave me."

"Won't everyone wonder how I've come by my finery?"

"They'll know soon enough when I bear you home," Joseph said dryly. "You best make ready to travel. Tuck those fine shoes in your pockets and put your stout pair back on."

Kira gathered her old shoes from before the hearth. Hannah had wiped off the mud and they were dry. She sat on the stool and reluctantly pushed her feet in—jumping at a loud knock. She leapt up. "I pray that's not Josiah."

"By heaven, if he harms a hair of your head, he'll not live to see the morrow." Joseph stumped to the door and threw open the heavy oak. His tall figure blocked Kira's view of their caller. For a wild moment, she contemplated hiding under the bed with the fox. Then Joseph called in welcome, "Get you in out of the wet, young man!"

To her surprise, Will walked in, his good looks still marred by last night's fight. That didn't seem to trouble him, though, as he swept widened hazel eyes over her. His jaw dropped. "Where in the world did you come by all that?"

Suddenly shy, Kira said, "Hannah. Do you fancy it?"

He stood as if rooted to the floor. "For pity's sake, girl, you surely make it tough for a fellow to wed elsewhere."

She returned his stare. "I thought I was like a sister?"

"Not hardly. Not *ever* if it were up to me. That was your doing. Are you certain you're wearing all of that gown? Seems like you're missing the top half."

Hannah smiled. "'Tis cut a bit lower than you're accustomed to. She has a lovely bosom, don't you agree?"

"Lovely," Will echoed, running his hand through wet blond curls. "Here, I expected her to be soaked through and as muddy as Bawtie and I find her looking like a duchess."

"It might be best if I wear my cloak," Kira offered.

Smiling, Joseph took Will by the arm and led him to the hearth. "Sit you down. Appears you could do with a drop."

"Can't tarry long, Mister McCue. I'm sent to fetch her."

Kira studied Will uneasily. "They know I'm

here?"

"You'll have to hide better than this if you want to stay out of reach."

She wrapped in the fine wool mantle. "Is Uncle Peter very angry?"

"He's none too pleased."

"What of you, Will Houston? Are you not frightened to enter the home of one called a witch?" Hannah asked.

"I've never thought ill of you, Ma'am."

"Precious few can say that."

"I'm sorry for the ugly accusations hurled at you, Miss McCue. And I'll smash the face of the next man who does so."

"That's the spirit!" Joseph clapped him on the back. "Stay a moment afore starting out." He pushed Will down onto a stool. Striding across the room, he tapped one of the kegs in the corner and filled a pewter tankard. "This'll take the chill off."

"Kira's already done that."

Joseph chuckled and passed Will the tankard. "Aye. She's a rare sight."

"That she is." Will knocked back a swallow, thumped his chest. "Good stuff."

Kira stood beside him. "I'm still me, Will."

He gave her an arched look and took another draught.

Shifting her feet, she asked, "What will Logan say?"

"Nothing. He took his horse and left early this morning. I don't know where he went. Typical of my cousin."

Her world suddenly went hollow.

"Don't fret, Kira. He'll be back."

"Maybe not after what I said."

Will reached out battered knuckles and covered her hand. "It couldn't have been all that bad and Logan's not easily scared off. Either way, whether he's here or gone, you would choose him over me. Always have done."

Kira met the yearning in his eyes. "How long have you felt this way?"

"Long enough. But there's only one man you'll have and he's not me." Will finished his drink and plunked the tankard down on the table. "Best be on our way."

"I should change first. I'll muddy these fine skirts."

"No need. I came on Donavan. You can ride with me."

"But I thought Donavan was stolen?"

"He came back this morning. Must have gotten free."

"That's a mercy." The gray gelding was a favorite.

Extending his hand to Joseph, Will said, "Many thanks for seeing to our Kira."

Joseph closed thick fingers around the young man's fight-roughened fingers. "I've done so since she were a mite."

With a nod at Hannah, Will added, "You too, Ma'am. Thank you."

"Would you thank me for loving one like my own daughter?"

Kira embraced Hannah as though it might be her last opportunity. "I wish I could stay."

"And I. You've brightened my dark days like sunshine."

"Joseph—" Wiping at her eyes, she turned and stood on tiptoe to fling her arms around his neck. She pressed her face against his shirt. "I wish Mama had wed you."

He hugged her tightly. "But then you wouldn't be you."

"Mama never said, but I believe she cared for you."

"Aye. But her heart was lost in your father. Can't any of us rule our hearts," he said huskily, and put Kira from him. "Take her on home, Will, before I say she stays."

"It wouldn't be just me you'd have to take on."

"Oh, I'd gladly rid you of Campbell, young man. Have no doubt."

Smiling wryly, Will fingered his bruised jaw. "If you can best that great ox you're one up on me."

"Did no one teach you to fight to win or run like hell?"

Will chuckled. "That sounds like someone I know."

Kira blinked at tears. "Logan."

Eyes narrowed, Will said, "I meant Papa." He picked up her discarded clothes and walked to the door. "I'll put these in the saddle bags and get mounted." He strode outside.

Hannah was thoughtful. "Will thinks a lot of you, lass."

"I didn't realize. Besides, he's to wed Jenny Lewis."

"A good girl and bonnie. Jenny will put all to rights, if his heart's not stolen entirely."

"I never meant to steal it at all."

"Aye, well, these things happen." Joseph slipped his arm through hers and ushered her through the door.

She paused to look back at the room, bathed in the soft glow of the fire. Alf peered down from the beam near the larger owl. The squirrels scampered past and the tiny fawn dozed by the hearth. Her creatures had settled in and would soon resume life out-of-doors. How contented they seemed in contrast to the raw emotions churning inside her.

"Gather those fine skirts, don't want you tripping."

They walked across the stoop and down the

steps to where Will waited on Donavan. The firm angle of his jaw reminded her of Logan's and bode no good. Joseph closed his hands around her waist and lifted her up to sit in front of Will, her legs and skirts to one side of the horse.

She reached down to Joseph for a final squeeze from his reassuring grasp. "Goodbye." Her voice was so tremulous she could scarcely speak.

His brown eyes glistened. "God speed, lass."

Kira raised her hand to the slight figure standing in the doorway. "God keep you, Hannah."

"And you, my dearest girl!"

Will prodded the big gelding into a canter.

"Never take off the cross. I've blessed it to guard you from evil!" Hannah called after her.

No doubt Kira would need all the blessing she could get.

****

"Come on, boy!" Will whooped. Digging his heels into Donavan's sides, he urged the big horse over a downed log.

Though he held Kira with one arm, she lurched forward as the gelding sailed across and thumped back against him on the landing. "'Twas risky. You should have led him around."

"Aw, he made out all right."

Will could be irritatingly stubborn at times and apparently he was just in the mood. She had no choice but to cling to him as he jumped Donavan over a fallen chestnut limb. They sped down the steep incline at a far swifter pace than any sensible person would've undertaken.

Loose stones scattered out from under the gelding's hooves as he fought for footing. Donavan slid the last few yards until the trail evened out. Then sprang into a canter at Will's nudge and the blurred ground fell away. Again, the horse hurdled across a log and pounded over the rocky path.

Beth Trissel

"Are you trying to get us killed!" she shouted.

"We're fine."

"Until we break our necks. I want off."

"Now?" he laughed. Mossy earth flew up from under Donavan's hooves.

Rather than view the misty rush of rain-slicked trees, she buried her face against his chest so tightly that his dark wool coat chaffed her cheek.

"It's all right, Kira."

"No it's not. Everything in my life is wrong and now I'm about to hurtle to my death."

"You just haven't ridden with me for a while. Do you think our fearless Logan takes these trails at a turtle's pace?"

"He's even crazier than you are, for God's sake. I thought you had some sense."

Rather than racing on, Will reined Donavan in. "You're right. I'm sorry." He tightened his arms around her.

For a time he said nothing more. She was content just to catch her breath and be still for a moment. Rain-drenched leaves dripped amid the gurgle of water and breezes blew, though not with southerly warmth. She shivered against him.

"Ah, Kira, I could get used to this."

Her reply was muffled against his coat. "I doubt your wife would be pleased."

"I don't have one yet." Again, the reluctance in his voice that he'd expressed at Hannah's.

"Do you really not want to wed Jenny?"

His chest rose and fell with a sigh. "I suppose I do, or would, if it weren't for you."

"I'm not so special."

"You can't convince me of that. We've lived under the same roof since you were twelve. I know you well, remember?"

"Then you know how strange I am."

"I don't mind."

122

"Come, now. You've ordered me about for years and not because you approve of me."

"I just don't want you doing something foolish."

"Like galloping over a stony trail?"

"Or running off with Logan."

The aching void Logan's absence had left inside her panged at his name. "He's gone. You said."

"Do you really think he would leave you to Campbell?"

"Maybe he's left me to you," she said in a small voice.

"He did that for seven long years and you're still his."

"I'm not...can't be. I told him so last night."

"You have an odd way of refusing. I saw you asleep in his arms. If you didn't want me the way you don't want him, I would be overjoyed. And you do want him, don't you?"

She sniffed disconsolately. "It makes no difference."

Will slipped the hood back from her face and smoothed the hair escaping her knot. "It makes a great deal."

"I won't let it matter, then."

"Why?"

"I can't say. I promised Logan."

"I have suspicions about him. No matter. If you're bent on refusing my cousin, will you at least give me a chance?"

"You are betrothed."

"So are you, according to Josiah Campbell."

"Ohhh, not him. What am I to do, Will?"

He bent nearer and his wind-blown curls brushed her cheek. "Marry me. I'll gain Papa's permission."

"Then Josiah will kill you instead of Logan."

"Maybe I'll get Mister Campbell first."

She looked up at Will's bruises and the half-dozen cuts Josiah's fists had left. "Have you lost all reason?"

"Quite possibly. Let me help you forget my cousin. Just one kiss," he pleaded.

"You'll pain your mouth."

Mirth shone back at her from his gray-green eyes. "I'll be brave."

In spite of everything, she smiled. "Oh, Will, I'm very fond of you."

He grimaced. "You could kill a man with kindness, Kira. It's a start, though. Could I have a bit more?"

She hesitated. "I shouldn't be kissing you."

"You don't know for sure until you've tried."

"Will—"

His seeking lips covered hers and put a halt to further argument. Not wanting to push him away, she surrendered to the moment. Sweet warmth flowed through her, soothing her troubled mind. He didn't evoke the tumultuous excitement Logan had, nor did she feel in danger of surrendering all. Still, it wasn't like kissing her brother. If she must wed someone, Will would be kind, but would that be fair to him when Logan possessed her heart? If she could determine where to love, she'd choose the young man whose lips sought hers now, but it seemed she'd made her choice long ago.

A horse nickered. Not Donavan waiting patiently.

Kira jerked in Will's grasp. If he hadn't held her, she would have fallen to the ground as Josiah spurred his black stallion alongside them. His bloated face was a mask of wrath. Suddenly, the blustery woods seemed a far more treacherous place then when they'd sped along on Donovan.

His battered lips curled in a sneer. "Like a brother, is he, Kira? How long has this been going on?"

She could hardly swallow, let alone speak.

"Not nearly as long as I would like." Will had the same cockiness as Logan.

Josiah narrowed blackened eyes at him.

"I've never been content with my lot as brother and was trying to discover where I stand in this lady's affections."

"Care to guess where you stand in mine?"

"No need, Campbell."

The stallion chewed the bit and sidled nervously. Josiah reined him in. "This foolishness is at an end, Houston."

"Ah, but you haven't inquired about my feelings for you."

"Will—don't!" Surely he had a death wish. Kira raced on breathlessly. "Josiah, if you harm him, I'll—"

"What? Never speak to me again? I can do without a woman's chatter," he scoffed through scabby lips.

"Can you do without your life? By heaven, someway, somehow, I'll kill you!"

"Kira!" Even Will seemed shocked.

Josiah glared at her. "This is how you speak to your betrothed?"

Kira could hardly believe she'd uttered anything so outrageous. Even more astonishing, that she'd meant it. Softening her threat, she reasoned, "If Will suffers at your hand, his father will never give me to you."

"He's feeling right beholden to me just now. I restored some of his stolen goods. Turn her loose, Houston, and get off that horse. I don't aim to hurt you too bad, just teach you a lesson."

"One moment." Will's tone was casual. "You'll want to see Kira's new gown first."

Josiah arched reddish brows. "I'll what?"

"Show the man, Kira," Will invited.

What he was up to, she had no idea, but shakily undid the ties at her throat and pulled the cloak apart. The hunger in Josiah's eyes made her feel disturbingly like dinner.

"Where did you come by all this finery, girl?"

"The faery queen gifted it to me."

His unbridled stare bored into her bodice. He nodded at the cross. "Papist, is she? Protestants don't wear that sort of cross, if they wear one at all."

"But doesn't it look well on her smooth skin, against that lovely bosom?" Will asked.

"Of all the bloody cheek. Will you discuss her bosom with me?" Josiah barked, shifting his fury back to Will. He tensed. "Why, you bastard."

The false frivolity had gone and in its place was steely grit. Will aimed the barrel of a pistol right at Josiah. He cocked the trigger. "One wrong move and I'll fire."

Josiah scowled in impotent rage.

"I strongly suggest you proceed on your way, Campbell."

With a slap of the reins, his restless horse sprang into action. "Be seeing you, Kira! Houston!"

"It had better not be in the next ten minutes!"

The instant Josiah was out of sight Will uncocked the pistol and shoved it under his belt. "Hold tight, girl. You're in for a wild ride."

She locked her arms around him and they raced away on Donavan. No cries of dissent escaped her. The swift gray couldn't canter through the hazy woods fast enough for her. She half-expected to see Josiah charging up behind them at any moment, but she didn't dare look back.

Relief flooded her as the Houston homestead came into sight. Her heart gave an unruly flutter. Maybe Logan had come back. But what on earth was she to do if he had?

****

Dusk fell and still no Logan. Fresh hurt raked Kira to think he might have gone permanently. Part of her was tempted to steal away to the McCutcheon homestead and seek for him. The more prudent part kept her seated before the hearth, her spirits as gray as the charred embers in the grate.

Donald and David huddled at her side and Bawtie sat at her feet as if the trio sensed her melancholy and shared it.

Donald prodded her. "When's Logan coming?"

"Maybe never," their father said moodily from his bed. "Best forget that scamp of a cousin and get to your chores."

They trailed out the door with the limp-eared dog.

Aunt Alice shut it behind them. "You needn't call Logan a scamp, Peter. I'm sure he has sound reason for going off."

"But will it be the truth? Your nephew isn't being straight with us."

"He's your nephew too. I'll not hear Logan so ill-used."

Each mention of his name was pure torture to Kira.

"You must be chilled through to sit wrapped in that cloak." Aunt Alice handed her a steaming cup of tea.

Kira nodded and sipped the spicy sassafras. After an initial scolding, her guardians had let her be, and no one had noticed the gown beneath her mantle. If she remained as she was, went early to bed, and changed in the dark, she needn't answer the inevitable questions. At least, not yet.

Aunt Alice hovered over her. "I should apply a fresh poultice to that knee."

"No need. I'll just rest here awhile."

"See you do," her guardian chided. "We can't be watching you every blessed moment. What did you run off for, anyway?"

Kira hesitated and then, "I can't abide Josiah."

"You said naught yesterday," he pointed out.

"It's different today."

"I see how the wind blows, Miss, and you can put my nephew from your mind. I know Campbell was heavy handed with you. But I've reprimanded him and he assures me this is not his way. The fellow's just rough around the edges."

"It might be best to give her some time, not press her to wed in such a hurry," Aunt Alice suggested.

"The sooner she's wed, the better. Let some other man trouble with the girl."

"But if she's truly frightened, you oughtn't—"

He waved aside her objection. "Don't tell me what to do. You've spoiled her. And her head's filled with notions."

Fierce barking erupted outside, jolting Kira's attention away from the argument. Bawtie had sighted someone he didn't know or didn't like. Then a loud rap sounded at the door.

Aunt Alice looked as if an attacker might lurk outside. "I don't feel easy with you robbed just last night, Peter."

"Thieves don't knock." He stood and limped to the door. His face broke into a grin as he opened it. "Campbell!"

Josiah stepped inside and Kira's heart dropped through the floor. Uncle Peter clapped him on the back. "Here's a man who knows how to pour whiskey. Alice thinks to stint me."

"Good to see you up, sir. I thought to find you abed."

"Enough lying about." He gestured Josiah to the hearth. "Sit you down and warm yourself, man. You'll find Kira a trifle broody, but I doubt that will trouble you."

"Not if I'm allowed to share the company of one so fair."

"Aye. That you are. You'll have a drink with me?"

"Gladly." Josiah hung his rust-colored coat from a peg and pulled over a chair next to Kira.

She retreated into herself as far as possible.

Uncle Peter fetched the bottle he'd hidden behind a low rafter and sat on the chair Josiah left vacant. He uncorked the spirits and offered him a swig. "My particular brew."

Josiah tilted back the bottle and took a pull. "The best I've drunk." He fixed smoldering eyes on Kira.

She shrank from the molten meld of anger and passion.

A faint smile turned up the corners of his pummeled mouth. "I've not only come to feast my eyes on this beauty, Mister Houston, but to restore yet more of your property."

"That so? What have you brought now?"

"Your roan mare. I found her wandering the woods."

Uncle Peter slapped his knee. "Welcome tidings, indeed. I think a lot of that horse. This calls for a celebration."

Passing uncertain eyes between them, Aunt Alice offered, "We're beholden to you Mister Campbell."

"My pleasure, Ma'am."

Uncle Peter further lowered the contents of the bottle and handed it back to Josiah. "You'll stay to dinner?"

"If I wouldn't be putting you to any trouble?"

"We should be happy to have you," Aunt Alice murmured, and darted an anxious glance at the door. Likely she feared Will discovering their *guest*.

Oblivious of his wife's discomfort, Uncle Peter

129

clapped Josiah's broad shoulder. "You've done us a good turn. Matters were bleak before you turned up." He nudged Kira. "Give the fellow a kiss, gal. Show him some gratitude."

Her stomach flopped like a fish out of water.

"Peter," Aunt Alice cautioned.

Josiah shrugged. "The girl's modest. I mustn't press her." He sipped from the bottle, handing it back to his host.

Uncle Peter took a pull. "She just needs encouraging."

"Perhaps a bit then." Cupping meaty fingers to Kira's face, he tilted her toward him and pressed a modest kiss to her cheek. With his mouth at her ear, he spoke words only she could hear. "Kiss me properly, or I'll tell your guardian his son threatened me with a pistol and his nephew's a renegade."

A hot tide of resentment welled in her as she pressed her lips to his—a revolting concession he took full advantage of.

"Told you she just needed prodding," Uncle Peter said.

She broke from Josiah's greedy mouth as discreetly as she could without arousing further attention.

He returned his chaffed lips to her cheek and drifted to her neck, his breath hot on her skin. "You smell all flowery."

Every piece of her clothing emanated the lavender scent.

His mouth hovered at her ear. "I'll have another kiss."

"Not on your life, Josie," she hissed.

He curled a tendril of her hair around his thumb. "You shall be mine, Kira. Final chance for surrender."

She ground out a reply. "No."

"Then it's war. One I'll win."

Intent on retreat, she stood at once. "I grow fatigued, Mister Campbell. Please excuse me."

A great paw imprisoned her hand. "Not yet."

Aunt Alice glanced round in consternation. "At least have your dinner first, lass."

Uncle Peter nodded. "The night's young."

Josiah pulled her back down. "Perhaps you're over warm. Why so bundled?" he asked in mock innocence.

"Been tucked up like that since she's come." Uncle Peter eyed her. "Think she was hiding something."

Aunt Alice cut wedges of meat pie from the iron skillet on the table. "Have you another of your creatures in there?"

Kira clutched her cloak with her free hand. "No, Ma'am."

"Not taking a chill, are you, lass?"

"I'm fine. Truly."

Smiling wickedly, his horsey teeth gleaming in the firelight, Josiah said, "Then you won't be needing this." He tugged the ties at her neck and whipped her cloak away.

The knife clattered to the skillet. "What in the world?"

Josiah frowned at Kira. "What indeed? For, surely, I was not the man who bestowed such finery on you."

Uncle Peter tightened his grip on the brown bottle. "Nor was it me. Have you a lover, girl?"

Kira warded him off with fingers gone ice-cold. "No!"

Triumph shone in Josiah's blue eyes. "Who else would give you such costly gifts?"

Uncle Peter set the bottle down and got to his feet. Clamping his hands on her shoulders, he jerked her up from the chair. "I'll have the scoundrel's name!"

She cried out in shock, "There's no one!"

"Don't lie to me, girl. Who gave you this gown?"

Josiah was on his feet. "And the cross at your throat? Is it a Catholic lover you've taken?"

"By heaven. 'Tis a Papist cross." Uncle Peter gave her a shake. "Vixen."

Aunt Alice rushed over and grasped his arm. "Let her go. She's no trollop. Didn't I nearly have the raising of her?"

"How do you account for this—"

"Hannah McCue gave it to her, Papa."

Every head turned as Will strode into the room.

"How did that old woman come by such costly garments?" his father asked. He gripped the cross. "And this?"

So shaken she could scarcely speak, Kira choked out, "Gifts from her betrothed, long dead."

Stunned silence followed her admission.

Will was somber. "The poor woman looks on the point of death. She's only passing onto Kira what's most dear to her."

His mother nodded. "I always thought there was more to Hannah then we knew."

Red and purple mottled Josiah's face. "She's a witch."

"She's a gentle lady." Acting on his promise, Will shot out his fist and punched Josiah's already bruised jaw.

He reeled back. "She's bewitched you both!"

"Never!" Hands clenched, Kira flew at Josiah and pounded his hard chest. "A good Christian is Hannah!"

Uncle Peter tore her away. "Calm, lass. Leave him be."

Sobs racked her. "I have no lover."

"Hush. I know that now," he said gruffly.

He released her to Aunt Alice who wrapped her in an embrace. "Now look what the pair of you have done. We'll have a time calming her without Logan."

"We don't need his help, Alice," Uncle Peter argued.

"But Logan's good with her. Like last night—"

"What the devil was he doing with Kira in the night?" Josiah demanded.

Aunt Alice hastened to explain. "Only comforting her."

"I'd be happy to *comfort* her myself, but I seem to be the last one at her."

"You can go to perdition, Josiah!" Kira fired back.

Aunt Alice gasped. "She didn't mean it, Mister Campbell. She's terribly upset."

"Or under some foul enchantment."

"Nothing of the sort, I swear it. Please say nothing to the neighbors," the shaken woman pleaded.

"Of course. I have no wish to endanger my betrothed."

"You'll still have her, then?" Uncle Peter asked.

"Oh, I'll have her," he grunted.

"And I say you won't touch another hair on her head!"

In all the confusion, no one had noticed Logan open the door and step inside.

Kira's heart doubled its beat and she stared at him in the sudden hush.

How handsome he looked, though grimy from his journey, and had he been digging? Mud streaked his face and spattered the brown wool coat he wore.

He ran widening eyes over her and swept his hand at her attire. "Where did you come by that gown, and the cross?"

"*Papist* cross," Josiah sneered.

"So it is," Logan said wonderingly, and then his face hardened. "I knew you were one for secrets, Kira, but this is beyond all bounds. What man gave you these gifts?"

Fresh betrayal stung her. "Not you too, Logan!" Twisting free from Aunt Alice, she fled in a swish of taffeta and ran to the back room.

Chapter Nine

Barefoot, wearing his shirt and breechclout, Logan slowly pushed open the door to the darkened chamber where Will and the twins normally slept. Kira had taken their place and the three brothers were bedded down up in the loft. After a brief scuffle, they'd sorted themselves out and fallen asleep. The whole household slumbered soundly, even Bawtie, as Logan tip-toed into the backroom.

Neither light nor warmth from the hearth penetrated the chilly gloom in here as he felt his way past the washstand to the bed where Kira lay. She'd refused even to see him earlier this evening and shut herself up in here. He wasn't taking no for an answer now.

Easing himself down onto the edge of her bed, he whispered her name. She stirred at his low summons then turned onto her side as if she thought him only a dream.

He gently clasped her shoulders and repeated, "Kira."

She jerked and rolled back over. He sensed her staring up at him in the blackness.

"What do you want?" Her voice was raw with hurt.

"I'm sorry I wrongfully accused you. Will explained about the gown, everything."

"He shouldn't have to. You should trust me, Logan."

It crossed his mind to ask why in God's name he should do that, given her unpredictability. Instead he replied, "It's difficult at times."

"For me too. Where have you been all day?"

"Where you thought I was."

"How did you know what I thought?"

"Will told me everything."

A faint, "Oh," escaped her.

Logan sensed her mood altering like a doe springing from one path to another.

"That kiss didn't mean anything," she blurted.

For a sharp moment, he had trouble getting his breath. "What kiss?"

She stiffened beneath his hands and whispered fiercely, "You said Will told you all."

"Apparently he left something out."

"Ooohhh—and now I've put my foot in it."

"Tell me what happened."

"Will brought me home from Hannah's on Donavan. He took me by surprise when he proposed marriage."

"That conniving snake. The moment I'm out of sight—"

"I didn't accept him. Please don't be angry."

Logan fought the strong inclination to bolt up to the loft and pound his back-stabbing cousin into the floorboards. "Isn't that toad betrothed to Jenny Lewis?"

"Yes. The wedding is day after tomorrow."

"What an odd bird. Why didn't he propose to you first?"

"Will said he didn't stand a chance of success as long as you were away."

"So he waits until I've returned?"

"And frightened me to death."

"Oh, for the—"

Instead of attacking his cousin, Logan gathered Kira in his arms as though it had been days, not hours, since he'd last held her. Aunt Alice had helped her change out of that voluminous gown into a shift. Her tantalizing curves pressed against his chest and a sweet scent hung about her. She took his breath away, though for a far different reason now, and despite her professed fear, clung to him in return.

Stroking her glorious hair, he whispered, "Dear Lord, how unbelievably wonderful you feel. I can scarcely recall what we were arguing about."

She didn't remind him. She didn't need to.

"What am I to do with you, Cricket?"

Face pressed against his shoulder, she replied with a muffled, "Help me."

"Anything, sweetheart. If only you would allow me, rather than seeing me as your enemy."

"I have a far worse one now."

"Thought you might."

She struggled for control over the tears he felt dampening his shirt. "Nothing I do puts Josiah off. Nothing. I even threatened to kill him."

"I heard. Just how do you think to carry this out?"

"Poison his food, shove him off a cliff, slit his throat while he's sleeping—anything."

"I don't believe I'm hearing this from you."

"You've never heard me this desperate before."

"Kira, you wouldn't cut his throat or hurl him to his death, even if you were able to succeed over that brute. Besides, you'd surely hang for it. Leave Campbell to me."

"And let you hang in my stead?"

"Who said I intend to dangle by the neck?"

"Josiah's wicked clever. He tricked me cruelly this evening."

"Poor Cricket. What a way to learn the truth. You're in deep with this man. Dangerously so, Will says. Don't openly oppose him."

"You don't understand. He's so awful."

"Oh yes I do."

"He hasn't made you kiss him or nibbled your

neck."

A battle cry resounded inside Logan. Will hadn't mentioned this. Perhaps he hadn't known. "Damn that blasted Campbell to Hell."

"I already have."

"I can well imagine. But don't—anymore. Let me."

"And have you die?" Her voice was a watery quaver.

"For heaven's sake, Kira, I've been with you less than a quarter of an hour and you've already buried me twice."

"Josiah is treacherous."

"I'm no fool myself. Stay away from him tomorrow. Hide. A talent you claim to possess. Only conceal yourself from him better than you did from me."

"You won't be here?" she sniffed, her tone bleak.

"I have a hunch to follow up regarding Campbell. I'll not say more about it until I know for sure."

"What of your treasure? You've not said a word about it."

"I haven't had the chance. Mercy, girl, I didn't think anyone could get into this much trouble in a single day."

"I feared you had gone for good."

Smiling in bemusement, he blotted her face with his shirtsleeve. "Like you told me to do? Not without you."

"I may have to go with you to keep us both from Josiah."

Her voice had the death knell of one choosing between execution and the unspeakable horrors of wedding that lout.

"At least the savages won't kill you," she continued.

"I do wish you would stop calling my friends

savages. Especially as one of them is your brother, and another, my sister. Besides, we can't meet with them yet. I haven't finished my search. There's too much fallen timber from the fire to do all the digging in one visit."

"Was your day wasted then?"

"I wouldn't say that." He reached into the pouch at his waist and felt for the small flat object. *There.* Taking her hand, he placed it in her palm then guided the fingers of her other hand over the round surface and the etchings marked on the metal. "What do you think of this?"

"A coin?"

"A gold sovereign, Miss. Worth a bit in itself."

She gulped, seemingly too awed at first to even speak. "Are there more?"

"Quite a few according to Shoka."

"How does he know?"

"Shoka put those coins there himself seven years ago as a ransom for Rebecca, to save her from a vengeful Catawba warrior called Tonkawa."

Kira shuddered. "I don't like that name."

An eerie sensation ran over Logan, like the chilled breath of a ghost. "Nor I."

"Is that warrior still alive?"

Logan clasped her tightly as if to shield her from all evil. "No. Tonkawa demanded Rebecca or her life. Shoka tried to buy her back with the same gold she'd given him, but in the end he had to fight Tonkawa for her."

Kira breathed out shakily. "Where did she get the coins?"

"From her late husband, a British Captain named Elliot. Remember, Rebecca was a lady."

"A very strange one."

"And very beautiful."

"More than me?"

"I've told you enough for now," he teased.

"Logan—"

For a tender moment, he found her mouth. What a world of pleasure there was in those sweet lips, tremulous as they were. All too soon, he heard a shuffling in the next room, followed by an oath and a watery hiss.

"My uncle is using the chamber pot. I must go before he discovers us. Remember what I said."

****

One striking difference between yesterday's dismal beginning and today's was Kira's renewed sense of hope. Logan had come back and would return again. Meanwhile, her task was clear; keep away from Josiah. She could walk, and if her knee held up, maybe even run. And by heaven, she could hide. But what was she to wear? Aunt Alice had tidied away her clothes.

Trailing from the bedchamber in her shift and shoes, uncertain of what awaited her in the larger room, she discovered Aunt Alice by the table up to her elbows in dough.

The mature woman brushed back fiery stray curls with her floury sleeve. "I thought I'd make chicken pie from this store of flour Mister Campbell brought."

"Am I payment for his generosity?"

Her hazel eyes dimmed. "Don't speak so." She nodded at the plate of cornbread and the brown pitcher. "Sit and eat."

Kira settled on the low bench by the table and bit into the warm bread. She glanced around the room as she downed the food and poured a tankard of creamy milk.

"The men are all out," Aunt Alice said. "And don't you take any notion of straying. Peter will have a right fit."

"But if Josiah comes, he'll find me easily enough."

The wooden rolling pin moved back and forth vigorously beneath Aunt Alice's deft hands. "That can't be helped, lass. He would find you soon enough anyway."

"Not if I hide, with your help."

Her jaw dropped. "Are you asking me to conceal you from the very man your guardian wishes you to wed?"

"Don't let Uncle Peter make me marry where I loathe to."

Sympathetic lines pulled at her flushed face. "If it were my say, you'd wed Logan before the week's out."

"I can't marry him if I'm wife to another. 'Twill break his heart."

"Indeed," his aunt said heavily.

"And mine," Kira added.

Her keen gaze explored Kira. "All that nonsense about Logan carrying you off to savages, you're past that now?"

"Aye. Help me, Aunt Alice. For his sake and mine."

"But to go against my own husband? I can't disobey him."

"You needn't. Just don't imprison me in this house."

Eyes darting over the room as though leery of being overheard, she was quiet for a moment, and then in hushed tones said, "I might look the other way. Where will you go?"

"Not far. I promise. Just away from Josiah's notice."

"Mister Campbell will be vexed to find you gone when he calls. And Peter will be furious. Lord help us both."

"Uncle Peter won't stay angry with you for long. He loves you too well. And I can bear his wrath if I must."

The flustered woman reached floury hands to her apron. "Love or no, we shall both bear his anger, and no mistake."

"Even so, will you help me?"

She gave a nod. "'Tis harebrained to think we can hide you for long."

"D. and D. will lend their aid. They loathe Josiah."

"Heaven preserve us. These are indeed desperate times to be looking to the likes of those rapscallions. Logan had best hasten back from wherever he's gone and see to you himself."

"He's—" Kira began to confide and thought better of it.

His aunt seemed not to hear her. "You can't go about in that shift. I'll fetch your clothes." She flew to the ladder and placed her shoe on the first rung. "You and Logan may have to go off together for a while. Mister Campbell's sure to be breathing fire, might try to make a widow of you."

"I fear the same. If Logan does take me away, you mustn't worry about me."

Aunt Alice looked over her shoulder, eyes misty. "I know Logan will care for you, but I would see you properly wed."

"Uncle Peter won't allow it."

"He may have no choice."

"What do you mean?"

Gathering her skirts, she climbed. "Never you mind, lass. There are ways."

Kira watched her ascent in confusion. "How am I to sway Uncle Peter if I don't know them?"

"Logan does. Just you stay clear of Mister Campbell 'til the deed's done."

Aunt Alice disappeared into the shadows and rummaged in Kira's trunk. She reappeared with her plainest short-gown and petticoat over one arm and scurried back down the ladder.

With an eye to the door, Kira hurriedly stepped into the drab petticoat and tied it. Her ear cocked for approaching footfall, she slid her arms into the short-gown. The color of mud, it hung just below her waist and fit her like a shapeless sack, but would blend into the trees. She waited in agonizing apprehension as Aunt Alice pinned the front together.

"This won't set Josiah's blood to boiling if he sees you. I ought to braid your hair back, less alluring that way."

"Less what?"

"Never mind." Aunt Alice rushed to the door and cracked it. She peered out, and beckoned to her. "No one's about. Peter and Will must still be looking at the hay. Make haste. I expect you back by dark."

"Shall we say I'm ailing and retired early to bed?"

"Oh, you'll be feeling poorly all right after Peter gives you the rough edge of his tongue."

Kira hugged her. "Thank you. For everything."

Aunt Alice closed floury arms around her in return. "No need for that. Besides, this isn't farewell between us."

"I'm sorry I've been such a handful."

"You're a good lass. Just a bit odd. Go now," she said with a catch in her voice,"and mind you watch for the wolf."

In her anxiousness to get away, Kira fled out the door and was halfway to the woods before pausing to wonder, *what wolf?* Uncle Peter and the other men in the settlement had hunted the beasts so vigorously that few remained to trouble the livestock. She must have missed talk of this one.

No matter. Unlike yesterday's foul weather, today was exquisite. Tree-covered ridges jutted up on either side of the narrow valley, glorious swells thrusting into the blue sky. Balmy warmth streamed down and mild breezes fluttered her skirts while meadowlarks trilled from the meadow.

Buoyed by anticipation, Kira walked beneath the sun-dappled canopy. Pink trillium colored the drifts of hay-scented fern. Green May apples spread over the forest floor, tiny parasols for the wee folk. Lavender redbud trees brightened the woodland tapestry, and white dogwood blossoms shone like the blessing of the Lord. This spring day was a foretaste of heaven, but she remained alert to every sound.

With the watchfulness of a doe, she knelt by the stream and cupped the icy water to her mouth, then tucked down at the base of a broad sourwood tree. She scooted back into the hollow in its trunk. Unless someone peered around the front, she shouldn't be detected here. Bees hummed in the blossoms overhead while she settled in to wait.

And wait.

Time passed slowly and she grew drowsy.

"Kira! I know you're there!"

She jerked at Uncle Peter's bellow. He had sharp eyes, indeed, or the twins had given away her hiding place. Not waiting to learn which, she scrambled to her feet.

"Don't run from me!"

She had no intention of doing anything else. Hitching up her skirts, she scattered like a frightened hare—not knowing which way to go, then darting down a path.

"Come back here or I swear I'll give you a hiding!"

The assurance that he'd reached the end of his tether didn't lessen her speed. A twinge shot through her knee and she half-ran, half-limped between the trees. She heard him sprint behind her. His leg must have healed faster than hers.

A log blocked her way. She hurdled over the lichen-encrusted bark, staggering at the sharp pang, and tried to go on, but crumbled to the leafy ground. Spying a deep groove in the log where bears had clawed for insects, she rolled partway beneath the wood. Perhaps he wouldn't spot her here.

"Kira Anne McClure!" Straddling the log, he glared down at her. "What do you mean running off like that?"

She gazed up tearfully at his taut face and slitted eyes. Dropping her gaze, she curled into a ball.

"What in blazes am I to do with you?"

Peeking out from between her fingers, she eyed him as she would a wild animal that might suddenly attack. "I don't know. But I'll not wed Mister Campbell."

"Damn and blast. First Alice defies me. Now you, a mere lass with no family, whom I've kindly taken in."

She started to remind him that she had family, her brother, Tom, but decided against it. Looking to her elusive sibling for help was useless.

"You shall wed the man I choose," her guardian scowled.

She lowered her hands. "Why must you choose Josiah?"

"Haven't I told you until I'm nearly blue in the face? Campbell will provide well for you."

"Is it me you're thinking of, or yourself?"

"Is it evil for us both to profit from this marriage? Your father entrusted you to me, and I've done right by you."

"But Papa would want my happiness. And Mama."

"They would all trust my say." He bent down and pulled her out from under the log and up onto her feet. "'Tis a wonder Mister Campbell isn't looking elsewhere for a wife."

She stood unsteadily. "Let him. He's welcome."

"You are coming with me before he does." Grasping her arm, Uncle Peter walked her back the way she'd come.

"Wait—if it's provision you're after, Logan has gold."

An abrupt halt, and he demanded, "Where in heaven's name would my nephew come by gold?"

"Sovereigns are hidden on the McCutcheon homestead. Logan's digging for them."

Uncle Peter absorbed this as he would the ravings of a madwoman. "Sure he has, and I've rubies in the barn."

"It's the truth. Logan showed me a coin in the night."

"While you were sleeping and *dreaming*?"

Caught off guard, she wondered if she might have imagined it. Her memory of his visit in the night was very dreamlike.

Her guardian dragged her over the ferny path. "'Tis these notions that have folks wondering if you've gone off your head. Now with this witch talk, matters only worsen. Still, Campbell can keep you from their wrath, if it comes."

"Can't you?"

"Not as well as he. And I'm fair worn out with chasing you down. Thank the Lord you're a bonnie lass, or I'd have your keeping the rest of my days."

All too soon, the trees gave way and the homestead came into view. A horse whinnied. Her stomach dropped like a stone at the sight of the black stallion tethered outside the stable. "Josiah's here?"

"Aye. Reverend Wilkins has come for Will's wedding. I thought we had best see to yours as well while he's about it."

If the very earth were closing around her, Kira couldn't have felt more trapped.

"Campbell's that eager. Give him a chance, lass.

He'll treat you right."

She wanted to run madly, giving voice to a thousand shrieks of "No!" But only a breathless cry escaped her.

"Don't you start taking on again. I won't have it, mind you."

Her panic heightened as Josiah bounded down the back stoop and strode past the outbuildings. He tracked through the grass leaving a flattened swathe behind. He was nearly upon her. She was caught between these two unyielding men.

A strange numbness came over her, like one facing execution after all struggles to escape the hangman had failed. She'd wed Josiah Campbell, and then, just as surely as she drew breath she'd find some means of stopping his.

"Mad wolf!"

Donald's frantic alarm burst on her ears from overhead.

Uncle Peter halted, Kira still in his grasp. Josiah stopped in mid-stride and both men scanned the meadow and woods. Uncle Peter didn't have his musket with him, but Josiah leveled his. Swiveling his head all the while for sign of the creature, he walked up to them.

"See anything?"

"No. Don't hear nothing either," Uncle Peter grunted.

The men stole in the direction of the shout, Kira at her guardian's side. Uncle Peter pointed up at Donald perched up on a sturdy limb. "Are you having us on, lad?"

With a shake of his coppery curls, he gestured ahead. "It ran up that trail!"

Josiah waved them back. "Take Kira to the house, Mister Houston. I'll get the beggar."

Uncle Peter loosed his hold on her and drew his hunting knife. "I'll back you up, Campbell. Go on to

Beth Trissel

Alice, girl. A mad wolf's bite will kill you slowly and horribly if the crazed beast doesn't rip you to pieces first."

A second terrified shriek rent the air. *David!*

Was the terrified child clinging to a branch while the animal lunged at his heels—or worse? She sped after the men.

"Kira! No!" Donald scrambled down from the tree.

She couldn't abandon David and hastened on, limping for all she was worth.

Donald shot in front of her. "There, Mister Campbell. Beside that hemlock! Hurry!" he urged, then fell back.

Despite the protests from her knee, Kira loped ahead of him and collided with his father.

"Stay back, girl. Give the man room to fire."

She didn't immediately see Josiah. He was rounding a bend in the trail, a *familiar bend*. And to one side of the sweeping hemlock tree was the hole she'd widened and—

"What the—" he yelled, then a thud. "Bloody hell!" carried up to her as if from a distance.

The boughs covering one of her secret places had broken through. She readily guessed who'd tumbled into the hole. Not a crazed wolf, though that might have been preferable.

"David! Donald!" their father bawled. "When I get hold of the pair of you I'm gonna whip your backsides!"

But Donald had vanished and David hadn't even been seen.

Uncle Peter pelted toward the hole. "Hang on, Campbell—" He broke off at the noxious scent exploding from the depths and dodged the furry form shooting from confinement.

Unable to scatter as nimbly, Kira glimpsed the black and white creature in passing. Large male

148

skunks had the most powerful spray of all and that one was huge. She staggered back, coughing and gagging from the overwhelming stench.

Similar retching noises emanated from the hole. Josiah must have borne the full impact of the potent eruption. At least there was some consolation in that.

"Damn!" His bruised face contorted, he heaved himself up over the side of the pit.

Kira only hoped he'd sustained enough injuries to further slow him. Covering her mouth, she stumbled back to the house where she collapsed on the stoop. Her all-consuming desire at that moment was to be rid of the overpowering stink.

Footfalls sounded in the yard and the noxious vapor heightened. She fought to retain what little remained in her stomach and glanced around through watery eyes. The men were only yards away from the house, her guardian a discreet distance from his repugnant companion. Josiah didn't look as stricken as she'd hoped, the hardened fox.

He freed the stallion's reins from the rail and swung up into the saddle. "I reckon you had nothing to do with this bloody prank, Kira, or you would have stayed clear."

Her only response was a low moan.

Uncle Peter stood beside her. "'Twas the lads, Campbell. Too high spirited by half."

"They won't be when I'm done with them."

"You'll never catch them," Kira managed to get out.

Josiah jerked his nervous stallion around in a circle. "See if I don't."

"I'll thank you to let me tend to my own boys," their father said tersely.

"As you like. Get cleaned up, gal. I'll return with Reverend Wilkins."

Uncle Peter bent over her. "Best leave the vows

'til the morrow. Give her a chance to recover."

"And run off again?"

"The lass is at my feet and in no shape to run."

"Just as well."

"I'll fetch the Reverend. Will And Jenny won't need his services until tomorrow evening. Come by in the morning."

"See the girl's ready this time," Josiah bit out.

Her guardian gave him a cold look. "I'm a free man, sir. I'll not live by any man's say."

Josiah reined in his impatient mount and himself. "Forgive me, Mister Houston. I'm somewhat out of sorts."

"A body would think you hadn't ever been near a skunk."

"It's those confounded boys. They tricked me."

Uncle Peter chuckled. "They surely did."

****

If Kira hadn't been under assault by Aunt Alice who knelt beside the wooden washtub before the hearth scrubbing at her until her skin was rosy, she might've appreciated the comic element in the affair of the skunk. Logan surely would. But the indomitable woman was bent on eradicating every vestige of the stench and Kira in no position to ponder anything in amusement. Wielding soap strong enough to take the hide off a cow, Aunt Alice attacked her streaming hair.

Kira sputtered, "Why don't you just cut it all off to my ears?"

"No ward of mine is going about like a sheared sheep."

"I won't be your ward this time tomorrow. I'll be Josiah Campbell's wife." What a horrible sound those words carried.

Pausing in her ministrations long enough to sigh, Aunt Alice said, "I thought Logan would have come by now."

150

"To steal me out from under Uncle Peter's very nose, not to mention Josiah's?"

"He might do." Aunt Alice was ever loyal.

"And if he doesn't?"

She briskly lathered Kira's hair. "I don't know."

"I'll deal with Josiah on my own, if I must."

"Have care, lass. You'll land yourself in more trouble."

"How can I be in any more than I already am?"

"Don't go tempting the devil to give you a lesson."

Squinting against the suds, Kira entreated, "I'll have no scalp left!"

"Very well." Petticoats damp, cheeks heated, the diligent woman stood and dipped the ladle into the kettle at the side of the tub. She poured the warm liquid over Kira's head repeatedly, but the pungent odor lingered.

"Shall I try my rose balm?" Kira asked hopefully.

"I'll pour vinegar in first, douse you with that."

The tang of apple cider vinegar mixed with polecat as Kira rocked in the tub under the renewed assault. "Enough!"

Aunt Alice wiped soapy fingers on her apron. "You need a good soaking. I can't air you out in the sun like linen."

"No. You'll just pickle me instead."

"Better that than you stinking at Will's wedding."

"Do you really think Josiah will take me to the Lewises once I'm Mrs. Campbell?"

"He had better. You're not having much of a do as is." Eyes glistening, Aunt Alice took her cloak from its peg. "Don't even think of bolting while I'm gone. I shall accompany Peter to fetch the Reverend in a bit. Will is supping with the Lewis clan, and the boys are hiding. Some of the chicken pie's missing and they took blankets. They'll not return until nightfall I don't doubt, the imps."

Kira had to admire the twins' calculated preparations. If she'd planned half as well herself, she wouldn't be soaking in brine awaiting her execution.

Chapter Ten

With the stealth of a panther in his moccasins, Logan crept into the house and over to the hearth. There lay Kira in the tub basking in the mellow glow up to her ears in brine, just as his aunt had disclosed without his uncle overhearing. Kira's eyes were closed and she seemed to be dozing. What a vision, all bare and curvy and so deeply arousing he could scarcely endure it. A man could search far and not find better than this beauty.

He had to smile at her predicament, though, one only she could manage. Kneeling by the tub, he spoke quietly. "Someone has annoyed a skunk."

"Ummm hmmm," Kira drowsily agreed.

"Caught in the crossfire, were you, Cricket?"

Suddenly alert, she sloshed in the water. Her eyes flew open and her eyebrows shot up. "Logan?"

"Expecting someone else?"

"No one—yet!" Crossing her arms over nicely rounded breasts, she sank lower in the tub. "I haven't a stitch on."

He reveled in her embarrassment. "I don't mind in the least."

Cheeks already heated grew pinker. "You shouldn't be looking."

"'Tis quite a fetching sight."

"Not all that fetching. Your aunt has pickled me."

"Not quite all, though you are redolent of vinegar and polecat."

"Can you stand me?"

"Just." More than anything, he wanted to strip

off his clothes and climb in there with her.

"Am I as bad as that?"

He picked up the square piece of towel big enough to cover part of her, but only part. "Let's see if you are."

"Oh, no. Give me that."

Holding the cloth out of reach, he invited, "Take it."

"I can't without shifting my arms, as you well know."

He chuckled. "But you can stand."

"That's even worse. Besides, my knee's gone again."

"Need help, do you?" He wrapped the towel around her shoulders and scooped her, squealing, from the tub. Her saturated hair streamed down around them both.

"Logan!"

Cradled squirming against him, her legs exposed and as much of her thighs as not, what a warm, wonderful, wriggling prize. Only his damp shirt lay between her bare chest and his. He savored her soft femininity. There was nothing in the world to compare this pleasure to.

He bent his head and asked, "Have you any notion what joy it is to hold you like this?"

The squirming lessened a little. "You shouldn't be."

"But I am."

In spite of her acute self-consciousness, she nestled closer. "Did you truly come to me in the night?"

"None other."

"I feared I might have dreamt you."

"Are you dreaming now?"

She lifted her arms around his neck. "Not unless this is a very real and lovely dream."

Triumph. The battle was half won. And then,

her lips trembled and she blinked at the moisture glistening in her eyes. "Are you going to weep every time you see me, Kira?"

"Will I see you again?"

"Sweetheart, I adore you. Why do you ask?"

"Because you are forever leaving me."

"And returning. I will always return to you."

"If you leave one more time, you will return to find me wed to Josiah Campbell."

Logan was torn between wanting to clutch her to him forever and letting go long enough to attack Josiah. "You shall never be wife to that brute."

"I might already be if not for the twins and that skunk."

"I swear I would have stolen you back before nightfall. But I'm right grateful to those mischievous lads."

She blinked moist lashes. "That wretched man is coming again in the morning to wed me unless you do something."

"I am."

"This is very soothing, but..."

"You were hoping for more?"

She gave a nod.

"I would gladly oblige, if you will cease weeping for an instant. It's difficult to kiss you when you keep breaking into sobs."

Her liquid gaze fixed on him in wonder. "We must get away at once if we're to escape. Don't you understand?"

"Perfectly." He freed the towel to blot her face and let it fall to the floor. "Even pickled, you look like an angel."

She froze as if uncertain what to cover first. "I'm utterly bare."

"And utterly entrancing."

"How can I flee in this state?"

"No need to run, just yet. Trust me," he said,

caressing her dewy cheek with his fingertips.

"But—"

"Shh," he hushed her, suspending further protest by lowering his mouth to hers and tenderly covering her lips.

He sensed her panic, as though she wanted to spring from his arms and flee if he lacked the sense. Firming his kiss, he held her tightly until flight seemed momentarily forgotten. How desirable were the lips beneath his...only a man carved from stone could resist her. Apart from one member of Logan's anatomy, he didn't meet that description, and that member throbbed. Fire seared through him body and soul as Kira answered his persuasion, slowly at first, and then more forcefully, as if this kiss were their last.

"I'll die if Josiah forces me from you," she said against his mouth.

"Do you truly think I would allow this?"

"But Uncle Peter—"

Logan drew back slightly. "I learned something of Mister Campbell today that won't please my uncle in the least."

Kira's eyes glowed, and she snatched at his piece of news. "Tell me."

"In a moment." Catching her back to him, he reclaimed her lips. The wondrous touch of her mouth, her bare arms around his neck, breasts rising and falling, sent a current charging through him from head to toe. Surely, he'd erupt into flames and take her with him.

"Logan," she said breathlessly. "Are you seducing me?"

He paused, equally winded. "I don't know what I'm doing, only that I want to do a great deal more."

"Then take me somewhere we can be alone."

Never, ever, had he expected those words to escape her lips. "Did you ask what I think you did?"

****

Footfalls intruded into Kira's bold request and she froze against Logan. Visions of her guardian's wrath nearly stopped her breath, though not her racing heart. "Quick—put me down."

"No, sweetheart."

She stared at him.

Still standing with her in his grasp, he said, "You'll understand in a little."

That she'd fallen in love with a madman was the only possible explanation. Choking back near hysteria, she hid her face against his shoulder and prayed her unbound hair covered what his arms left exposed.

The door opened. *There! Uncle Peter's heavy tread.*

"What in the name of—" he broke off, apparently, at a loss for words.

Not for long, though. Not this man. She cringed as she awaited the full force of his fury.

Stomping over to them, he hissed, "Reverend Wilkins is scarcely two paces behind me. You beat all, Logan. Bloody all."

Aunt Alice uttered a low cry. "Oh, my."

"May I come in, Mrs. Houston?" a man asked pleasantly.

"Certainly—Reverend. Ummm, you remember our ward—Kira McClure? And I don't believe you've met my nephew, Logan McCutcheon. My sister Mary's son. You remember Henry and Mary McCutcheon?"

Was the woman actually making introductions?

"Ah. Yes. Seems we've chanced upon them at rather an awkward moment," the good man said with remarkable calm.

"Rather," his flustered hostess agreed.

Too mortified to speak, Kira kept her face against Logan. Let the Reverend think her a deaf mute, anything but lewd.

Aunt Alice rushed on. "The McCutcheon's are kin to—"

"Alice!" Uncle Peter barked.

"Logan recently returned to us from captivity with the Shawnee," she finished weakly.

"I see," their guest murmured.

"Perhaps I ought to fetch a blanket," she offered.

"I believe that would be best, Mrs. Houston."

Her footsteps trailed away as he added, "Well now, Miss McClure, 'tisn't quite the meeting I'd expected with you, but I assure you this is one I shan't ever forget."

Uncle Peter didn't waste words on niceties. "I damn well won't. What in hell are you playing at, Nephew?"

"I should think that obvious."

The hot waves of anger emanating from her guardian burned into Kira's bare back. "How dare you come in here knowing my sentiments regarding my ward and make love to her?"

"I'm more concerned with her feelings, uncle. I gained her approval."

Reverend Wilkins spoke again. "It seems to me the question is why I've been summoned to wed Miss McClure to Mister Campbell, when 'tis plain she has formed quite an attachment to young McCutcheon here?"

"Because I won't have her fancying him!"

Unseen hands closed the welcome blanket around Kira and Logan stood her on her feet. Huddled between him and his aunt, she lifted unwilling eyes to Reverend Wilkins. What a contrast his fashionable gray wig and broad-brimmed black hat made with Logan's reddish-brown spill and the gray-streaked mane Uncle Peter had pulled back. Reverend Wilkin's black tailored coat, high shirt collar, gray breeches, white stockings and leather shoes were in keeping with a proper gentleman's. Logan's wet loosely belted shirt, breechclout, leggings and moccasins better suited to a white warrior, and his uncle's tan, open-necked shirt, brown breeches, and worn leather boots the garb of a frontiersman. The reverend seemed out of place, and yet he eyed everyone with goodwill.

Her focus shifted back to her irate guardian.

"You can't make the girl love where you choose, Peter," his wife reasoned.

"Balls!"

"Peter—the reverend."

"That's quite all right, Mrs. Houston. Your husband is understandably upset."

"Uncle, hear me," Logan interjected. "I'm not just being free with the lass. I want to marry her, and despite what you think, I will care for her."

"As well as Mister Campbell?"

"Far better I hope."

His uncle eyed him scornfully. "How, pray tell?"

"I'll never strike her for one, or force myself on her. You know damn well he'll do both."

"Campbell might be a bit rough, but he's not as bad as you make him out to be."

"He's a right scoundrel!"

"And you're a savage, snatching the girl from her bath!"

"I didn't snatch her. She came willingly."

Red in the face, the older man hurled back, "She shouldn't have come at all."

"You'd have done the same if you were me," Logan said.

Uncle Peter let his fist fly and cracked Logan in the jaw. The solid crunch reverberated in the room.

Logan glared back at his relation and fingered his chin. "You want to take this outside?"

Aunt Alice grasped her husband's arm. "For God's sake, stop. The pair of you."

Laying a restraining hand on his host's broad shoulder, Reverend Wilkins said, "I implore you to discuss this rationally as befits civilized Christians. What, apart from your nephew's youthful passion, do you find so objectionable? Surely if he ardently desires the girl he will see to her needs."

"Uncle Peter, please," Kira summoned shakily.

He glowered at her from beneath bushy brows. "What have you to say for yourself, lass?"

"'Tis Logan I love. If you wed me to Josiah I swear I will run away from him the first chance I get."

"That's so, is it? Which of you is delivering these tidings to that great ox when he comes in the morning to fetch his *virgin* bride?"

She stiffened at the skepticism implied in his use of the term. "I'm still a virgin, sir."

"After what we just walked in on?"

"That's as far as I got," Logan said coolly.

"This time."

"Are you calling both of us liars, Uncle?"

Tearful eyes on her husband, Aunt Alice pleaded, "Let them wed. Kira's fancied Logan since she was a wee lass."

Reverend Wilkins nodded. "Consider carefully before you reply, Mister Houston. Much heartbreak is incurred when women are forced to wed where they do not love."

The narrow lines at Peter Houston's mouth remained drawn.

"Hear Logan, sir," Kira pleaded, as she'd sworn to Logan she never would.

"Very well. Speak to me, boy. Where do you intend to keep a wife and the wee ones that will swiftly follow? Here, under our roof? Is it farming you want, with Will and me?"

Logan's expression was as tightly drawn as his uncle's. "I hardly think that arrangement would suit either of us."

Uncle Peter fingered his beard. "Where will you go?"

"To the McCutcheon homestead."

"'Tis burnt to the ground and lies on the edge of the frontier."

"I know. I've already visited the site."

"Have you, now? Found any gold?" he scoffed.

Logan gave him an arched look. "Should I have done?"

Uncle Peter nodded at Kira. "This one says so."

Plainly, she shouldn't have. Holding the nubby blue and brown blanket shut with one hand, she reached to him with the other. "I'm sorry. He's so bent on me wedding Josiah. I thought maybe you could—" she hesitated.

"Buy you?" He reached inside the buckskin pouch at his waist and withdrew the gold sovereign. Taking her outstretched hand, he placed the coin in her palm. "Give this to my uncle for all his care and as proof that I do indeed have the means to provide for you."

Three pairs of eyes widened at his find. Even though Kira had felt it in the night, a sense of unreality cloaked the gold glinting in the firelight. She held it out to her guardian. "Here, sir."

With a low whistle, he closed his hand around the coin. "By heaven, the lass wasn't dreaming. Are there more, Logan?"

"So I'm told. I've not had ample opportunity to search."

Respect warmed Uncle Peter's eyes, an expression Kira never thought to see. "I'll not ask how you know. I expect you'll not say. If there's gold hid on your place, you've the right to it, but if word of that stash leaves this room your life won't be worth a farthing."

Kira's stomach made a sick flop. She was

161

responsible for it spreading this far.

Uncle Peter faced Reverend Wilkins. "Have we your promise you'll not speak of this to a single living soul?"

He extended his hand. "As God is my witness."

His host seized it warmly. "And you'll wed these two?"

"That I will. And I'll do you one more. I shall tell Mister Campbell he can seek elsewhere for a bride."

"Nay, sir. You possess the courage of ten, but it's my place to tell him."

"I have news that will make your task easier," Logan said. "I did some scouting today. The tracks from your gelding and mare led back to Campbell's holding."

A red flush stained his uncle's face and neck, what showed of it apart from the beard. "You mean to say Campbell himself is mixed up in this thievery?"

"Don't you wonder how he restored your goods so quickly?"

Aunt Alice leaned weakly against Reverend Wilkins.

Not her husband. He exploded to life. "And made me beholden to him for it, the bloody scoundrel! To think I nearly gave him our Kira. Can you find it in your heart to forgive me, lass?"

She nodded numbly.

"Good girl. Never you fear. I'll deal with Campbell." Uncle Peter dashed forward, snatched his musket from the horns above the hearth, and spun around. He charged to the door.

Aunt Alice called after him. "For God's sake, Peter, do have some sense! Don't go tearing off after him alone."

"I'll go too." Logan grabbed his musket from where he'd propped it against the wall and dashed out after his uncle.

"Get the whip, Nephew! We'll give that bastard a lace jacket he'll not forget!"

Aunt Alice turned helplessly to Reverend Wilkins.

"I'll see what I can do, Ma'am," he assured her, and hastened to the door. Pausing, he looked back over his shoulder. "Your husband has the devil of a temper and your nephew's not a great deal better, if you'll forgive my saying. And yes, dear lady, I remember Henry McCutcheon well. Logan's father was quite similar."

Kira stared after them not at all certain what she was to do, other than dress with all possible haste. Then what, go after the men while they confronted Josiah?

Not on her life. If she'd learned one thing today it was to stay clear of him. She just prayed the scoundrel didn't appear in their absence.

****

"Will you wait the night out here, lass?"

Kira shifted from where she sat huddled on the stoop to see Aunt Alice silhouetted in the doorway behind her. She beckoned. "It'll be dark soon. Come inside and get warm."

The evening breeze was light but carried a chill nip in its breath. Drawing the blanket more snugly around her shift, Kira shook her head. "I'll do."

"They'll be all right." The slight tremor in Aunt Alice's voice detracted from the reassurance she'd intended.

"How can you bear not knowing if Uncle Peter will return safely?"

"There's nothing else for it other than to wait and trust."

"It's not right putting us through all of this worry."

"Thank heavens Reverend Wilkins is with them."

"They should have gotten some of the neighbors to go as well. Not gone off half-cocked."

"What they ought to do and the deed is rarely the same. If you're bent on watching for them, see if you can scout up the boys. Likely, you'll know best where to look."

"I have a notion." Kira limped down the steps.

Twilight blue spread across the heavens while gold and rose traced the ridges. A mantle of green encompassed the woods and meadows, receding into shadows. White dogwood blossoms stood out in the descending dusk. The first stars winked through breaks in the leafy canopy as she passed beneath the branches. If Logan were with her, these bright lights would seem magical. Now they lacked luster. Was he to color her whole world?

"Too too too."

The mellow whistle of the saw-whet owl floated down to her. She gave a whistle and the diminutive form fluttered down to her shoulder. Taking the bird in hand, she stroked his brown feathers and walked toward the old oak. She'd discovered the tunnel hidden at the base of its gnarled trunk. The agile duo could vanish into the burrow in an instant. If not hunkered down there, they might be any number of places. The tree loomed above her, a gentle giant, as she stole beneath its limbs.

Dim light prevented her seeing the boys, but sounds of bickering emanated from beneath the ground. "You ate most all the corn bread." That was Donald.

Scuffling followed. "Bawtie did. Give over!" David argued. "That's my piece."

She squatted beside the tunnel. "You can come out now."

"Nuh uh. Papa'll skin us alive."

"No longer. He and Logan have gone after Josiah."

Two tousled heads emerged. "How come?"

"Logan discovered Josiah had a hand in the robbery."

The twins tumbled out and Donald gave a whoop. "Papa'll give him such a thrashing. Logan will too."

David jumped up and down. "Wish we could see the fight. That conniving thief will rue the day."

Neither ventured a doubt as to the outcome of the encounter, only unadulterated jubilation. "We got Campbell first," Donald reminded her.

"Got him good," they chanted, gyrating around her. Even Bawtie joined in their merriment.

"Stay clear of Josiah or he may get you back. Go on to the house now. Supper's waiting."

The scampering figures vanished down the path with the dog. Like pint-sized warriors, the boys embraced the violence and uncertainty inherent in frontier life, as natural to them as breathing. Kira longed for a gentler, more ordered world, if such a place were possible this side of eternity.

Nestling her feathered companion in the crook of her arm, she sat against the tree. Logan came and went with all the predictability of the wind. Was it in him to settle down? Resentment churned in her amid anxiety for his well-being.

"Is he capable of true devotion?" she asked the owl.

The wise bird had no answer.

Night breezes picked up, and stars shone through the tossing branches. Chilled, Kira wriggled back into the cramped space recently vacated by the boys. Maybe she'd stay where she was and let Logan seek her out for once.

Men's low voices carried on the wind. Was that him? Who was he with, Will or Uncle Peter?

She crawled from her retreat and called, "Logan?" then froze. Why were the two men approaching from behind the tree instead of coming from the direction of the house? Unless they'd spoken with the twins they couldn't know where she was.

"You hear something?" one man asked.

Not a voice she recognized. Clamping her mouth shut, she tucked back into the hiding place.

"You're too nervous, Jesse. Just the wind playing tricks on you," the second man answered.

Whoever this Jesse was Kira prayed he agreed because the other voice belonged to Josiah's cousin, Nate Campbell.

"I tell you I heard a woman," Jesse said.

"You mean you want one." That was Nate.

"Not enough to haul some girl off like your fool cousin."

"You want to go back and call Josie a fool to his face?"

"Hell, no. He's mad enough to eat straw and not notice."

"Come on, then," Nate urged.

"He should have come here himself."

"Only if she's downwind of him," Nate chuckled. "Josie ain't sneaking up on nobody the way he stinks."

"That girl ain't gonna be sitting there waiting on us."

Horror struck her. Until a short while ago, she'd been perched on the stoop.

"Better do as Josie said." Their voices faded as they slunk past her toward the house.

Straining to hear more, she scooted from the hole, but the ominous exchange was lost on her. Heart hammering in her chest, she struggled to think. She couldn't just hide. Not this time. Those two might endanger Aunt Alice and the twins, and what if Logan returned and encountered them unawares? A stealthy blade could pass across his throat. She had to go after them, a bizarre tactic as she was the one they sought. But she had an idea, possibly her most daring yet.

The owl in hand, she tiptoed behind the dark forms, careful to keep out of the moonlight filtering through the leaves. Hidden among the trees, she called, "Nate," the wavering in her summons lending it an eerie inflection.

Their footsteps halted. "You hear that?" Nate asked.

"Ain't no damn wind this time." Jesse sounded shaken. "Indians say if an owl calls your name, it means your death."

"Nate," she quavered again.

"That weren't no owl." For all his former bravado, Nate's voice reflected his companion's apprehension.

The hunter was now the hunted, or the haunted, a rare reversal that gave Kira sharp pleasure. She thrust the little owl aloft. Wings flew and "Too, too, too," sounded overhead.

"Bloody hell—" Jesse gasped. "I'd rather face Josie than some damn ghost."

"We'll grab the girl later," Nate agreed.

Flattened against a tree, she remained undetected as the men shot past her. Her triumph diminished, though, at the question surging in her mind; when would that be? She couldn't depend on conjuring another haunting—might even be caught off-guard. With that unnerving thought, she made for the house intent on bolting the door.

Chapter Eleven

Kira scrunched down in her nest of blankets before the hearth, jumping like a singed cat at the tread of boots outside the door. "Don't unbolt it—might be them."

"More likely to be Peter." Laying aside her sewing, Aunt Alice rose from her chair.

The door rattled. "Wait to be certain," Kira cautioned.

"Open up, woman! Can't a man get into his own home?"

"Give a body half a shake."

Kira wasn't waiting that long. Ignoring the twinge in her knee, she flew to the door, slid the bolt and flung it wide. "Uncle Peter—" Coherent speech not immediately in her power, she hugged his reassuring bulk.

The surprised man closed his arms around her in return. "Don't take on so, lass. No one's suffering."

Aunt Alice stepped beside them. "What happened at Campbell's place?"

"Not as much as we would have liked. We left the fellow mad as a crazed hornet. Couldn't find the stash of goods and turned the place upside down looking. 'Rooted around like pigs,' Campbell said, but he'll not say it again."

"Oh my," his wife murmured.

"Reverend Wilkins kept us from too much mischief. Campbell declares thieves must have come by his place while he was over here and that accounts for the horse tracks."

"You don't believe that nonsense?" Aunt Alice

was indignant.

"Not on your life, but we've got no proof to arrest him."

"His sins will find him out. The Lord will see to it."

"If the Lord doesn't, Logan or I will."

Still locked to her guardian, Kira asked,"Is he with you?"

"In the stable seeing to his horse."

Aunt Alice gently detached her. "Let the man get his breath. Where all have you been, Peter? You were gone ages."

"We went on to the Lewis place, left Reverend Wilkins there, and fetched Will back."

"What about your supper?"

"They fed us royally. And it's just as well we stayed on a while. As set as Will was on Kira, we had a time prying him away from Jenny. He can hardly wait to bed the girl."

His wife colored. "Mind your tongue. Don't speak so before the lass."

"Won't hurt her modesty none after the display she put on for the reverend."

"She never meant to."

"Likely not. That Logan's a crafty one. At least Will's seeing sense now, says it's better to have the girl who wants him than one pining her heart out for another."

Will's teasing grin appeared through the door. "I heard about this afternoon, Kira." Concern displaced his good humor. "What's happened?"

"Kira's had quite a scare," his mother said.

Spying Logan at the base of the steps, she left Aunt Alice to explain and tore out the door and down the stoop, stumbling in her haste. He caught her as she lurched forward. If she could have, she would've wrapped her legs around him. As it was, she clung to him like a drowning woman. He held her close,

seeming only mildly surprised at her near panic.
****

What now, Logan wondered. A horse ready to bolt couldn't have seemed more frenzied. "Not that I mind, sweetheart, but why the anxious welcome—again?"

"Take me away now!"

"Barefoot, in your shift?"

She pulled back. "I'll get my things. We haven't a moment to lose."

He grasped her shoulders. "Calm down, Kira."

"What good will that do? I want a pistol—muskets are too heavy—and I'll need shot, powder, and a knife."

"You'll be asking me for a tomahawk next."

"A bit unwieldy for me. I'd rather the pistol." She broke away. "Yes, just the thing."

"I wasn't being serious."

Pacing and gesturing with her hands, she insisted, "I was. You don't understand."

"How can I? You're sidling like a high strung mare." He was beginning to see why his aunt dosed her regularly.

"I've every right to be nervous. I overheard two men, Nate Campbell and Jesse somebody—don't know him—they're after me."

"What do you mean?"

"To snatch me for Josiah."

Logan weighed her assertion. "No one was with Campbell when we left him."

"Maybe they were hidden."

"Damn good if they were. We took that place apart."

"Maybe they came by just after you had gone?"

"Perhaps…" She tensed at the doubt he'd failed to conceal. "Campbell must have given them their marching orders mighty quick," he continued. "When did you hear the voices?"

170

"Soon after dusk."

"On foot or horseback?"

"Foot. They could have left their horses back a ways."

"Could have, I suppose," he allowed.

"I *heard* them, Logan. By the great oak."

"What were you doing up there?"

"Fetching the boys. I stayed behind after they left."

A thought occurred to him. "Are you certain you were awake?"

"Of course," she snapped.

"I just wondered if you might have dozed—"

"I didn't dream it!"

"Very well." He adopted a soothing tone. "What then? Did they just walk away?"

"No. I scared them off."

He slid his arm around her waist to coax her up the steps. "How? You're not that frightening."

She limped beside him. "They never saw me. I called out to them like a haint."

"A what?"

"You know, a creature that's there, but ain't?"

"For heaven's sake, Kira, a *haint*?"

"It worked," she muttered as they walked into the room.

At a glance, he saw his disbelief mirrored in Uncle Peter and Will's faces, as must Kira who rounded on Aunt Alice. "Didn't you tell them what happened?"

She replied gently, "I did, lass. It's just...you're subject to imaginings. Not that we're saying it was that."

"'Tisn't notions!"

Uncle Peter threw his hands up. "Have it your way, gal."

Eyes filled with reproach, Kira swept her gaze over the circle. "Aren't you going to do anything?"

Beth Trissel

"You want us to take out after Campbell again and his cousin and God knows who else?" Uncle Peter asked.

"If you don't, they'll come for me."

"Don't fret, gal. We'll keep you safe," the grizzled man assured her.

Will gave her an affectionate pat. "Try and get some sleep, Kira. You'll feel better in the morning," he yawned, and headed toward his room.

"No one's listening to me."

Logan propped his musket against the wall. "I am."

"Good. You see to her then. I'm all in." Uncle Peter limped to his shadowy bed and sat down, tugging at his boots. "Come on, Alice. Get you to bed. You look worn to a thread."

"The brandy's by the hearth, Logan, and I've brewed some betony. So good for nervous hysteria," his aunt advised wearily, as though turning Kira over to him like a troublesome patient. "Heed him, lass." With this admonition, she retreated to bed.

Kira glared in their direction. But what could she expect after this latest outburst? Her imagination was getting out of hand.

Narrowing her eyes at Logan, she drew herself up and hissed. "I'm not doing a blessed thing you say if I don't want to."

Her will wasn't daunted in the least. One moment she'd clung to him for all she was worth, the next she fumed in defiance, the little vixen. "Is that so?" he countered.

"Why should I when you don't credit a word I say." Turning coolly away, she hobbled to the hearth and crawled under the blankets.

Not easily put off, he laid his tomahawk and knife aside and slipped in next to her. Tucking the coverlet around them, he asked, "Have I rebellion to quell from the start, Miss?"

172

Logs settled in the hearth, sending up a shower of orange sparks. Her gaze was fixed on the red coals in the fire. "You know I hate it when you won't believe me."

"I never said I didn't."

She rolled over and punched him on the shoulder. "You never said you did either."

He grasped her hand. "Save your strength. You have a big day tomorrow."

"I suppose I shall be at Will's wedding after all, along with everyone else from miles around."

"Without a doubt. Jenny Lewis has graciously agreed to share her day. Likely to keep you from her husband."

"I'm not after Will."

"You let him kiss you."

Flickering flames revealed the regret hazing her eyes. "Before I realized."

"Never mind. Just so Jenny doesn't find out. She fairly pounced at seeing us wed."

"Did she?"

"By heaven, she would have had Reverend Wilkins conduct the service this very night if she could have. But tomorrow will do."

Kira's eyes widened, almost as if she'd actually seen the haint she'd pretended. "I'm wedding you tomorrow?"

"Why so surprised?"

"I—just didn't expect us to marry quite so swiftly."

He studied her in bemusement. "You begged me to take you away not a quarter of an hour ago."

"I still would if I thought you'd listen."

"If I took you off this instant, what do you expect would follow? That we would live together as brother and sister?"

"Hardly, but to be your wife—marriage makes matters between us rather more binding."

"Do you fear having to obey me more than if you weren't?"

That stubborn look settled over her face. "I shall do as I please either way."

"We'll soon see about that." He snuggled her against him, preferring something far more sensual, but his relations were close by. Whether or not the girl was entirely sane, he wanted her. Dear Lord, how he wanted her. "Ah, Kira. I've had eyes only for you from the moment I saw you in that tree."

"With my petticoats over my head?"

"Especially then. It just took some doing to bring my uncle round."

"Not such a lot. Less than a week."

"A great plenty, the way I feel. Just be glad I'm taking you properly."

"There's nothing proper about everyone finding us together as they did today."

He smiled. "Everything worked out as I intended. Aunt Alice told me Uncle Peter and Reverend Wilkins were coming."

"You meant for them to discover us?"

"It's one way to hasten a wedding."

She socked him again. "I was never so mortified in all my life."

"Sorry, Cricket. But I never had so much pleasure while waiting on a preacher."

****

Everyday clothes had been laid aside. Aunt Alice wore the olive short-gown with the skirted waist and quilted green petticoat she saved for best. "Do stand still for two seconds together," she entreated Kira, laboring to lace her corset while she held to the side of Will's bed in Hannah's freshly aired shift and fine petticoats.

"I can barely breathe."

"Fitted stays won't hurt you for a day, your wedding day at that. I'd far rather you and Logan

174

were married here," she sighed. "But with Mister Campbell breathing fire, we'd best see you joined straight away."

"Give over, Will!" His father's shout carried above the jocular bathing out in the main room. Logan's laugh sounded alongside Will's in the watery battle that followed, while the twins cheered them on.

"Are you two cleaning up for a wedding, or just giving each other a good wetting?" Uncle Peter scolded, but humor underlay his rebuke.

"That floor's awash," Aunt Alice predicted. "No matter. Let them have their fun." She gathered Kira's well-brushed hair into a knot on her head and held the curling mass in place with the ivory comb. "Such a fair bride you are."

Wistfulness tugged at Kira as she surveyed the blue-flowered jacket Aunt Alice had laid out. "I'd be a sight fairer in Hannah's gown."

The older woman tucked stray tendrils into the auburn braid coiled on her head. "Come, now. You have all else, and I've left the cross at your throat."

"But Hannah wanted me to wear her gown at my wedding."

"That bodice shows far too much of your bosom, my girl."

Logan's chuckle drew Kira's eyes to the doorway. Toweling the excess moisture from his hair, he stuck his head into the back room and gave an appreciative whistle. "Is this the same girl who raced me and smacked into a sheep?"

Aunt Alice smoothed the lilac bows at Kira's corset. "I never thought to see her in such frills."

"He should see me in the gown, too," Kira pressed.

"He did."

"Just. She fled the room and me." Logan stepped inside, bare-chested, with blue-printed fabric draped over his arm. "I'm enjoying you without it, but I should like to see you dressed like gentry. Couldn't you line the bodice with a kerchief or cover her with a shawl, Aunt?"

"'Tisn't only the neckline that troubles me. Her gown is far grander than other girls. I fear they'll be envious."

"Kira will stir that, no matter what she wears."

The gown receded in importance as Kira watched him pull on his shirt. Small silver cones shone over the colorful fabric alongside beads sewn in a bright design. Creamy elkskin breeches were molded to his muscular legs, while quill and beadwork ornamented his high-topped moccasins. The bold dress coupled with his handsome figure was striking, but a question mounted in her mind. Where had he come by these things? While he was with the Shawnee, of course, but who made them for him?

His attire wasn't lost on his aunt. "My, aren't you grand. All the unwed gals will hunger for you and some of the wedded ones too. Kira will be envied even more."

That tumultuous emotion seethed in her already. "Sewed it yourself, did you, during those long winter hours?"

"I'm not quite that handy with a needle and thread."

"Thought not," Kira said frostily. "Some woman took great pains outfitting you. I'll wager she wasn't elderly and in want of a son."

"Not a son of my years, anyway."

Resentment flashed in Kira like fire set to dry kindling. "Perhaps you should take yourself back to her."

"Oh, lass. Let the past be," Aunt Alice pleaded.

A lump rose in her throat. She swallowed hard. "But I waited for him and—"

"He was gone a long time. You two sort this out. I'll fetch Hannah's gown and we will see what Logan thinks," plainly a concession by his aunt to soothe Kira's feelings.

She pivoted away from him. "I shall wear what I please. You certainly are."

He encircled her from behind, closing one arm over her corseted breasts and the other around her waist, his energy enveloping her like a pulsing star. "Fair enough. But I'll not have you defy me at the Lewises because you're hurt."

"Why should I not be?"

"What if I told you Tessa sewed my breeches and applied her skills to my moccasins?"

Kira was slightly mollified, but that wasn't the most stunning garment. "What of the shirt?"

"A gift."

"You ought not to accept gifts from unmarried women."

"Would you prefer married ones?" he asked.

"It's impossible to speak seriously with you."

"Not impossible. She was wed and very lonely, her husband much away."

"So you comforted her?"

He made no denial.

Turning slowly in his arms, she lifted her eyes to the man she was to wed this very day. "Didn't her husband wonder at the half-breed children she bore him?"

"I know of none. But if there were any, he wouldn't have. He was a French trapper."

She gaped at him.

"You demanded honesty, sweetheart. I know you think I'm a rake, but I did care for Meketha."

"So, she has a name."

"Not one I'd intended to share, but as you're insistent."

"Did you care a great deal for her?"

177

"Nothing like the adoration I possess for you."

"You might have had these passions for her at the start."

"Not like this. I swear it."

The intensity in his eyes, his tone, everything about him seemed sincere. And yet, "How can I be certain?"

"By taking me at my word."

"You ask much."

"I will give much in return. When I hold you I'll not think of Meketha."

"I will."

He pressed his lips to her neck and sent tingles shimmering down her spine. "I shall make you think of me."

"'Tisn't fair."

"Why? Because you prefer to brood over a woman I knew before falling in love with you? Brood if you must, dear heart, but behave yourself today or I will take you off without the good reverend's blessing."

"You wouldn't taint what reputation I have left?"

"Indeed, I would. 'Tis most improper to hightail away with a renegade let alone in a state of sin."

She was silent a moment. "We must away, mustn't we?"

Somberness filled his eyes. "Even apart from Josiah's threats, yes. Time wanes. There are those counting on us. You've never been deep into the frontier, Kira. It's no place for squabbling. Stand with me, or you'll fell us both."

Trepidation mingled with a sense of anticipation and a chill ran through her. She felt the truth behind his warning.

Chapter Twelve

The earthiness of straw and horse droppings scented the musty air inside the stable. Wooden rails divided the cramped space into stalls. Uncle Peter's draft mare and gray gelding were already outside. Logan's chestnut stallion snatched at hay as he bent beside him to adjust the cinch strap on the saddle. He lifted his head to see Kira hike up her skirts and tiptoe in, mindful not to spook the horse or soil her shoes. What a proper lady, adjusting her mother's lace-edged shawl over Hannah's sumptuous gown, and a rare beauty. It made her tempestuous nature all the more intriguing.

Stepping nearer to him, she said, "Uncle Peter is eager to depart."

"I'm almost ready."

She lifted uncertain eyes to the stallion. "Is he friendly?"

"To me, always."

"What of me?"

Logan straightened and patted the horse's sleek neck. "Who could resist you? Come and meet Tequi."

She edged closer to the seemingly placid animal.

"Be kind to Kira, Tequi. You must carry us both."

Reaching tentative fingers to the horse's velvety muzzle, she crooned, "What a handsome fellow you are."

"Me or Tequi?"

"Both and you know it."

"Will you deny all knowledge of your beauty? Let me see this gown before we go."

179

She slid the shawl from her shoulders. "Do you like it?"

He steadied himself with a hand on Tequi's powerful neck. "Splendid. You would make a fine lady."

At first pleasure shone, then hesitancy hazed her eyes. "You're not intent on living in the frontier, are you, Logan?"

"Only temporarily. Perhaps we should return to Scotland and make a claim on the family seat?"

A fleeting smile and she shook her head.

More softly, he asked, "What of Quebec?"

The uncertainty in her expression deepened. "Is that the only safe place for us?"

"It may be."

He smiled in encouragement. "Don't fret about that now. We've a wedding before us, and I think Aunt Alice is right. I shouldn't take you to the Lewis stronghold dressed like this."

Disappointment keen in her eyes, she said, "You'll not insist I change?"

"No. I'm relishing the sight far too well, but I'll have to fight the men from you."

"Not today, surely?"

"I take nothing for granted where you're concerned."

"I feel the same about you, Logan, and with more cause."

"Come now, I'm not entirely unreliable. Haven't I always been your friend?"

"And an enormous tease to boot."

He closed his fingers around her smaller hand. "I'm in earnest. Whatever I've been, whatever I've done, my heart is yours now and forever."

"What of your body? Will you stray?"

"I will be faithful to you. I swear it."

"And I to you."

A sweet pain pierced him. "You always have

been."

"For all that it's meant."

"Quite the contrary. Don't you think I want to be the first man with you, the only man?"

"I'm treading dangerous ground taking you to husband. Yet, I shall have no other."

He touched the spray of lily of the valley tucked in her hair; the purity of the minute white bells suited her perfectly. "I wish we were already wed. I would spend the day reassuring you."

"Logan! Are you coming?" That was Uncle Peter.

"I'd rather make use of that haystack, but as they're waiting on us." He gestured Kira forward. "After you."

She swished from the stable ahead of him, while he led the stallion. "Up you go, darling." Closing his hands around her waist, he lifted her onto Tequi, skirts and legs over one side. Then slid his musket over his shoulder and mounted behind her. He held her securely. "I've got you."

The roan mare was harnessed to the wagon. Uncle Peter and Aunt Alice sat on the seat with the twins in the wagon bed beside the keg of whiskey and smoked ham Uncle Peter was taking to the festivities. Bawtie whined, but had been ordered to stay behind.

Will stopped alongside them on Donavan and swept his gaze over Kira. "Wearing that, are you?"

"It's my wedding too."

Challenge glinted in his eyes. "So it is. First one to Lewis's gets the loft after, Logan."

A rosy blush stained Kira's cheeks. "Will—"

"What else did you think would follow the nuptials?"

Her eyes sparked at him. "Must you be so blunt? You've the manners of a boar today."

"Sorry. I forgot we had a gentlewoman among us." He prodded Donavan into a canter. "Loser gets the stable!"

Logan urged Tequi after him in a drum of hooves.

Kira called out, "I don't mind the stable!"

"Nor I! But he's not winning this!"

No man or beast would win against Logan if there were any earthly way to prevail. It crossed his mind that he might need more than earthly aid to fulfill his mission at the McCutcheon home place. An unsettling thought he drove from his mind. The race was on.

****

The rutted road was little more than a widened trail, but Logan had galloped Tequi over worse. Raucous crows flapped up from the newly planted cornfield as they flew by. Buttercups and tiny red poppies in the grassy verge were a blur of color.

"Slow down!" Kira yelled over the pounding gait.

"Can't. Will's still ahead." Logan just made out the swiftly vanishing horse and rider.

"I'll not be going to the loft if I'm lying along this trail with my neck broken!"

He laughed. "Tequi won't fail us."

"You had better slow down or I'm not going anywhere with you."

"You're going—damn. Will's clean out of sight."

"Donavan's not carrying two like Tequi. Give it up."

"Not that easily." Logan could still overtake Will and jumped Tequi across a shrubby tangle at the side of the road.

Clenched in his grasp, Kira was in no danger of pitching to the stony ground but gripped him for dear life. "Logan! Where are you going?"

"Shortcut." He headed the stallion across the sunny hay field toward the darkened woods. The clear whistle of "bobwhite" rang out and the warm fragrance of hay rose in the mild air. Ruddy-brown quail flushed from cover and rabbits scattered. "Wish I had time to hunt."

Leaving the tall grass behind, he cantered Tequi into the shadowed trees. Giant chestnuts loomed on every side. He urged the horse down the steep path winding between tall green hemlocks to the narrow trail below. The loose ground fell away and stones slid beneath the stallion's hooves. Kira lurched over Tequi's neck then jolted back into Logan.

"You're as wild as any Scotsman!"

"Worse than some."

He charged Tequi at an oak lying across the path. They sailed over. The stallion hurtled across a second uprooted tree and stumbled as he landed on the uneven path.

Jerked forward, she cried out in alarm.

"It's all right."

"No it's not!'

Tequi nimbly recovered his footing and bolted ahead. He splashed knee-high through the stream running hard from rain.

A shower of water sprayed up and splashed droplets over them. Tequi bounded up the mossy bank, slipped, and threw Kira over his neck again. As before, he was instantly back on his feet.

He sprang into a canter, but she cried out, "Please, Logan! Even Will slowed when I begged him."

Guilt pierced Logan's conscience, and he reined the chestnut in. Kira sagged against him as he halted the horse beneath a white-flowering crabapple. Tendrils of hair had torn loose from the knot on her head and her flowered skirts were spattered with wet. Worse, her face was pale, eyes wide. The poor girl was all dressed up for her wedding. Now, he'd disheveled her and frightened her to death. Sometimes, he really was a savage.

"I'm sorry, Kira. I hate to think I treated you

183

worse than that cousin of mine."

"Don't you see? Will knew you couldn't win with me along, the weasel. You must think me the most frightful coward."

"No. Just not keen on horse racing."

"Are you very disappointed about losing?"

"Naw. The fairest woman in these ridges is in my arms. Will knows that, too."

Snowy blossoms wreathed her face as she gazed up at him. A beam of sunshine streaming through the perfumed bouquet shone on her glossy hair and the dizzying blue in her eyes. "You really are quite nice sometimes, Logan."

"I'm not an utter lout."

A smile tugged at her lips. "Not utterly."

"I get the most exquisite pain when you smile. You truly look angelic. If I'm especially nice, will you smile again?"

"I might."

He badly wanted to win another from her and prove he wasn't beyond civilizing. "Say, are you thirsty?" He rooted around in the saddle bag for the flask, twisted it open, and offered her the first swallow.

"What is it?"

"Cider," he grinned.

She smiled and sipped the apple brandy. Bees hummed overhead as they passed the flask back and forth.

"Hungry?" he asked.

"Breakfast was rather hurried."

Reaching his hand into his waist pouch, he took out a yellow chunk wrapped in linen. He unwrapped the cornbread, split in two and oozing with honey, and held it to her lips.

With a laugh that delighted him, she bit into the cake. "Never expected honey in the middle of a horse race."

He grinned. "If one plan fails, I'm ready with another."

Again, she eyed him with that melting light. "This is the first ordinary thing we've done since you returned."

"Eating on the back of a horse is ordinary?"

A wistful quality in her eyes, she said, "For us."

"We will share hundreds of ordinary things, all the bits and pieces of the life you crave. You'll see."

So radiant was she, he felt inclined to coax far more than a smile from her. "Have you any idea how tempted I am to lie with you beneath this tree?"

"I would happily stay."

"I believe you would, with nary a struggle."

"'Tis expected we will attend our own wedding," she reminded him.

He groaned. "Indeed. Lovemaking won't be as simple there as here, though."

She looked mystified. "Why do you prefer the ground to the stable?"

"Solitude, sweetheart. I could do without curious ears, and eyes, if we have intruders."

"I don't covet them either. We could slip away after saying our vows."

"Before all that feasting and dancing and being properly seen to bed? They'll not let us out of their sight until we oblige them. Still, we had best make haste to this wedding."

Logan prodded Tequi into a lope with Kira nestled against him. He had to admit this was better than tearing all over the countryside like a madman.

Pointing to drifts of yellow and scarlet blossoms nodding in the breeze, she said, "Columbine are my favorite flowers."

"Shall I pick a garland for your hair, my lady?"

Another heart-paining smile and she shook her head.

"Quite right. I would tarry." How he'd love that.

Tequi whinnied a low warning.

Instantly alert, Logan slowed him to a walk. He patted the horse's sleek neck and peered through the leaves. "What is it, boy?"

"I see nothing amiss. Do you?" Kira asked softly.

"No, but Tequi senses something. He's a wary one."

Ears pricked, the stallion walked on. He nickered again, a sort of signal between them. Logan reined him to a halt and nodded ahead. Two horses were tethered to a birch tree. Their rear ends partially blocked the narrow trail.

Kira froze against him.

"You know these mounts?"

"The gray is Nate Campbell's gelding. I don't recognize the piebald mare. She might belong to Jesse, the second man I told you of."

"So, you heard rightly." He could've kicked himself for not believing her and suspected she could have too.

He pointed at the steep slope that led back up to the road they'd traveled earlier. "Appears we are expected. These two left their mounts behind thinking to spot us up there. Must be lying in wait."

"Dear God. It's monstrous. What of Josiah? I don't see his black stallion."

He hated to further panic her. "Campbell could be anywhere."

She darted glances at the trees on either side and strained to see beyond the waiting horses. "Does he intend to snatch me on my wedding day? Folks won't stand for it."

"He may just think to harass us. Target the bridal pair with some sort of mischief."

Skepticism creased her eyes. "Do you really think they simply intend to discharge their muskets and cover us in smoke?"

"No." He fully expected an attempt on his life

and an all-out battle to claim her.

"Nate's a wicked rider, Logan, and his horse is as fast as the very devil. Can you get past them?"

"I'd sooner dismount and sneak up behind those sons of bitches and give them the surprise of their lives."

She jerked against him. "They might ambush you."

"A chance I'll take."

"And leave me to face Josiah alone?"

Biting back the curse rising to his lips, he muttered, "You're right. Hang on. We're going through."

He nudged Tequi and edged him toward the tethered horses. Nate Campbell's mount rumbled, flattening his ears against his head. He kicked out a warning leg, but Tequi skirted both horses. That done, Logan spoke to him. "*Memequiluh.*"

Tequi's stretched out his long legs at the Shawnee command to run and galloped over the trail as if the Hell Hound was on his tail. As far as Logan was concerned, it was. He fervently hoped the stalwart horse wouldn't falter. This ride was all important.

The faint beat of hooves echoed over Tequi's.

"They're behind us," Logan grunted.

"At this speed?"

"They're bloody well not chasing me down." He wheeled the lathered horse toward the steep rise.

Blowing hard, Tequi scrambled up between the rocks and trees. Stones gave way and he slid. Kira bit back any shrieks, seemingly more fearful of those in pursuit than taking a spill. Tequi lunged upward and reached the top.

"Now we can really fly," Logan crowed.

In comparison to the lower path, this road was a thoroughfare, but the ruts remained. Tequi sped around the muddy curves. Trunks and branches flashed past as they pelted through the dark hollow where ambush might lurk. Logan thought he glimpsed a big black horse. It might have been a bear, but he didn't linger to be sure.

They broke through the trees and the road wound past fields of corn and hay. Up ahead, the Lewis homestead beckoned like the Promised Land. If they reached it intact, all would be well. Anyone following wouldn't dare enter into an assembly of hardened men.

"I think we lost them. We're nearly there, Cricket."

Breathless silence spoke for her.

Tequi charged up the hill and through the sheltering grove of evergreens. Then they were pounding up the lane, slowing to a trot as they neared the barn. Chickens cackled and flew up. The large log house rose before them. Holy ground.

Logan trotted Tequi into the yard and reined him in. He swung a leg over the saddle and sprang to the ground. Just as quickly, he reached up his arms for Kira. She bent forward dazedly and he lifted her down, holding her to him with the supreme knowledge that he'd won his own race.

"You're safe now," he assured her.

But for how long? They were up against a more determined foe than he'd realized. Damn that Campbell.

Chapter Thirteen

Thank God. Kira could've kissed the ground in gratitude that they'd escaped their pursuers and arrived intact.

The door banged opened and people streamed outside and down the steps. Will dashed up to them first. "What happened, Logan? We feared you must have had an accident."

"Too close by half. I'll explain all in a minute."

Aunt Alice threw her arms around them both. "Poor lass. She looks frightened to death. Will Houston, you had no business egging Logan on to race."

"Sorry, Kira," the contrite young man offered.

"Doesn't she suffer enough without the pair of you causing her more distress?" Uncle Peter chided, stumping over to them. "Poor girl won't have a nerve left."

Unusually solicitous, Donald and David patted her arms. "Are you hurt? Were you tumbled off? Can you walk?"

As appreciative as Kira was for everyone's concern, it seemed she'd entered a tempest of a different sort. "I—we—are fine." Unstable emotions rendered her response even more disjointed and her trembling legs weren't entirely reliable.

Jenny Lewis swept up to her in blue homespun skirts, auburn hair streaming down her back, and sympathy in her thickly-lashed brown eyes. She slipped an arm around Kira. "Poor girl. You've gone white. Let's get you inside."

"There, there." Like a plump hen, Mrs. Lewis

clucked, "We'll put you to rights. Come sit by the hearth."

Aunt Alice supported Kira on the other side. "You'll soon feel better."

"Good. You see to her then. I'll tend my horse." Releasing her to the cluster of women, Logan beckoned, "A word in your ear, Will. You'll want to hear this, Uncle." Reins in hand, he strode toward the stable with Tequi. Will and Uncle Peter hastened after him with the twins at their heels.

Jenny Lewis ushered Kira through the gathering in the yard and up the steps to the house. High-spirited men, women, and children parted to allow them passage to the great hearth in the central room of the sprawling homestead. Savory scents escaped the black kettle hung over the cheery blaze and the Dutch oven tucked in the hot coals. Roasted hams, wild turkeys, baked spring onions, stewed rhubarb, crusty partridge pies, and molasses cake heaped the platters on the trestle tables. Brown bottles of whiskey and pitchers brimming with ale waited in readiness and more stood on the oak cupboard.

Weddings being the only festive gatherings that didn't first require the back-breaking work of harvest or house-raising, these hardy Scots had come fully prepared to revel. Hearty chatter buzzed on every side of Kira and from the back room where the people had spilled over. She nervously surveyed the robust gathering. Some folks were still out on the stoop, in the yard, or the stable. It was impossible to say exactly how many people had come, but she'd counted several dozen at least and more were arriving.

Boisterous young men in brown hunting shirts or more refined linen thumped each other on the back and flirted with the young women. Some of them had tried to court Kira before Josiah's fierce threats put an end to their ardor. The more roughly dressed among them wore deerskin breeches, leggings and moccasins, though not with the adornment Tessa had sewn onto Logan's. No one had a shirt to equal his.

Reverend Wilkins' black frock and white collar stood out in the crowd. The good-natured man conversed with a rugged frontiersman. Spying Kira, he nodded cordially, but didn't entirely conceal his surprise at her attire.

He strode to her side. "Good day to you, Miss McClure."

"Good day, Reverend," she managed, wanting to sink through the floor at what he'd seen of her the day before. She prayed no one else here knew.

Humor hinted in his kind eyes. "You look lovely. A rare blossom in these ridges."

"Thank you, sir."

She'd never been at ease in large assemblies and was acutely self-conscious now. Every eye in the room fastened on her and a questioning murmur replaced the merry chatter. What on earth had possessed her to flaunt a gown so superior to the petticoats and short-gowns around her? One woman wore a jacket fashioned from flowered cloth similar to the one her brother Tom had given her. Here and there a lace-edged kerchief trimmed a bodice, or ribbons lent color to the braids and knots of hair, but little ornamentation was to be had in this hard pressed settlement.

Even the minister must be shared among them and journeyed between rough-hewn churches on various Sundays when he could spare the time from broader travels, and never in the depth of winter. The call had gone out for another man of the cloth, but none had yet answered.

Aunt Alice's quilted petticoat and short-gown, part of her dowry, were the only articles she possessed not woven by her own hands or the Irish weaver. Kira must seem like a visitor from another world and not necessarily a welcome one. She shrank under the barrage of scrutiny and wrapped her shawl more tightly around her, but it was too little too late.

Jenny's brown eyes traveled her wonderingly. Her own mustard colored short-gown and blue petticoat were quite plain by comparison, as were those of every other woman present.

She tugged Kira's shawl apart for a better look. "Heavens above. Wherever did you come by such a gown?"

Aunt Alice pushed beside Kira and gave her shoulder a cautioning squeeze. "'Twas her mama's," she answered for her.

If she'd declared fairies gifted it to her, Kira couldn't have been more surprised. As far as she knew, Alice Houston had never told a lie in her life.

Mrs. Lewis darted brown eyes over Kira with amazement equal to her daughter's and something else, a suspicious gleam. "I never saw Margaret McClure decked out in this."

Calmly, Aunt Alice replied, "She kept it hidden away," amazing Kira with just how well the woman fabricated.

But Mrs. Lewis did not appear convinced. "Why that?"

"Saving it for best maybe."

"Did *best* never come afore she died?"

"Reckon not, poor soul."

"More's the pity." Trailing work-worn fingers over the lavender-flowered fabric and lilac bows at Kira's bodice, their hostess observed, "This must have cost a bit. I don't recall Robert McClure ever having more'n the rest of us."

Aunt Alice didn't waver. "There was more to the man than you knew, Mary."

Like a hen hunting spilt grain, Mrs. Lewis's sharp eyes spied the gold cross at Kira's throat. "What's this, then?"

Again, Aunt Alice intervened. "A keepsake. You know Margaret was Papist before Robert made a Protestant of her."

"Tried," their hostess interjected.

Waving her intrusion aside, Aunt Alice bore on. "'Tis only natural Kira would wear this token at her wedding."

Disapproval etched weathered features that bore traces of Jenny's fresh beauty. Out thrust Mrs. Lewis's jaw. "We'll have no Papist symbols in this house. 'Tis enough the girl comes dressed as a kept woman."

Never had Aunt Alice looked so forbidding. "By heaven, if I weren't a Christian I'd give you the rough edge of my tongue, Mary Lewis. A good lass is our Kira."

Hands on her hips, the outraged woman hurled back, "There's many who agree with me and not one that won't say the girl's peculiar."

Reverend Wilkins bravely interposed himself between the indignant females. "Now then, Mrs. Lewis, these are strong charges to lay against Miss McClure without just cause."

Jenny linked her arm through Kira's. "I certainly never said such a thing about Kira. And *Will* esteems her highly, Mama," the emphasis on his name plain to Kira, while her stubborn mother stood in lip-protruding defiance. "Mama's just not used to finery, sir," Jenny said to the reverend.

"Few are in this settlement, or the others I visit." He turned to the gawking assembly. "I assure all you good people that I have seen such fashion among the ladies in Philadelphia and Williamsburg. Very fetching, is it not? Particularly on this young lady."

A congenial murmur ran through the gathering. The men seemed especially willing to oblige the reverend. "Bonnie lass! A right beauty!" several shouted out.

"We could do with more fashion around here," chuckled one of Jenny's many red-headed brothers.

His mother fired him a look that would've withered most men, but the Lewis clan seemed accustomed to her dark threats.

"Don't be contrary, Mama. We want to see Kira wed to Logan McCutcheon today, do we not?" Jenny pleaded, emphasizing each word as though the perturbed woman were hard of hearing.

"Aye," Mrs. Lewis said gruffly. "I'll say no more against her gown, but I'll not have that cross in my house."

Here, Kira entered the fray. "I won't wed without it."

Her jaw jutting out even further, Mrs. Lewis declared, "You'll not thumb your nose at us. Good Protestants we are."

"No one is disputing this, Ma'am. It's only a cherished token the girl wishes," Reverend Wilkins reasoned.

"And a Papist one."

His eyes grew stern. "Haven't enough precious souls perished and innocents been burnt at the foul stake in endless Holy Wars? The Lord desires forbearance among his people."

Mrs. Lewis muttered her reply. "Very well, Reverend. I'll not stand in the way of Kira being properly wed."

"Nor anyone here," Jenny quickly added.

"A fine way to treat folk soon to be your family, Mary Lewis," Aunt Alice scolded. "And poor Kira's nerves worn to a thread."

With a significant glance at her obdurate parent, Jenny offered, "Mama didn't mean to be hurtful."

Mary's downturned mouth didn't convey significant remorse, but she allowed, "Will's a good man. We don't want hard feelings with his people."

"Like a sister to him Kira is," Aunt Alice reproached her, as though she didn't know otherwise.

An assenting grunt from Mrs. Lewis was as near as they were likely to come to an apology.

Aunt Alice's grudging demeanor reminded Kira of the expression she wore when reluctantly allowing a wild creature into the house that had better not give her cause to evict it.

"Your tongue always did have a way of running ahead of you, Mary. Still, I'll say no more," she agreed.

"Well then, that's sorted out nicely. Now our brides are come, I'll scout up our grooms and summon the rest of the guests," Reverend Wilkins said briskly. He made a slight bow to the women and walked to the door. That he didn't bolt from the house seemed to Kira a mark of extreme self-control.

Jenny turned to her mother. "We must make amends."

A curt nod came in response. "Please, take some refreshment. Daughter, fetch a drop to steady Kira."

The soon to be wed young woman appeared in need of something to steady her own and grasped a brown bottle from the table. Pouring the clear fluid to the rim of a stoneware mug, she held it out to Kira.

She sipped and liquid fire burned a path to her stomach. "Very kind," she coughed.

Unlike the ill-tempered Lewis matriarch, their eager to please hostess poured another cup and extended it to Aunt Alice.

"No thank you. I'll just go see to my men," she said in clipped accents, and swept after Reverend

Wilkins.

"I have a young man to see to myself," Mrs. Lewis fumed.

Jenny caught her mother's arm. "Wait, Mama. I fear Mrs. Houston is deeply offended."

"No more than she should be."

"Mama!"

Mrs. Lewis shook off her daughter and bore down on the more outspoken of her sons. The little woman backed the strapping young man into the corner like a bantam hen baiting a bear. Only in this instance, the hen would win out.

"Oh Lord," Jenny groaned. She lifted the rejected cup to her lips and gulped with nary a cough.

Despite the diversion their aggravated hostess offered, Kira still found herself the center of much unabashed masculine appreciation. "I never should have come. I've spoiled your day entirely."

Rosy mouth quivering, her fellow bride insisted, "No you haven't. I want you here. Mama's just—Oh, you know how she is."

"It's not just her. Every eye is boring into me."

"That can't be helped the way you're dressed."

"They'd stare anyway." Kira pivoted away from onlookers toward the hearth. She knocked back another fiery swallow and gasped. "Enough of this and I'll take no notice."

"Nor I." The girl stood beside her and drained her cup. "Kira…what of you and Will?"

The firelight played over Jenny's red hair as Kira met her searching gaze. "He's like a dear brother and always been kind to me, except when he's bossy."

"There's more between you than that." This insightful Lewis female didn't seem angry, just sad.

"Did Will say so?"

"He doesn't have to. 'Tis plain he adores you."

"Will knows I love Logan."

"Even so, a well-placed word from you and Will would walk away." Jenny's voice caught. "What would I do without him?"

Kira met the appeal in her moist brown eyes. "'Twill be all right. He'll not leave you."

"He would, if he thought you'd have him."

"No. He'd rather wed the woman who loves him than one who loves another. And you do, don't you?"

"With all my heart."

"Good. Your love will keep him."

"But to always know he'd rather I were you?"

Slipping an affectionate arm around Jenny's slender waist, Kira said, "With such a wife? Will isn't so foolish."

"Do you really think so?"

"Don't I know him well?"

A tremulous smile from Jenny was her reward. "I can't tell you what a relief this is." She circled her arm around Kira in return. "Thank you."

"Glad to be of service." Her words slurred a little and she clung to Jenny's support. The room wasn't as stable as it had been only a short time ago. "Just keep some distance between him and your mother."

Jenny giggled—an infectious giggle. Holding to each other, they dissolved into laughter.

"Best of friends now, are you?" Will asked from behind.

"Or had a drop too much?" That voice belonged to Logan.

They spun around and came face to face with their prospective husbands. "Both," Kira admitted.

Will shook his head. "Can either of you stand unaided?"

Kira considered the sloping room. "I don't know if I can make it up the hill."

"Do we need to?" her new friend giggled.

"Unless the good reverend makes no objection to

conducting the service from the floor," Logan said dryly.

Jenny convulsed into laughter. "Your cousin's witty."

Will rolled his eyes. "Hilarious."

Wiping at tears of mirth, Jenny gazed up at Logan. "And so handsome."

Will took a firm hold on his intended's arm. "Don't you go falling in love with him too."

"I won't," she said solemnly, and broke off into giggles.

"I hope Reverend Wilkins can make himself heard above this," Will said, elevating his own voice.

Logan detached Kira from Jenny, closing his arms around her as she staggered. "I never thought to support you through our wedding because you're too intoxicated to stand."

"If you could have seen what I've been up against."

"We heard. Blow by blow," Will said.

Jenny sniffed. "I'm so sorry Mama's caused such a fuss."

Will touched her cheek. "It's not your fault."

Fresh moisture welled in Jenny's eyes. "And everyone's staring at Kira—"

"That's not your fault either. Don't weep."

But Jenny had swung from laughter to tears and convulsed against him. Will held her tightly and stroked her hair. "It doesn't matter. Nothing does, just so you say yes."

"Yes—" she sobbed.

Reverend Wilkins approached, his questioning gaze passing between the two couples. "Are we ready to begin?"

"As ready as we're likely to be. One bride can't stand and the other is hysterical," Logan replied.

The reverend nodded, lips twitching. "I've seen worse."

"What might that be?"

"A bride giving birth."

"Far worse," Logan smiled.

Beckoning for them to follow, Reverend Wilkins made his way to the center of the room. Exuberant well-wishers parted to allow the happy couples through. Kira held to Logan and put one unsteady foot in front of the other. Laughter rang out as he scooped her up in his arms. Grinning broadly, Will did the same with his precious bundle, petticoats bunched up, red hair streaming over them both.

"Jenny!" her mother bawled. "'Tis no way to behave."

Mr. Lewis frowned down at his wife. "Not another word, Mary. It's your fault the girls have been at the whiskey."

Aunt Alice held herself stiffly, but seemed somewhat appeased. Uncle Peter grinned. Without further interruption, Kira swiftly found herself before Reverend Wilkins.

Lowered to her feet, she half-stood half-sagged against Logan who kept his arm around her while surrounding faces looked on. Most were friendly, some not, but they failed to hold the power over her that they had before. True, the whiskey had eased her self-consciousness, but it was more than that. Jenny's friendship warmed her and Logan's love gave her courage. At that moment, Kira felt she could do anything.

Reverend Wilkins surveyed them with gentle solemnity. "Dearly beloved, we are gathered here today in the sight of God to join these two men and two women in holy wedlock…"

Was it truly possible these sacred words were intended for her and Logan? Events of the past week had happened so fast. Somewhere along the way she'd gone from adamant refusal to acceptance of his proposal. And here she was on the verge of uttering the vow that would make her his wife.

Gravity lessened her surge of confidence, but the shadows of the future didn't bear contemplation now. Not with golden sunshine streaming through the open door and Logan only a breath away. He smiled at her and she knew very well how she'd come to be here. There was no turning back.

"Stand united, facing life's struggles, joys and sorrows together. For divided you will surely fall."

Listening to Reverend Wilkins with only half an ear, Kira glanced at Jenny. Her glistening eyes were fixed on Will with tender hopefulness. Judging by the warmth in Will's expression, he seemed prepared to offer Jenny equal devotion.

"Therefore a man leaves his parents and cleaves to his wife and the two shall become one flesh."

The ancient words from *Genesis* recaptured Kira's distracted thoughts. Her heart quickened and not entirely from expectation; uncertainty mixed into the emotional blend swirling inside. Earlier with Logan, she'd had few qualms about intimacy. Now, in a house overflowing with people...

"Above all, love each other. And remember, 'Love beareth all things, believeth all things, hopeth all things, endureth all things. Love never fails.'" Here, Reverend Wilkins smiled and his perceptive eyes targeted Kira. "You have some understanding of what I speak. More will come. Trust in God and each other. And now, the exchange of vows. But first, I must ask, is there anyone here who knows of a valid reason why either of these couples should not be joined together? If so, let them speak now or forever hold their peace."

Her stomach caught. She half-expected Josiah to charge into the assembly with Captain Winn at his side bearing orders for Logan's arrest. Tense moments passed and she sensed she wasn't alone in her fears. But only a restless infant wailed and meadowlarks called from beyond the door.

The reverend seemed to share her relief. "Let us proceed. Logan Wallace McCutcheon, do you take this woman as your lawfully wedded wife, to have and to hold, to love and to cherish, in sickness and in health so long as you both shall live?"

"I do."

"Kira Anne McClure, do you take this man as your lawfully wedded husband, to have and to hold, to love and cherish, to honor and obey, in sickness and in health so long as you both shall live?"

All eyes were on her as she briefly contemplated this awesome undertaking, and shakily answered, "I do."

Nodding his approval, Reverend Wilkins turned to Will. The remainder of his words fell about her like soft rain.

"And now by the power vested in me, I pronounce you both man and wife."

This declaration regained her attention.

The minister beamed. "You may kiss the bride."

Anticipating only a quick kiss in front of onlookers, Kira was unprepared when Logan swept her up, covering her lips as though this was what he'd wanted for a very long time.

Cheering and clapping broke out. "McCutcheon's been gone ages. It's high time he got her!" one man said loudly.

"Campbell won't thank him!" another man countered.

"By heaven, that lass is worth risking Campbell's ire!"

"Ah, Cricket, you surely are."

She prayed so. He'd gained a menacing foe.

Chapter Fourteen

"Come and eat!" An eager stampede of guests heartily accepted Mister Lewis's invitation.

Logan watched women in linen aprons and white caps assist Mrs. Lewis serve up the mounds of roast pork, turkey, wild game, partridge pie, stewed vegetables, rhubarb, and cake. Clearly the Lewis clan intended to see to it that no one suffered from hunger. Places of honor had been reserved for the bridal pairs at one of the long trestle tables. Will and Jenny sat on the bench beside Reverend Wilkins. Across from them, Uncle Peter and Mister Lewis engaged in lively conversation as they ate.

Folks spilled throughout the house with laden plates and trenchers. Some settled on stools, chairs, and beds. Several young men sprawled on the floor. Scampering children, including Donald and David, fought for spots on the ladder to the loft, the stoop, or shared the steps with three black and tan hounds. The dogs, happily occupied with a meaty bone each, took scant interest in the children's portions.

Thrusting well-heaped trenchers into Logan's and Kira's hands, Aunt Alice urged, "Go on now. Sit you down."

Logan followed Kira's gaze up beyond the clamoring children to the shady trees at the edge of the meadow. He knew she'd far rather retreat to a secluded nook than face further scrutiny by the boisterous gathering.

Aunt Alice shook her head at Kira. "Oh no, my girl. March yourself over to that table."

Logan grinned. "No getting around you is there,

Aunt?"

"Not when you've had her care as long as I have. Take hold of your bride before she legs away like a spooked doe."

Chuckling, he gripped Kira's elbow and guided her through the jostling crowd toward the table. "Folks are counting on us, sweetheart," he said under his breath.

"There are so many."

"You can't hide every time you're uneasy."

"I could if—"

He'd anticipated her argument and wasn't letting go.

Bottle in hand, Mister Lewis waved them beside him. "Logan! Sit you down with your bonnie wife. 'Twill be a bit of a squeeze, but I don't reckon you two will mind that."

Nudging Kira ahead of him, Logan said in her ear, "Can't have you escaping off the end."

Blocked from retreat, she scooted along the bench and sat between him and Mister Lewis. And there she must remain until dinner was finished. The company could be worse, though. Mister Lewis was as unlike his wife as a friendly dog from a spitting cat. He was rough, as were his clothes. The grizzled brown hair pulled back at his thick neck matched his graying beard. He smelled rather like the big bear he resembled, but his eyes crinkled in a grin and his weathered face beamed warmth upon them.

"What a sight you are, Kira. Does me good to look on you." He chucked her lightly under the chin with thickened fingers. "Not to slight my own. Jenny does us proud. Seeing you gals together, why, there's none finer." He took a lengthy draw from the brown bottle, wiped his mouth on his plain homespun sleeve, and passed it to Logan. "You young fellows are mighty fortunate in your brides."

"We are that." Logan took a long swallow and returned the bottle.

Beaming at him, Mister Lewis said, "Not one to let the grass grow under your feet, are you, lad? Been back, what—a week—and already snatched up Campbell's woman?"

Uncle Peter frowned. "I wouldn't let that rascal have her anyway. Not after what he's done."

"Now Peter, you don't know for certain Campbell had a part in that thieving," Mister Lewis pointed out.

"Not that I can prove. But I damn well know he did."

A cautioning hand upraised, the reverend advised, "Don't lay charges against Mister Campbell until you have evidence."

"The fellow's already madder'n a treed coon. And he won't be getting a leg over this beauty, will he?" Mister Lewis chuckled.

Kira turned pink and Jenny's cheeks flushed. "Papa—"

His hearty laughter drowned out her protest.

Uncle Peter thudded his fist down onto the table. "By heaven, you're right, man. And I've my stolen goods back from the fellow and a bit more besides. Very generous of the man." Leaning across the table, he clapped Logan on the shoulder. "You've done me right good service wedding our Kira."

"My pleasure, Uncle."

"It will be!" Mister Lewis roared. "Haven't got her to yourself yet, have you?"

Jenny hid her face in her hands and Logan sensed Kira battling a strong impulse to flee.

With a snort, their host passed the bottle to Reverend Wilkins. "These girls carry on like they've taken the veil."

He simply smiled and raised the bottle. "For the bridal pairs, here's to your health. May the Lord richly bless you and keep you in his care."

Gratitude in her eyes, Kira said, "Thank you, sir."

"Blessings on you, lass. On you all." The reverend took a swallow and held the bottle out to Uncle Peter.

He lifted it high. "Here's to your health. May you have thumping good fortune and great children."

"Aye! Good fortune and great children!" Mister Lewis belted out. Men on all sides raised shared bottles and mugs of ale and echoed his salute.

Will inclined his head. "Thank you all. I'll do my best to bring on the children."

Hearty laughter resounded.

Logan lifted his cup. "And I shall do my part. The rest we must leave to God."

Mister Lewis reached behind Kira and walloped him on the back. "Well spoken. Good to have you among us, McCutcheon."

A chorus of approval swelled the gathering.

His host continued in a more pensive tone. "I thought a lot of your father, lad. 'Tis proud Henry would be of you."

The old pain pierced Logan. "I like to think so, sir."

Uncle Peter gazed at him with approval. "You've gone the long way round, Logan, but I'm right glad you've come home."

Guilt drove through him. He hadn't been straight with this man, with any of them. The fact that he couldn't be didn't erase the deed. To have such hard-won acceptance offered to him now twisted a knife into feelings he'd pushed deep inside. But he kept these sentiments to himself.

"I'm grateful to you—"

The promising pluck and whine of fiddles being tuned interrupted him. Glad for the change, he glanced at the corner of the room where the two oldest Lewis brothers readied their instruments.

Their father clapped his hands overhead. "Eat Up! The lads are about to begin!"

Anticipation eased the self-consciousness in Kira's face. "I love dancing," she said between hurried bites. "Three and four-handed reels, square sets, jigging, all of it."

"Rotten luck, Cricket. Your knee won't hold up to much."

"It will for a bit," she insisted.

"Yesterday you could barely walk."

"That was yesterday."

"You will end up troubling Mrs. Lewis for a poultice."

"I'll not trouble her for anything after this morning."

He frowned at her. "Then you'll be hurting and I won't have it."

"Logan, I'm not going to sit and watch the dancing at my own wedding."

"Dance a little then. But only a little, mind."

Stubbornness glinted in her eyes. "I shall dance for as long as I like."

"And when your knee gives out, what then? Have me haul you about?"

No reply. She chewed in silence.

"You'll stop at my say if I see you're suffering."

Still, she ignored him.

"You're as stubborn as a dog-eared horse!"

Mister Lewis grinned broadly. "At it already, are you? Give her what for, Logan. You'll soon make it up."

Uncle Peter smiled knowingly. "Didn't I say you were doing me a favor, lad? Enjoy your fair wife, but remember you must take the sour with the sweet."

No arguing with that wisdom. Kira was a challenge and would likely remain so, but he loved her more than his life.

****

Rollicking music filled the room and the colorful sight of the dancers lifted Kira's spirits. She might feel out of place here, but not while dancing. The fiddlers arms flew and the floor shook under all the stomping feet. She couldn't deny the growing ache in her knee, though, and glanced up breathlessly to see Logan shake his head at her.

"Rest a spell!" he shouted over the riotous festivity.

With great reluctance, she released his hand and stepped back to sink onto a stool in the corner. Plucking the kerchief from her lace-edged bodice, she patted her warm forehead while Logan jigged and whirled with the best of them. Absence hadn't lessened his appreciation of dancing, nor his ability. He stepped expertly around the room, the beads and silver cones on his shirt catching the light from the hearth.

Surrounding faces reflected their admiration. As much as Kira wanted him entering into the merriment, she wasn't eager to share him with the giggling young women. Before the dancing commenced, many people had given him an effusive welcome. The girls were especially pleased to have him back among them. Men also cheered his return. In one afternoon he'd become the center of the gathering with the approval of almost the entire settlement. Even Will, exceedingly popular in his own right, didn't command the draw his captivating cousin did. But jealousy wasn't evident in his smiling face. Will's admiring gaze was on Jenny and she sought him.

Both fiddlers paused to down mugs of ale before the next set and Emily Stewart rushed up to Logan. Tossing her blond curls, she wagged her finger at him. "You ought not to go getting wed before I even knew you were back!"

As if he would've chosen Emily instead. Serve her right to be carried off to the Shawnee or the French. None of the women casting long looks at this new arrival knew of Logan's divided loyalties or had any notion of the risk Kira had taken in wedding him.

The musicians struck up a reel and she saw him partnering the preening Emily. Warmth flashed through Kira and it wasn't tender passion.

"Have a drop, gal," a man invited.

Jared Lewis, another of Jenny's many red-headed brothers, stood quite close to her. It was apparent from his unsteady condition that he preferred drinking to dancing.

"I've had enough strong drink. Tea, if you please."

He gave her an odd look, but walked unsteadily toward the table. Returning with a cup, he held it out to her.

"Thank you, Jared."

"Most welcome." Clutching his bottle, he staggered back while she gulped cold sassafras tea.

Getting stiffly to her feet, Kira slipped from the resounding room. How long would it take Logan to notice her absence? A parting glance at him twirling Emily Stewart did nothing to further the expectation that it would be soon.

"Any man foolish enough to be taken in by that simpering creature is not as sharp as he thinks," she muttered to herself, stepping past the children on the stoop. Granted, Emily was fetching in a way some might find appealing, but Kira certainly never had. She passed excited children playing tag in the yard and limped past outbuildings and the garden.

"Where you going, Kira?" Donald called.

"To get a breath of fresh air."

"At your own wedding?"

"Especially then."

A shrug and he pelted after eight-year-old Elizabeth, the youngest member of the Lewis clan. "Got you!" he yelled, tumbling her to the ground.

Not content with that, he seemed bent on pinning the girl as he did David. Auburn ringlets flew as she kicked up a valiant fight. "You oughtn't to wrestle girls!" Kira chided.

"Why?"

"'Tisn't proper."

"Why?" he repeated, struggling to gain victory over his tenacious opponent.

Elizabeth threw him over and emerged on top. "Got you back, Donald!"

Leaving them to their rough play, Kira lifted the latch in the slatted gate set between two posts and pushed it open into the large split rail enclosure. Sheep watched idly as she traipsed across the meadow to the spring and knelt at the edge to cup mouthfuls of the cold bubbling water. Wetting her handkerchief, she sponged her face and neck. The vibrant music reached her here, but she had no desire to return. If Logan wanted her, he could jolly well seek her out.

Late afternoon sunlight slanted through the emerald leaves of nearby trees. She rose and limped to the shade of a locust dripping with snowy panicles and settled at the base, inhaling the sweet scent. Mild breezes cooled her heated cheeks, also her temper. Bees hummed overhead, lulling her with their soft drone. She leaned against the trunk and closed her eyes. Perhaps she'd been too hasty to take offense with Logan. After all, he'd only just returned and this was his first dance. And he was far more sociable than she—

"Well, well. Weary of your husband already, Kira?"

Her heart nearly stopped and she jerked her head around. Not twenty yards away was Josiah on his horse. Scrambling to her feet, she shouted, "You've some nerve turning up here!"

He swung his leg over the stallion and dropped to the ground. "Can't a man wish his neighbor happiness at his wedding?"

"Not a man who wants to be the groom." Snatching up her skirts, she spun away, shrieking, as he caught her arm.

He whipped her back around to face his cold fury. "I can still be the groom, once you're a widow."

"Donald! Josiah's come!" she shouted, praying he heard over the music.

"They'll know soon enough."

The menacing calm in his reply alarmed her more than his previous threats. She pulled wildly to free her arm from his grip. "If you think to just walk up to Logan and attack him, I warn you he's well liked."

"That will change once they know the truth."

She froze. "None will believe you."

"Captain Winn was most interested in every detail. He wants to question your husband."

Ragged breaths made speech difficult. "Winn can't charge Logan. You've no proof—only that you saw some white man with a party of warriors. It was growing dark. You can't be certain who shot you."

A slow smile curved Josiah's lips. "How did you know the hour of the day?"

She gulped. "You said—I'm sure you said."

"Never. I wager I know who did, though."

Horror welled at her blunder. "It makes no difference!"

"Ah, but it does. Let's get along to Lewis's and recollect some more."

"They want nothing to do with you after learning our horses were tracked back to your holding."

The insinuating smile still lurked at his mouth.

"Who's to say it wasn't Logan making it look like I did it?"

"Only a fool would believe that."

"Folks can be made to believe anything, little darling."

As Kira knew all too well. With the fury of a gathering storm, she drew herself up and lashed out, "Hear me well, Josiah Campbell. If you go anywhere near my husband you shall rue the day."

"Will I indeed?"

"Leave us be or I'll put a hex on you."

He arched reddish brows. "Did I hear you rightly?"

"You did."

Cold blue eyes glittered at her like a snake's. "Claiming to be a witch now, are you?"

"What do you think Hannah's been teaching me all this time?"

"You're mad."

"Am I? Ask your cousin about the owl calling his name."

Disbelief widened his narrow gaze. No turning back now. "I was that owl."

"Like hell you were."

As much fear as anger underlay his retort. "I can assume any shape I like. A horse. A hare. An owl. And I can find you *wherever* you go."

He scowled, "You're just trying to scare me off."

"Maybe. And maybe I'll hex the life out of you!"

"Kira!" a woman cried from behind her. *Jenny*.

She turned to see people swarming out of the house and across the meadow. Logan and Will were out in front and Jenny ran for all she was worth to keep up. Uncle Peter, Mister Lewis and Aunt Alice were further back with the others.

"A witch and a traitor," Josiah sneered. "You deserve each other. I wonder what they'll all make of this?"

"Nothing. One word against Logan and you'll discover just what kind of power I have," she whispered fiercely.

Logan reached her first and jerked her away from Josiah. "What are you doing here, Campbell?"

His contemptuous gaze passed between them. "Ask the witch."

A guttural yowl tore from Logan. More incensed than Kira had ever seen him, he hurled himself at Josiah and flung him to the ground. He slammed down, grunting from the impact.

Will sprang forward and Kira started toward them.

"My fight!" Logan yelled.

She waited uncertainly beside Will as he dodged Josiah's fist and struck out hard. Again and again Logan pummeled him. Josiah threw him off, but not for long. Logan launched at him anew. He'd fought well at the Houston home place, but now it was as if he possessed the strength of ten men coupled with the wrath of a wounded grizzly.

His relentless fist slammed Josiah then he bent over him and slicked his knife from its sheath. Pressing the blade so closely to his throat he drew blood, Logan hissed. "Serpent. Call Kira that again and I swear you die now."

Crimson ran from Josiah's swollen lips. "She says it of herself."

Logan's eyes burned, the gold-flecks, hot coals. "Want to live, Campbell?"

Josiah scotched him with equal rage, but said nothing.

"Shut your mouth, get back on your horse and ride."

A hush came over the gathering. All wondered what Josiah would do. Kira waited in agonizing uncertainty. At a nod from the beaten man, Logan straightened. Josiah staggered to his feet and reeled to his waiting stallion. Cheering and whistling broke out as he rode away.

Mister Lewis spoke first. "Hell of a fighter, that nephew of yours, Peter."

The ridges had a new champion, but Kira feared the old one would battle again with even greater treachery. She flung herself into Logan's arms.

His chest heaved from the fight as he clutched her to him. "Not a word out of you," he breathed into her ear with more than the hint of a growl.

She stiffened. Not all of his anger had departed with Josiah. Plenty remained for her.

Uncle Peter seemed unaware as he clapped Logan on the back. "Hurrah. I couldn't have fought him better myself."

"High praise indeed, Uncle."

Aunt Alice hugged them both tearfully. "I was never so frightened hearing Mister Campbell was with our Kira."

Donald and David pressed around her. "You all right?"

Swallowing hard, she nodded.

Logan tousled their copper heads. "She'll be fine. Don't fret."

Over the hubbub, Uncle Peter bawled, "I reckon it was bound to happen, Campbell picking a fight. I just didn't expect the cheeky bastard would turn up today."

Will kept his arm around a silent, shaken Jenny. "It didn't surprise me any."

The crowd rumbled in agreement. "The fellow hates like the very devil to give her up," Mister Lewis said. "He'll be brooding on what he's missing tonight."

"Enough of that talk," his wife chided. "Get the girl inside. What's she doing out here alone in the first place?"

"Kira likes it out of doors," Aunt Alice said in

her defense. "Go back in now, lass."

Logan retained his hold on her. "You all go ahead. Kira and I will be along shortly."

"You'll have her to yourself soon enough."

"Allow us a moment please, Aunt."

Mister Lewis nodded vigorously. "The man has earned the right. And more besides. Come on, folks. Let's see if there are any tunes left in these boys of mine."

A chorus of approval rose and people headed back toward the homestead. Smoke from the gray stone chimney drifted up into the lavender swirling across the pinkening sky.

"Will, Jenny, stay a moment," Logan requested.

Both stood as they were.

Uncle Peter swiped fondly at his son. "Your mama and I are heading back home now. Chores are late. Take good care of that sweet wife of yours, you hear?"

"You can count on it, Papa. I'll see you all soon enough."

"That you will. I'll expect you home in a day or two."

Eyes glistening, Aunt Alice embraced her new daughter-in-law. "I'm right proud to have you in the family."

"Thank you, Mrs. Houston. I'm proud to be a part."

She gave Will an affectionate pat and beckoned to the twins. "Come along, boys."

"Can't we play a wee bit longer?"

Their father clamped a hand on each small shoulder. "You've had enough of a day," and then to Kira, "Heed Logan, lass. He's your husband now."

"Do," Aunt Alice sniffed. "He's not the boy you used to scrap with."

"He'd whup you good if you tried," Donald said. "Someday I'm gonna whup that Elizabeth."

Smiling, Uncle Peter guided his sons toward the stable. "Someday you'll have very different notions of what to do with Elizabeth Lewis."

What did Logan intend to do with her, Kira wondered nervously. Grim lines edged his mouth, and he kept a tenacious hold on her arm. Worst of all, he emanated wrath.

****

Only Will and Jenny remained behind. Logan didn't doubt Kira was tempted to flee the anger she sensed boiling just beneath the surface of the front he'd put on. Likely she wished to return home with his aunt and uncle until he simmered down. That, he prevented.

In a barely perceptible voice, he said to Will and his new wife, "I know you heard how Kira threatened Campbell."

Will leaned in closely. "We'll be fortunate if we're the only ones who did. She fairly shouted it."

"I don't think anyone else heard. They said nothing. Please, don't breathe a word of this."

"I surely won't," Will promised.

But it was Jenny Logan was really appealing to.

Her troubled eyes searched Kira's in the descending twilight. "I won't tell a soul. Why did you say such a dreadful thing? Are you that afraid of Mister Campbell?"

"Terribly," Logan answered before Kira could reply. "She sometimes says crazy things to put folks off."

"Really crazy this time," Will added.

"You don't understand—"

"We do, sweetheart." Logan wasn't about to let Kira worsen an already intolerable situation. "Campbell's a great brute. 'Tis behind you now."

The shock in Jenny's face diminished and she hugged Kira. "Don't fear so. He's not likely to trouble you again after the beating he took." She gazed up

215

admiringly at Logan. "You fought mighty fine, Mister McCutcheon."

Flashing Jenny a smile, he coaxed, "None of that mister stuff. Call me Logan. After all, we're family now."

Her lips curved responsively. "You must call me Jenny."

"Certainly, Jenny. What a lovely name."

Will shook his head and gave him a look as if to say, *you're doing it again.* "Excuse us, cousin. I think I'll bear my wife away before she pays you any more mind."

"Come to the house soon," Jenny invited over her shoulder.

"Indeed we shall!" Logan answered.

"I'll have you know I whipped Campbell myself several days ago," he heard Will tell his new bride as they walked away in the dusky light.

The instant the two were out of ear shot, Logan rounded on Kira. "Are you completely out of your mind? Do you wish to become an utter outcast?"

Despite forewarning, she seemed taken aback. "I was trying to prevent you from becoming one and being hung to boot. Josiah's spoken to Captain Winn just as he threatened. Now Winn wants to question you."

"Winn's got no proof," Logan said tersely.

"He has a bit more now than he did," she said shakily.

"What are you saying?"

"Logan, I'm sorry. I said Josiah couldn't know who shot him, that it was growing dark—a detail he never told me."

Logan cursed under his breath. "Even so, you had no call to go and make yourself out to be devil's spawn."

"Josiah was going to tell everyone about you. I had to do something. I didn't realize I was overheard."

"Campbell heard you and will tell anyone who'll listen."

"Maybe not. You scared him pretty badly. And say what you like, I surely did."

Grasping her upper arms, Logan gave her a shake. "For God's sake, this isn't one of your games. You claimed to be a damn witch."

"For you—I did it for you," she choked out.

"I never asked you to. Let me fight my own battles."

"You might have lost this one."

"Have a little faith. The Houston and Lewis clans are highly regarded. I'm aligned with both. They'll not readily turn against me."

"Folks loathe Indians, Logan, and wouldn't easily forgive what you've done."

"They aren't overly fond of witches either. Besides, I don't think they would believe what Josiah says of me."

"Will suspects the truth."

He groaned. "Have you said something to him as well?"

"No. And he'd never betray you, so long as—" she heaved a shuddering sigh. "You don't betray the family."

"Dear God. Do you think I'd turn on my own?"

"Not willingly. But if you had to choose sides—"

"Kira, every warrior acquainted with me knows who my people are and where the homestead lies. They will not be attacked."

"Is there to be fighting, then?" she asked in a small voice.

"Not that I know of. But war is inevitable."

"At least it's not imminent. You still have Captain Winn to deal with."

"Not unless he comes for me tonight. I doubt the *gallant* captain is eager to storm the Lewis

217

stronghold."

"Cowards are sometimes the cruelest. He's had men beaten and hung."

"I'll stay ahead of him. As for you, I've yet to hear a word of regret from those fair lips. Have you no fear for your immortal soul?"

"When did you become a preacher?"

"When you became a witch."

"I didn't mean any of it—just words to frighten Josiah."

"Words matter, Kira. And God heard every one you spoke."

Faltering under his rebuke, she said with less assurance, "God knows my heart. Surely he will forgive me."

"Do you truly wish forgiveness?"

"Yes."

"Swear to me you will never again speak anything so dangerous."

"But you're asking me to concede my best defense."

"You're a healer, Kira. With such a gift, surely you can trust in God, not in your odd ways?"

She said nothing.

"I am waiting for your assurance and I'm not relenting until I receive it."

"All right. I swear not to speak any more witchcraft."

"No more hiding or pretending. We're taking what comes together, beginning with seeing this day through."

She shrank from him. "I can't go back in there. Not after this."

"If we don't return they'll come looking for us."

"Let them. It'll soon be pitch dark."

"No more hiding, remember?"

"I never promised that!"

"I'm promising for you."

"Logan—no!"

Ignoring her protest, he lifted her up in his arms and bore her back toward the cabin. The music and accompanying revelry drowned out any further dissent.

Chapter Fifteen

Deaf to her pleas, Logan carried Kira back inside the lively homestead. She'd promised what he demanded but still sensed his underlying vexation. Maybe because she wasn't as sorry as he wanted. Well, it was easy enough for him to face Josiah—he could pound him into the ground. She had only her wiles, and desperate times called for desperate measures.

All right, maybe she'd gone a bit too far this time. Being labeled a witch would get her shunned—or worse.

Did the gathering know of her outrageousness? Acutely self-conscious, she gripped his neck and surveyed the figures stepping to an English Country dance played by the hard-pressed fiddlers. People not on their feet sat in any available space. Young women occupied many a young man's lap and no one seemed to mind, particularly the men. Exuberant children joined in the celebration while the littlest ones slumbered in shadows.

Mister Lewis sat at one of the tables with several older men engaged in animated conversation while lowering the level of a brown bottle. Other bottles passed from hand-to-hand, mostly male, although the women weren't averse to a swallow.

Wiping her hands on her striped apron, Mrs. Lewis trotted up to Logan and Kira. Sharp eyes passed over him and bore into Kira. "Had to haul you back here, did he, girl?" She turned away with an affronted sniff.

Laughter rang out from onlookers who'd noted

Kira's manner of arrival. Mister Lewis pounded his fist on the table. "Not taking a chance on her getting away, are you!"

Logan smiled. "None."

"I can walk," Kira reminded him.

"Right out the door," he answered through smiling lips in a voice only she could hear.

"Logan—I swear—"

"Not here, you don't," he corrected in that maddeningly amicable manner he'd adopted.

Mister Lewis beckoned. "Come on over here."

"Find some excuse to get me away from them," she pleaded.

"Very well." Still bearing her, Logan strode to the table. The men made room and he sat on the bench with her on his lap while surrounding faces studied them in amusement.

A highly amused Mister Lewis held out the bottle to Logan. "Got her right where you want her, eh?"

Logan grasped the drink and took a swig. "Not quite."

The table broke up in laughter. Other folk glanced around to see what the joke was, prodding their neighbors until it had circled the room. Everyone seemed in high spirits except Kira, whose toes curled, and Logan whom she sensed was a better actor than she when he chose to be.

Mister Lewis walloped him on the back. "Want to get her alone, then?"

Logan choked on the swallow he'd just taken. "I'd not put up a fight," he managed in a strangled voice.

Their host threw back his head, laughing harder. "Just as well. No man wants to challenge you. Mary! See these two settled. Will and Jenny, too."

"Now? 'Tis hardly time yet," his wife argued, as

221

if any intimacy commencing before ten o'clock was a blatant sin.

Her husband wiped at streaming eyes. "Don't get high-handed with me, woman. Jenny won't put up a fuss. Not certain about Kira, though. Nearly had to hogtie you to get back in here, didn't he, gal?"

Wishing herself most anywhere else, she forced a smile. "Logan's just playing about."

"Well then," Mister Lewis, chuckled, "if nothing's wanting, let's get you four seen to."

Kira rushed to extricate herself. "I would much rather see to myself, sir."

He waved her protest aside. "In my house? We'll see you properly put to bed."

There'd be little propriety about it, Kira had no doubt, and eyed the door longingly.

"Oh no you don't," Logan said in her ear.

Emily Stewart detached herself from the frolicsome company. Jenny Lewis joined in and they pounced on Kira. "Come on!" they giggled, tugging her from his lap.

Releasing her with an apologetic shrug, he left Kira to her fate—the toad.

"I'll come to you, sweetheart," he said, as the two vixens herded her across the room.

More peals of laughter. "That he will."

They must all be intoxicated.

Emily put her foot on the first rung of the ladder and climbed toward the loft. Her green petticoat rose over Kira's head as she climbed.

Jenny nudged her. "Now you, Kira."

She much preferred the relative privacy of the stable, dark and musty as it was. "You should be the one in the loft, Jenny. 'Tis your home, after all, and Will won the race."

"Never mind about that. You've had more than your share of troubles today. 'Tis the least we can do to make amends."

"How kind," Kira made herself murmur, envisioning Aunt Alice's mortification if she refused their hospitality. Not to mention Logan's displeasure. She dutifully placed her foot on the ladder and followed Emily.

Clearly pleased with herself, Emily reached down from the loft and gripped Kira's upper arms to help her up the final rung. "Must be awkward for you in such heavy skirts. My, what glorious cloth," she said, pulling Kira beside her. They straightened, and Emily smoothed the creamy lilac-flowered fabric and the lavender bows at Kira's bodice. "I've never seen such a gown. Have you three petticoats on under?"

"Two. One is embroidered and the other's all ruffles."

Emily arched dark brows. "Really? Let's have a look."

Instantly, Kira regretted her words. "I can't undress up here."

"Sure you can." Emily caught up the woven blanket from the narrow bedstead in the corner and spread the burgundy cloth over the rail at the edge of the loft. "Don't be shy. You have to change out of that gown anyway."

"But the men—"

"Won't be along with Logan for a bit yet." Heedless of Kira's discomfiture, Emily began unlacing her bodice.

The light in the loft was much fainter than in the room below, but Kira wasn't invisible. "How long is a bit?"

"Long enough for us to ready you."

"Why must I be ready?"

Emily giggled. "You think Logan will bed you clothed?"

Jenny joined in as if at the merriest joke. For the life of her, Kira couldn't imagine what she'd said to cause such amusement.

Emily rustled the taffeta down over her shoulders. "With so many men after you I'm surprised you don't know more."

"I ran or hid."

Feminine laughter chorused around her. And Emily whisked away her gown. "You can't take off tonight, not that any sensible girl would want to run from Logan McCutcheon."

Whoever said Kira was sensible? Not a claim she'd made, though she was likely the only sane and sober female present. Arms wrapped around her chest, she wanted nothing more than speedy flight.

Emily smoothed the whispering cloth. "What a feel," she sighed, passing the gown to Jenny. She pushed Kira's arms aside to better see the beribboned corset. "How pretty."

Jenny nodded with a wistful air. "Isn't it?"

The next thing Kira knew Emily spun her around to attack the laces in back. "Louise, come see her corset and petticoats!" she shouted above the fiddles and revelry.

Men roared, and Kira wanted to crawl under the bed.

Moments later, Louise's curly brown hair appeared at the edge of the loft. She squealed. "So many bows and lace."

Not to be left out, her younger sister, Sally, climbed up. She drank Kira in. "Oh, my. How are the seams done?"

"Let's see." Emily tugged at the ties keeping Kira's petticoats in place.

A faint cry escaped her as they fell down around her ankles. Stumbling out of the vanishing skirts, she stood, shaking, in her shift. Then Emily jerked the cord at Kira's neck and stripped the embellished underdress overhead.

Naked—she was naked!

Oblivious of Kira's strangled croak, she pronounced, "Such fine linen, ruffled at the neck and hem."

Jenny distractedly passed Kira the remaining blanket from the bedstead. She clutched it about her as they turned the coveted clothing inside out and examined every minute detail.

"The light's mighty poor up here," Sally lamented.

Emily snatched the blanket from the railing. "Bring the gown nearer the edge."

Springing onto the bed, Kira huddled in her coverlet.

"Can we have a peek?" more women entreated from below.

Emily called back, "There's not room up here!"

"Fetch everything down, then."

If a rattlesnake hid beneath her covers, Kira couldn't have been more startled. "The men will all see!"

"Men aren't concerned with such stuff," Jenny said.

"This time they will be—"

Excited chatter drowned her protest. Gathering her clothes, the girls rushed down the ladder. The music dwindled under the onslaught of feminine enthusiasm.

Benjamin Lewis rested his fiddle. "Are we dancing or looking at Kira's finery?"

"Finery!" the women chorused.

Mary Lewis feigned indifference. Bless her. If swoons came for the asking, Kira would faint dead away and be done with this torment. Painfully conscious, she turned her back on the gaiety below and gazed out the small window cut in the logs. Stars winked at her and the moon shone milky white. It would be full soon, and like the changing orb this humiliation would pass. She'd never live it down, but it would pass.

"Give that poor girl back her things!" Mister Lewis boomed. "'Tisn't right to go carrying them off like magpies. Let's commence the dancing."

Thankfully, both fiddles resumed. Jenny and Emily reappeared in the loft, arms overflowing with cloth. They reluctantly laid her clothes over a leather-bound trunk.

"We'll send Logan up with the men now," Jenny said.

Reaching out, Kira clasped her hand in a near death-hold. "Please—just send Logan."

"It breaks with tradition to have him come up alone, but I'll try to persuade them. You know men, though."

"Not nearly as well as you."

Jenny squeezed her fingers. "You'll be all right. Logan knows what he's about. Any woman can see that."

Kira would rather that weren't so obvious.

Head cocked to one side, Emily scrutinized her. "Be grateful you wed where you did. I wish I could be half as fortunate as you and Jenny."

"So do I." Kira badly wished Emily were away with her husband now, unable to attend the wedding and strip her of her finery. Starving vultures couldn't have picked her cleaner.

"How sweet, Kira. I didn't realize you cared so."

"Heartily."

"You're a dear."

"Indeed she is." Jenny bent over Kira and gave her a quick hug. "I'm off to the stable now to await Will." Glad expectation welled in her words.

"Are there any men left worth having?" Emily moaned.

Jenny stepped toward the ladder and gathered her skirts. "Why not think on Jared? He's quite tolerable, really."

"Jared can hardly stand," Emily pointed out.

"Not now, but he can when he's sober. And that's most days," Jenny said, and disappeared over the edge of the loft.

Lord, spare me any more, Kira implored the Almighty, and slid further beneath the coverlet. One thing was for certain, she was never being wed again.

****

With the wariness of one fearing to be shot, Logan raised his head up over the side of the loft. By the orange glow radiating from the room below and the moonlight streaming through the small window above her, he spotted Kira curled in a ball beneath the blanket, her face turned to the wall, shoulders heaving in a tearful sniff.

"Kira, I'm here."

She looked around with a mournful expression.

"Is it safe to join you, or will you toss things at me?"

Wiping at her eyes, she said, "What would I throw? They've taken most everything."

"Your shoes?"

"I'm still wearing them."

"In bed?"

A shuddering sigh, then, "Oh, Logan. I was never so mortified."

He climbed the rest of the way into the loft. "Poor Cricket. You sound like a wounded kitten."

"We should have run away when we had the chance."

"Too late for that now." He stood and restored the blanket at the railing, their sole concealment apart from the shadows. "These truly are fine petticoats," he offered.

"Which every man in this house has seen. And my stays."

"They didn't mind," he assured her

227

"I do. Told you I didn't want to come back here again."

In a few strides he reached her and lowered himself onto the side of the bed. "I never said coming back would be easy, just right."

Glistening eyes reproached him. "Then I'll settle for wrong. I want to go home."

"Wearing only your shoes and stockings?"

"You could help me dress."

Her hair, more down than up now, tumbled all about her. He stroked a luxurious length. "That's not what I've been sent up here for."

"You don't have to do what they sent you for."

Trailing his fingers over her smooth cheek, he said, "I'd very much like to."

For a tremulous moment she made no reply. "Would you?"

He smiled. "More than I can say."

She uncurled a little from her tight ball. "This morning so would I. Now I'm wretched."

"I can be very soothing." Bending lower, he covered her quivering lips with his firm mouth. She tasted salty-sweet and infinitely desirable. Slipping his arms around her, he drew her up against him. Kissing Kira was the most natural, and yet, thrilling thing in the world.

As if drifting into a dream, she relaxed in his arms, her supple lips returning his kiss—then she tensed again and broke from his mouth. "What of all the people?"

"They can't see us back here."

"Are you certain? Someone may come."

"I threatened to pound any man who did."

Breath escaped her in an evident relief. "None will challenge you after your fight with Josiah, but the women will bring food."

"Not for quite a while. I warned them as well."

"That's even braver than threatening the

menfolk." Admiration in her voice, Kira reached for his hand. "But I still want to go home."

The trusting feel of her slender fingers moved him more than he could say. He tightened his grip on her smaller hand. "We can't return there now. Josiah and his men will be watching for us. Besides, you know where we must journey."

"The McCutcheon homestead."

"Yes," though it chilled him to think of it. Something about that place made his blood run cold, and it wasn't sentiment alone that unnerved him.

Her gaze lifted to the window and the moon. "'Tis nearly full."

The white orb shining through the trees silvered every bough. "And nearly time. I have a rendezvous to keep."

"Do you still intend to go away with your friends?"

"Half of me wants to remain here among my kin, while the other half longs to rejoin my sister and adopted family."

Her eyes turned back to his. "Which half is stronger?"

Holding her fingers to his lips, he warmed the chilled tips with his breath. "Don't ask me that now."

"When?"

"Another day. Tonight my thoughts are all for you."

She curled her hand at his mouth. "Only me? Has that ever been?"

"All the time, sweetheart. Remember, whatever I choose, I will keep you with me always and guard you with me life."

For a long moment neither of them spoke, the silence between them filled with a world of emotion no words could truly capture. "Kira, I love you to the depths of my soul. Please trust me."

Eyes searching his, she said, "I'll try."

A concession he cherished and as much as he could hope for. Cupping her face with his hands, he tenderly covered her mouth with his then pressed his lips over her cheek...her neck and shoulder...down the length of her arm to her palm, spreading goose bumps as he went. Pausing to ask, "Tell me, Mrs. McCutcheon, is there room in that bed for two, or must I spend the night sitting on the edge?"

"There might be room, Mr. McCutcheon."

Pleasure shimmered through him at her slightly breathless invitation. "I hoped there might."

"I rather like my new title, Logan. Don't go changing it to some Indian name."

He smiled. "I won't." Releasing her hand, he undid his belt, adding that and his sheathed knife to the feminine pile on the chair. Then he pulled his shirt over his head.

Bathed in moonlight, she pushed up on her elbows, the blanket falling down over her exquisite shoulders. "Why is it you're allowed to disrobe unaided?"

He tossed his shirt aside. "The men aren't nearly as taken with my attire as the women are with yours. But you can help me if you like," he teased, and unfastened the top button of his breeches.

She glanced away. "I think not."

"Suit yourself."

Hugging the blanket around her with one hand, she reached to her feet with the other and slid her shoes to the floor. "You're fortunate the women didn't have your shirt off and your breeches too. Many wanted a closer look, I don't doubt."

"At me or my clothes?" he chuckled.

"Both."

"The difference between us, dear heart, is that I wouldn't mind."

"Good heavens. Haven't you a shy bone in your

body?"

"Not really."

Her innate modesty was appealing, but he hoped to coax her into deeper revelation. He unbuttoned the rest of his flap and stepped out of his breeches. Only the narrow woven belt at his waist remained, and that he never removed. Shawnee tradition held that he'd forfeit his manhood if he did so and he wasn't inclined to take any chances.

"Kira, sweetheart…" Stroking his fingers over her cheek, he tilted her face toward him. "Don't you think you ought to see what you've married? I suspect there's a prominent part of my anatomy that will take some getting used to."

She slanted her eyes at him and dropped her jaw. Then clapped her hand over her mouth, uncovering it again just as quickly to blurt out, "You're quite handsome—most of you, anyway. I'll wager other women have said the same."

He laughed. "Not droves of them. Besides, it means far more coming from you."

"Let's keep it that way."

"Fine," he agreed, sitting back down on the bed, "if you'll share that blanket with your poor, cold husband."

She lifted a corner of the coverlet and he scooted in beside her. "You're not the least bit cold."

"You're like ice, but not for long." She sucked in her breath as he gathered her to him, not wanting to frighten her, just *wanting* her.

"*Ahhhh*, that's more like it," he said, savoring the sensation of skin against skin and her rounded breasts pushing against his chest. How unspeakably worth all the trouble she was and how he relished this dreamlike moment. It seemed as though she couldn't be real, but she was. He lightly kissed down the curve of her neck until tremors rippled through her, almost too much exhilaration to bear.

231

She gasped, "You tingle me to my toes."

"Better than mortified."

"Much." She circled her arms around his neck and boldly sought his mouth.

"You move very fast, darling," he teased.

"Not so very fast. I've waited seven years for you."

And it seemed as if she couldn't get enough of him, while urgency to have ever more of her swiftly mounted in him. "Whew…when did you learn to kiss like that, my girl?"

"From you."

"It had better have been me. You're a fast learner."

"Oh, yes."

He bore down harder on her mouth, bending her under the force of his ardor, before letting her pause for breath.

As if sensing their passion, the fiddlers departed from lively jigs and reels and played a lilting melody, rich and full, that blended with their surging love.

Kira arched, shivering, as he trailed his lips over her shoulders and delved lower, tugging at her irresistible breasts. Her nipples ripened beneath his mouth…tempting him to linger there while she squirmed delightfully. Like a balmy summer breeze, she wafted over him. At least, that's the only comparison he could make to her glorious warmth pressed against him, her soft, heated lips seeking his.

"Still with me?" he said, knowing full well that she was.

She slipped her fingers through his hair. "What if I wasn't?"

Curling his hands around the supple curve of her bottom, he promised, "I would coax you along."

"Where are you going, Logan?" she asked in a whisper.

"I expect you can guess."

As if floating on the currents, she let him direct her path. His heart doubled its already pounding pace. And she scarcely contained the sighs of pleasure and small breathes escaping her.

"If I didn't know better, I'd say you'd done this before, Cricket," he chuckled.

"I have...with you."

Her hair tickled his cheek as he bent over her. "When, wouldn't I remember?"

"In my dreams, only you're taking me much farther now."

"I'll take you farther still." Wrapping her in his arms, he reclaimed her mouth.

"Are we racing?" Kira asked against his lips, panting as though she were.

His chest rose and fell above hers. "In a way...but we'll both win this one."

Chapter Sixteen

Wheeeeee!

Like a summons shrilling across the years, the whistle pierced the mantle of sleep enveloping Logan. His groggy thoughts sailed back to his father standing on the front stoop, fingers to his lips, calling him back to the house. That whistle easily carried across the meadow.

Logan!

He could've sworn his father had called his name, but that was as impossible as the whistle. Cradling Kira in that place between wake and sleep, he strained to hear.

Logan Wallace McCutcheon!

Good heavens, his whole name, and shouted just as his father used to do. He'd wanted to call Logan, William Wallace, after the Scot's hero, but his mother had preferred Logan. And Henry McCutcheon deferred to his adored wife.

Was Logan really hearing him? *Papa?*

A rugged frontiersman approached through the mist, chestnut hair pulled back beneath a dark felt hat with rust-gold pheasant feathers and a red fox tail attached to the brim, just as his father had worn. Creases borne of wind and sun furrowed his face, a kind face and well-featured, with intent blue eyes. There was no mistaking this man.

To see his father again after all these years, if only in a dream, brought a lump to Logan's throat. He'd never had the chance to bid him farewell. When he strayed from the fort to hunt that day, he hadn't any idea it was their final parting. Then came the

234

terrible news from Cousin Rebecca of his father's death during the assault on Fort Warden. By that time he and Tessa were captives and there was nothing Logan could do but see to it they survived.

With the aid of several powerful warriors, not only had they lived, but thrived, and Logan grew accustomed to his new life. Now...this odd homeward call. He lay as if drugged while his father drew near and stopped a few feet away.

His sharp gaze scrutinizing Logan, he ran callused fingers over the brown beard roughening his chin. "I'm calling you, lad. Do you hear me?"

"Yes." Logan struggled to reach out to him, but sleep weighed him too heavily.

His father bent and laid a hand on his bare shoulder. The heat from his palm felt as if he were really there.

"I've been waiting on you for some time now, lad."

"And Mama?"

A smile warmed Henry McCutcheon's earnest gaze. "She never really left us. Get on home."

Regret welled in Logan. "I can't stay, Papa."

Vexation flickered in his blue eyes. "You can come, by heaven, before you go again. A task awaits you."

"Finding the treasure?"

He snorted. "Besides the coins."

"What of Kira?"

"Bring her. She's a vital part of what lies ahead. And you're one fortunate fellow to have her. You want to keep her in your care, get a move on before day breaks." With that, his father turned and disappeared into the haze.

And Logan lay wondering what in the world that was all about, a mystical visitation from beyond, or simply a dream. If the latter, that was one vivid dream, the ire in his father's face as clear as when he'd annoyed him as a youth. Despite the love between them, they'd often butted heads. Here they were separated by death, and still at it.

Another question crossed his dazed mind. How did his father know of the gold? Shoka hadn't left it in the cabin until after Henry McCutcheon's death at Fort Warden.

****

Encircling Kira with one arm and holding the reins with his other, Logan guided Tequi over the darkened trail. The moon shone through gathering clouds and the woods were still, as if waiting. Deep inside, so was Logan, though he didn't know for what. His strange dream, if that's what it was, left him disturbed. Uneasiness at visiting his old home place didn't gladden his heart any.

Thank God Kira tucked drowsily against him. Now, to keep her safe. Sliding his hand down his side, he fingered the handle of his tomahawk and knife, worn to fit his grip. His musket, an old friend, hung across his shoulder. Even the weapons didn't make him feel secure enough, though.

Gradually the birds awakened and birdsong accompanied their stealthy journey. The stars shining between the clouds faded and pale light filtered through the forest. Soft rose colored the rim of the eastern sky, and a watery sun rose above the trees. Trunks, rocks, and leaves took form. A stream tumbled nearby, familiar sights and sounds.

The land was far less traveled since the Indian wars. Only large parties of warriors dared come this near the settlement now, but mistrust ran deep and few settlers ventured here except frontiersmen, and possibly Josiah Campbell along with Captain Winn and his party.

Alert to the slightest snap of a twig or movement in the underbrush, Logan continually scanned the woodland for anything that didn't belong. He'd bet Josiah expected him to take Kira back to the Houstons' holding, and she'd dearly love to go. But that wasn't possible now, maybe not ever. Strangely that thought grieved him too.

The chill breeze snatched lengths of her hair from beneath her hooded cloak and tickled his cheek. How he wished he could've stretched out the night and made love to her again before they left. He ought to be able to cherish his new bride for more than a few short hours before tackling only God knows what.

Miles fell away beneath the steady tread of hooves. Gray clouds covered the sun. This rough-hewn path made the road they'd traveled yesterday seem smooth by comparison. Mountain laurel thickets and green briar hedged them in. Branches snapped from trees during winter ice storms, even entire tree trunks, lay across their path.

Logan dismounted and led Tequi across a log capped with yellow toadstools. "We're almost there," he said over his shoulder, his voice low to safeguard their presence. "I hope Josiah and his curs are watching the wrong trail, but can't be certain. Or if he will try and catch us up later."

"What can you be certain of?"

"That I adore you, Mrs. McCutcheon." And that they were in grave danger if their pursuers caught them before they reached the loyal band awaiting him deeper in the frontier.

****

The gravity in Logan's face dimmed the pleasure Kira felt at her new title. Gone, the humor he normally exuded. He hadn't seemed himself since he'd awakened her before sunrise and they'd slipped away. But she'd said nothing. Reluctance at leaving the others and fear over what lay ahead heavily weighed her. With a somber look, he remounted Tequi and secured her in his hold.

As the stalwart horse carried them near the homestead, the dense trees thinned out and they passed into what had once been a generous clearing. The surrounding woods were fast reclaiming the open space. Young maples, oaks, black walnuts...flourished where hard-won crops had grown. No green shoots of corn poked up from freshly tilled earth. No lush hay waited to be cut and fill the air with that new mown scent. If Logan took her to live among the French and Indians, she might never inhale fresh-cut hay again.

Hannah's finery lay across the bed back in the Lewis's loft. Over her shift, Kira wore the shirted bodice, flowered jacket, and crimson petticoat Logan brought for her in his saddle bags. This attire was far more suited to the journey, but she'd hated to part with that gown.

He'd left his fine shirt behind and changed back into his hunting shirt, breech clout, leggings and moccasins. They fit him like a second skin, and he was as ruggedly handsome as ever. Delicious thoughts of his passion in the night made her heart race. He was all to her, and yet, would his love be enough to compensate for all she'd left behind?

Almost as if fearful of losing her, he tightened a strong arm around her waist and urged Tequi on. The split rail fence enclosing the meadow took shape in the haze. Many of the rails leaned drunkenly and portions of the fence had given way. Land meant for grazing livestock had succumbed to the dictates of nature. Patches of grass struggled for light among weeds and saplings. These fields bore scant resemblance to the thriving farmstead Henry McCutcheon had fought to build.

Logan had been a part of the grinding toil. Sadly, it had come to nothing. She tilted her face up at him. "What was it all for?"

The haunted look she remembered touched his

eyes, but his mouth was set. "A dream not meant to be."

"'Tis the dream of countless Scots, your own people. Your father came here with his beloved wife to build a life in this new land. What hopes they must have had."

Logan's taut features betrayed a slight wince, but he said flatly, "This land isn't new nor does it belong to us."

Kira blew out her breath. "Your father had a deed."

"From whom, King George? What right has that despot across the sea to land the tribes have held time out of mind?"

"For pity's sake, treaties were made."

Brows drawn together, he glowered at her. "And broken."

"The tribes sold their land, including your precious Shawnee."

"And were cheated of its true worth, or had it sold out from under them by Iroquois claiming ownership."

"Oh, I can't talk to you when you're like this. If Josiah weren't on our tail and you facing a noose, I'd—"

"What?"

She socked him in the shoulder. "Wrestle you to the ground and pound some sense into you."

His lips twitched in a faint smile, the first all day. "Think I'd rather enjoy that. Better spare your knee."

Leaving her to sputter, he swung one leg over the stallion and dismounted. He led Tequi through what remained of his family's fight to tame this piece of earth. Grass and weeds were knee high.

She pursed her lips as they neared the dilapidated outbuildings. Years of wind, rain, and snow had taken their toll on the logs. Shingles were torn off. The sides of the smokehouse sagged and portions of roof were gone. The barn was only slightly better.

As for the garden, it pained her to see the once cherished plot abandoned. The rhubarb Logan fondly remembered struggled for life among a host of burdock. Generations of earth-loving Scots rose in her veins. "Fetch me a hoe and I'll have a go at that garden."

He eyed her in bemusement. "We've little time, and a treasure to find."

She voiced the doubt growing in her like a lengthening shadow. "I sense this gold may not belong to us."

"It's on my father's land."

Raising her arm, she pointed an accusing finger at him. "You claim this plot when it suits your purpose."

A smile crinkled the corners of his eyes and the flecks in their brown depths shone. "Touché, Cricket."

"There's so much to be done here, Logan."

The light in his expression faded. "We've not come to farm. Put that nonsense out of your head right now."

"It may be nonsense now, given our plight, but later, maybe we could return?"

He clenched the bridle so tightly his knuckles turned white. "We've been all through this. Whether or not you agree, you took a vow to obey me. We're here to find the coins and leave, not reclaim the past. Let it go. I have."

"You haven't. I see it in your eyes."

He set his jaw at that stubborn angle she knew well. "I'm not arguing with you anymore."

"Fine. You're infuriating."

"And you're not?"

Glancing away from his exasperation, she spied

another survivor from the past. A leafy peony covered in white blossoms thrust up among the weeds.

"Look there. Your mother's favorite flower."

"Must be as tough as boot leather to survive."

She angled her eyes back at him. In that instant, she saw more of the inner man than she suspected he wanted her to. "Beauty isn't always fragile. Wildflowers live to bloom another year."

"Are you such a one, Kira?" He loosely tethered Tequi to a sapling, then bent to pluck a snowy blossom and held it up to her. "Live and prosper like this flower."

Burying her face in the moist petals, she breathed in one of the most exquisite fragrances on earth. "I'll try."

"You'll do more than that. You shall succeed and I will guard you with my life." With unexpected fervor, he pulled her down from the horse and caught her to him.

Alarm twinged through her and she gasped in his tight hold. "Pray God it doesn't come to that."

He lightened his grip. Smiling, as if to shake off his forbidding mood, he stood her on her feet. "I didn't mean to frighten you. Come, my lady. You've more to see of the McCutcheon estate."

Linking her arm through his, she walked toward the burned-out cabin. The enormous chestnuts that once sheltered the house had sprouted offspring that hid all evidence of its existence. But indications of Logan's former trip were visible in the grapevines and branches he'd chopped to clear a path.

"'Tis plain you labored here."

"With a handful of gold sovereigns to be claimed, I should think so."

"*That* many?"

"Cousin Rebecca's late husband, Captain Elliot, gave them to her before the battle that took his life.

She believes he knew he would fall and sold all he had to make provision for her."

"Very generous provision. And yet, she wed a warrior?"

"Not just any warrior. I wish Shoka were here now."

"Whatever for?"

"Something's amiss," Logan muttered.

Kira glanced around her, stating the obvious. "Your homestead's in ruins."

"Beyond that. I could use his aid and hawk-eyes."

She couldn't imagine seeking assistance from a warrior. Logan needed to understand who his allies and enemies were.

Saying no more on the subject, he helped her across the fallen vines and rubble. He swept her over a scorched log and held her aloft. "Somewhere hereabouts is the threshold I'm to carry you over."

Before them, lay the heap of blackened timbers. The ax and shovel were on the muddy ground beside the hole he'd dug among the tree roots. Rocks and stumps displaced the hand carved furniture the cabin had housed. He shoved a moldering log aside with his foot. Stepping over the rest of the debris, he lowered her to stand beside the charred hearth.

Virginia creeper climbed up the once much-used chimney, the heart of every home, so strongly built it had withstood the fire and all the elements of nature. She smoothed the worn stones. "What glad times you must have had here."

"Don't make me recall those memories now."

She shifted her gaze to his. Pain glistened in his eyes. "You are determined to forget, aren't you?"

"And to think only of you."

"What of your treasure?"

He curled his fingers around hers. "I can see to both."

****

Nothing about being here again felt right to Logan. He didn't belong. Neither did Kira, he was certain, for all her insistence. Huddled in her cloak in the weedy grass, she watched him unsaddle Tequi. Sunlight didn't penetrate the clouds and the raw damp reddened her cheeks. What a joyless place to bring her, poor girl. He swore he'd make it up to her somehow, as soon as may be.

"I wish today was like yesterday." Raw emotion made her voice quaver.

It was time to hearten the troops before she dissolved into tears. Difficult when an unsettling rhythm drummed in his head. He summoned a smile. "We shall have a wealth of fair days to store up before winter, you'll see."

He slid the saddle, bags, and bedroll from the waiting stallion. Handing her the saddlebags, he grabbed his musket. "The stable appears the least in ruins. Come on, Mrs. McCutcheon. I'll see you settled in grand style for our stay on the estate."

Hoisting his load, he headed for the weathered building with Kira following behind. Hinges creaked as he pushed open the graying door and an ancient mustiness greeted him. Brushing the cobwebs from his face, he walked inside.

Despite the webs spun throughout the dim, dusty interior, a sense of order remained. The stalls that had housed his father's prize mounts still stood. Mangers held old hay. A harness and bridle hung on the log wall above an oak bucket as though left there to be used the next day. In one corner, a plow, hay fork and two hoes idled in readiness. He envisioned his father walking behind the plow and nearly unbearable pain pierced him.

Kira laid the saddlebags down. "Much was left behind."

Logan steadied his voice. "We left in a hurry

after the alarm, thinking to return after forting up for a time."

"But no one ever came back after that fateful summer," she said quietly.

"That's not entirely true. I later learned Shoka and Rebecca sheltered here as they fled Tonkawa." A chill ran down his spine at the thought of that vengeful Catawba warrior who'd chased them here. Alarm crossed Kira's face.

She startled as two barn swallows swooped, scolding, above them, and then vanished through the hole in the roof. Loud peeping drew his eyes to the nest tucked between the rafters and the open mouths. "Only birds," he soothed, and shifted his load against the wall furthest from the hole.

Shaking off his dark mood, he undid his bedroll and spread the wool blanket over an antiquated mound of hay. He swept his hand at the stable. "Our chamber, my lady."

She swiveled her head at the musty corners. "It could do with a good cleaning."

"We're not giving it one."

"Me, then."

"I won't have you wearing yourself out for nothing." He followed her eyes. "And I'm not patching that roof."

Up went her chin. "Why are we forever at odds?"

"We needn't be."

Her wistful gaze touched the plow and tools. "These are still serviceable and we're young and strong. Uncle Peter and Will would help us rebuild and likely the Lewis men. Have you forgotten all your father held dear?"

He grimaced. "If only I could."

She threw her hands up. "The land is everything, Logan."

He knew the creed she lived by. All the work that went with a homestead was deeply rooted in her and in him once. "There are other ways of caring for it."

"None I can conceive of."

"You may come to."

Kira blinked furiously. "Whether I will or won't, I have no choice other than to do as you say."

"You make me sound like a tyrant."

"Hardly, but I can't stay and rebuild without you."

She was so damn appealing, he hated to be unbending. But he must. "No. You can't. In your zeal for the homestead, have you forgotten Josiah Campbell?"

She shot a glance at the darkened doorway. "Do you really think he'll come here? He doesn't know of your digging."

"Unless he's been watching the trails." Logan laid his musket down and took a pistol out from one of the saddle bags. The wooden stock, lock and side plates shone from his polishing. Fine engravings were etched in the brass.

Reaching out her hand, she lightly touched the stock. "That's beautiful. Where did you come by it?"

"Shoka gave it to me."

"You never said," she chided.

"I hadn't need of it yet."

"And you fear you may now. Shouldn't you arm me too?"

"Any weapon you have can be wrenched away and used against you, or me. And I didn't carry extra."

"Very well then. What else did you bring with you?"

"Your balm, kerchiefs, brush, extra cloth for—" he hesitated. "Women's needs."

"If you're determined to treat me solely as a woman, let me remind you I have other needs, like food."

245

He laid the pistol down. Rummaging in the saddle bags, he spread provisions wrapped in cloth on the blanket. "Partridge pie and molasses cake left over from the wedding. Eat hearty." He extracted a bottle. "And apple brandy, to celebrate our first wedded breakfast. Will insisted."

"You saw him before we left?"

An ache fast becoming familiar reasserted itself. "Briefly."

Her chin trembled. "I miss him already."

"I see I must keep you from brooding over my cousin."

"Not just Will, all of them."

"I promise to do my utmost to comfort you." Logan uncorked the bottle and saluted her. "To us, Kira."

He downed a warm mouthful and passed the bottle to her.

She took a dejected swallow.

He lay back upon the blanket and opened his arms. "Come here, Cricket."

She burrowed into his embrace. "I feel so lost."

Enfolding her, he said, "I'll find you."

Chapter Seventeen

"Rest, sweetheart."

Warm and wonderfully washed in Logan's love, Kira had only the drowsiest awareness of his soft words.

His lips lightly pressed hers. "I'm off to dig."

Something about his excavation stirred that nameless disquiet within her like the rustling overhead in the eves. Her deepest senses told her a menacing darkness brooded over those coins. She must warn him.

Speaking was such an effort. "Stay," she breathed out.

He kissed her cheek, and tucked the blanket more snugly around her shift. "I can't. I've a treasure to find. Come to me when you've rested and dressed."

She tried to lift her arm and catch his sleeve. Her hand was like lead. "Danger," she said in a bare whisper.

"I know. I'm watching for Josiah and his henchmen."

Not only them. "More danger."

"No doubt Captain Winn's after me too. Never fear, sweetheart. I'm cagey."

She had to make Logan understand. If only she could open her eyes and sit up. "Don't go."

"I must find this gold. Not for us alone. Times are hard for the tribe after years of war. My friends suffer."

It was as though she'd been given an opiate, and all she could do to shake her head.

"You don't want Tom and Tessa to face want, do you?" He sounded slightly exasperated.

Of course not. How could she make him understand?

His warmth left her as he stood, then she detected the clink of the stable door closing. She struggled to rise and go after him. But her body was too weighted. She must be far wearier then she'd realized. Perhaps some forgotten nightmare accounted for her mounting apprehension. Perhaps...

Sleep tugged at her like a strong current spiraling her down into the black well of unconsciousness. How long she floated like this, she didn't know. Gradually she became aware of iciness blowing across her. Probably the chill came from the hole in the roof or some other crevice. The gloomy day must've grown mightily cold. It was too hard to open her heavy eyes and find the source of the draft, far easier to slide further beneath the blanket that had slipped from her bare shoulders.

When had her shift slid down? She thought she'd retied the neck. If only she could move. What was this strange malady that possessed her?

Summoning all her will, she pulled at the cover.

The stubborn cloth resisted her like a living creature. Was it caught on something?

Had Logan returned without her knowing and was teasing her? Just the sort of thing he would do.

Logan? She called sleepily. At least, she thought she did. She couldn't be certain if she were awake and speaking, or dreaming she was.

He made no reply.

Yet she sensed she wasn't alone. Who was here?

Her heart pulsed as if squeezed between two great hands. Dear God, had Josiah come?

No. Even worse.

An ill presence hovered, one more insidious than

he. She must get to her feet, get to Logan, but she was too heavily weighted.

Rebecca.

She froze. Was she dreaming or had she heard the faintly whispered name?

Rebecca.

There! Again the eerie summons rasped the name in masculine tones...real, yet not real. Embodied and yet without form.

How were both possible? She envisioned skulls and old bones.

Coldness blew across Kira's bare shoulder. Her skin crawled under the icy breath.

So fair.

The faint whisper, if that's what it was, seemed louder than before. And she thought she felt fingers, clammy with cold as if from beyond the grave, drift over her neck.

A scream rose in her throat but wouldn't pass her lips. Everything in her cried out for flight. Still, she lay there.

Rebecca.

Who was calling for Rebecca, and why? She was Logan's cousin, the woman who'd wed Shoka and taken refuge here before the cabin burned.

Grayish smoke clouded Kira's mind. As if the fire still burned, she detected the acrid scent of burning wood, heard the crackle. A fearsome warrior painted green and black took form in the inferno, eyes burning with the hunger of Hell. This terrible image could only belong to Tonkawa, the warrior who'd hunted Shoka and Rebecca. Tonkawa, killed seven years ago. But still here.

He reached out his hand dripping in blood. *Mine, Rebecca. Mine now.*

A voiceless shriek rose in Kira's throat. *I'm not Rebecca!*

Fiery eyes bored into her. *You lie.*

No!

Always you lie. Your lover can no longer protect you.

He's my husband!

The warrior's pale lips twisted in a sneer. *Go. Seek for Shoka, if you can.*

Billowing smoke concealed his dreadful countenance.

Then sleep fled Kira like a potion spent. The scream tore from her and she opened her eyes.

Chest heaving, heart thudding, she sat up in dread of the fearsome sight awaiting her. No malicious stare seared into her, no bloody fingers grabbed her hand or hair. Only the murky gloom of the stable met her horrified scrutiny.

"Kira!" Logan shouted from beyond the stable. A moment later he flung open the creaky door and sprang inside.

Shaking violently, she stumbled to her feet. "We must go from here now."

He caught her to him in a rush of strength. "Why? What's all this about? I heard you scream for dear life."

"I did. Tonkawa—" Kira hated to speak his name for fear it would call him forth again. "Thinks I'm her."

"Who?"

"Rebecca."

"Calm down, darling. You aren't making any sense."

"He's after her—me. I saw him."

Logan cradled Kira like a frightened child. "Shhhh...It was just a bad dream."

"No. I heard him. Felt him."

"Now, Kira."

His manner reminded her maddeningly of Aunt Alice. "I'm telling you this place is cursed."

"Maybe so. But I'm not ready to go yet. Let's get

you dressed. You can wait by me while I finish my search."

Like a malignant vapor, she sensed Tonkawa lurking out of sight. "We've no time, Logan."

"I didn't come all this way to leave without the coins. I'm nearly to them. I know it."

The sickening realization came. His digging had disturbed Tonkawa's spirit. "Choose me or the gold, Logan. He'll not let you leave with both."

He was rigid. "Now you're being ridiculous."

"I wish to God I were."

"Listen to me. We will leave, together, with the coins." He snatched up her petticoat. "Step in."

Gulping shallow breaths, she stepped into the red cloth. He did the ties at her waist.

On went the stays and he helped her push her arms into her jacket. She watched his actions as she might a rising stream just before the water covered their heads.

He laced the front and wrapped the cloak around her. "A drizzle's falling out now."

She thrust her feet into her shoes. "Tequi?"

"Grazing." Logan hurried her from the stable, leaving their saddle and supplies behind.

"You must saddle him."

"After a while."

"Logan—"

"Kira Anne McCutcheon. It was a dream, horrific I'll grant you, but a dream. By tonight we'll be gone."

"Tonight will be too late."

"Enough. You're only upsetting yourself more." He guided her past the vines and timber to the tree beside his excavation. "Wait here."

Chest drumming, she sank beneath the far-reaching branches while he resumed his work, and tried to gain a shaky hold over herself. Maybe he was right and it had only been a dream. And yet, she couldn't rid herself of the impression that her dreadful encounter held far more significance.

The drizzle intensified into wind-swept rain. Ignoring the ill weather, Logan shifted aside more timber and scooped shovelfuls of dirt. He sorted through his finds, dropping the collection of broken crockery into the iron kettle he'd already unearthed. Everything was encrusted with dirt, his earth-colored shirt more so now, as was the rest of him.

Bone-cold damp seeped through her, but she wouldn't have left him to go back inside the stable if she'd been threatened with catching her death.

Holding out his grubby hand, he shouted excitedly, "I found one!"

The chill wind blowing in her face, she stood and walked to the edge of the hole. Even in the low light, she saw the cylindrical object was a coin. Even one gold piece was more wealth than most settlers ever saw.

"That coin must have scattered from the others. It's simply a matter of discovering where Shoka flung them." Rubbing the gold between his fingers, Logan washed the mud from its surface in the rain and slid the sovereign into the pouch at his waist. He bent over the site where he'd made his find, speaking over his shoulder. "Shoka said to seek the cellar Papa and I dug under the floor where we hid our belongings in the event of an attack. It was right in front of the hearth, but with all this debris and trees growing up—it's quite a job."

He heaved another log aside. "Wait—there's more."

She watched in disbelief as he plucked coin after coin from the mud. Some had lodged between the roots of trees.

Clutching a handful, he waved them triumphantly. "Ten!"

Triumph wasn't the emotion surging in her.

This gold had been tossed as an offering to appease Tonkawa. It only stood to reason, he still wanted it.

She beckoned to Logan. "Hurry, please."

He waved a dismissive hand at her. "I might find more."

"You've found enough."

"Each coin matters. Everyone's counting on me." He clinked their newly acquired wealth into his pouch and returned to his task.

The gleam of gold must have blinded him to the danger. She leaned over the side of the hole, pleading with every fiber of her being. "We have to get out of here now!"

"For pity's sake, Kira."

She flung a leg over the side. If he wasn't coming out, she was going in. "I mean it!"

"I'm coming." Logan grudgingly straightened and started toward her—staggering back with a gasp as a scorched timber at the side of the hole flew forward and struck him on the head. He crumbled to the ground.

It happened so fast Kira could hardly believe her eyes. The wind wasn't strong enough to propel that log. "Logan!" Shrieking his name, she scrambled down into the diggings.

No answer.

She slipped in the morass of mud sucking at her feet and went down on one knee. Clambering up, shoeless, she wrestled with the timber. Splinters dug in her palms as she heaved it from him. He lay silent, unmoving. Blood ran from the ugly cut on his forehead.

God, no. "Logan!" Crying his name, she crouched beside him and pressed trembling fingers to his dirt-streaked neck. His pulse was weak.

Terror engulfed her. She knew with awful certainty this was Tonkawa's doing. She'd thought his vengeful spirit was after her, but it was Logan.

253

Tonkawa must have been bent on killing Shoka first and was substituting her and Logan for the couple who'd eluded him.

Kira strangled on a sob. Without Logan, her heart would be shattered. But she wasn't giving him up without a fight. Rage coursed beside her wrenching grief, empowering her with newfound strength. Maybe it was for this moment she'd been gifted. She shouted into the wind,"You're not winning this, Tonkawa! I'm a healer!"

Cradling Logan's head in her lap, she pressed her fingers to his wound. This injury was far worse than the bleeding alone. Had she the touch to heal such a wound? She'd thought her gift only lay with the stopping of blood.

Praying with all her heart, she gulped out through streaming tears, "Give me aid, Lord. Restore him to me."

Again the words of Ezekiel flowed from her. "'And when I passed by thee and saw thee polluted in thine own blood, I said unto thee, live.' Live, my dearest love, live."

If she could give him her spirit to give him life, she would. Then they truly would be one.

As before, tingling flowed through her fingers and the unmistakable scent of roses perfumed the air, as unlikely a fragrance as blackberries in winter.

The blood lessened, and then stopped. His breathing grew stronger. But could he hear her?

"Logan, speak to me."

He groaned in reply.

Relief beyond expression filled her and weakness seeped to her very marrow. A vital part of her had entered into his restoration.

He opened dazed eyes. "Kira?"

She was too overcome to speak immediately.

"What'd you hit me for?"

She shook her head.

Struggling to sit, he asked,"Who?"

"Never mind." She was terribly aware of *who* and tore the ruffle from the hem of her shift. "We must go."

He stared up at her. "Do you smell roses?"

"Yes." She bound the bandage around his head.

"You've pulled off another healing, haven't you?"

Her skin crawled as she sensed the dreaded coldness stealing up behind her.

"Come on!" She tugged at Logan. Exerting every bit of energy she had left, she helped him to his feet.

Who will heal you, Rebecca?

Whether Tonkawa had spoken aloud or in her head, Kira didn't know. With the suddenness of the timber he'd flung at Logan, chilled hands closed around her throat.

"Logan—" his name was all she got out.

Clutching at her neck, she tried to fight off his unseen presence, but his relentless grasp was overpowering. Helpless, choking, she fell backwards onto the muddy ground.

Logan bent over her just as she had done to him only minutes ago. "Kira! What's happening to you?"

I will have payment.

Logan must not have heard the sinister demand.

He gathered her to him, his voice breaking. "Tell me what afflicts you!"

She couldn't. The iron grip prevented her from speaking a word.

"Kira!"

His plea grew fainter. She had scant breath left. No strength to fight this menace. Tonkawa's would be the ultimate revenge. And Logan would never even know.

Remember the cross, child. It was Hannah's voice.

Logan's precious face faded and Hannah's took

his place, shining like an angel. As promised, she was here at Kira's greatest need. Even now, Tonkawa couldn't fully close off her breath. The cross at her throat prevented him. But neither could Kira prevail. He was too strong, and she was weakening.

Hannah's gentle countenance disappeared and she looked again into Logan's desperate eyes.

His urgent gaze pleaded with her. "It's the gold, isn't it?"

Tearing the pouch from his waist, he threw it down. "Take your treasure and be gone, damn you, Tonkawa!"

The force at her throat instantly lessened—then returned with a vengeance. *Rebecca stays.*

****

Logan wasn't certain if he actually heard the poisonous hiss, or if it sounded in his mind. But it could belong to only one malign spirit.

Yelling his fear and fury, he struggled to lift Kira. "Let her go! She's not Rebecca!"

Normally he would've easily lifted her. Not now, and not only from the lingering effects of his injury. The very earth seemed to have laid claim to her. His knees buckled and gave way under the tenacious pull.

Sinking down beside her, he beat his fist on the wet ground. "Go to Hell, Tonkawa, where you belong!"

"Hold on, Logan!"

He must be delirious. That sounded like the winded shout of Joseph McCue.

"I'm coming, lad."

Logan jerked up his head. "Over here!"

Wild hope filled him as Joseph's reassuring bulk appeared at the edge of the hole. Though it seemed an all-powerful priest was needed to banish this evil.

"Hannah sent me. She had a vision," Joseph

panted.

"You've not come a moment too soon. A vile demon has Kira by the throat."

The rugged man dropped into the hole and hunched beside them in his sodden coat. He eyed them from beneath the broad brim of his brown hat. "Quick. Hannah gave me the words to speak." He grasped Logan's muddy fingers and Kira's blood-stained hand. "Join hands and don't let go."

It was all Logan could do to lift her other hand from the greedy earth. He closed his fingers around hers and gripped Joseph's. "Nothing in heaven or in hell is breaking this circle. I swear it, Kira."

Deathly white, she gave a faint nod.

"What now, Joseph?"

"Pray with me. Both of you."

Joseph lifted his weathered face, rain running down his cheeks over his graying beard. "In the name of God the Father, God the Son and God the Holy Ghost, may this distressed soul be relieved of his obsession with this world and sent to where he belongs."

Logan repeated the sacred words aloud, trusting Kira echoed them silently. That would have to do.

Was that the wind or had an enraged roar bellowed from behind them? Logan rocked under the rushing force. And he sensed an almighty struggle between Heaven and Hell, angels and demons wrestling in some unseen battle.

Freezing fingers clawed at Logan's hand to tear him from Joseph and Kira. He held on for dear life, shouting at the unseen malevolence. "Begone! Damn you!"

The earth shook beneath them. The storm howled like a banshee. Hail rained down, stinging his head, shoulders, and the back of his neck. Squinting against the gale, he ducked down over Kira to shield her from the fury.

The darkness would not prevail. Somehow, someway, the heavenly light would shine again. He had faith.

Then the deluge of hail pattered to a halt, the gusting wind to a cool breeze. Only a misting wet fell around them. With the storm's departure, Logan knew Tonkawa had gone.

Kira took a gasping breath. A great heaviness lifted from him at that sweet sound. She gulped in air again and again as if she couldn't get enough.

"Thank God." Logan held her to him so tightly he feared to stop her returning breath, and lightened his grip. His voice broke. "I thought I'd lost you."

"And I, you," she said faintly.

He looked around at Joseph. Ice pellets sprinkled the rim of his hat. "I owe you an immeasurable debt."

The older man wrapped a drenched arm around his shoulders. "No. She's like a daughter to me. There's nothing I wouldn't do for her."

"There's nothing greater than storming the gates of Hell. That took great courage."

"Hannah said it might."

A tear glistened in Kira's eyes. "She appeared to me like an angel."

Joseph's eyes were also moist. "She may be one by now. I left her weak as a newborn lamb, but she said I must come to you."

Kira reached her hand to his face. "You must return to her as soon as may be."

Joseph covered her fingers with his work-worn grasp. "There's not much to be done for her, I fear. I'll see to you two before I go. If I can build a fire in all this wet I'll cook us some supper." He rose and held out his hand to Logan. "Come on, lad. Appears you could use some help."

Logan took his outstretched fingers. With Joseph's help, he got to his feet and pulled Kira up with him. His head throbbed. "I have one hell of a headache."

She swayed in his arms. "I'm not surprised. What of the gold?"

Joseph didn't reveal any surprise. "The coins Hannah spoke of?"

Logan nodded. "Do we dare take them now?"

"Tonkawa has no use for gold. Besides, whatever payment he demanded was already made years ago."

Logan slapped Joseph on the back. "So it was, and we've just sent him off, so the treasure is free for the taking." He offered a coin to Joseph. "Beginning with you."

"Nay lad, I have no need of it. See to your own. There's more than this lass alone depending on you, are there not?"

"Indeed. And Josiah Campbell to keep it from."

Chapter Eighteen

Everything was different today. Kira felt the change in the soft air, and gold light poured down over the abandoned homestead as though God himself had upturned a bottle of liquid sunshine. Spider webs sparkling with dew festooned the split rails. Blue sky spread above her as far as she could see and met blue-green ridges rising on every side of the narrow valley. Warmth rose from the newly washed earth, spreading hopeful promise over yesterday's evil like a balm.

A bobwhite repeated its name as Logan rose from the clear spring, wiping his mouth on the back of his hand. His forehead was bruised purplish-black, but the nasty gash had closed and color returned to his face. "I feel a new man."

Kira patted her damp face on her kerchief and tucked it at her waist. "You look one. Though Aunt Alice would have fits if she saw us." They were both muddy and bloodstained, despite their efforts to clean the worst of it off.

He shifted his somber gaze toward the excavation site. "She'd have fits if she knew how close we came to not being here. That hole was very nearly our grave."

Wonder and dread mixed together in Kira. "It's a shame people will never know of our deliverance, or Hannah's goodness or Joseph's courage, unless we return home."

"It's not our home anymore, Kira. Besides, would anyone believe such a bizarre tale?"

"No one, if I told it, but they would hear you."

He shook his head. "You know where we must go."

Melancholy washed over her. "Poor Joseph, burying Hannah alone. She gave all for me. I should be there."

Logan's eyes held pity. "I'm truly sorry. I told Joseph our suspicions about Campbell and where we're going if he wishes to seek us."

Relief eased the ache she felt for her old friend. "Thank you. Seeing him again would be a precious gift."

"He said he has a hunch of his own to pursue first." Logan studied her closely. "Why is there such a bond between you?"

"Didn't you realize? Joseph loved Mama dearly."

"Did she return his affections?"

It pained Kira to recall. "Not as Joseph wished. Mama was devoted to my father, though he broke her heart."

Logan frowned. "I wish you wouldn't say that of him. Do you still fear I'll break yours?"

"Not so much as I did. Not after yesterday."

"Thank God some good came of that horror."

Kira gazed pleadingly at him. "Much did. Your land is no longer cursed. Isn't this why your father summoned you?"

Logan tightened his lips in a hard line. "Papa put us through hell if that was his aim."

Dropping his hand from her face, he whistled for Tequi. The grazing stallion perked up his head and trotted to them.

Kira looked around at the homestead glowing like a jewel in the burnished light.

Logan took the reins. "I know what you're thinking and I am not reclaiming this land."

"Later?"

"Ever."

Annoyance bit at her. "You're stubborn as ever."

261

"Did you think a knock on the head would alter me?"

"I thought it might have softened you a bit."

"No. Let's go on foot awhile. There's something I must see to before we leave."

His solemn demeanor puzzled her. "What?"

"Mama's grave."

Without another word, she walked at his side across what used to be the meadow. Elusive meadowlarks trilled from the dewy grass while her shoes and skirts grew damper.

He ran pensive eyes over the field. "It ought to be right around here. The spot will be rough and overgrown." He pointed to the large gray stone in a green mound at the edge of the field. "There."

Split rails surrounded the small plot. He left Tequi outside the disordered enclosure, laid his musket aside, and climbed over the fence. Taking the tomahawk from his belt, he chopped at the tangled growth to clear away space by the stone. He brushed vines and weeds from the weathered surface and beckoned to Kira.

She gathered her petticoats and crawled over the rails to step beside him. A chiseled inscription was still visible on the granite. The dates of Mary McCutcheon's birth and death were also given. A leafy vine had been etched into the stone and wound around the words.

"Here lies Mary Elizabeth McCutcheon, dearly beloved wife and adored mother. God rest her soul," she read softly. "It's a lovely tribute."

"Papa fashioned the stone."

Kira envisioned his handsome, rugged father carving this painstaking memorial. "It must have taken him hours."

"Yes. I remember him bent to his task." Logan hesitated as though he wanted to say something more, but was uncertain. "I've wondered...where does Papa lie?"

"Oh, I thought you knew. But of course, you wouldn't," she faltered. "I don't know how to tell you, Logan."

"Just give me the truth."

"The men couldn't get your father out of Warden with the battle and all. Fire consumed him. Though he'd already fallen by then," she hastily added. "I'm deeply sorry."

Logan was silent then said, "I wish he could have been buried here with her."

"They're together now."

"I hope so." He traced the chiseled vine with his fingertips and laid his hand on top of the gray stone. "Goodbye, Mama. Forgive me. I just can't stay. I suppose Papa already knows," he whispered, and turned away.

So did Kira. She faced him squarely. "Logan McCutcheon, you're running away."

Sunlight glinted on the moisture in his eyes. "Because I can't bear to stay?"

"Because you want to and won't." She planted her hands on her hips. "I know running very well."

"True enough, only I'm just going back where I belong." Winking furiously, he swung his leg over the rails.

She snatched up her skirts. "You belong here."

He took hold of the bridle and stroked Tequi's dark brown muzzle. "You don't understand, Kira."

"I think I do." She climbed across the fence and raised her eyes to his. His jaw was set and she knew he'd made a stand.

"I'm not quarreling with you anymore about this," he said flatly. "If you argue, you'll argue alone."

Hurt stung her. "You've never turned a deaf ear to me before."

"I will now if you persist."

She took a final look at the fields crowded with young trees, the weedy garden, the crumbling vine-covered fence and run-down buildings. "So we're truly not coming back?"

"We'll find our way."

"You mean, *you* will. I'm not so certain about me."

He lifted her up onto the horse. "You're a strong lass, Kira. Surely you can face friendly warriors with fortitude, after battling a demon?"

"Friendly and warriors are not words I'm in the habit of using together."

"Come on. We've a treasure to share and no notion where Josiah and his henchmen have gotten to."

Logan grabbed his musket and mounted behind her. Circling his arm around her, he prodded Tequi into a canter. And Kira braced herself: Lord only knew what lay ahead.

****

"Kira, we're there."

There…the word held grave significance, though Kira couldn't at first think what. The past two days were a jolted blur of pitching back and forth on Tequi.

In some places thickets of rosy-pink mountain laurel and rhododendron were so tight they scarcely had room to pass. But anything was better than thorny green briars snatching her cloak. Icy water had soaked through her petticoats and stockings more than once as the sure-footed horse splashed through mountain streams swollen with rain.

Worn to a thread, she'd dozed while Logan kept her from toppling to the stony ground. She could have slept five minutes or five hours, the disorienting effects were the same. Yawning, she shifted stiffly in his arms, her sore muscles protesting every move. "We're where?"

"Camp, sweetheart. We've come."

She blinked her eyes wide open. Snowy dogwood blossoms shone in the twilight and a great golden moon rose above the trees. The river tumbled to her right while mounded stones jutted from the ridge on her left. The rock ledge sheltered a campfire. It was before this Logan had halted.

At least four warriors sat among the eight to ten shadowy figures silhouetted in the orange glow. Feathers hung from their scalp locks or longer, loose hair. The feathers fluttered in the breeze. Heart racing, she pressed back against Logan. "Oh, God."

"You'll be all right. Remember, Tom's here somewhere. And they have a fire and dinner cooking."

His words were lost on her. The gathering rose and started toward them, the warriors out in front. Why them? Why not let the women come first?

Stomach churning, she clapped one hand over her mouth. "Oh, God," she repeated, muffled by her palm.

The men hailed Logan. "*Awassolepo neneaway, Alaquoi! Weheapealo.*"

She lifted her hand just far enough to gulp out, "What did they say?"

"They're glad to see me, and my name, Alaquoi, remember? They're asking me to come."

"Don't go to them," she pleaded breathlessly.

"We can't just sit here all night on Tequi."

She clapped her hand back down. "Oh, God."

"Will you stop saying that?"

"I can't." She repeated it like a wordless prayer, and thought she might faint dead away, but sat transfixed as the oncomers closed in on Tequi.

Even in the fading light, the terrible scars carved onto the older man's face were visible. That warrior's hair was plucked in a severe scalp lock. Silver cones shone at his ears, the lobes split and

265

wrapped with wire in a bizarre fashion. He and the other men wore cloth shirts in colors or prints, buckskin breechclouts, leggings, and moccasins.

The Shawnee patriarch stood watchfully while the others crowded around Tequi. He didn't like Kira, she was certain, but the assembly momentarily took her breath away. Surely, this was the strangest of all reunions. She shrank back even further as Logan bent low in the saddle and held out his hand to their outstretched fingers.

"*Bezon*," he greeted each one in turn.

The same odd word echoed back at him.

One young brave with a scalp lock like the older man had an unlikely Scottish haversack slung over his shoulder and a sheathed dirk at his side. No doubt, he'd lifted both from some unfortunate Highlander in the recent Indian wars.

He gestured at Logan's forehead.

"I must look the very devil," he said to her, and then to the gathering, "*Ne weshelashamamo*," apparently assuring them he was firmly among the living.

Kira felt anything but reassured. And shuddered to think how many English lives these warriors had taken.

"Hang on a moment," Logan said.

She required no instruction to cower on Tequi while he dismounted. He threw his arms around one man, then another.

"Meshewa—Neeake—" A jumble of unrecognizable names issued from her husband's lips.

He embraced the fierce-looking scarred warrior for an especially lengthy moment. "Notha, I'm come." Logan glanced up at her. "This is Wabete, my adopted father."

Dear Lord. What a change from Henry McCutcheon's warm appeal. If she searched to the far side of the moon she couldn't have found a more forbidding father in-law. How could Logan be the man she loved and this *Alaquoi* they claimed kinship with?

He was insane, there was no other explanation. He'd hidden it from her well. There was no time to wonder how. The women were surging around them. Colorful skirts embellished with beads and ribbons swirled around their moccasins. Long black hair fell to the waists of all except for one. This striking young woman had a blond braid down her back and fair skin.

Good heavens, Tessa. Only fifteen when taken captive, the slender, petulant girl had grown into a fine looking woman with much of Logan about her; the bulge at her middle evidence of her warrior husband's affection. God help her, Kira was in a heathen camp surrounded by madness.

Logan engulfed Tessa in a hug, lifting her up and swinging her around before returning her to the ground. "Neeshematha, you've grown. Part of you anyway," he teased, and smiled down at the dark-headed little boy at her skirts. "Are you bigger too, Newe?"

The child nodded, grinning as Logan scooped him up. "Come and meet my wife."

Two small girls looked on inquisitively as he set the boy up beside Kira. He was just past the toddler stage. Wide brown eyes studied her rather like a trusting fawn's.

"You can't possibly be frightened of a child, Cricket. This wee lad is Newe, Tessa's son. Newe, this is Kira."

"Keera," the child repeated, playing with the new sound. He patted her face with chubby fingers. *"Keera paca tamsah."*

Logan smiled. "He says you are a beautiful woman."

"He's darling," she admitted.

"Isn't he?" Logan laid his hands on the heads of the girls. "What of these? Kitte and Melassa are your nieces."

She searched their faces for some resemblance to her brother or anyone else in the family. Their dominant features were Shawnee, but there was some McClure in their hazel eyes and the shape of their mouths, and they were undeniably pretty with glossy black braids.

Logan drew a shy woman nearer. "Laneke, Tom's wife."

Kira eyed the female who'd kept her brother from coming home. Granted, Laneke possessed the same dark beauty as her young daughters. Why couldn't Tom have found contentment with a woman from his own race, though?

Evidently, his wife also had questions. Unintelligible sounds fell on Kira's ears as Logan made explanation, coaxing hesitant smiles from Lanake and the children.

"Didn't Tom teach them any English?" Kira asked.

"A little. It's faster this way, though."

"For you. Ask her where Tom is."

"Koonah stands watch," one young warrior offered.

Logan closed an affectionate arm around his shoulder. "Meshewa is Tessa's husband and my good friend. He speaks English well."

Kira was relieved someone did. She looked more closely at the brave. Meshewa was about Logan's height, with a lean muscular build. Loose black hair fell around his shoulders, and no scalp lock or weird earrings marred his undeniably attractive face. His blue shirt was the hunting style frontiersmen wore and he seemed friendly.

Not only that, there was something familiar

about him. She'd seen his face before. But where?

She gasped in recognition. "Oh my."

Logan glanced up sharply. "What?"

"It's him. The brave who saved me from the fire at Fort Warden."

****

Logan shook his head to clear the feeling of unreality. He looked wonderingly at his long-time friend and brother. "You saved Kira's life?"

A peculiar expression came into Meshewa's eyes. "Yes."

Gaping from Meshewa to Kira and back to her husband again, Tessa scolded, "You never said."

Meshewa shrugged. "I did not know her name. Only she was a girl whose cloak caught fire."

Logan angled his head at Kira, eyeing Meshewa with a blend of amazement and uncertainty. "Seems you owe him a debt, darling."

She made no reply, only gaped.

"Shall I thank him for you?"

Kira simply nodded.

He chuckled and slapped Meshewa on the back. "*Megwich.* You saved her for me."

A ripple of amusement ran through the group, though his adopted father, Wabete, looked none too pleased.

Then Kira actually ventured a question to Meshewa. "When will my brother come?"

"Soon. He saw Alaquoi ride in." Meshewa turned to Logan with a quizzical expression. "How long has this woman been your wife?"

"Barely three days and we've spent most of that on Tequi or battling for our lives."

Meshewa arched black brows like the wings of a raven. "Who attacked you?"

"I shall tell you the whole story later. This isn't a tale for children, particularly not at bedtime."

Tessa reclaimed her small son. "I'll put him to

sleep now. Goodness Kira, I'd hardly know you if you weren't the very image of your mother. Poor girl. You look frightened to death and exhausted.

"Both. Come on, darling." Logan reached up for Kira.

She entered his arms with seemingly no intention of leaving them again. He lifted her down and she pressed against him practically standing on his feet.

Meshewa took the reins. "You want help with Tequi?"

Logan nodded. "I think Kira won't be parted from me."

The gathering, except for Meshewa, closed ranks around them as Logan walked with her to the campsite. He gently pushed her down on the shale and mossy earth before the fire and settled beside her. Shadows from the flames flickered on the stone walls and ledge overhead as Laneke passed them warm slices of venison.

He tore hungrily into his portion. Kira ate with less enthusiasm, eyes continually straying to the warriors seated on either side of the campfire.

Tessa smiled at her encouragingly. "You're all right here, Kira. None will harm you."

Logan guessed whom she feared most. He gestured at Wabete's powerful figure. "*Notha* is father in Shawnee. You may call him that."

"I'm not likely to call him anything," she whispered.

Wabete narrowed his eyes at her. The man could hear a mouse tiptoe across damp leaves. Taking an indignant draw on his pipe, he blew a smoky ring overhead. "You endanger us coming here with this woman."

"I couldn't leave her behind, Notha. I love this woman. Besides, she belongs to me."

His fervent protest did nothing to lessen the

older man's displeasure. "Her people will follow. Fight to regain her."

"I wed her properly. I didn't just carry her away."

The censure in Wabete's expression remained unaltered. "The English Colonel demands the return of all captives. We risk much to hide your sister, Koonah, and you. Must we conceal another white woman?"

"Soldiers will soon go from our village. Then we may safely return."

Wabete took the pipe from his lips and snorted. "Soldiers may find you both, if her people do not."

"We can travel to Shoka in Quebec."

Frowning eyes met his assertion. "A long and dangerous journey lies between these mountains and the land of Capitaine Renault. Would you take her on such a trek?"

"I'm not giving her up." Logan would put her back up on that horse and ride. After all he'd done to bring her here he couldn't believe she wasn't wanted.

Wabete broke off the argument to stab his pipe at the figure treading silently into camp. "Koonah comes."

Logan nudged Kira. "Your brother is here," he said, wondering how in the world she would react to Tom. And what Tom would have to say to him.

****

The great moon shone down on the man Kira had known as Tom McClure. She strained to see him as he stepped into the circle around the fire, wanting yet not wanting to be reunited with this traitorous brother. The flames revealed a clean-shaven face strongly chiseled in the image of their handsome father. She couldn't clearly see Tom's eyes, but knew they were colored like the sky before a storm.

Brown hair pulled back at his neck was the way he'd always worn it. There the similarity ended.

Three golden hawk feathers trailed from the back of his head adding an undeniably Indian touch, as did the silver arm bands and the beaded shot pouch hanging around his bare shoulder. He didn't have a shirt on, only a buckskin breechclout, fringed leggings, and quilled moccasins.

Despite the rough transformation, there was no mistaking his ancestry—like having Tom back from the dead.

She stopped in mid chew, choking on the bite she'd taken, and called out in a sputtering cry, "Tom!"

He stood stock-still. "Kira? You're the woman Alaquoi brought?"

"She is." Logan offered nothing more, apparently leaving the immediate explanation to her. Difficult when she could make no intelligible response.

The gathering fell silent. Every eye fixed on them, every ear tuned to their conversation except for the sleeping children. The fire crackled above the distant howl of wolves as Kira scrambled up and hurtled at her brother.

He caught her with a grunt and hugged her to him.

How solid and good he felt, scented with wood smoke and the outdoors. His unique musk was the same as before. It really was Tom.

He kissed the top of her head. "God in heaven, I never thought to see you again, little sister."

"Nor I—" she choked out, fighting to regain her breath and not burst into tears. "It's been so long."

"Ages. You were scarcely more than a child when I last saw you. Let me take a better look." He held her at arm's length, gray eyes exploring her intently. "You've grown up, little sister."

"'Twas bound to happen."

He pressed his lips to her forehead. "I suppose so. Somehow, I still imagined you as the girl I left."

"Frozen in time?"

"Something of the sort. Ah, Kira, you're very like our mother."

"So I'm told, and Papa could be standing before me now, apart from your attire."

Tom's brow, shaped very like their father's, creased in surprise. "Indeed? No one has remarked on it."

"I remember Papa well."

Moisture glinted in his earnest gaze. "So do I. How have you fared, Cricket?"

She could hardly speak. "You still remember calling me that?"

"Of course. I've not forgotten you."

"It seems that way."

Cupping her face with roughened fingers, he said, "Never. Have the Houstons treated you well?"

"Yes. Though I've tried their patience."

He smiled faintly. "No doubt. I left you in good hands, then?"

"Are you trying to ease your conscience?"

Dropping his hands, he shifted from one moccasin to the other. "A bit, maybe."

"They've treated me like their own, but it's not the same as family. You were all I had, Tom."

"I know. I'm sorrier than I can say." He looked beyond Kira to the woman gazing up at him. Deep affection warmed his eyes. "I couldn't return home with Laneke and resume my former life, and I couldn't bear to leave her."

"I've met your reasons for remaining behind. All three of them."

"Laneke is a jewel, and the girls," he said huskily.

"They are that. But do I mean nothing to you?"

He returned his focus to her, his rugged face drawn with regret. "A great deal. How pale and shaken you look."

"I'm sore, weary, and frightened to death."

Holding her to him again, he asked, "Of whom?"

She gestured shakily at Wabete. "Just now— him."

"Wabete will do you no harm."

"He doesn't want me here," she argued under her breath.

"Neither do I."

She pulled back, staring up at her brother. "What are you saying?"

"As glad as I am to see you, Logan oughtn't to have brought you."

"I'm his lawfully wedded wife."

Tom's jaw dropped. "What?"

If Kira had declared she'd run off with pirates, he couldn't have seemed more unprepared. "Reverend Wilkins married us three days ago at the Lewis homestead."

"With Peter Houston's blessing?"

"It wasn't easily gained, but Logan managed."

"Did he, indeed?" Tom flashed narrowing eyes at Logan. His voice dropped menacingly. "*Nepahloh*, Alaquoi."

"In English, if you please," Kira pleaded, taken aback by Tom's anger.

"I require a word with your *husband*."

Logan rose from the campfire as if anticipating a knife in the chest. "I thought I'd give you two a moment first."

"We've had one. I want one with you now."

The terseness in Tom mirrored the resentment in Logan, reminding Kira of two dogs bristling before a fight.

Logan eyed him coldly. "May we sit and talk, or do you prefer Kira to fall at your feet?"

Tom prodded her back down onto the blanket before the fire, but remained standing. "I prefer you had left her safely tucked away at the Houstons'."

Arms crossed over his chest, Logan faced the more mature man head to head. "You make her sound like a bird in its nest. Even they're not safe from being plucked."

Fists clenched, Tom demanded, "Who has plucked her, besides you?"

Logan looked ready to punch him in the mouth. "For pity's sake, man, I wed her."

"I didn't ask you to wed her, just to be certain she was all right."

Wabete rose from the fire and inserted his bulk between them. He faced Logan, his mouth downturned. "I asked you to have much care when you returned to the English."

Logan raked his fingers though his hair. "I did."

"By bringing this woman to us?"

"She was in much danger there."

Tom shot Logan an arched look. "She said the Houstons treated her well."

"Except for my uncle's blind spot. He was about to marry her off to Josiah Campbell when I arrived. The man hungers after her like a crazed wolf."

Driving his fist into his palm with a loud smack, Tom erupted, "Damn! I thought you shot him."

"Seems I only clipped the blackguard's shoulder."

Kira looked uncertainly from one man to the other. "Josiah figured out who shot him and told Captain Winn."

"Another bastard," Tom muttered.

Wabete laid his hand on Logan's shoulder. "This captain wishes your death?"

"Winn would gladly see me dangle from the end of a rope, but Campbell has no proof I'm the man who shot him."

"Does the captain need proof to do as he likes? Campbell, his men, they may all come. We are not too far for him to track."

Tom warned, "Particularly if he goes to the McCutcheon homestead and follows from there."

Somberness settled over the gathering. Wary eyes looked outward at the moonlit trees.

"Do you want me to leave, Notha? Go back and settle with Campbell?" Logan asked.

"I fear you would not live."

Tom rubbed his fingers over his chin. "He would have more of a chance if I went with him. I've a score to settle with Campbell." He glanced down at Kira. "Two, now."

Meshewa spoke out. "I also. This man shot Skaki."

Kira hadn't noticed Meshewa join the circle.

"It's too risky for a warrior to come so close to the settlement," Logan argued.

"I will take the risk."

Logan rolled his eyes heavenward. "Then God help us. I guess the three of us are going."

Getting determinedly to her feet, Kira said. "Make that four."

Chapter Nineteen

A fiery ball blazed across the night sky in a trail of light. Logan had lived among superstitious people, both the Scots and Shawnee, long enough to know a falling star of this size was portentous. He prayed it foretold something good.

The night air had a cold bite in its teeth. Moccasins pointed toward the warming campfire, he leaned against the rock wall with Kira tucked beside him. If only they could remain like this for more than a few hours. And he longed to be alone with her again. For now, she needed rest. He was relieved she didn't seem nearly as intimidated by the warriors as she had when they'd first arrived earlier this evening, and was even beginning to trust Meshewa.

Tessa huddled beside her warrior husband, clutching him. "Don't go. They'll fire on you if you're seen."

Wrapping his frightened wife in his arms, Meshewa soothed. "None will see. Shoka taught me to move like a shadow."

Wabete drew on his pipe and looked at Logan. "My brother also taught you. Even so, the danger is great."

"For outright ambush against Campbell, yes," Logan agreed. "We'd have the whole bloody militia swarming after us. But there's one matter that might aid in bringing him down, like an elk in the jaws of a wolf."

Every head in the fire-lit circle bent toward him.

Logan ran his eyes over each man's alert gaze. Even Tessa glanced around, tearful, but expectant,

277

and Kira perked up at his side. "Campbell is the leader of a pack of thieves. I tracked stolen horses back to his place, but couldn't find a thing. If we can discover where Campbell hides his take, the settlers would turn on him."

Tom clapped his hand on his thigh. "Then by heaven, we'll track him to his lair."

Logan smiled. "The hunter becomes the hunted."

Kira sat up straighter. "I'm coming with you."

Lips pursed, Tom shook his head.

Logan spoke before Tom opened his mouth. "We've been all through this, Kira. It's too risky for you to go."

Pipe in hand, Wabete gestured at her with a stabbing motion. "Campbell will come for you."

Her lower lip quivered, but she lifted her chin. "Then we shall just have to get him first."

Logan tightened his arm around her. "Not you, *us*."

"I must go too."

Wabete fixed her with a look that forbade refusal. "If Alaquoi says you stay, you stay."

Most men would quail under such censure, but Kira didn't back down. "Alaquoi needs me."

An up swell of love flooded Logan, painful in its intensity. "I do, sweetheart. But not for this."

"Yes, for this. I'm a healer, remember?"

"Not for everything. I won't put you in such danger—"

She covered his mouth with chilled fingers. "I already am. Besides, I think I know where Josiah's lair is."

Logan weighed her assertion skeptically. "How?"

"A feeling."

Tom raised his hands, palms up. "A hunch?"

"I've been right before," she reminded them.

"True. Tell us then," Logan invited.

"Oh, I will. When we're halfway there."

Humor flickered in Tom's exasperated expression. "You're one stubborn lass, Cricket."

Despite all they were up against, Logan chuckled. "Never underestimate her. Or me," he added quietly.

****

Moonlight silvered the woods in a sort of half-light. That, at least, should make night travel easier, Kira thought as she stood shivering beside Logan.

The fire's orange glow illuminated his solemn expression. "Keep them, Notha." He pressed the hard-won coins into Wabete's hand.

The mature warrior shook his head. "When you return."

"There's no sense in my taking the gold back and risking Campbell seizing it."

Still, he didn't close his fingers around the coins.

Logan swept his hand at the gathering of men, women and children, some still asleep. "Use it as you see fit for these. Please."

Wabete withdrew two coins and pressed them into Logan's palm. "For you."

A poignant look of understanding passed between him and his adopted son. Then Wabete slipped the valuable glint of metal into his pouch and Logan did the same.

"Be clever like the fox, Alaquoi." Wabete turned his uncanny gaze on Kira, gently lifting fingers to her cheek that had dealt vengeance to others. "Have care, *Neetanetha*, my daughter. You are soft. *Ouishicattuoui*, be strong."

Wonder stirred in her. "How strong, Notha?"

"Like the wind when trees bend."

"You ask much."

He gave a nod. "Much is needed."

She squared her shoulders. "I'll not fail you."

A faint smile crossed his scarred countenance, incongruous with those intimidating features. "Good.

You have the pale beauty of Sister Moon. Shed light on the evil ones who would wrong you. Show them for what they are."

"With my help, she will." Giving Wabete's arm a parting squeeze, Logan turned away. In one swift motion, he boosted her up onto Tequi.

Every muscle protested and she failed to suppress a groan. So far, the hardest part of this adventure seemed to be how beastly uncomfortable it was. And the hour before dawn had to be the most wretchedly cold of all.

Logan swung up behind her and circled an arm around her middle. "Sorry, Cricket. You must be terribly saddle sore."

Achy and weary to the bone as she was, it seemed worse for the women left behind. Tom murmured unintelligible words to his tearful wife and cradled her before stooping over his sleeping girls. Snuggled together like contented cubs, they were unaware of his departure.

Tessa exhibited far less restraint than Laneke and clung sobbing to Meshewa. He pressed his lips over Tessa's face, offering assurances, and trying to part from her without success.

Calling down to her old friend, Kira promised, "Tessa, if it's any way in my power, I swear he shall return to you. And Koonah," she said, uncertain what else to say to Laneke.

Wabete pried Tessa from Meshewa. She turned and stifled shaking sobs against him.

"Rebecca once made that promise to me," Logan said.

"Did she fulfill it?" Kira asked.

"Tessa's alive, isn't she?"

"So shall Meshewa be," Tom said. "We best be off. This isn't getting any easier." Breaking from Laneke, he mounted a brown mare, saddled and ready.

Logan raised his arm in farewell, one everyone solemnly returned except his weeping sister and the slumbering children. Wabete approached Tequi, the unintelligible words he murmured lost on Kira.

"*Tanakia*," Logan offered in parting. Leading the way, he guided Tequi back over the trail they'd followed not many hours ago.

"What did you say to each other?" Kira asked.

"'Until our paths cross again.' And he called you his daughter of the moon."

Strangely touched, she fell silent.

Tom rode behind them and Meshewa brought up the rear on foot. After a while, she asked, "Why doesn't he ride?"

"He can seek cover more quickly this way and better stay out of sight. If we'd come by foot we wouldn't be as easy for Josiah to track. Horses leave prints."

"You wouldn't have left Tequi behind."

"Nor did I want to put you through the ordeal of walking on a recently injured knee."

"Perhaps you should have done."

"Perhaps. There's nothing for it now other than to right this wrong."

Holding her against him, he trotted Tequi past shadowed trunks and branches. The moon sailed overhead and glinted off the river where the tumbling water peeked through the leaves. Rocks loomed in the strange light and disappeared again. White blossoms stood out like sentinels. All other colors receded in this wild moonlit garden.

Finally Logan spoke. "Will you tell me your hunch now, or must I wait until tomorrow?"

"Will you take me back if I tell you?"

"God knows I should."

"Are you glad I came, then?"

Tightening his arm around her, he said,"To have you near me, always. But if anything happens I'll

281

never forgive myself."

"It won't," she insisted, with more bravado then she actually possessed.

"You're going into a battle of sorts, Kira."

A shudder ran through her, and not only from the cold. "I better go ahead and tell you what I know, or think I do."

"Let's hope it gives us an edge. We'll need one."

"Do you remember the cave we used to explore that lies several miles beyond the Houston homestead in the woods between them and Josiah's holding?"

"Sure do. Aunt Alice had fits if we went there. She said it was haunted."

"Most folk believe that and stay away."

Logan considered. "It's not a really big cave, but roomy enough. That could be his lair."

"One matter puzzles me. If Josiah's using the cave as his hideaway, why did he take the horses to his place?"

"He didn't. His cronies did. Campbell was with us when Will and my uncle were attacked. You'd think he would have spared the people caring for the woman he was bent on wedding. Likely he instructed his men to hold on to the horses, intending to return them and the goods, and make himself out to be a hero."

"You mean Josiah planned the whole thing?"

"Right down to being with you when they were robbed to put people off any suspicion. He didn't count on me showing up, though."

"Thank God you did. I could be the wife of that vile man by now."

"The danger isn't over. And it's not a wife he wants if he gets hold of you now, Kira. If we're apprehended, I'll draw Campbell away. You hightail it back to the cave."

The dead earnestness in his tone alarmed her,

but she shook her head. "I couldn't just leave you."

"You can and must. It's vital to alert the Houstons. Only if people know can they take our side."

Wishing Logan could always be this near, she pressed tightly against him. "What if I'm wrong about the cave?"

"I'm hung."

"Not if I have anything to do with it, you're not."

****

After pausing for a hasty meal of cold venison, the party slogged on, Logan and Tom on horseback and Meshewa following unseen somewhere behind. Ominous clouds covered the sun and a storm broke. Thoroughly miserable, Kira huddled against Logan. Wind-swept rain pelted her face, seeping beneath her cloak and chilling her to the marrow. Trees swayed under the assault and a torrent of water rushed across their path. Then they reached the churning stream.

The muddy deluge overflowed its banks. She braced herself to cross. "I wish Tequi could fly over."

"Sorry sweetheart. He hasn't sprouted wings." Logan prodded Tequi into the brown tide.

She tucked her knees well up, but the icy water climbed to her ankles. Logan was already drenched halfway up his legs and his shirt clung to him. He said nothing at the fresh soaking, but she gasped then screeched as Tequi lurched in the swirling tumble.

Logan gripped her. "Hold on. We're almost across."

Tequi recovered his footing and plowed up the muddy bank. He slid on a moss-slicked stone, righted himself, and lunged to higher ground. Blowing hard, he paused in swords of dripping fern.

Kira pitied the winded horse. "Do stop, Logan. He's all in."

"Tequi's tougher than that. But we'll stop soon."

"Thank goodness. Surely reaching the cave can wait until tomorrow?"

"We'll see what a rest does," he hedged.

"Logan—"

"You'll get through this and live to see better days."

Kira wasn't so certain.

Evergreen boughs sprayed her with cold droplets as he guided the horse past saturated hemlocks. Not that it really mattered anymore. Up ahead, a massive limb took shape in the haze blocking their way like a giant's arm. She blinked up at the enormous chestnut arching over the trail. The great limb must have ripped off during all the bluster and left a jagged tear.

Logan halted Tequi. Rocks mottled with gray-green lichens mounded on their right and barred any outlet that way. She could worm through the snarl of vines and branches on their left, but not the horses. "Can Tequi jump it?"

"He might injure his belly. I'll try to shift it."

Swinging his leg over Tequi, Logan splashed down to the trail running with wet. He propped his musket against a furrowed trunk and bent over. Muscles bulged beneath his rain-drenched shirt as he strained to lift the cumbersome branch. "It's wedged between stones," he grunted.

Tom tethered his mare to a misty tree and trudged up to Logan. The downfall had diminished, but the nearby stream roared in Kira's ears. She squinted from Tequi as the two men struggled to wrench the gargantuan bough aside.

"Damn heavy," Tom panted.

"And stuck," Logan said through his teeth.

Their chests rose and fell while they stopped to catch their breath. Logan wiped the rain from his face. "Let's have another go."

This time they shifted it far enough for the horses to squeeze through. Then straightened, panting, and threw a companionable arm around each other.

"Any trees you want to heave from the ground while we're at it?" Logan chuckled.

Kira was glad to see them more at ease, but every part of her cried out for respite. "Could we rest awhile?"

Tom nodded, and Logan reached up for her. "Let's have you down."

Perhaps she could persuade them to seek shelter beneath the rocky outcropping farther up the ridge. More than anything she wanted to collapse before a warm blaze, eat and sleep, mostly sleep, a piece of heaven compared to this endless trek.

Logan swept her past the puddles and stood her on the spongy ground. He held her to him, kissing her cold face. "Poor Cricket. You should have stayed in that tree where I first found you. You'd have been better off."

"Never. I wouldn't trade a moment I've had with—"

"Not another step!"

She startled at the angry bark. Her heart nearly stopped, then pounded so loudly it was deafening. She lifted unwilling eyes to the rider fast taking shape in the whiteness. Josiah's long musket barrel aimed right at them.

Logan tensed against her. "Damn," he said under his breath. "My musket's at the tree. So is Tom's."

Other riders trotted up behind Josiah. She couldn't be certain how many. Frontiersmen, likely acting as the militia Winn had summoned. The nightmare rapidly worsened as the captain himself rode into view. The corpulent officer reined in his roan gelding and glared at them, eyes like hobnails, jowly face pink and moist.

"I've some questions for you, McCutcheon. Who's the man with you?"

Josiah sneered. "McClure, I'll wager. You're keeping poor company these days, Tom."

"No more than you."

Thick eyebrows drew into a bushy 'V' across Winn's glare. "I want a word with you as well, Mister McClure."

Logan clutched Kira as if in defiance of the inevitable. He and Tom couldn't possibly fight off so many.

"What's this about, Captain?"

"You are accused of an attack on Mister Campbell committed in the company of warriors, fraternizing with the enemy, treasonous behavior. Need I go on?"

"You've only that rat-assed bastard's say to support any of these charges!"

"I'm satisfied with his word, sir," Winn said coldly.

"Perhaps you should examine his character more closely," Logan countered icily.

"Or are you in league with the thief?" Tom tossed out.

Kira cringed at his boldness.

Every visible part of Winn's fleshy face reddened. "One more outburst like that and I'll have you flogged." He waved to the soldiers accompanying him. "Bind them both."

Josiah fixed hungry eyes on Kira. "What of the witch?"

"I'll cut out your lying tongue!" Tom shouted.

"She says it of herself, McClure," Josiah spit back.

"Bind her with the others," Captain Winn ordered. "No doubt she's used her craft to aid them."

"The hell she has." Tom whipped out his knife

and hurtled between the limb and the rocks at Josiah. Two burly soldiers snagged him and narrowly evaded his blade. One dashed the knife from his hand. Tom kicked out and flung the men off, only to be seized again.

Kira shrieked as Josiah hammered her thrashing brother and bloodied his mouth. Josiah drove his fist into Tom's middle. He doubled over with a groan.

"For God's sake, stop!" she screamed, and looked in horror at Logan.

Molten anger glinted in his eyes. Another quality was also there, steely calm, and he was still like a mountain lion about to spring. Slipping the hard butt of a pistol into her hand, he whispered, "Run."

She instinctively hid the firearm beneath her cloak, but hovered beside him uncertainly. How could she just leave him to his fate?

Men were dismounting and striding forward.

"Go!" Giving her a push, Logan charged at the nearest man and threw him back. "Now, Kira!"

Chapter Twenty

Like a stunned rabbit sprung to life, Kira darted at an opening in the woodsy tangle.

"Get back here, woman, or it will go all the worse for you!" Captain Winn bellowed after her.

She squeezed through the vines and sprang away again.

Someone thrashed in the underbrush behind her.

"Take these prisoners on, Captain! I'll fetch her!"

Josiah! She fled down the side of the ridge. Scrambling over slick stones, she grabbed wet branches to steady herself. Chipmunks scurried into hollow logs and quail flew up. The brown and white birds scattered into the mist. Unlike them, she had no idea where to go or hide—just away. Brambles caught her hair and cloak, scratched her hands, but she scarcely heeded the sting.

Desperation for Logan pounded in her mind. Was he bound, helpless? Had the soldiers struck him down? What of Tom, were bony knuckles pummeling him again and again? Anxiety for them surged alongside terror for herself.

The pistol Logan shoved into her hand held one shot. She had no powder or lead to reload and little experience in firing. This one volley would have to count. Breath rasping in her fiery chest, she ran through bracken fern. Sweet fragrances rose from the wet spring woods in contrast to the scent of fear permeating her.

No dread of becoming lost assailed her, only of

being found. And she slapped through branches seeking an opening in the trees. A river tumbled up ahead, but thick haze and leaves concealed its bank. She bit back a yelp as the ground dropped away and her feet slid out from under her. Grabbing at branches flying by, she thudded down the steep incline. Leaves slid through her fingers. Nothing anchored her. Over and over, she tumbled. She wound up sprawled on her back in fern and mud, too breathless to moan.

Josiah would come any moment. She must get up, take cover and ready herself to fire. With him behind her and the river in front, she was trapped.

Too late—his towering figure appeared on the hazy bank.

Winded from the chase, he stood with his hands clasping the tops of his legs. "Damn fast, gal. Not fast enough."

She lifted the pistol with trembling hands and pointed it at him. "Stay away!"

Rain streaked the grime on Josiah's scornful face. "You think you can shoot that, Kira?"

She cocked the trigger. "I'll have a bloody good go."

"You won't fire." He lifted one great boot.

"Stop!"

An insolent smile curved his lips. "I'm coming for you."

He stuck out his foot. And she pulled the trigger. The smoky explosion tore from the weapon in her fingers out across his shoulder—the same shoulder Logan had shot.

A loud yelp and Josiah clasped the crimson stain oozing from between his fingers. "You bitch!"

God help her, she was going to die, or worse. Kira watched in horror as he clamored down the bank. No living creature had eyes like that. There was haunting familiarity between Josiah's and

Tonkawa's fiendish stare.

Crouched beside her, he struck the pistol away then cracked her across the cheek. "Bind this wound."

Face stinging, she sat up. Her hands shook so hard she could barely do as he bid, but tore a strip from the hem of her already shortened petticoat. She tied it around the red furrow on his upper arm and stared at him numbly.

He shoved her back down and bent over her. "Nothing to say? You said plenty the last time we met. What of the shapes you can take? If I were you, I'd change myself into an owl right about now."

"I'm no more of a witch than you are."

"Shouldn't have lied then, should you? You'll do anything for your precious Logan. Can't do anything to aid him now, can you? And he can do nothing for you."

She could scarcely swallow past the lump in her throat. "Will you kill me?"

His evil grin better suited a fiend. "You're no use to me dead. I shall do as I've longed to then haul you back to Winn, a shamed, beaten woman. No one in the settlement will keep company with a witch, wife to a traitor hanged for treason. Your fate will be worse than Hannah's. The first I'll take from you is the witch's cross." Ripping the treasured crucifix from her neck, he tossed it aside.

Anger flashed in her terror. "Give that back!" She lunged at him.

Hands snapped around her wrists and he forced her back down. "You'll have to do better than that, Kira," he jeered, pinning her arms over her head. She collapsed under his weight as hated lips claimed hers. "Don't fret, lass," he said against her mouth. "When all others have cast you off, you'll still have me."

"Then I pray the captain hangs me too."

"Winn won't. I'll see to that."

Twisting beneath Josiah, she cried, "I'll confess to treason!"

He reared back and struck her cheek again. "You'll do as I say."

Pain sharpened her resistance. Then a shadow caught her eye. Blinking at hot tears, she glanced over Josiah's broad shoulder. Her heart lurched at the stealthy figure gliding up behind them, his tomahawk upraised.

"You've had your say, Josie."

"Like hell."

She lay unresisting as he grasped a handful of petticoats and jerked the sodden skirts up to her thighs.

"Any last words?" she asked.

He reached toward his breeches. "Enough talk."

"Agreed." Closing her eyes, she braced for the blow.

All she heard from Josiah was a guttural grunt.

Smothering weight fell over her. Gasping, she struggled to escape his death hold. "Get him off me!"

"I will. Calm down."

"Hurry—he's horrible!" His stench intensified with the terrible load bearing down on her. If she'd had anything left in her stomach she would have lost it all.

Meshewa heaved Josiah's bulk from her. While she gulped in air, he pried the scarlet-edged tomahawk from his back, and rolled him over.

"Oh, God." Staggering to her feet, she recoiled at the blood pooled under his lolling head. He seemed to be staring at her with a look of madness in his sightless gaze.

A hand over her mouth, she stumbled back, tripping over a stone. She crawled farther away and slumped on the wet earth like a child clinging to its mother. Her teeth chattered. "I thought he had me for sure."

Meshewa bent over her with all the gentleness Josiah had lacked. "This evil man will trouble you no longer."

She heaved a shuddering breath. "I forgot you were there."

"Alaquoi remembered."

"When Logan told me to run he knew you'd come?"

"Would he send a dove to flee an eagle? You could not defeat one so powerful. Even with the pistol he gave you."

"Thank you—that's the second time you've saved—" she hesitated, uncertain how to express her gratitude.

"You owe me no thanks. Alaquoi is my brother."

She looked shakily into Meshewa's steady gaze. "I'm beginning to understand why."

Fear for Logan and Tom returned in a dizzying rush. "What do we do now?"

"First, warm you. So cold, weak, you are." He stood and helped her up. She swayed against him. He circled a strong arm around her and half-carried her along the river, stopping before a rocky shelf. "Go under."

She ducked her head and scooted beneath the overhang. Dry leaves cushioned her and the chill wind couldn't reach her here, but her wet clothes offered no warmth. Meshewa took off his bedroll and spread the deerskin on the earthen floor for her to sit on. He untied her cloak and laid it aside, then wrapped his blanket around her. She was grateful for the dry wool, but trembled violently.

He tucked her against his warmth. Never in her wildest imaginings would Kira have thought to shelter in a warrior's embrace. "Won't Tessa mind?"

"To keep your life, none would." He said nothing more.

Weariness washed over her. "I should rise. We must—go." A yawn intruded on her insistence.

"Rest first."

She battled the deepening urge to lose herself in slumber. "But Logan and Tom are depending on us."

"Yes. Sleep, gain strength to aid them."

Conceding the wisdom in this, she closed heavy eyes. But release didn't come immediately; a thought nagged at her like a thorn. "Meshewa?" she said drowsily. "Josiah tore the cross from my neck. It was dear to me." Tears slid down her sore cheeks. Such a tiny thing would be impossible to find among the stones and plants along the river bank.

"I regret he took this. He would do far worse."

"I know." Meshewa must think her foolish to cry over a lost keepsake when he'd rescued her from such dire peril. Anger brewed alongside her sorrow. "I want Josiah's knife."

"We will get it later. He moves not."

"I want his pistol too."

"Have care not to shoot yourself."

"I'll be careful," she sniffed, pressing her face against him. He smelled like the rainy woods, smoke, and wind. "I'm so frightened for Logan and Tom."

"Do you know where this captain will take them?"

"Most likely Fort Rudd—" she said, another yawn splitting her reply. "Smaller than Warden and not many miles from where it stood."

"First we seek this cave. How far have we to journey?"

"I'm not sure where we are, but a goodly trek." Not one she felt equal to. "I wish we had a horse."

"There is much you want."

"Just Logan and Tom alive."

****

Gradually Kira became aware of the noises

293

around her, the rapid water, shrill cry of a kestrel, and it came to her that she was alone. Meshewa had gone. His presence had brought badly needed comfort. She was fast growing dependent on him and strangely fond, as though in some sense he was her brother as well as Logan's. Her thoughts swept back to Logan and Tom and a sharp pang shot through her.

She must reach the cave and get help. Her bruised body ached all over but she had to keep going and sat up under the rock ledge. She gingerly rubbed her tender cheek. It was hard to believe Josiah's hand would never again be lifted against her. Was Meshewa bent over his gruesome corpse now? She had no desire to see.

Trailing the blanket, she crawled from beneath the stones. The fog had lifted and white clouds scattered before the breeze. She stood, brushed back lengths of hair whipping her face, and wrapped the blue cloth around her. The sun hung low. He must've let her sleep several hours.

If anything happened to him, Logan and Tom's fate rested solely on her. With that grim thought, she knelt by the swift river and cupped water to her mouth. Her growling stomach reminded her that she'd had no food since early morning. She ran her eyes up and down the river bank seeking Meshewa's sinewy figure among the stones and leaves glistening with rain. Swallows swooped over the water, but no warrior greeted her.

Another unsettling thought occurred. If he didn't come soon, darkness would close in while she waited—alone. And Josiah lay not far downstream. She washed his foul touch from her mouth and face with a shudder. *Please God, don't let him be a ghost, too.*

"So, you are awake?"

She straightened and spun around. Meshewa

was a few yards behind her. She ran to him, stumbling. "Thank God—"

He steadied her. "Why are you frightened?"

She didn't care what anyone thought and flung her arms around his neck. "I feared you wouldn't come back."

Closing a consoling arm around her shoulders, he said. "I will not leave you alone. I will give you aid to restore your husband and brother."

"And if you cannot?"

He spoke gravely. "Take you to Wabete. What else? This Captain Winn will seize you."

What cruel irony to be driven from her people and forced to seek sanctuary with those she'd feared the most. "I couldn't bear to live without Logan. I'd rather die."

"Do not fear so. The battle is not yet lost. First eat, gain strength. I found food in Campbell's saddle bag."

She heartened immediately. "I forgot about his horse. Bryan doesn't like strangers. Did he give you any trouble?"

Meshewa shrugged as though a kick or nip was of little consequence. He led her back to the rocky shelter and they sat together on the deerskin beneath the ledge. He took slices of smoked ham and cornbread wrapped in leaves from inside the front of his shirt, like a pocket.

She chewed hungrily. "Where did you leave the horse?"

He nodded in the direction of the trail she'd fled. "I watered him, tied him there."

"This is welcome news. We can ride the remainder of the journey."

"If he does not throw us to the ground."

"Bryan knows me," she said in between mouthfuls.

"We shall see."

She started in on the corn bread. "Aren't you eating?"

"I have done so."

She wolfed down the last of her food, relishing the smear of molasses. "I feel more like battling now."

"Good. We journey tonight."

She licked a sticky forefinger. "I'll need arms."

He angled a guarded eye at her. "Did you ever fire a pistol before today?"

"Will Houston let me fire his sometimes."

Taking the coveted firearm from his belt, he handed it to her. "This is loaded, Kira. I have no wish to be shot."

"I'll leave the trigger guard in place until time to fire." She traced her fingertips over the fine craftsmanship. The wooden stock was even more ornately carved than Logan's. All the furniture on the pistol was brass, and scrolled with serpentine designs. "It's French-made. Josiah took it from a French officer he killed."

"I see this."

For a moment it slipped her mind that Meshewa had sided with the French during the war. How odd to be united with him now in a common purpose. She examined the small ramrod beneath the barrel. "What of the powder and shot?"

"You know how to load?"

She envisioned the steps. "Will showed me."

Meshewa patted the extra shot pouch and powder horn hanging across his front. She'd been so distracted she hadn't noticed the duplicates. He slid the woven straps over his neck and passed them into her eager hands. She slipped them over her head and across her left shoulder. The powder horn hung just above the shot pouch. Both dangled down further on her than on Meshewa and much further than on Josiah's big frame.

"You want this?" He held out the knife.

The hardwood handle wrapped with leather and the well-honed blade called to her. "Beautiful."

A faint smile touched his lips as he passed it to her. "You need a belt to hold your weapons. I cut Campbell's down. Come." Gathering his bedroll, he scooted out from under the ledge.

Clutching her weapons and cloak, she crawled after him, tripping over her skirts. "You must think me very clumsy."

He helped her to her feet. "No. Weary and you hurry too much."

His response was kind, though she'd detected some amusement. Not that she blamed him. She'd done little but stumble and fall since they'd met.

She hated to ask, but had to know. "What did you do with Josiah's body?"

"In the stream." Taking the improvised belt, he tied it around her waist. The knife hung in the sheath on her left side and he stuck the pistol through the belt at her right.

The added weight was strange, but reassuring. "How do I look?"

"Like a warrior woman."

"I'm angry enough to fight. Also afraid."

He reached back into the pouch and withdrew something. The fading light shone on the cross gleaming in his palm. He must have cleaned off the mud and polished the gold.

Placing it in her hand, he said, "Have courage."

She slipped the cross into her bodice where it rested between her breasts near her heart, and followed him back up the ridge she'd flown down. The tethered black stallion lifted his head and whinnied.

Meshewa edged up to him and grasped the halter. He raised his moccasin to get a leg into the stirrup. But Bryan tossed his head and backed away.

Again Meshewa tried. Ears flattened, Bryan kicked out and danced to the side. Meshewa dodged his powerful hindquarters while gripping the reins, but was no further along.

If they were to ride the remainder of the journey, Kira would have to calm the unruly animal. Though skilled in taming forest creatures, she'd never been adept with horses. She inhaled deeply. "Let me have a go."

"He has much temper."

"So have I. Steady, boy. Steady," she crooned, easing closer. She grasped the halter and jerked it as the stallion tried to break away. "Enough nonsense, Bryan."

His defiance lessened under her stern admonishment and familiar voice. "Easy, fellow. I know you're upset," she said gently and stroked his velvet nose. He stilled as if listening. "I'm counting on you to make amends for all the trouble your wicked master has caused."

The stallion nuzzled her battered cheek. It was time to act. "Meshewa, give me a boost up."

He did and she found herself sitting astride the horse, skirts bunched up around her legs. She gripped the reins. "Quick, get on while I hold him."

Meshewa sprang up behind her. "You did well."

After battling Tonkawa and Josiah, confronting this temperamental animal didn't seem as daunting as it would have not long ago. Loosening the reins slightly, she urged Bryan into a manageable trot. How was it possible she was riding Josiah's stallion, with a warrior mounted behind? Her life seemed to grow continually stranger. But then everything about this night had an air of unreality.

The moonlight filtering through the forest added to that other-worldly feeling. She wondered if she were dreaming. The cool breeze and the horse trotting beneath her persuaded her she wasn't. She must remain alert to maintain control over Bryan and find her way. Meshewa's knowledge of the area wasn't as detailed as hers, though he'd been with the war party that attacked Fort Warden.

Noises accompanied their ghostly journey. Scuttles in the underbrush, foxes barking. Deer snorted and sprang across their path. These weren't the only creatures prowling the dark woods. Kira was especially grateful for Meshewa's presence when the thin howl of wolves trailed across the night.

Miles wore on broken only by the occasional need to dismount and lead Bryan around downed branches and fallen trees. Gradually, the blackened path took on a more familiar and traveled appearance. She kept a sharp eye out and trusted Meshewa's keen gaze would do even better. They must be prepared to stop in an instant if anyone approached and let him slip into the trees.

Crabapple blossoms perfumed the air as they paused to drink from the stream and eat the rest of Josiah's food. How far removed Kira felt from the girl Logan wed only a few days ago. What would he think if he saw her now, armed with Josiah's weapons, commandeering his horse?

Her stomach knotted, and she wondered how far ahead of them Logan and Tom were and how they fared. She fought against paralyzing fear. Only by keeping a clear head could she hope to help them.

A twig snapped and she swiveled her head—a black bear. She breathed out in relief. Given their lot, a bear was less of a menace than many humans. But those were to come.

Chapter Twenty-One

What a hellish day and fast fading into a hellish night. Tied to a damn tree, Logan couldn't move. He hadn't been forced to endure this maddening restriction since he was first taken captive by Wabete and Shoka seven years ago. Nor had Tom, bound to the other side of the scaly trunk just as he'd been back then. The confounded cords dug into Logan's arms and chest. Thankfully his shirt was woven of thick cloth or he'd be worse off than he already was.

Even so, his limbs grew numb. And he was bone-tired, hungry, thirsty, his eyes swollen from more than one man's fist, jaw sore, lips bloodied. His ribs were bruised and he ached all over as though strong men had beaten him from head to toe with a stout stick. They might as well have. Tom had suffered just as harshly.

At least the rain had stopped, but that was about the sum of their blessings. If Captain Winn hadn't wanted them both alive for hanging, they'd likely be dead by now. And who would know? At least, who with any influence? Once they'd dangled by their necks, it would be too late anyway.

With the Indian Wars stark in everyone's memory, only their nearest and dearest would grieve their loss. It occurred to Logan that the release of death might be preferable to his current state, but there was no way in Heaven or Hell that he'd ever give up on finding Kira. He had to be with her again—had to.

Straining at his bonds, he groaned. Pray God,

she was safe. He was nearly half crazed with worry over her. It was maddening to be restrained this way. He couldn't even scratch the itch on his chin or swat an annoying gnat.

A shower of sparks flew up from the campfire crackling about twenty yards away from him. He ran swollen eyes over the men gathered around the orange blaze. The meaty scent of roasting game tormented his empty stomach, but Captain Winn was more likely to feed a stray dog than his prisoners. Settled by the fire, his back to them, he swigged from a flask. Nor was he the only one guzzling brandy or whisky. A brown bottle passed from hand to hand. Let them drink up. The more intoxicated the men grew the better.

"Hey," Tom grunted through a throat that had to be equally parched. "I know one of them."

Logan had a better line of sight than Tom whose back was to the rough assembly gathering. He peered at the figures silhouetted against the flames. "Which one?"

"The fellow who didn't hit us with any real teeth in his fist. Name's Jason Rudd, son of the late Captain Rudd. He was little more than a boy back then, decent sort, as was his father. I taught Jason to whistle through his fingers. Think he may be trying not to let on he knows me."

"To put the others off?"

"Yeah."

The lanky young man was partly hidden under a wide-brimmed hat decorated at the back with a white deer's tail and pheasant feathers. A three week's beard darkened his chin and he'd caught his shoulder-length brown hair back at his neck. His dun-colored hunting shirt, breeches, and worn riding boots the garb of most frontiersmen. Nothing about Jason Rudd stood out in Logan's memory, except that he was Captain Rudd's son. But Tom was older than Logan and serving in the militia when he was taken captive.

In a husky croak Logan asked, "Might Jason aid us?"

"I damn well pray so."

Maybe it was a good thing Tom had come along after all. He'd feared all Tom had accomplished thus far was getting himself beaten and condemned to the noose alongside Logan, which would break more than one heart, including Kira's. For the first time since they'd fallen into the hands of Captain Winn and his men, Logan had a glimmer of hope. He fixed his sight on the fellow slouched by the fire.

Now and then, Jason glanced their way, his manner guarded. Unlike the others, he didn't enter into the conversation, but watched and listened. Savory rabbits and pheasants were sliced, trenchers filled from a kettle of bubbling cornmeal, and portions passed around. Ample food remained to share with Logan and Tom. That lout Winn even had seconds. But no offers came. Then the sated gathering sank around the fire and the ribald exchange died off. Snoring took the place of talk.

With the utmost casualness, Jason got to his feet.

The man beside him muttered,"You taking a piss, Rudd?"

"Uh huh."

"See to the fire while you're about it."

Logan watched Jason bend down and gather an armful of kindling. He didn't toss the wood on the fire, but fed the flames quietly, as if not wanting to rouse the others. That glimmer of hope in Logan grew. The fellow was definitely behaving in a stealthy manner.

"Think you may be right," he whispered to Tom.

Rather than slipping behind a bush to relieve himself Jason crept toward the tree where they were bound. As he neared, Logan detected an object in his hand. *Damn, a knife.* Was Jason going to free them or slit their throats?

"He's got a blade, Tom."

"He would have, wouldn't he?" Tom said in a dry voice.

Logan wasn't so certain and held himself rigid as Jason slipped beneath the overhanging boughs. The young man squatted beside them, his face lost in shadows.

"There'll be hell to pay if I'm seen," he said, his low voice gruff, "but I don't care a lick for Winn, and Tom and I go way back. I think a lot of your cousin, McCutcheon," he added, sawing at the cords around Logan's chest and arms.

"Thanks." He could hardly believe Jason's kindness after all they'd suffered today and was grateful for Will's popularity with the young soldier.

"I saved some game for you and your mounts are ready. Look sharp and be on your way before the others wake."

"I can't thank you enough. But what of you?" Tom asked. "Winn will cry foul at our escape."

"As far as I know, you had a blade hidden on you."

Logan hoped Winn accepted their rescuer's account, but didn't dwell on his fate. They had miles to go and he had to find Kira. There was only one place he knew to look.

****

Still Kira and Meshewa had encountered no one. Wistfulness welled in her as they neared the holding that had been her home for years. "We're close to the cave now and not far from the Houstons." If only she could see them again. Bryan perked up expectantly, conveying a sense of journey done. "He knows this place."

"Well," Meshewa pointed out.

The stallion balked as she halted him outside the cave entrance she and Logan had used years ago. She hauled back on the reins, but he seemed intent on continuing. "This is the way in, unless Josiah discovered another."

"His horse will know."

She gave Bryan his head. Without hesitation, he picked his way between the tall fern and woodsy brush that hid the familiar entrance. He picked his way to the other side of the tree-lined hill and stopped.

Stones blocked any view of a secret opening. "If there's another way in, it must lie somewhere beyond those rocks."

"We will see." Meshewa dismounted first and swung her to the ground.

Riding astride had not diminished her aches; in fact, she'd developed new ones. She stifled a groan and stretched her sore limbs.

The bright moon didn't pour much light down on the shrubs and mound of stones here. "How will we find our way?"

He tethered Bryan among the weedy grasses. "Come."

"Can you see in the dark, like a cat?"

"Almost."

Following his dim figure, she said, "Logan also."

"Shoka, Wabete taught us," Meshewa explained in low tones.

She successfully rounded some of the rocks, only to collide with another. "Ouch. I'm awkward enough when it's light, let alone dark."

He took her arm. Under his direction she made better progress through the rocks. The moonlight illuminated a gaping hole in the stone. "We need a torch," she whispered, sensing they were precisely where Josiah, were he alive, wouldn't want them to be. "Even in midday you can't see to explore inside."

Pointing to one side of the yawning entrance, Meshewa said, "I will make a small fire there to light the torch."

She helped him gather twigs and strips of bark, anything remotely dry and combustible. He took the flint and steel from his pouch and struck them together.

The sparks combined with a pinch of gunpowder brought his small pile to glowing life. "I have little powder left."

"Josiah's horn isn't suffering. Take what you want."

He tipped some of the powder into his horn and spoke in her ear. "Stay here."

Sinking onto a stone by the small fire, she rested while she waited. He soon returned with a pine branch and lit the resinous knot at one end, then smothered the blaze. "Come." She ducked her head and scrambled after him, bumping into him in the process. "Slow, Kira. I will not leave you behind."

"You better not. I'm not fond of tight places. I only came to this cave as a girl because Logan dared me and Aunt Alice said not to."

"Give me your hand."

She clung to his reassuring fingers and followed just behind him. Cold droplets wet her head as they navigated the rocky maze. The cramped space seemed worse now that she was older and taller. "Surely it widens soon. Josiah couldn't store supplies in this narrow place."

Meshewa held the flickering light over the damp floor. Traces of tallow had left a waxy trail on the sandy stones. "This way."

Chill air permeated the cave and she was glad for her blanket, gladder still when Meshewa found a second torch stuck in a crevice in the wall and lit it. The tallow-soaked cloth gave out a brighter flame than theirs. Any added light in this nether region was welcome. Grasping a raised torch in each hand, he padded through the winding passage with her at his heels.

"Still no signs of stolen goods," she whispered.

"Yet men came this way."

The dancing flames illuminated an opening into another stone chamber. He went first. She squeezed through the rocky hole behind him and found herself in a far bigger room than anything she remembered.

Meshewa swept his torches at the chamber. "You ever see anything like this?"

"Never."

Bizarre shapes hung from the high ceiling or sprouted from the floor. Some even joined those above. Their pearly surfaces glistened in the torchlight with the dripping wetness that had formed them. Trickles of water spilled down the rock walls and collected into a small pool. She couldn't be certain how high the ceiling was because impenetrable darkness, blacker than night, swallowed every nook not illuminated.

"The part of the cave Logan and I explored was much smaller."

"Many caves lie in these mountains. Some very large. Rebecca and Shoka spoke of such a place."

Kira pressed closely to Meshewa. "This one?"

"No. Larger still, and farther to the South."

"This one is big enough for me. I don't like it here."

"No." He held the torches high and they walked over the uneven ground spying out more of the secret chamber. Wooden kegs, skins, furs, muskets, saddles, and sacks came to light like sins hidden away. "I like this better."

She gaped at the pile of goods. "Where on earth did Josiah and his men come by all of this stuff?"

"They stole from many people."

Bending over, she peered into a sack of pewter

spoons, plates and cups. "Josiah said he was off on hunting trips when really he was raiding the ridges and up and down the Shenandoah Valley from the look of this."

Meshewa stuck both torches into chinks in the stone. "My people would be glad for this wealth."

"We can't take it all with us."

"Perhaps a little." He slid a second powder horn over his shoulder and exchanged his musket for a more finely crafted flintlock.

"I wouldn't begin to know who it belongs to," she said. "But that makes no difference. We have proof that Josiah is a scoundrel and a liar."

Meshewa's keen gaze met hers. "Captain Winn may say you have no proof Campbell is the man who did this. And dead men make no confessions."

Despair rolled over her at the realization. "That's just the sort of thing Winn would say, especially if I carry the tale. You certainly can't tell him. We need someone reliable the captain respects."

"You must make someone hear you. What of this Will Houston you speak of?"

"Yes. Will would listen to me. He and his new wife should be at the Houston homestead by now."

"Go to him, Kira. Tell him what your eyes see here. Speak to him of the danger to your husband and brother."

"I'll tell Logan's uncle and aunt, too. It won't be easy to persuade them though, Meshewa."

"Why is this?"

"I'm not known for always telling the truth. Not lies exactly, what folks call *notions*." A tendency she heartily wished she'd better kept in check.

"This wealth is real. Show them."

"Where will you be?"

"I will stay from sight. Do not fear for me."

"But I do. Once I'm gone how will I find you

again? What if I need you—how will I know you're all right?"

He clasped her shoulder. "Fear not. I will be well. You will find your way."

She had better. All their lives depended on it.

Chapter Twenty-Two

"What the hell are you playing at, Josie?"

Kira jerked at the angry bark breaking into her and Meshewa's exchange. He held a finger to his lips.

The growling voice continued. "I ran into Winn hauling McCutcheon and Tom McCue to Fort Rudd. He thought you were catching him up, not bringing the girl back here."

Too stunned to move, Kira managed a breathless whisper to Meshewa, "It's Josiah's cousin, Nate. He must have spotted Bryan outside."

Eyes hard, the warrior in him evident in his taut face, Meshewa pulled her into a recessed corner of the cavern. He gestured her farther back and she scrunched into a fissure in the damp rock. Flattened against the shadowed stone, he kept furtive watch.

Nate's exasperation grew louder. "Winn's bedded down for the night, but I wouldn't care to be you come morning."

"More than he knows," Kira hissed to Meshewa.

"Malcolm's furious!" a second man added.

Totally unprepared for his presence, she said under her breath, "I don't know this voice. Why is he calling Captain Winn by his first name?"

"He is a good friend or brother," Meshewa suggested.

"Come on, Josie, we know you're in here!" That was Nate again. "Have you lost your head? The girl will talk. As odd as she is, someone will listen."

"Malcolm won't have it. You'll have to get rid of her," the stranger added.

309

Two thoughts occurred to Kira; first, Josiah's men would have to do his dirty work for him. Second, Winn was somehow involved in the theft—so much for persuading the captain of their discovery. They must contrive another scheme and fast. She darted her eyes over other dark recesses in the cave. Worming her way farther back into a black hole held no appeal, but their present position would soon be detected by the approaching pair.

Heart in her throat, she whispered, "What now?"

"Fight them." Meshewa lifted his newly acquired musket and pointed its long barrel at the gap in the rocky maze that adjoined their spacious chamber. It was a distance of roughly fifty yards with strange cave formations rising between. Not a straight shot.

A chill ran through her. "Kill them both?"

"One. Take the other alive."

"Why?"

"He must speak to the Houstons."

Steeling herself, she watched the opening with the intensity of a cat stalking a mouse. "Leave Nate, then."

His bulk appeared first, his manner and look awfully reminiscent of his cousin's. Waving a torch around the cave, he stepped through the gap. "Are you deaf, Josie? Girl got your tongue?"

"Give over. You've screwed with her enough—" his companion argued, halting in mid-cry at the explosion shattering the air.

Kira hadn't heard a musket fired at close range in confined quarters. It was all she could do not to scream. If she had, the shriek from the stranger would've drowned her out. Still screaming, he clutched his side and fell to the sandy stone.

Nate flung down his torch and dove behind an unlikely formation shaped like wings, tinged pink. "Have you gone mad, cousin? It's Nate! For God's sake, man, you just shot Brewster."

Brewster...the name was vaguely familiar, but Kira couldn't clearly see the bearded man writhing on the cave floor. Meshewa uncorked his powder horn with his teeth. She must buy him a few vital moments to reload and lure their fugitive into the open. "Trust me," she pleaded.

He frowned at her. "What are you doing?" he asked past the cork gripped between his teeth.

"You'll see. Please, I have to do this." Fighting to steady her voice, she said softly. "Nate, do you remember me?"

He peered around the winged stone, eyes wide, reddish hair catching the torch light. "Who in blazes?"

"I followed you through the trees," she called in the eerie tone she'd used when he mistook her for the owl.

"Like hell. Where's Josie?" he flung back, not entirely concealing the tremor in his reply.

"Dead. You'll not find him here."

"I don't believe it."

He sounded as stunned as she felt, yet a sense of power came over her. "No? Ask the river where your cousin lies."

"Who killed him?"

"Come closer and see. Or do you fear me?"

"I fear no woman."

"Are you certain that's what I am?"

"Bloody right! I'll not be fired on like Brewster."

"No harm will come to you, if you do as I say. If not, you will die like Josiah."

"Damn witch!" He leapt out from behind the stone, musket raised, and fired. His shot passed harmlessly over their heads.

She drew Josiah's pistol and rushed at him. "Not another step!"

The big man froze. "Kira?" Staring eyes fixed on the pistol in her hand. "That's Josie's."

She cocked the trigger. "I have his knife and his horse too. Drop your musket."

It clattered to the floor.

"Knife on the ground."

The lethal blade thudded beside the musket. All the while, Brewster moaned and twisted only a few yards away.

Still Nate seemed not to believe his eyes. "How in hell did a slip of a girl kill Josiah?"

"Never mind. You're going to tell the Houstons what's been going on here."

"And if I refuse?"

"I'll shoot you and tell them myself."

Scorn curved lips all too reminiscent of Josiah's. "They won't believe you."

"I'll make them. Or get Brewster to speak. He has some life in him yet."

"Not much. Do you think Winn will thank you for killing Josiah and shooting his brother?"

"That's Brewster Winn?"

"Sure is, little darling."

"Don't call me that!" Momentarily taken aback, she struggled to think. "The Houston and Lewis family and others won't stand idly by when they learn Captain Winn is involved in this thievery along with the rest of you and your late cousin."

Challenge gleamed in Nate's hazel eyes. "Shoot me, then. I'll not speak."

She hesitated. This wasn't the same as firing at Josiah when he was bearing down on her. "Come now, Kira. You and I played together as children," Nate wheedled.

"One of us grew up to be a snake. You were about to get rid of me, Nate Campbell. I heard you."

He stepped toward her. "Just talk, to put Josie off. I wouldn't hurt you."

"Stay back!"

He smiled. "You can't shoot me, can you?"

Meshewa strode from the shadows, his musket aimed right at him. "I can. I have no difficulty cutting you into pieces, like a deer."

Outrage overran the mocking in Nate's face. "God damn savage. You killed Josiah—not Kira. And you shot Brewster. I thought that blast was too loud for a pistol."

"Now I must kill you," Meshewa said flatly.

Kira looked from one to the other in alarm. "But what of his confession?"

"He will not speak."

"Couldn't you make him?"

"You want me to cut him into pieces first?"

She couldn't be certain if Meshewa were serious or bluffing. Judging by the horror in Nate's expression, he took the grim-faced warrior at his word.

His voice broke like an adolescent boy's as he faltered,"I might be of some help."

"You will," Meshewa assured him. "Or I will cut off your hand. Take the cord from my pouch, Kira. Bind him." Reaching shakily into his pouch, she drew out the length of buckskin. "Give me your pistol." She left it with Meshewa and cautiously approached Nate.

"One move, I fire," Meshewa warned. "Hands behind your back."

Nate grudgingly complied and she wound the cord around his wrists, tying it as tightly as possible. A strangled oath escaped her prisoner. "And his ankles," Meshewa said.

"But how will he walk?"

"He won't. You must bring the Houstons here."

She wrenched Nate's boots off and bound his thick, stocking-clad ankles together. "What will you do?"

"Go."

She didn't dare ask where in front of the men,

even though Brewster was paying scant heed to their exchange.

"I'll not forget I saw you, you godless savage!" Nate hurled at him.

"Bind his mouth, hard." Meshewa tossed her a coarse strip of linen.

She snatched the cloth and tied it over Nate's virulent lips, then breathed her own threat. "Speak one word about my friend and I will track you down wherever you go. Remember the owl you heard call your name? I was there that night, yet you never saw me."

He stiffened and fear crossed his face. Her implication had touched a nerve. God forgive her.

"Lay this whole sordid business on Josiah and the captain if you like. Say you were forced into cooperating. I'll not argue. Nor will Brewster, I think." Eyes brimming with resentment, Nate gave a nod. It would seem a bargain had been struck. "I will hold you to this," she said, and turned away.

She paused inexplicably by the suffering man lying face down on the cave floor. Blood stained the back of his once white linen shirt, yet the shot had entered his front. "Meshewa, give me a hand with Brewster."

Incredulity in his gaze, he asked,"Why?"

"I want to examine his injury."

"You must go from here *now*," he said, as if speaking to one of slow wit.

"I know," but a will stronger than hers bid her to linger. "Please, just for a moment."

Shaking his head, Meshewa rolled the groaning man over. She knelt beside him and tore the stained cloth away to examine the hole in his side. "The shot passed clear through." If she stemmed the vital flow, he had a chance. She had no desire to see him live, but felt compelled to give him that chance. "Brewster Winn, I can help you."

"How?" he gasped.

"I'm a healer."

"Help me then. I beg you."

"Why should I aid one who would hang my husband, kill my friends, kill me?"

Eyes closed, he stretched out shaking, bloodied fingers in helpless appeal. "I'll not. I swear it."

She didn't know if he spoke the truth, or was simply desperate. Nor did it matter. She must do as she was lead and pressed both hands against the streaming wound. An unwanted prayer rose to her lips. Rather than the heart-felt desire for life that had surged in her tearful petition for Uncle Peter and Logan, she felt only a sense of duty as she spoke the sacred words.

Tingling coursed through her like a charge from heaven. Not in a jolting way, she was a channel of healing. The blood seeping between her fingers lessened, and the moans issuing from the suffering man faded. As before, the scent of roses perfumed the cave in sweet contrast to the musty stone, smoky torches, and human sweat. Awe stirred in her. She cared little if Brewster Winn lived or died, yet he was visibly improving, his face less ashen.

Eyes shut against the pain fluttered and opened. His blue gaze lifted to her. He said weakly, "You're no witch. You're an angel."

"An unlikely one. Bloodied, armed, and ready to fight any who'd harm those I love."

"Yet you are. Beautiful angel." He gazed past her to the unusual rock formation. "There's your wings."

She doubted Nate shared Brewster's seemingly drastic alteration. He was watching, though, a peculiar expression in his eyes. It was all too strange for her to grasp.

Meshewa touched her shoulder. "If I did not see, I would not believe what you do."

315

"Nor I. God chose to spare you, Brewster Winn. Not me. He may reclaim your life if you break your pledge."

"I'll not."

It seemed unnecessary, even cruel to bind him, yet neither did she fully trust this bizarre alliance. "Remain as you are, Mister Winn. I will return with the Houstons." She rose wearily, drained from her efforts on his behalf, found a blanket among the plunder and covered him.

"Bless you," he murmured.

Reaching to Meshewa for support, she said, "Show me the way out and I'll ride for help."

He lit the discarded torch from one lodged in the rock wall and ducked through the opening in the stone. Keeping her hand on his arm, she followed. Extreme anxiety to reach the Houstons, and rush them to Logan and Tom's rescue, reasserted itself. "I hope my delay hasn't cost us."

"Why did you aid that man?"

"I just knew I must. But if helping him harms Logan and Tom how will I bear it?" Or understand her part in it all. The gift she possessed was sometimes a hard taskmaster.

She pondered in silence as they wound back through the stone maze and scrambled through the yawning hole into the earliest light of dawn. "Where will you go?"

"I will stay here for a time to guard the prisoners."

She hated to think of him being detected. "Have care." Mindful of the torch, she closed her arms around his neck. "Thank you for everything."

He enfolded her in turn then released her. "Go now."

She stopped at a warning whinny from Bryan. Meshewa reached for his musket.

"Kira?"

Had she heard rightly?"Logan?"

Joy surged through her and she shook all over, relief almost as debilitating as fear had been. By the light of her torch she saw his familiar form. And Tom's right behind him.

"Thank God!" Passing the light to Meshewa she hurled herself at her husband who caught her to him with a groan. Reaching out an arm, she clutched at Tom. "I can't believe you're both here."

Logan held her to him. "And you, my dearest love. Are you all right?"

"Yes, thanks to Meshewa. What of you?"

"Sore."

Tom grunted in agreement and squeezed her hand.

Peering up into their faces, she took in the welts, bruising, and blackened eyes. No wonder Logan groaned. They'd both been beaten rather badly. Might have suffered cracked ribs and Lord only knows what else, but they were alive, and she was determined they'd remain that way.

"Sweetheart," Logan summoned, his voice gruff from his ordeal and strong emotion,"did you find what you sought?"

****

Cantering Tequi over the trail in the pale light sent a charge of renewed energy pulsing in Logan. And racing alongside him on Josiah's stallion was Kira. *Unbelievable!* He almost slapped himself to be certain he was conscious when he learned she'd tamed the high-strung horse and now wore the fallen man's weapons, even had Meshewa calling her warrior woman. After all she'd been through these past few days there was no holding her back now. Despite her fear of speed—or former fear—they fairly flew.

Familiar trees rushed by like old friends, the lopsided hemlock struck by lightning, the gnarled

apple, and the great chestnut he and she had
climbed as children. The meadow came into sight,
grayer than green in the early light, and the fence
rose before them. He galloped Tequi at it. Kira
charged alongside him. Both mounts sailed over the
rails and took off again the instant their hooves
touched down.

Sheep dodged to the side. Turf flew up under the
horses tearing across the grass. They charged up the
hill. The ground fell away beneath their assault.
Tequi gave it his all and Bryan didn't flag. Once
won, his loyalty never wavered. Logan wouldn't be
surprised if he preferred his new mistress to his old
master. Josiah had handled him roughly.

The dim silhouette of the stable and other log
outbuildings took shape, and then the blur of plants
in the front garden. Fragrant herbs mixed with wood
smoke and the earthiness of the homestead as the
horses trotted into the yard. Breathless from the
ride, aching from head-to-toe, he reined Tequi to a
halt before the house. All would be decided based on
whether or not his relations believed them.

Pray God Mesehwa made it safely back to camp.
Well-armed and supplied with provisions, he'd
slipped away after Tom insisted on staying behind to
guard their prisoners. If Captain Winn arrived
before Logan and Kira returned with help all might
yet be lost. Would Brewster Winn hold to his
promise and speak against his thieving brother, or
tell tales against them? Kira's miraculous
intercession might prove a Godsend. They'd know
soon enough.

Likely the family was at breakfast. Famished,
Logan wished he could join in. She must be hungry
too, and beyond exhausted. But there was newfound
strength in her.

Will burst from the stable and pelted up to
them. Bryan whinnied warning. He stepped back,

taking in their arrival with a sweeping stare. "Kira—Logan—Good Lord!"

The door swung open and Aunt Alice flew onto the stoop, a wide-eyed Jenny and the twins at her heels. "Gracious, girl. Whatever's the matter?" Her gaze swiveled to Logan. "Just look at the state of them, Will! She's covered in blood and Logan's battered something frightful."

"I see. And whose stallion she's riding."

"Oh, my." Aunt Alice clapped a hand to her mouth.

Uncle Peter pushed past his wife and pounded down the steps. Bryan snorted and flattened his ears. He halted in his tracks. "Logan, what in blazes! Where's Campbell?"

"Dead."

"You kill him?"

"I wish, but no, a friend felled the brute. Campbell was bent on molesting Kira."

Uncle Peter scowled. "Man doesn't deserve to live."

Will eyed them with a trace of skepticism amid his shock. "Where's that *friend* now?"

"Gone." Logan wasn't giving details. "Tom's waiting at the cave folk think is haunted with two prisoners. Turns out it's a great place to hide stolen goods."

Even in the early light, the red flush spreading over his uncle's face was evident. "Is he, by heaven?"

Logan urged, "You and Will mount up and we'll ride back before Captain Winn arrives."

"What's Winn got to do with this thievery, Nephew?"

"Everything," Kira asserted. "As his brother will attest. Please come, we must hurry."

"Yes, yes. At once."

Aunt Alice beckoned to her, "You're in a right state, lass."

"Most of the blood's not mine, Aunt."

"Even so, let the men see to matters from here."

Kira shook her head. "Brewster Winn owes me a debt—the Lord, really—and I aim to see he honors his pledge."

Jenny came urgently to life. "Saddle up Donavan for me, Will. I'll ride hard and fetch my father and the others. They'll not stand for this."

"Ought you to ride alone, Jenny?" Aunt Alice asked worriedly. "Will can fetch the Lewis men later."

"They may be needed sooner. I know how to ride, Mrs. Houston. And shoot, for that matter. I have six brothers and my sister Elizabeth might as well be a boy. You know Papa's an old bear and they're all as tough as cinders. I grew up scrapping. Will and Mister Houston had best go on with Logan and Kira. I'll bring the Lewis clan."

"That's my girl," Will smiled, and turned away.

Voice cracking with emotion, Kira said, "Thank you."

Jenny met her tearful gratitude with heartening warmth. "You and Logan have had some mighty bad troubles since he came back. Maybe he doesn't even think he belongs here after all those years with the Shawnee. But I aim to help clear his way and hope you'll both see that's not so."

Logan tipped his hand to her in deep appreciation. His cousin wed a fine woman. But he'd married a jewel. Kira had finally stopped hiding and come out fighting for all she was worth—for him. And the battle wasn't won yet.

David and Donald clamored, "Bring Winn back hog-tied!"

****

Kira hauled back on Bryan's reins while Will swung up behind her. Uncle Peter was astride his big mare and Logan waited impatiently on Tequi.

320

Aunt Alice held up her hand in farewell. "Bring my nephew back safe and sound, Peter Houston. You too, Will. I don't care if he has a wild streak. We'll settle him down. And look after our Kira."

"That we will, woman."

The three horses sprang away with the boys running excitedly behind to see them off. They galloped down the hill Kira had recently ridden up and sailed over the split rails. The stallion couldn't churn up the turf fast enough to suit her, but she let Logan and Uncle Peter lead the way.

"I don't believe you're the same girl!" Will shouted.

"I've had to fight like a mad dog just to survive."

"We can see that from looking at you. Bet I can guess who killed Campbell."

"What makes you think it wasn't me? I have his pistol, knife, and horse."

"You're wrapped in an Indian blanket."

"Oh." She'd forgotten Meshewa's gift. "Logan's blood brother saved me from a horrible fate."

"I've no love for savages, but I'm right grateful to this one."

"There's another thing," Kira admitted. "Winn wants to arrest me. Josiah told him I'm a witch."

Will's arms tightened around her from behind. "Like hell you are. We'll just see about that."

They cleared the meadow, slowing as they entered the trees. She made out the two riders ahead of her rounding the grove of chestnuts before cave hill. Bryan trotted between the branches and she and Will ducked their heads. Ahead of them rose the mound of stones and leafy tangle that hid the entrance. Brewster Winn's piebald mare and Nate Campbell's dark brown gelding were tethered outside snatching at clumps of grass. Logan and Uncle Peter were there ahead of her, and to her surprise, Joseph McCue's black mare and a fourth

321

roan horse. She hazily remembered seeing the white streak on its head, but wasn't sure where, like trying to remember the details of a dream.

Puzzled, she reined in Bryan. Uncle Peter and Logan slid to the ground and tethered their mounts. Will dismounted first and grasped the halter. Bryan tossed his head, but Will took charge. "Behave yourself, boy. You're not the only fellow who cares for her."

Logan appeared at her side and held up his arms. "Poor girl," he said gently and pulled her down from the horse, so stiff she could barely hobble. But he looked far worse.

Uncle Peter muttered, "There's mischief afoot. We best slink in. Logan, Kira, keep back till we see what's what." He and Will led the way past the rocks and brush at the entrance. Kira held to Logan's arm and followed just behind him. They stooped under the yawning mouth in the stone and walked inside.

Voices carried from the larger cavern, the words unclear. Uncle Peter picked up the flaming torch stuck in the wall. It threw up garish shadows on the damp stone. They padded through the maze with the stealth of a fox. The voices grew louder and she heard the speaker.

"Think you're tough, McCue? I'll not tolerate an old coot coming in here accusing me of thievery. Bad enough hearing it from that renegade McClure."

Captain Winn. It was his roan mare she'd seen yesterday. Logan and Tom's disappearance on top of Josiah's must've alarmed him and he hightailed here to search, after parting company from his men. Else they'd have seen what he was about. But how had Joseph known to come, that hunch he told Logan about? And what had happened to Tom!

Anger shook in Joseph's voice. "You just happened to show up at this very place, did you? No notion there's a load of goods hidden inside."

"I'm looking for Mister Campbell and his men. I saw horses, theirs."

"Who did the thieving, then?" That was Tom's croak.

"You know full well, McClure. Logan McCutcheon and those savages he bands with. I reckon you're in on it too."

"I know different. So do Nate and your brother," Joseph argued.

"You're talking foolishness, old man," Nate said tersely. "You heard the captain. It was McCutcheon and his thieving redskins. And McClure here." Tom groaned under what sounded like a kick.

Fury inflamed Kira. "The lying toad," she hissed. "Winn must have unbound Nate. Now Tom's taken his place."

Eyes as hard as the stone around them, Logan held a finger to his lips. All four of them listened intently.

Captain Winn spoke again. "Now we just have to arrest the witch."

"You'll not touch her!"

"You're in no position to stop me, Mister McCue."

A shattering volley erupted, then a sharp cry.

Logan covered her mouth before she screamed Joseph's name. She sobbed, shaking, beneath his palm while Uncle Peter, already out in front, ran over the remaining passage, Will at his heels. Logan followed behind half-carrying her. Pistol cocked, Uncle Peter peered through the gap in the stone that led to the wider cavern. Motioning for them to wait, he bent his head and ducked through.

"Who the devil?" Captain Winn demanded.

"Devil's the word for you, right enough. Drop that pistol and get your bloody hands up. You'll swing for this Winn, cutting Joseph McCue down."

Kira heaved silent sobs while Logan clutched

her, tears streaming over cheeks and his hand still at her mouth.

"Nate shot him," Winn insisted, sounding a bit rattled.

"The pistol in your hand is smoking and it had better hit the ground," Uncle Peter warned.

"It's plain Nate handed it to me, Mister Houston."

"The hell I did! Enough, damn you!"

Will sprang through the rocky hole with Logan on his tail and Kira stumbling after him to see Nate hurl his knife into Winn's chest. The pistol clattered from his fingers to the cave floor. Gripping the knife handle, he staggered to the side. He lurched down onto his knees, shuddered, and thudded onto his back, gurgling in this throat.

Uncle Peter, Will, and Logan halted in stunned silence. A silent Nate Campbell stood like one of the strange rock formations. Then Kira ran to Joseph's motionless figure. He'd fallen not far from where Brewster lay, weak but still alive, she saw at a glance. It was otherwise with Joseph. The hole in his chest had finished him in an instant, unlike Winn gasping his last.

Tears streamed down her cheeks as she bent over her dear friend, smoothed his grizzled face and pressed her lips to his forehead. "No Joseph. Not you, too."

Logan stooped beside her. "He was a good brave man."

"He died for me—" she choked out.

"No, sweetheart. He lived for you." Logan caught her to him, smoothing the hair from her tear-streaked cheeks and kissing her face and lips. "I'm so sorry about Joseph. So sorry. Thank God you're all right."

She clung to him as though she'd never let him go. Her words strangled in her throat, and she was only vaguely aware of Will cutting Tom free. He staggered to his feet and over the uneven floor.

Rubbing at his bruised jaw, Tom said hoarsely, "A damned shame about Joseph. Funny how we were all headed to the same place."

"If only we had gotten here a little sooner." Logan's voice was equally husky.

Uncle Peter turned to Kira. "Joseph McCue was a finer man than I knew. I'm powerful sorry to see him fallen, lass." Through her tears, she watched him stride to Tom and wring his hand. "I'm mighty glad to see you, Tom McClure. By heaven, it's like having you back from the dead."

"I'm mighty glad to see you, too, Peter Houston. But I'm just passing through."

"So be it. I'll not ask why. You'll stay to see Alice, let her tend your wounds and feed you before you go?"

"That I will."

Will clasped Tom's hand then engulfed Logan in a hug. "I didn't get the chance to say before, but it's good to see you in one piece, cousin. Are you here to stay?"

"I might be willing to give it a try. Wish I weren't leaving such fine friends behind."

"I heard that warrior brother of yours saved Kira."

Logan looked at her with glistening eyes. "I'd say she did plenty to save herself."

"And me. She's an angel," Brewster said faintly. "No witch. An angel."

The statue that was Nate Campbell spoke up. "I'll say no different if we leave the matter as it is. Captain Winn and my cousin, Josiah, headed up this thievery. Brewster and I were forced into it."

A loud bellow echoed in the cave, like a bear finding his den invaded. "You're a lying snake, Nate Campbell! Lewis and his boys will say the same!"

Uncle Peter roared.

"But I think you'd rather they not know some of the details of your nephew's treason, or Kira's witchery."

Logan was on Nate before the startled man could swallow. Knife at his throat, he backed Nate against the wall, pressing the blade so closely that blood creased the lethal edge. "They had better not hear a word from you Campbell, if you want to take that next breath."

Kira got to her feet. Joseph's blood mingled with Brewster's down the front of her jacket and blanket. "No tricks this time, or I'll be an avenging angel."

Nate nodded slightly, all he dared with the blade nicking his flesh. "Whatever you say."

Logan lowered his knife. "Go. Don't ever show your face in these parts again. If she doesn't get you, I will."

Stumbling in his haste to get away, Nate scrambled up and fled. Uncle Peter clapped Logan on the back. "You two are quite a pair. I'd say you have the makings of one hell of a McCutcheon, lad."

Kira fell into Logan's arms. "Maybe you have a home here after all."

"Maybe I do."

A word about the author...

Married to my high school sweetheart, I live on a farm in the Shenandoah Valley of Virginia surrounded by my children, grandbabies, and assorted animals. An avid gardener, my love of herbs and heirloom plants figures into my work. The rich history of Virginia, the Native Americans, and the people who journeyed here from far beyond her borders are at the heart of my inspiration.

www.ingramcontent.com/pod-product-compliance
Lightning Source LLC
Chambersburg PA
CBHW070830280626
47161CB00015B/427